Critical praise for Carole Matthews's previous novel, *For Better, For Worse*, a "Reading with Ripa" Book Club selection:

"It's a big five points for humor."
—Kelly Ripa, *Live with Regis and Kelly*

"British author Matthews makes her American debut with this light, funny novel. A natural for the beach, it will charm Bridget Jones fans on both sides of the Atlantic."
—*Library Journal*

"...she entertains her readers with serendipitous trysts and near misses."
—*Publishers Weekly*

"...her humorous storytelling resurrects the power of romance to conquer all."
—*Booklist*

"...a cheeky romp from a best-selling Brit with a great sense of fun."
—*Kirkus Reviews*

"Warmly written..."
—*Express*

"You'll love this...."
—*Essentials*

"She's good...."
—*The Bookseller*

To my beautiful boy.
It just gets better….

Carole Matthews

A Minor Indiscretion

First North American edition August 2003

A MINOR INDISCRETION

A Red Dress Ink novel

ISBN 0-373-25033-9

Visit Red Dress Ink at www.reddressink.com

Printed in U.S.A.

ACKNOWLEDGMENTS

To Joan, Margaret and the team at Red Dress Ink
for your wonderful enthusiasm.
You're a delight to work with.

And to Helen—
for being a great agent and a very special person.

CHAPTER 1

I, Alicia Isabelle Kingston, am miserable. Absolutely miserable. Not just normal Monday morning miserable, but bone-deep, mind-numbing, fist-curling, toe-twitching miserable. The sort of miserable that makes you scowl at your perfectly well-behaved children and snarl at your husband when, for once, he really doesn't deserve snarling at. And the worst thing is, I have no idea why. Really, I don't.

Admittedly, my coffee is stone cold, but that isn't reason enough to be in this anxious state of suppressed aggression blended perfectly with utter desolation. I'm sitting outside the appropriately named Covent Garden Café in Covent Garden's main piazza—if you can use the word "piazza" in London and not appear too poncey. It's supposed to be spring, yet I'm frozen. I've tried pulling up the collar of my coat and nestling down on this very trendy, but rock-hard aluminum chair, and now its slats are digging even more deeply into my bottom. The sky is the startling blue of Paul Newman's eyes, and the brash yellow sun, brazen as a bottle blonde, lacks any form of warmth. I glare menacingly at some passersby so that they are aware of my discomfort, but they ignore me and this feeling just doesn't go away. Do you ever wake up feeling like this? I do. More and more often.

Marie Claire tells me it's my age. My children tell me it's my age. My husband tells me it's my age. My sister tells me it's because I'm a moody cow and always have been, but then, she can talk!

I stir my coffee and spoon up some cappuccino froth, which, let's face it, tastes okay whether it's cold or not. By now, I'm getting rigor mortis of the buttocks, and I cross my legs and wriggle about a bit in the vain hope of finding a portion of my cheek that isn't yet dead.

"Don't move," a voice instructs me.

I turn and say "What?" in my snappiest voice. A boy is sitting there with his easel, his young, untroubled forehead creased with the intensity of sketching me.

"I'm drawing you."

"I don't want to be drawn." Told you I was grumpy.

"I've nearly finished."

"I'm not paying you."

"I don't want to be paid."

"Then why are you doing it?"

He looks up and smiles, and for a moment shows the lackluster sun what it should be doing. "You have beautiful hair."

"I do not have beautiful hair." For the record, I have hair that would be considered flamboyant on a film star. The sort of hair that Nicole Kidman can get away with, no problem. To me it's just plain irritating. Hair that gave me a nightmare time all through school. It's red to the point of a ginger-nut biscuit and corkscrews into dreadlocks the minute it hears the word "damp." I was the person who wept with relief when John Frieda invented Frizz-Ease.

"Swish it about a bit."

"I will not."

He grins, very cheekily, and whizzes his charcoal around like a true professional. I turn away from him and stare out into the piazza in the hope that he will go away and find a less reluctant model.

I'm supposed to be at work. Work being an assistant to a C List interior designer with a "studio" just around the corner from here next to a Mexican-themed bar on Maiden Lane. She's the sort who pops up on *Changing Rooms* or *Richard and Judy* for guest appearances every now and again when they're desperate and can't get Laurence Llewelyn-Bowen or that other posh chap who paints everything beige. But she isn't sufficiently into monochrome or orange or brushed-steel tubing to make the grade regularly, harboring as she does an unhealthy appreciation for chintz, which isn't at all the thing for a hip, up-and-coming designer. And she looks sort of normal and has a boring name, which she can't help, even though I can testify that she's as mad as a March hare and organization is not a word in her vocabulary. She's as daffy and arty as they come, even though she looks like someone who's running a bit late for her Women's Institute meeting.

It's only eleven-thirty, but I was starting to bark and niggle at perfectly nice customers who wanted nothing more sinister than their living rooms made over or their kitchens kitsched, so I thought it was time to take an early lunch, even though I'm not the slightest bit hungry.

I've been sitting here for ten minutes, and now I'm not only miserable, but I'm getting bored too. Before the intrusion by Andy Warhol here, my thoughts were wandering on to the barren plains of what we might have for supper tonight and the fact that no matter how many times they eat them, my children never get tired of chicken nuggets and oven chips. I have tried to bring them up not to be philistines, but hey, I'm a funky millennium working mother and time is short. Time is short for everything.

Covent Garden isn't what it used to be. There's hardly anyone here this morning, and usually the place is packed with tourists and street entertainers and pickpockets. This was once the old flower market—until the developers got hold of it and jazzed it up, but I expect you all know that. You can't imagine it now, can you? There's not a flower in sight. Everything looks gray and dirty, or maybe I'm back to that mood thing again. Too many sweet wrappers drift across the cobbles on the slight breeze, making the whole place look like no one cares for it. Perhaps that's why I'm feeling like this. Perhaps I feel no one cares for me either.

One of the street performers in front of the graffiti-covered facade of St. Paul's Church is strutting his stuff. He has a thin, ragged audience that looks to be comprised of truanting children who are heckling him, and bemused Swedish tourists. He is juggling, very badly, and his shirt is grubby and looks terminally unwashed and I can understand why his audience is keeping its distance. I used to love the spontaneity and creativity of the street entertainers. Oh, the courage of just standing up before a crowd and laying your soul bare for the meager reward of gaining its pleasure and a few grudgingly spared pounds! Then I found out that all the performers have to book and pay for their pitches in advance and turn up come hail, rain or shine to entertain the tourists whether the tourists want to be entertained or not. They're not fickle, will-o'-the-wisp artistes, here today, gone tomorrow carefree performers. They have day jobs like the rest of us after all. Disillusionment, thou art a cruel bedfellow.

"I'm done."

I look up and my artist smiles at me again. And I smile back, because it's really hard not to when someone turns the full force of their white, twinkly teeth on you, isn't it?

He sidesteps the scraggly bushes and plastic chain-effect fence that ineffectively mark out the territory of the Covent Garden Café and comes toward me. His own hair isn't too bad. It's dark blond, mussed up, and looks like it too is tempted to take on a life of its own. He has gone down the spiky hair-gel route to tame it, although bits of it still fall forward in an artily foppish way, and he pushes it back with his fingers, which seems particularly unwise as they are very dirty.

"Here." He holds out the drawing.

"I'm not paying for it." I have reverted to grumpiness and refuse to succumb to any cheeky street vendor charm.

"If you like it, you can buy me a cup of coffee," he says.

"If I don't like it?"

"Then I'll buy one for you."

I take the drawing and, believe me, it's all I can do not to gasp. It is utterly fantastic. It looks absolutely nothing like me. It is a drawing of some fabulously gorgeous person with a wild, flowing mane and searing eyes. Although the nose is a bit like mine… Really. And the sulky lip is very me at the moment.

"Do you like it?"

"Who is it?"

He smirks. "That's how I see you."

"It looks nothing like me."

"Then I'm buying." And before I can protest, he's called the waiter—a miracle in itself—and orders two more cappuccinos. He pulls up a chair and plonks himself down, and I have to tear my eyes away from this wondrous drawing that could look vaguely like me on a good day. A very good day. "As well as beautiful hair, you have sensational bone structure. Classic."

Any minute now he is going to whip out a bill for fifty quid and I'll have been stung. I just know it. The waiter brings the coffee, and he settles back in the chair, looking an awful lot more comfortable than I do. And I don't know why, but I start to examine his bone structure—like I know anything about it! His cheeks are high, sharp, his jaw square and he has soft, pale lips that pout like they've been stung by a bee. He has youthful, fresh skin with hardly a trace of stubble and eyes that are the color of nuts, whole hazelnuts. You see, I've gone silly already. I don't usually carry out this sort of analysis on the faces of strange young men I meet. This is definitely a first for me.

"I'm Christian," he says, making me blush as I become aware that I am staring at him with my mouth pleasantly agog. "Christian Winter." He has a posh, upper-class accent that he probably peppers with swearwords and the hip slang of youth to make him seem less educated. Why do the young do that?

"Alicia," I say. Even though no one calls me Alicia except when they're telling me off. "Ali. Ali Kingston."

"Well, Alicia, Ali Kingston," Christian says. "It's been a pleasure to draw you."

And now I've gone all shy and pathetic, which is ridiculous because I'm about a zillion years older than he is and should know better. "Do you do this for a living?" I ask, sounding like he shouldn't.

"I wouldn't call it a living. I've just finished college. Fine arts degree. I'm doing this for the summer, until I see what else comes along."

"You're very good."

Christian laughs.

"No, really. You are. You just caught me on a bad day. I got out of the wrong side of the bed this morning or something."

"Perhaps you got out of the wrong person's bed?"

"I'm married. I get out of the same bed every day." I wonder why I'm embarrassed by how that sounds to this confident, good-looking young stranger.

"Married?"

"Very."

"Children?"

"Three."

"Wow. You don't look..."

"Haggard enough?"

"Old enough." *And you don't look old enough to be flirting with me.* I smile to myself and then realize I didn't do the "to myself" bit and he smiles back.

I scrabble round for my handbag for something to do. "I have to be going. I only popped out of work for a coffee to see if I could shift my mood."

"Did I help?" His eyes appeal to me like a puppy desperate to be loved.

I laugh and suddenly my heart wants to bleed or stop and I'm in severe danger of dropping my handbag and spilling its contents onto the cobblestones. "Yes, you did." And his puppy-dog eyes glint with wolfish mischief. I glance at my watch to break his gaze, which has gone on for far too long. "I really must go."

"Where do you work?"

"In a design studio around the corner." I'm not about to tell him that I answer the phone and hold the tape measure when required. I realize I am making a fuss about leaving and stop.

"Don't forget this," Christian says, and holds out the drawing.

I take it and regret that our fingertips don't touch, even though his need to be scrubbed with a Brillo pad. I walk off across the ever-widening expanse of the piazza, trying to keep straight yet sexy and not fall over any of the rubbish that is lying around. I don't look back, so I don't even know if he can see what an effort I've made in walking away from him. "Don't forget this." What a laugh. By the time I've bashed out three lots of chicken nuggets and chips tonight and two frozen lasagnas with two tepid glasses of Chianti as a softener, I'll have even forgotten his name.

CHAPTER 2

"I could die before we finish this." Ed put his head in his hands. "Why, oh why, am I doing this?"

"Because you have a wife, and several more children than is good for one person, to feed."

The two men were in a corner of a vast warehouse on the premises of Performing Power Tools, which had been turned into a temporary set. They were attempting to film a blonde in a minuscule white crocheted bikini, who in turn was trying to drill a hole with a dual-action hammer drill into a two-inch-thick plank of wood.

"And action!" Ed shouted encouragingly, ever hopeful that in his role as Executive Producer of this promotions video he might at some point be able to produce something.

Nothing. The Performing Power Tool was not performing. Neither was the blonde. Out of all of them, the plank of wood was doing best.

"Okay. Let's take a break," Ed called out.

The blonde tottered into her waiting terry-cloth dressing gown.

Trevor eased the camera from his shoulder. "Smoke break?"

"Why not?" Ed tried to get a crack to come from the tight bones in his neck, but, like the dead drill, it wasn't playing ball either. He addressed no one in particular: "While I help Trevor in his quest to develop lung cancer, can someone please find a drill that actually works?"

He followed the cameraman out into the relatively fresh air of Brent Park industrial area and they leaned on the hood of his four by four, which saw its only action in the car park at Sainsbury's rather than the rugged terrain that God and Mitsubishi had intended.

Ed closed his eyes and pretended he was somewhere else. Somewhere hot and tropical with swaying palms and rolling surf, somewhere that didn't smell of engine oil and spent fast-food cartons. "I was that far away from stardom, Trev." He indicated a metaphorical inch with his fingers. "That far."

"Don't give me the Harrison Ford routine again, Edward. You usually save that for when you're drunk."

"He was nothing before *Raiders of the Lost Ark.* That film made him what he is today. It could have done the same for me."

"It's made you into a boring old fart. Ciggie?"

"I haven't had one for four years—you know that. And I'm not about to start now. Just blow the smoke in my direction, I'll inhale."

Trevor obliged, filtering a stream of Benson & Hedges toxins through tight lips. Ed widened his nostrils and snorted deeply.

"I don't know what more you want," Trevor nagged him. "You run a very successful corporate video company. You have a great staff. A great wife. Great kids, if you like that sort of thing."

"I have spent two days in a warehouse trying to get fantastic camera angles on a woman drilling a hole in a piece of wood." Ed sighed. Heavily. "I was the man who blew up the plane at the end of *Raiders.* Did I tell you about the time Harrison and I were in a bar in Morocco and he said..."

"Yes. Yes. A thousand times, yes. I know about the time the camel nearly bit him on the arse. I know about the effect that having sand permanently down his underpants had on him. I know about what a great bloke he was because he always remembered Ali's name. I have worked with you for five years. Long enough to have heard all your Harrison Ford stories several times. And they're great. They really are. But not today, Ed. Not today. Let me finish this cancer stick and we'll get on with Miss Driller Killer showing the old folks down at B&Q how to get the best from their DIY."

"I gave it all up for Ali, you know."

"You didn't. You gave it up because, like the rest of us, you were fed up with the insecurity. The fear of being only as good as your last explosion, the trailing halfway round the world for a few months' work only to be forgotten at the bottom of a very long line of credits; the nights spent propping up seedy bars in dubious Third World countries with the likes of Harrison Ford and living on diarrhea pills when you'd rather be at home on your own comfy little sofa watching repeats of *Frasier*...with a nice cup of tea."

Ed huffed in an unconvinced kind of way.

"There are an awful lot of extremely talented people out there, Edward, chasing a tiny handful of jobs. Be grateful that you had the big time and can now settle for cozy suburbia on a fat executive salary. Life could be worse." Trevor took the last drag of his cigarette.

"Can I grind the butt out for you, mate?"

"My pleasure." Reverently, Trevor handed the glowing butt to Ed, who kissed it to his lips with a quivering sigh.

"I still miss it desperately. It doesn't get any easier even when you've given it up."

"Are we talking about films or cigarettes now?"

"Maybe both." Ed dropped the cigarette to the floor and ground it out with his heel.

Trevor gazed across the weed-ridden expanse of car park. "Did I say life could be worse?"

"You did."

"I'm bloody psychic," he sighed. "It's the Ogre."

Ed looked up. Orla O'Brien was out of her BMW and heading toward them. She already looked tetchy and she didn't even know what a cock-up they were making of the nonperforming Performing Power Tools demonstration video. And, being blessed with an ultra-feminist heart, she'd probably go ballistic when she saw the blonde in the bikini.

Orla had been put in place by the owner of the company as a management consultant. Her remit was to downsize, upsize, modernize, rationalize, digitalize and all sorts of other "izes" that were bound to arouse suspicion and engender hatred in the work force. She had been with them for a month, and everyone loathed her except Ed, who for some chivalrous and inexplicable reason found her merely misunderstood. Despite her leanings, Orla wore tight skirts and filmy blouses and her hair piled on top of her head as if she were an extra in *Pride and Prejudice.* Wispy ringlets of jet-black hair escaped when she shook her head, which she did often. Ed thought it was supposed to make her look stern and unapproachable, but it didn't. It made her look sensual.

And she was American, which didn't help. She was brisk, efficient and didn't understand most of their jokes, and when she did she complained about them being sexist, which they invariably were. Her sense of humor bypass didn't allow her to click into the more usual response of the other women in the office, which was to riposte with an equally risible comment or throw a missile at the offending person—paper clip, elastic band, Kit Kat wrapper (used) or plastic cup (preferably empty, though not essential). Orla thrived on punctuality and schedules and forecasts, and Wavelength Films had existed happily for several profitable years on a sublime blend of chaos, camaraderie and sheer goodwill. They had a loyal if disorganized staff, and there was an unwritten rule that when the shit was about to hit the fan no one ducked—they all closed their mouths and faced it together head-on. It worked. Sometimes well, sometimes less well, and it didn't fit into Orla's brief at all. And she said so, frequently, in a seriously kick-ass sexy accent.

"She is scarier than Cruella De Vil," Trevor muttered.

"She's okay," Ed said and, without realizing it, crossed his arms defensively across his chest.

Orla stopped in front of them.

"How's it going?" she asked without preamble.

"Great," Ed replied with an easy smile.

"I thought I'd stop by for the last hour—if that's okay with you. There are some things I want to go through." Ed noticed her bulging briefcase with something approaching resignation. "Maybe we can go for a drink when you're done?" She looked from Ed to Trevor and back.

"Count me out," Trevor said and pushed himself away from the car. "I'm going home to watch *101 Dalmations* on video." He sauntered back toward the warehouse with all the alacrity of a man who knows he's about to meet his maker.

Orla wrinkled her nose crossly. "Is that another one of these jokes that I don't get?"

"Search me," Ed said, suppressing the smile that threatened to curl his lips.

"What about you?"

"I can't be late, I'm going out tonight."

"With your wife?"

"With my brother."

"Oh."

"What about tomorrow after shooting?"

Orla's chin lifted. "I have a date tomorrow night."

"Oh."

"I can do this without your help," she said, and shrugged her shoulders with such indifference that it created an unexpected and empty little hole in Ed Kingston's heart. There was a time when he had felt truly needed. Now Ali didn't need him, the children didn't need him and even management consultants didn't need him.

Orla marched off after Trevor, her heels clicking resolutely on the concrete. Ed, wishing he had something else to grind into the floor with his foot, followed meekly, hoping beyond hope that someone might have found a drill that drilled.

CHAPTER 3

"Good day today, darling?" At my question, Ed glances up from *Broadcast* magazine and forces a smile. He looks tired and frazzled and in need of more sustenance than ready-made lasagna will offer.

"Yes. Fine. You?"

"Yes."

"Hurray, chicken nuggets! Chicken nuggets! Chicken nuggets!" I do wonder about my children sometimes. This is my youngest, Elliott. He of the chicken-nugget addiction. He is bobbing about at the table with a faintly insane glint in his eye for one so young. Before the plate has hit the table, it is already an inch deep in tomato ketchup. I once dreamed of going to the Pru Leith School of Food and Wine to train as a trendy chef. How soon we forget our ambitions when faced with the relentless onslaught of daily life. I put a sprig of coriander on the side of Elliott's plate in an attempt to assuage my guilt. It doesn't work. For me or for Elliott, who whips it off as quick as a flash lest it poison him, and fills the vacant space with more ketchup.

My other son, Thomas, is twelve and a parent's dream. He doesn't yet have acne, his trainers don't smell and he likes to read. Harry Potter, what else? Thomas probably hates chicken nuggets but would be too polite to mention it and would eat them anyway. He is considered intelligent, chatty and sociable, and I do hope he doesn't grow out of it. My third and eldest child is Tanya, and she once was intelligent, chatty and sociable and now she's a teenager. A girl-woman of fifteen and don't we all know it. We are all waiting for her to grace us with her presence at the table while our convenience food grows steadily colder. She's heavily into Trance music. Now don't ask me what that is; I did once and got tutted at. I think it's because it's so monotonous and repetitive that it makes her go into a trance. All it does is make me want to bite my own ears off. Sod painkillers, you could have babies with it, it's so numbing to all the senses. Tanya has the permanently glazed look of the terminally bored and only perks up to the point of silliness when Enrique Iglesias appears on telly. (Nicky to me.) She wears skirts that aren't anywhere near long enough and shoes that will ruin her feet, but I've given up moaning.

Tanya graces us with her presence, and I bite back the urge to ask her whether or not she has washed her hands. At fifteen, I guess she is old enough to decide whether she can eat with grubby digits.

"Not chicken nuggets *again.*" I have tried lasagna with her, honestly I have, but she complains about that too.

They all swoop on their food like vultures, which I should be grateful for. But I'm not. Even though it hasn't taken a great deal of effort, someone should say thank you somewhere. Actually, Ed has headed for the glass of wine option first.

"I'm playing squash with Neil tonight," he mutters as he tackles his pasta. I doubt it, faced with this lack of enthusiasm. Neil is Ed's younger brother. He's handsome in a laddish way, a sort of thinking woman's crumpet and reluctant heartthrob. Neil is softer and smilier than Ed, but then he hasn't got three children and a wife to nag him. He seems so lovely, but he must be emotionally crippled in some way because, although he has loads, he can never keep a girlfriend. Ed and Neil arrange to play squash every week. One in three weeks they actually *do* play squash. The rest of the time they go to the pub and talk about how unfit and old and hard done by they feel now that they don't get the time to play squash regularly.

"Jemma's coming over," I say, and no one looks the slightest bit interested. Jemma's my baby sister, and they all adore her in their own low-key, offhand way. They do.

"That's nice," Ed manages.

We are going to get drunk on a bottle of cheap Chardonnay and discuss the genital inadequacy of the last three men she's dated, as we often do. She is still searching for someone who's hung like a stallion rather than My Little Pony. And then we might possibly laugh like hyenas at an old episode of *Friends.* Sometimes, it seems that I get all my excitement filtered down through Jemma's sex life. Which, I have to say, is going through a bit of a lean patch at the moment. Much like my own.

Ed and I never get time for a bonk. And if you saw the size of my ironing pile, you wouldn't even need to ask why. We fall into bed every night just grateful to have survived another day. It's not the best recipe for getting mushy, is it? But, hey, don't 99.9 percent of the population live like that? I can't believe we are the same people who used to make love for hours and then lie in bed entwined, watching the shapes the clouds made as they wandered past our window. Naturally, that was pre-Pampers life.

"Did you all have a good day at school?" I ask those responsible for ruining my sex life.

"No," Tanya says.

"It was fine," Thomas says. "Thank you."

"Great." Elliott has not yet learned that enthusiasm is uncool and is still at a nursery prep-school place down the road that costs us a small fortune each month but is worth it because he will grow into a balanced, confident and self-sufficient member of society. Or so we tell ourselves every time we nearly faint when we get the bill. "We had to be trees." A look of confusion darkens his face. "Or was it elephants?"

I wonder if excessive consumption of chicken nuggets can cause long-term brain damage and our fee-paying will all be in vain.

There is the synchronized clattering of forks, and I can sense the dishwasher bracing itself. I have eaten my lasagna without even tasting it, something for which I should probably be eternally grateful.

"What are you doing tonight?" I ask next.

"Nothing," they all say.

I tell you, we could have a parade of the Moscow State Circus, the entire lineup of Steps and half the Arsenal football team in here every night, and what would my children say had happened? "Nothing."

"Well, go and do it quietly," I say.

The children evacuate the table without asking and disappear. I had every intention of bringing them up better than this. Really, I did.

I squeeze Ed's hand. "You look tired."

"I'm knackered. I'm not sure if I feel like squash tonight. I think it might be better if we just go for a drink. I'll see what sort of mood Neil's in."

Neil is always in a good mood. He's one of life's shiny, happy people. My sister should snap him up and marry him before someone else does. But she won't. She says it would be incest. Technically, it wouldn't, but I can see what she means. Marrying your own brother-in-law could be considered a bit close for comfort, even though it wouldn't necessarily line you up for genetically challenged offspring. Besides, my sister seems to prefer men who are already married.

There is a deep, growling sound three streets away in the soft underbelly of suburban Richmond and, after I count the statutory twenty seconds, Neil arrives on his motorbike, riding over the remains of my daffodils and spraying gravel to the four corners of the earth. It suits him, this laddish mode of transport, and he insists it isn't just a toy. He says it is his antidote to driving round London in the beat-up old Citroën estate that he uses because of his work. Neil is a photographer. One who spends more than his fair share of time photographing reluctant schoolchildren rather than the fashion models he so desires. But he's great at it. He has a natural rapport with kids. Or so he tells us.

"Yo! Bro!" Neil says as he comes in through the back door. I'm grateful that he doesn't kick it in. He always goes into *Terminator* mode when he's on that wretched machine. It's a Honda something or another—flashy, racy, the sort of bike that makes grown men drool and weep silently for a time when they were young and didn't have a mortgage or a pension fund. You know the sort. Usually Neil is a very sane and reliable person, but the minute he sits on that thing, his brain cells deplete.

"Hi, Neil."

He kisses me and punches Ed playfully. "Squash or pub?" he says. Maybe he senses that Ed is stretched too.

"Not in the mood for squash?" Ed queries.

"Nah! Let's do some damage with the old Amber Nectar."

"Leave that thing here," I say, indicating the bike. "Why don't you stay here tonight? I'll throw the boys in together. You can have Elliott's room."

"Sounds good to me!" He high-fives Ed, and I'm relieved to see my husband laughing.

Ed stands and stretches. He is still a very handsome man, despite a slight sagging in the tummy area due to too much sitting behind a desk. But then, that's like the pot calling the kettle black. Gravity and multiple childbirth have not been kind to my stomach muscles either. He does very well to keep in shape on a limited timescale. Ed is rugged and manly and looks like he ought to play rugby, but he never has. Although, strangely, we met at a rugby club do. Goodness knows what either of us was doing there, and time has, unfortunately, rubbed out that part of our memory banks. Why does it happen like that? Things that you think you'll never forget are suddenly gone, off into the ether, with little hope of them ever coming back.

Ed has dark brown hair, which he combs and preens within an inch of its life, and it grows like a weed, so apart from the week when he's just been to the barber's it always looks like it needs cutting. His voice is sexy and growly and he'd make a great television sports presenter. His eyes are the color of new denim jeans, and he has full red lips and eyebrows that are a bit too heavy and look even worse when he frowns. Which he does now. "What are we waiting for?"

Jemma pops her head round the door. "Not me, I take it."

"Hello, Jems." Ed kisses her and gives her a hug.

"Jemma." Neil pecks her cheek.

"Where are you two off to in such a rush?" she asks them as she kisses me distractedly.

"They're going to talk about squash, rather than get involved in the sweaty, messy end of it."

"We're going to have a tactics meeting. It just so happens we're going to do it at the Queen's Head."

"I might join you later," Jemma threatens.

"This is man's talk." Ed grins. He brushes my cheek with his lips. They feel dry. "See you later." And they are gone.

Jemma sits on a kitchen stool while I start to tidy up. "God," she says, wriggling to get comfortable, "when did Neil get so gorgeous?"

"It's the tight black leather," I advise. "Does it every time."

"Oh."

I find the corkscrew and head for the wineglasses. "Open something decent," Jemma says. "Raid Ed's stash for something pre-2000. I've had a hell of a day. We always drink stuff that's only fit to splosh in a Bolognese sauce. I want to get drunk on quality grapes, not plonk. I can't afford to have a headache tomorrow. I have a shop to run."

My sister enjoyed the high life as a British Airways purser for several years and lived off several married pilots while she saved all her hard-earned cash to open an antique-clothing emporium. She sells 1920s dresses to television actresses for awards ceremonies and stuff like that, and is an endless source of celebrity gossip. Personally, I think she reads most of it in *Hello!* magazine, but she won't have it.

I smile and open something decent. Not that either of us will be able to tell the difference after a few glasses. I start to stack the dishwasher and wonder if it's not harder than just washing up in the first place.

Jemma sips her wine, sighing with pleasure. "What's this?"

She has pulled the loosely rolled-up paper from the corner of my workbag and waves my portrait at me. "A drawing," I reply helpfully.

"I can see that! Who is it?"

"Cow."

"You look utterly, utterly gorgeous. When did you have this done?"

"Today. This morning."

"God, it's good. Isn't it?" I turn my back to her, intent on my stacking. I can't bear it when you don't stack the things properly and you get all dried-on stuff left inside or scummy water in the cups. It's a nightmare, isn't it?

"So?"

"So."

"So, it's not like you to splash out on something like this. This is the sort of thing I do. You spend your money on washing powder and school fees and the world microwavable meal mountain." My family take the piss out of my inability to produce good wholesome meals on weekdays. A lot.

"The guy did it for free."

"No!" My sister is examining the drawing from every angle, and I want to grab it from her and hide it. "Why?"

"I don't know. I was sitting having a coffee and he drew me. I think he was bored," I add hastily, seeing her skeptical look.

"He singles you out of a crowd to come and draw you because he's bored?"

"There wasn't a crowd. There was no one else around."

"Ohmigod, this gets more romantic by the minute!"

"It does not. He was only a boy."

"Was he?" Jemma grimaces. "How disappointing." She turns the drawing back to the right way up. "Well, he must have fancied you to make you look like this. God, Ali, you're fourteen film stars rolled into one…." Jemma catches my eye, and I put the oven chips dish down. "You're blushing," she says, looking horrified.

"I'm not."

"You are."

"I'm having a hot flush."

"Bollocks."

I pick the oven chips dish up again and try to swish my unruly hair forward to hide my face. Jemma and I look a lot alike. Except she has a slinkier figure, a great nose and more sensible hair. Her hair is burnished chestnut rather than two-day-old carrot and it's long rather than wide, fashionably crinkly and curly instead of making her look like the Wild Man of Borneo.

"You've gone all girly." She's also like my mother, who doesn't miss a trick.

"Now it's my turn to say bollocks."

"What was his name, this handsome young man?"

"Who said he was handsome?"

"I bet he was."

"He was called…Christian," I blurt out. My legs have gone all weird and wobbly. "And you're right—he was *gorgeous.*"

"You old tart!" My sister howls with laughter, and I sit down with her and gulp my glass of wine because I'm blushing and having a hot flush all at once.

CHAPTER 4

"That Jemma is one hell of a woman," Neil said appreciatively as he lifted his pint.

"She's a man-eater and a commitment-phobe," Ed said, examining a cheese-and-onion crisp before eating it. There were loads of trendy bars in Richmond, but they always went to the Queen's Head. It was a proper man's pub that sold draft ale even though the brothers never drank it, and it didn't play music at a million decibels, so that you could actually have a conversation. Neil did, however, rue the lack of scantily clad women, not counting the barmaid whose breasts always looked like two ferrets having a fight down her crop-top. "Jem's always whining on about not being able to get a man, and yet she's got a queue of them battering down her door. Then she always manages to pick the ones who are totally unsuitable."

"That's women for you," Neil agreed.

"She'd be far too much effort for you."

"Rubbish."

"Does she look like the sort of woman who'd let you wash your socks by putting them down the toilet and flushing it?"

Neil looked hurt. "I don't do that anymore! Never ever! Well, hardly ever."

"You couldn't stack take-away cartons in your kitchen until

they walk out all by themselves in disgust. You're not the type to be able to handle a high-maintenance babe. You're one of life's laid-back bodies. Enjoy it. Find a slovenly woman who will love you for what you are."

"A slob?"

"If the cap fits..."

Neil glared at his brother over his beer.

"Remember what happened with Penny?"

Neil shuddered.

"You had three years of hell with her. She stopped you playing football, *and* watching it. She stopped you smoking. She stopped you getting pissed at parties. She made you sell the Alfa Romeo and get a Citroën and complained constantly that you didn't have a proper job."

"I thought that's what people in love did."

"And then, when she'd done all that, she dumped you for a physiotherapist with no hair who smoked and played football."

"Bet he doesn't now." Neil grinned.

"I love Jemma...like a sister," Ed claimed. "But she'd try to change you too."

"Jemma could change instead. She could lower her standards."

"Never. Women don't change. Until you marry them."

"I saw Penny the other day. She was in Tesco with two kids, one still in a pushchair. She'd got fat." Neil smiled and helped himself to Ed's crisps. "But at least she'd moved on. Here I am, three years later, same job, same flat, same life."

"How is the glamorous, drug-fueled world of school photography?"

"Same as ever. I spent the day trying to herd tribes of unruly five-year-olds into some semblance of order. How would you like to spend your entire waking moments saying 'Smelly Sausages' in order to get some toothless, hyperactive urchin to grin?"

"I spent my day trying to get a blonde in a bikini to drill a hole with a broken drill. Tomorrow, I will no doubt spend an equally futile day trying to get her to saw with a broken saw. Don't ever buy any Performing Power Tools, by the way."

"At least you get to look at a bird in a bikini. What do I get? Horrible little tykes who could learn some sartorial elegance from *Just William.*" Neil leaned back. "Oh, when is *Vogue* finally going to get on the phone and insist that I fly to Ecuador at a moment's notice to photograph Elle or Helena or Liz for the front cover?"

"Maybe when you get off your lazy backside and compile a decent portfolio."

"I shall treat that with the contempt it deserves. Still, the wedding season will soon be upon us," Neil said, cheering up. "The brides may be lost causes, but I've pulled some very nice bridesmaids with my sparkling repartee."

"Be grateful that life is so simple, my brother."

Neil paused over his pint. "Not trouble at home?"

"No. No. Not at home. Everything's fine. Well, nothing that winning the lottery and giving three children to a passing circus couldn't fix."

"Work?"

"Same as ever. You're not the only one who hankers after bigger and better things."

"Oh, not the Harrison Ford stories, bro."

"I haven't told them for ages."

"Christmas. One glass of port too many."

"That was months ago!"

"If I wasn't so certain of our mother's cast-iron morals, I'd swear he was our third long-lost brother."

"Three weeks ago, I spent ten days filming a man dressed as a tin of tuna flakes. That was a major contract for Wavelength. Don't you think I miss the good times?"

"Everything's relative, Ed. How do you think the man inside the tin of tuna felt?" Neil nodded sagely.

"True."

"Hindsight always gives things a rosy glow, mate. You know that."

Ed sighed. "Sometimes it's very easy to forget it. And sometimes I just wonder where I might be now, if I'd stayed the distance."

"Probably filming *The Mummy Returns* in a sandpit in the Home Counties purporting to be the far-flung desert sands of Egypt."

"Probably."

"It wasn't all sun, sand, sea and sex. You said so yourself. Did you ever spend the night in Sharon Stone's trailer?"

"No."

"What was the point in it all then? A few beers with Harrison Ford doesn't amount to much. It can't have been the great job you make it out to be."

"Maybe you're right."

"There must be something that's brought on this little black cloud. Have you still got the brisk and terrifyingly efficient Orla with you? Perhaps she's getting you down."

"Orla's all right. She's just doing a job."

"I'll give it another month. She'll be turning you inside out by then, psychoanalyzing you, questioning every decision you've ever made."

"If it wasn't her, it would be someone else. And they might be short, fat and bald and have body odor. At least while Orla's picking my life over, she's pretty stunning to look at."

"Is she?" Neil perked up. "I thought you only had eyes for Ali?"

"Everyone's entitled to look every now and again," Ed said and gulped his beer, chasing it with the last cheese-and-onion crisp and wondering why his cheeks and his ears felt as if they were glowing.

CHAPTER 5

I really can't believe I'm doing this. Really, I can't. I have taken an early lunch from work and am sitting—yes, you guessed it—at the Covent Garden Café eating a baguette which might be a lump of cardboard for all I know. And that's not a criticism of the food here, it's more to do with the state of my mind. I lasted a week before I did this though. Which, I think, all things considered, wasn't bad going. And until I got here, I'd almost managed to convince myself that all I wanted was a cold coffee and a cardboard sandwich at a convivial hostelry and wasn't the slightest bit interested in seeing if Christian was still around and how many other older women with dubious hair he might be drawing as an act of kindness.

I don't know if you can understand how I feel. It's like when you used to leave a disgusting, fallen-out tooth under your pillow at night and, miraculously, in the morning the tooth would have vanished and in its place would be a shiny fifty-pence piece. (Although the going rate in our house now ranges from a pound to a fiver depending on the level of pain endured in pulling out the offending tooth. Tanya lost one of her front teeth going over the handlebars of her bike, which is worth five pounds of anyone's money.) But, in my heart of hearts, I always knew that it was too good to be true. Why would anyone, let alone a fairy, want a manky, bloody tooth in return for money? The tooth fairy always seemed to get a raw deal, and it left me with a nagging sense of doubt. Why would anyone do that? And that's what this feels like, in a peculiar sort of way. Although I'm not sure I can really compare Christian to the tooth fairy, I think I can empathize wholeheartedly with the manky tooth.

Life was very quiet at the Kath Brown Design Studio this morning. See, I told you she had a boring name. Not that there's anything wrong with being called Kath Brown, per se. It's just not a sexy designer-type name, is it? Perhaps if she changed it to Kathy or Katy Brown or even Kat Browne, it might perk it up a bit. Anyway, whatever. Things are quiet and I'm going to take a whole hour for lunch. So I might just eat this baguette quickly and nip off into Neal's Yard to see if I can find something quirky or pretentiously New Agey that I don't need so that I can justify my being here.

The square is busy. Maybe that's because the sun has deigned to come out. By the café there is a man painted from head to foot in gold with a squeaker in his mouth; not unexpectedly, he is squeaking at passersby, who in turn throw him money. There is a puppet theater called The Amazing International Theatre of Dolls, which consists of row upon row of wrecked-looking Barbie and Ken dolls and the odd Action Man thrown in who are dressed in bizarre clothes and are being made to mime along to popular hit tunes by an equally bizarrely dressed man who is desperately trying to make it look like there is some sort of skill involved. Across the street, a beautiful bohemian brunette is playing Vivaldi like an angel on a battered violin and making it look like there's no skill involved at all. It's a strange world, isn't it? But, try as I do not to look, there is no sign of Christian anywhere.

I pay my bill and wander into the market. I could take the direct route up James Street and past the Tube station, but you never know, I might find something in the market that I can't live without. Well, I might. As I pass through the rows of painted glass and silk T-shirts, it seems unlikely, and then, as I get to the other end near the back of the Opera House, he's there.

He has his back to me and he is drawing a middle-aged woman and she is laughing and flirting with him. I don't know why, but I feel sick. Maybe there was something dodgy in that damned baguette. I had my suspicions all along. I thought the lettuce looked way too limp to be fresh. I edge closer and see that the drawing is good. Excellent. But not as good as my drawing, and she laughs again and swishes her hair about. Christian puts his charcoal down, and she rummages in her handbag and pays him. Oh yes, she pays him! And then she "ooo's!" at the drawing. It is a good likeness, but he hasn't given her tempestuous hair or eyes that wouldn't look out of place in *Wuthering Heights.*

I stand behind him for a second, unsure whether to stay or whether this is the moment I should walk away and get on with my life. You know that feeling when your gut tells you something, and another part of your anatomy, your brain or your heart or your feet, tells you to ignore it. And before I can decide whether to follow my gut instinct and leave, he turns round.

His eyes light up. They do. I have never seen anyone's eyes light up for me before. I'm sure I haven't—not even Ed's eyes. And, my God, is it a heady feeling. "Ali," he says. "What are you doing here?"

"Watching a master at work," I say with a laugh. How can I tell him what I'm really doing, when I'm not even sure myself? There's an awkward moment where we both fidget and then we should both start to speak at the same time, but we don't. I do. "I came to say thank you for the drawing. I was in such a foul mood on Monday, I wanted to thank you for brightening my day."

"You brightened mine," he says, and if it's a line, it works.

"Well, thanks." Fidget, fidget. "I wish you'd let me pay you."

"It was a gift."

"Well, thanks." Fidget, fidget. "I'd better be off."

He stands hurriedly and nearly knocks his easel over. "Have you had lunch? I could have a break now. There's no one waiting."

And he's right. There's just the two of us in all this crowd.

"I've had lunch."

"Coffee," he says. "Have you got time for coffee?"

I look at my watch as if I'm undecided.

"There's a nice little place down here." Those eyes are so hard to refuse. "They do great cakes."

"I'm on a diet." I'm not, but I probably should be.

"I'll eat one for you."

I laugh. He is so eager to please. Eager to please me. Me, so used to pleasing everyone else but myself.

"Or we could go for a walk. There's no calories in that."

Or harm? I ask myself. "The sun's out."

"Walk it is, then." Christian smiles and packs up his little box with bits of charcoal in it and tucks it into a Nike rucksack and slings it on his back. He's wearing a huge white T-shirt smudged with the fruits of his labors and beige combat trousers that hang loosely on a frame that has not yet developed its full quota of muscles. The sort of clothes that Tanya's friends wear. We smile uneasily and set off toward Neal's Yard, not touching but not far away. And this just feels wrong, so wrong.

It's impossible to talk as we try to stroll casually along. We keep having to part to let crowds of chattering French teenagers barge through. Why do they all dress in navy blue and behave badly? And why do they never have a schoolteacher with them? We cross over by Marks & Spencer. I head automatically for the Zebra crossing while Christian prefers to dodge the traffic, and I avoid thinking about tonight's supper while I have this beautiful, beseeching boy by my side. This side of the road is more interesting, in my opinion, and quieter. We drift together again, still attempting to act like comfortable old friends.

"Have you been busy this morning?" I ask, and sound as if I'm talking to my children.

"Steady," Christian replies with a shrug. "I hoped you'd come back. I've been hoping all week."

"Why?"

"Why?" He laughs. "Do you believe in fate, Ali?"

"Not really," I say. I actually believe in paying your credit-card bills on time, washing strawberries before you eat them and always wearing clean underwear in case you're involved in an accident that requires hospital treatment and showing a young, attractive doctor your pants. See my earlier discourse on the tooth fairy, if you want to be assured of my essentially skeptical and unromantic nature. "Do you?"

"Of course."

I want to say, "But that's because you're a child and you haven't been worn away by the daily grind of just getting through life and your head is still filled with ideas and hopes and fanciful notions." I don't, because behind that boyish facade there is a developing man and I don't want to crush his unfettered spirit. Not on a bright, sunny day like this. I turn and smile at him. "Let's go for the cake option instead," I suggest, and he grins back and we head for the nearest place, which looks tatty, but at least has tables outside.

La Place Velma serves enormous cakes. Christian opts for the no-holds-barred full fruit stall on a cream doughnut affair. My children eat like horses and look like stick insects too. It isn't fair, is it? I plump for the more sedate strawberry tart and I think of my sister. Not because she's a tart, but because she called *me* one, if you remember. And I think at this moment she might be right. Although I'm sure Christian isn't trying to impress me, because he dives straight into his cake and pulls bits out with his fingers, something I'd go mental at if Elliott did it, and he has cream on the end of his nose and he must know but he seems entirely unconcerned. He eats with relish and is taking such joy in a simple cake that I can't stop watching him. It makes me smile. A smile that comes from deep down inside my tummy.

"Where do you live?" Christian asks as he wipes his mouth.

"Richmond."

"Nice. Big house?"

I shrug. "Yes. We bought it when property there cost an arm and just half a leg." I'm horrified. I sound as if I'm talking to my bank manager, and can do nothing about it. "It was a wreck when we bought it. We've done a lot of work."

"You and your husband?"

"Yes."

"And you travel in to your design studio every day."

"It's not my studio. I just work there. But, yes, I travel in every day." And the weird thing is, Ed works just down the road. Well, in Soho. His office is a stone's throw from the Groucho Club. Very trendy address if you're a media type. But, you know what? We never travel in together. Never. Well, once in a blue moon, but that's all. Ed's often out on location, I suppose, and he works later than I do, but it's never occurred to us to meet up for lunch, and I always belt back the minute I finish to collect Elliott from his school, so a relaxed drink at the end of the day is out of the question. It seems such a waste. Maybe I'll suggest it to him. I realize I'm drifting and turn my attention back to Christian. "What about you?"

"Notting Hill," he says. "We get a great view of the carnival."

"Expensive?"

"Yeah. Where isn't?" He flushes slightly. "My parents still help me out. Until I get myself settled, of course."

"Of course."

"I'll write down the address for you," he says, scrabbling in his rucksack for a pen. And I wonder why on earth I'll ever need to have his address. He grabs a business card from the holder on the table, crosses out the address for La Place Velma and scribbles his own on the back. His handwriting is languid and flowing, and even if you didn't know, you'd probably guess it was an artist's hand. "You might find yourself passing that way and want to drop by."

I take it from him and politely study the card. "My sister has a dress shop near there. She sells vintage clothes."

"Cool."

"Cool," I echo with a laugh, and suddenly Christian looks shy. He can only be twenty-two or twenty-three and here am I, thirty-eight, fast approaching thirty-nine. What are we doing here together?

"I've put my mobile number on there too." He points it out. Even impoverished art students have the latest technology these days, just like fifteen-year-old daughters do.

"Thanks," I say, but I've no idea why. I start to gather my belongings and my senses. "I'd better get back. Things to do." Yeah, like typing and filing and a bit of staring out of the window.

"Can I see you again?"

"See me?" I resist the temptation to snort incredulously.

"I'd like to."

"Why?"

"Ali!"

"I don't know...." I chew my lip uncertainly, and there is the sweet lingering taste of strawberry on it.

"We can be just friends," he insists. "There's nothing wrong with that."

"No." I chew my lip some more.

He takes my hand and, I'll tell you this for nothing, no other friend has *ever* sent a jolt through my fingers like that before.

CHAPTER 6

"I'm in love." Christian doled the curry out of its carton and into a chipped Wedgwood serving dish that he put in the microwave. The gold edge had long worn off, and the dish no longer hissed and crackled viciously as it heated up.

Robbie looked up from the *Metro* paper that he'd picked up at the Tube station yesterday morning. "You said that last week."

"I did not."

Rebecca had her foot up on the table and was painting her toenails and wearing a painstaking expression. She was daubing them with lime-green varnish. "You did."

"See?" Robbie returned to his paper.

"I did not."

"You did," Rebecca insisted. "It was that pasty girl from the late-night deli. You'd been going on about her for weeks. You said she'd got eyes like Michelle Pfeiffer." Rebecca looked up. "Personally, I thought she'd got a squint."

"It doesn't matter when they're closed in ecstasy," Christian countered pleasantly as he arranged pilau rice as artistically as he could manage on three matching Wedgwood plates. "Besides, that wasn't love. That was merely a boyish infatuation."

"She blew you off when you asked her to go for a drink," Robbie reminded him.

"Then more fool her," Christian huffed. "Anyway, I shan't tell you if you're going to be pedantic about the whole thing." The microwave pinged and Christian retrieved the bowl.

The kitchen was huge, fitted with stripped pine that had seen better days and was due a revamp before too long. An original terra-cotta tiled floor made the room sound echoey rather than cozy. The big refectory table was at one end and looked out through the French doors over an enclosed garden that had run wild due to lack of gardening knowledge or enthusiasm among its current residents. A Clematis Montana, the only thing in flower, rambled freely over the walls, threatening to engulf everything in its path. The other shrubs were fresh, green and burgeoning due to the extremely wet winter and equally sodden spring, and were in need of judicious pruning. A tumbledown shed with broken windows nestled at the bottom and hid from work-shy eyes the myriad of spider-laden tools that had lain unused for some considerable time. It was the sort of charming chaos that would probably win a prize at the Chelsea Flower Show. The three friends had been living here for nearly six months, and it still looked nothing like home.

Robbie folded his newspaper and brushed the crumbs from this morning's toast from the place mats on the table. He ambled to the drawer and clattered about until he found three forks, which he plonked on the table while Christian dished out the curry.

Rebecca finished with her nail polish and slid it back into her handbag as she admired her handiwork. "Has your allowance come through yet, Christian?"

"Should be in the bank today if Pater and Mater haven't disinherited me for some imagined misdemeanor."

"Can you give me a sub? I'm a bit short."

"Sure." Christian brought the plates to the table. "I'm going to have to tap P and M for a tad more cash. This pittance just isn't keeping us in the style to which we have become accustomed. I don't make enough at the market to keep me in beer."

"Speaking of which..." Robbie opened some Tiger Beers and passed the bottles round. Christian drank from his gratefully.

"The tourist season is just beginning," Robbie said. "A couple more weeks and your earnings will soar."

"Not quite to the levels my father would have hoped for in the city job he managed to wangle me."

"Maybe you should have taken it, Chris."

"I'm an artist, for heaven's sake. Can you see me in an Armani suit, crunching numbers in front of a screen all day? No thanks, old man. My spirit would be crushed by the weight of responsibility within days."

"You mean you'd have to get off your lazy arse and do some real work."

"You're beginning to sound like my father." Christian flopped down. "How *is* life behind the counter of HMV?"

"You're a bastard." Robbie laughed and Christian joined in. They clinked their beer bottles together.

"Here's to being idle beggars all our lives!" Christian toasted enthusiastically.

"Have we had any more letters?" Robbie asked as he dug in.

"One from the electricity company, threatening disconnection." Rebecca raised her eyebrows and teased round the edge of her food with her fork.

"Damn!"

"We're going to have to do something about it, Christian," Robbie said.

"I know. I know. I'm just not sure what."

"Can't we just pay it?"

"How can we do that?" Christian asked. "There must be someone we know who can sort it."

"Pater and Mater," Rebecca mimicked.

"They've rescued *you* more than once," Christian reminded her. "These companies are all talk. They hardly ever disconnect anyone these days. They'd be sued for violating human rights, or something. We need you to get preggers, Becs. Then we could all get a council house together."

Rebecca gave him a stony look. "Ha, ha."

"Don't worry," Christian assured her. "We've probably got ages to get it sorted."

"I hope you're right," Rebecca said, and finally swallowed a mouthful of food.

They all ate silently as the sun in its last throes moved over the garden, filling the kitchen with a warm, golden glow which brought out the best in it.

"So, who is it this time?" Robbie said.

"What?"

"Who's the lucky lady?"

"Oh," Christian said, happy to push away thoughts of unpaid electricity bills. "Her name's Ali. Alicia."

"Top totty?"

"More than top totty, my uncultured little friend. Destined to be the love of my life. I'm talking soul mate, Robert, my boy. Soul mate."

"Ooo," Robbie said. "This is a new departure."

"I am a changed man," Christian admitted.

"I've heard that before."

"This is different." Christian settled back in his chair and folded his arms contentedly across his chest. His eyes glazed slightly and his mouth turned up in a little smug smile of satisfaction. "She is beautiful. Stunning. Gorgeous. Beautiful."

"You've said beautiful twice," Robbie noted.

"Beautiful, beautiful, beautiful." Christian looked wistful. "I can't say it enough."

Rebecca put down her fork. "He's off again."

"I am not."

"And where did you meet this many times beautiful woman?"

Christian put his hands behind his head. "Ali? I met her at the market. I drew her. I drew her for nothing, just because she was sitting there looking so beautiful."

Robbie nearly choked on his beer. "You did something for free? It *must* be love!"

Christian smiled ecstatically. "It is."

"Well, I for one can't wait to meet her," Robbie said.

"All in good time, Robert. All in good time."

"And is this one over sixteen?" Rebecca asked.

Christian let his hands drop to the table, and his smile turned to a thoughtful pout. "I think you could safely say that," he said.

CHAPTER 7

"It always takes an age to get served here." Ed shook his head with resignation. "All the waiters seem to be bustling about, busy doing nothing." He was sitting in the Groucho Club with Orla, and to prove him a liar a charming and efficient waiter came over straight away to take their order. "See what I mean?"

Orla laughed. It was a beautiful sound, made all the more startling because she did it so rarely. When she ordered a white wine spritzer, Ed confessed that he could never understand the joy of watering down wine. For himself, he ordered a beer, ignoring the desire of his taste buds for something infinitely stronger. Although the thought of diluted wine didn't hold much appeal, the lure of neat whisky was becoming increasingly hard to resist at the end of a long working day.

The Groucho Club was overridingly black and scuffed. Very laid back in an overstated manner. The carpet was very nightclubby in a you-wouldn't-want-to-see-it-during-the-day type of way. The club always had young, fashionable alternative comedians huddled into corners hoping no one would recognize or overhear them, and groups of brash, loud-talking, champagne-drinking nobodies hoping that someone would. It was the place where anyone who was anyone went to be ignored. Heaven knows why Wavelength held a membership, but it was only round the corner from their offices and it meant that the owner could stay in London in relatively cheap, convenient and trendy surroundings on his rare visits to the city. And you got a complimentary dish of peanuts with your media-type-priced drinks. What more could an exclusive club offer?

"You got finished on-time at Performing Power Tools?"

"Yes," Ed said, stretching out and failing to add "just about." Orla crossed her legs, but still sat bolt upright on the worn leather Chesterfield, despite it using all its guile to lull her down into its depths. She didn't do relaxed well. Social chitchat seemed beyond her powers of comprehension, as if the whole thing was rather pointless, which it was but it certainly helped the day to go by. "The tape's going into editing tomorrow. I'm sure they'll be pleased with the results."

"Good. Good."

Their drinks arrived and Ed signed for them. He held his beer aloft. "Cheers," he said.

"Cheers." Orla sipped her wine. Ed wished she'd unbutton her jacket or do that "plain librarian" thing and loosen her hair and turn into a sexy vamp or do something to indicate that she wasn't on duty now. But then, Orla always seemed to be in work mode. He sighed.

"Something wrong?" she asked.

"No." He eased his neck against the sofa. "Just weary." He wanted to curl up in a ball and go to sleep or be massaged with aromatic oils until his muscles let go of their seemingly permanent tension and softened to the point of helplessness.

"You look like you could do with a back rub," Orla said, and Ed straightened up slightly, wondering if this frighteningly perceptive and astute woman could also read minds.

"I am due in Slough at some ungodly hour in the morning," Ed supplied, "to film Digital Computers sales training." And I really, really don't want to go. "The thought of it is sending my spine into spasm already."

"Did they decide on a presenter?"

"Jeremy Clarkson. Big budget," he added with a trace of irony.

"Who?"

"Maybe he's not made it on your side of the pond, but he's very popular here. Except with car manufacturers. I think they would rather have Lucifer himself presenting their corporate videos."

"Oh."

"He's good. Professional. We'll get the job done quickly." Unless the managing director decided to make a cameo appearance, as they so often did. Ed blamed Victor Kiam—he of "I liked the shaver so much I bought the company"—for an awful lot of tacky homegrown advertising videos. It could slow the whole thing down by a day if someone was particularly determined to make their screen debut. Still, the customer was always right. And, even if they weren't, they paid the bill.

Orla leaned back and seductively unbuttoned her jacket, nearly causing Ed to spit his beer back in his glass. "Trevor was telling me that you started out in movies."

"Yes." *Be casual, Edward. The words "Ford" and "Harrison" must not pass your lips or you will be the laughingstock of the postproduction suite.*

"Ever miss it?"

Ed looked round. Was Trevor hiding behind the sofa ready to spring some *Candid Camera*–style joke on him? He turned back to Orla. "What?"

"The world of corporate videos is a little different from Hollywood."

He was tempted to say "No? Really? I hadn't noticed." But then he remembered that Orla didn't do irony either and said instead, "Yes, it is. A bit."

Orla took a long, slow sip of her wine and fixed him with a stare, as she was prone to do. "I won't be here for very much longer," she said.

Ed chuckled. "It makes it sound like you're dying."

"I am," she answered coolly, "in some ways. If not physically, then mentally. This just doesn't get my juices flowing. I can feel them stagnating in my veins. This whole management thing desiccates the creative process. It's not for me. I don't know how you've managed to keep fresh for so long."

"Er..." Ed said, realizing that Orla could have no idea of the size of his mortgage, which had been his prime motivating factor for an equally sizeable portion of his life.

"Don't you feel the same way?"

"Er..." It was true to say that Ed's juices had not recently been known for the quality of their flowing. But why did it matter to Orla? Had she suddenly found her small-talk button, or was this all being noted for a damning report about his future at Wavelength? He could see it now—"Edward Kingston, Managing Director. Creative juices all dried up. Desiccated. Recommend 'izing' in some way with large golden handshake." But, no doubt, not large enough to allow him to retire in luxury to a deserted Caribbean island. Good night, Vienna, for poor old Ed, and back to scouring the job ads in *Broadcast.*

"You're good, Ed," she said flatly. "You're good, but you could be better. You have some great ideas, which will never *ever* see the light of day as long as you stay at Wavelength."

He wasn't sure he liked the emphasis she placed on *ever.* "Er…"

"Can I be frank with you?"

When Orla was frank, it was usually quite painful. "Er..."

She leaned forward conspiratorially from her sofa toward the low occasional table that separated them. "When I go back to the States, I'm going to be heading up a small independent film company."

"That's nice," he said for lack of anything more inspirational.

"It's also confidential." Orla put her glass and seemingly her cards on the table. "They're young, funky, going places. We have some great British scripts that we have backing for."

Ed nodded. "Good."

"I want you to come with me."

"Me?" He laughed.

"I mean it."

He checked the back of the sofa for Trevor again. Any minute now he was going to jump out with a camera, going, "Ha, ha, got you!" He didn't. Ed frowned. "I have no doubt, but why me?"

"You have a good, all-round knowledge of this business. I think I could put that to good use. British directors and producers are hot stuff in the States now. Look at Sam Mendes."

"Look at Sam Mendes indeed!" Ed was tempted to say, "But I get women in itsy-bitsy teeny weeny bikinis to drill holes in wood," and then he realized that false modesty was not a quality recognized by Hollywood either.

"You run a very eclectic but efficient organization with precious little in the way of assets or support from your management. You're a great motivator."

Only of other people, he added mentally.

For a moment he saw himself driving down Rodeo Drive in

some racy, top-of-the-range convertible, sun shining, Beach Boys on the radio. "Ali would never go for it." He shook his head. "She's not a great fan of America. She's the only person I know who doesn't like *Frasier*."

"You've been married a long time?"

"A very long time."

"Then what Ali thinks is important."

"Yes." Ed sighed heavily and wished he'd ordered the scotch. "This is no slur on your fellow countrymen, believe me. I love America. I would move there tomorrow. But Ali thinks Ronald McDonald is the Antichrist."

Orla laughed.

"I think she would rather our children were brought up somewhere really, really awful than in Los Angeles."

"Like where?"

"Like… Like… Budleigh Salterton."

"I have no idea where Budleigh Salterton is," she said with a smile.

"Neither have I," Ed confessed.

"It sounds pretty."

"It does, doesn't it?"

"Maybe nicer than L.A."

"Maybe."

"We should go there one day. Together."

The hairs on the back of Ed's neck all stood to attention. "Maybe." He finished his beer. "The District line calls," Ed said ruefully.

"Think about this, Ed. I don't need an answer right away," Orla said as she stood up and smoothed a wayward curl from her forehead.

Think about it! It was going to occupy his every waking moment and probably most of his sleeping ones too. It was the opportunity he had longed for, dreamed of. A chance to get his foot jammed back in the door of real filmmaking. Get his career riding on the fast-track once again rather than shunted in some sleepy siding. No one else would give him a second look on his current CV, he knew that. It had taken someone inside, close to him, to realize that he could still make the grade.

Orla picked up her perpetually bulging briefcase. "But I won't wait for you forever," she warned.

"Of course not," Ed agreed, and realized his tongue had gone dry and he was desperately in need of another drink.

"We can talk about this some more." Orla headed to the door and he followed in her wake.

Oh, he could sit here all night and talk about this! He might even be persuaded to share his Harrison Ford stories, given the right moment. But the person he needed to talk about it with most was Ali.

"Maybe over dinner one night?" Orla suggested casually.

"Yes. Yes. Great idea," Ed agreed readily. "Dinner. Dinner."

Would Ali be prepared to pack up and go halfway round the world to satisfy his ambition? Would she realize how long he had waited to hear the sorts of things that Orla was saying? Would Ali, whose ambition stretched only as far as putting seven vaguely edible meals on the table each week, understand how much this ache had been suppressed in him? Until he'd heard that there might be a way out, he hadn't even realized how much himself.

Ed glanced at his watch. They had closed the Venetian blinds and switched on the lights at the club, giving it a softer, more intimate feel. The inside of the much-vaunted Groucho might be disappointing, but there was a strange comfort in knowing that. At least there was one place where he didn't feel he was on the outside looking in.

The alternative comedians were sinking deeper into the sofas, and even the brash boys were heading for home. It was late. He had said he'd be back ages ago. Ali would be worried. His dinner would be dried up or in the microwave or in the dog, if they'd had one. Perhaps he should have suggested supper to Orla tonight and phoned Ali to say he had an unexpected meeting. But then he ought to do the groundwork with his wife first. There was no point discussing the niceties when Ali might flatly refuse to consider it. They must sit down with a nice glass of wine and talk. He could rehearse his speech all the way home on the Tube to make sure he got it right.

He and Orla pushed out of the door and stood on the pavement. Before he had a chance to behave like a gentleman, Orla had hailed a cab. It pulled up next to her. "Good night, Ed."

He held the door open. "Good night, Orla." Ed stood there feeling ridiculously grateful. He wanted to hug her and kiss her and whoop enthusiastically and generally give some sort of emotional demonstration to show her how much her throwing a lifeline to his drowning film career meant. Instead, he stood there like a statue, being tongue-tied and British and fiddling with his hands. In the end, all he managed was, "And thanks."

She smiled out through the open window and waved her hand dismissively. The cab drove off, leaving him alone on Dean Street. There was a chill in the night air that felt more autumnal than springlike, more reminiscent of closing, ending, rather than of beginning. Ed shivered and wished he'd worn a thicker coat. At the same time he wondered what the temperature would be in Los Angeles.

Yes, he and Ali must talk. Tonight. But he wasn't entirely sure that she would want to listen when she found out what he had to say.

CHAPTER 8

"Oh, Daddy! How could you!" Tanya is tearful and possibly premenstrual, which at this age is a frightening condition that turns her into a hormonal psychopath. I'm sure I was never like this at fifteen. I was always so good.

Ed has just walked through the door. He is desperately late and is looking extremely bemused. "What?"

He looks to me for support, but I have my hands on my hips and am in no mood to placate anyone, as I've had to listen to three hours of how Tanya doesn't concentrate in lessons (any of them, apparently) and how, if she doesn't stop yapping to her friends and eyeing up the boys and start doing some serious work pretty damn soon, then she's going to end up working on a checkout in some shabby supermarket. Not exactly the teacher's words, but I'm paraphrasing and it amounted to the same thing anyway.

Ed looks at Tanya. "Well—what?"

"You have missed my parents' evening," she wails, and crashes upstairs, managing to knock all the Gustav Klimt prints askew for maximum effect. "You don't care about me at all," she shouts down over the banister rail. What she really means is that she's had to listen to me moaning at her for the last hour, telling her how she is going to be grounded for three whole weeks while she catches up with her homework, and how she probably won't get any pocket money until the same year she starts drawing her pension and that "Daddy, how could you!" would probably have smoothed it all over for her.

Ed turns to me, looking vaguely mortified. "I completely and utterly forgot," he says.

"Oh, Ed! How could you!" I say, taking up my daughter's refrain.

"I got caught in a meeting."

"Yes. I can smell it on your breath."

"I had *one,*" he insists. "At the Groucho. A quick one."

I glance at the clock to make a point.

"Oh, Daddy! How could you!" Elliott is in his best striped pajamas and is holding Barney, the chipper purple dinosaur, by his one remaining ear. His eyes roll round his sockets and he pouts petulantly. Clearly, my youngest child, when he has finished his extortionately priced schooling, is heading straight for a career on the stage. We both try not to smile at him. "You've missed Tanya's parents' evening. And all her schoolwork is really, really bad," he says triumphantly.

"I hate you too, Elliott, you little snitch," Tanya shouts over the banister.

"Tanya!" I'm the one who shouts in this house.

Elliott rolls his eyes some more. "Women," he says with a campy flick of the wrist and flounces upstairs to bed.

"Elliott. Wee and clean your teeth. I'll be up in a minute."

I march through to the kitchen because I want to shout at Ed too and I don't think you should ever row in front of your children. He puts his briefcase down and shrugs out of his coat in a weary way, and somehow, instead of making me feel soft toward him, it incenses me even more. With drooping shoulders, he follows me through to the kitchen.

"I forgot," he repeats before I can launch into him.

"It was the last thing I said to you when you left the house this morning."

"I have dealt with a million things since then, Ali. It slipped clean away. I didn't do this on purpose."

"Sometimes I wonder whether you care at all. They are your children too. Next year is Tanya's exam year. This is important to her."

"It's important to me too...."

"Is it?"

"You know it is."

"I have been trying to ring you for hours, and your phone is switched off."

"The battery was low. I was trying to save it."

"A fat lot of good that is to me."

"I'm sorry."

I know that you can't use mobile phones in the Groucho without threat of expulsion for such a hideous flaunting of the rules, and this makes me cross because it bothers Ed more than his daughter's entire future. But I can't stay angry, I'm too exhausted. What I really want is a big cuddle and for Ed to tell me that my daughter isn't going to end up as a juvenile delinquent and a single-parent family. I'm so upset that she can't see the opportunities she has to make a great life for herself and is, instead, content to watch *Buffy the Vampire Slayer* and spend her days at school goofing off. Am I such an awful role model for her? Where have I gone wrong that she doesn't want to be a geneticist or a corporate lawyer or a Shakespearean actress? Why does she have no ambition beyond how many times she can get one ear pierced?

I pretend that all I want in life is her happiness. But it is lip service. I don't. I want her to work hard and earn lots of money and be able to make informed choices about her future and have a great job that I can boast about to other mothers with less successful daughters. I don't want her to be pregnant at sixteen and be saddled with looking after her baby while she tries to claw back some of her childhood. I want her to travel the world and break some hearts while not having hers broken in return, then I want her to meet a wonderful, financially secure, emotionally stable Ben Affleck look-alike when she's twenty-nine and then think about having babies. Am I being unreasonable? I don't think so. And I wish I could share this—with Tanya, with Ed, with anyone. But I can't. No one understands me. Ed would laugh and say that I'm getting it all out of proportion just because some tight-arsed lesbian teacher who's never had a proper job thinks it's unusual for a fifteen-year-old to have the attention span of a flea. It's all right for him. He was hopeless at school, did badly in all of his exams and has carved out a great career for himself in a job which he loves, through sheer determination. I worked really hard and achieved zip—unless you count a relief map of the Andes in stretch marks on my stomach.

I crash about and put the kettle on. "Your dinner is all dried up." I sniff. "It looks disgusting." It looked disgusting before it dried up and it tasted fairly awful too, but I won't tell Ed that. I'll let him discover it for himself. He'll eat it without complaint, because despite the fact that he has a memory like a particularly leaky sieve, he's not a bad man.

I watch him lift his dinner from the depths of the oven with something approaching horror. He lays it gingerly on the table. "What is it?" he says.

"I can't remember." I put a cup of tea down next to him. "Something from Marks & Spencer. Mexican, I think. It looked okay three hours ago."

"It looks very nice now," he says, and my cruel, upset heart melts. "Thanks."

I sit down at the table opposite him. "You need to go and talk to Tanya. She's doing really badly at school. I don't know what's wrong with her."

"Can't you do it?"

"No, I can't."

"You're so much better at it than me." Ed is whining and I dig my heels into the kitchen floor.

"You're the one that's upset her."

"I'll go up in a minute," he promises. I hear the sigh hidden in his voice. "I'll see to Elliott too. Where's Thomas?"

"In bed with Harry Potter, where else?"

Ed smiles tiredly. "Two drama queens and a pervert. We're doing a great job."

"No one said it would be easy."

He puts his fork down for a moment, and I fear he is about to abandon whatever it is I cooked for him. "No one said it would be this hard either, did they?"

"No. I guess not."

Sometimes I would like to stop being a parent and just walk out of the front door without thinking about anyone else. The last time I did that I was about twenty. I wonder if Ed ever feels the same? He picks up his fork again and stabs it into his food determinedly.

"What was your meeting about?"

Ed keeps his head over his food and takes a long time before he answers.

"It was with Orla. She's setting up a new company."

I vaguely remember who Orla is and "Mmm" my interest.

"Ali." Ed looks up, and his eyes are deep and distant and I can't see what's behind them at all. "Would you ever consider moving to the States?"

I'm taken aback. "America?"

"Yes."

"No."

Ed puts down his fork and pushes his plate away. "I thought not." He gets up from the table. "I'll speak to Tanya."

CHAPTER 9

Kath Brown comes into the office. When I say office, it's really a glorified cupboard filled with bulging files and bits of fabric and colorful storyboards to give people a sneak preview of how their house will look when they recklessly abandon their magnolia walls to Kath's flowery clutches. It's always the same. Whoever the client. They start off tentatively with the first room—a little change here and a swag or a tail or two there—and then they get bolder with each room. Their confidence grows as they progress through the house—a touch of gilt here, a bit of glitz there, more plasterwork, perhaps a bit of handcrafted something—and the suppliers become steadily more exclusive. Perhaps that's why having a name like Kath Brown works. It's a name you can depend on. You're never going to get ripped off by a Kath Brown, are you?

I am typing invoices. Like the choice of fabrics, they also grow a little bolder with each room. I am in ultra-efficient mode and my fingers are positively smoking over the keyboard. This cupboard-cum-office may look like utter chaos to the untrained eye, but I can lay my fingers on anything I need within a millisecond. Kath, on the other hand, cannot. I look up at her and smile benevolently. She needs me more than I need her.

Looking very worried, she slides her glasses down to the end of her nose and peers over them at me. "There's a boy in the shop," she says hesitantly. I stop the flurry with my fingers. "A young boy. He says he knows you. He's asked to see you."

I can't even kid myself. I know exactly who it is. And so do you. Only Kath Brown is in the dark. I frown as if to say, "How intriguing!" while I try and think of something to say to her. I stand up and my knees are shaky and I wonder if I've gone as white as I feel.

"You'd better go through," Kath says when it's clear I'm not about to offer an explanation. And what could I tell her? "He's waiting."

"I won't be a minute," I promise her, and in the three steps it takes me to cross the office, I mentally check out how I must look. I'm wearing a black trouser suit, which is great because it's quite trendy and makes me feel younger and everyone was very civilized at breakfast this morning so it hasn't got any puke or jam or tea stains on it. A major plus when you want to look good, I think you'll agree. And, I know it's stupid, but I do want to look good. I don't possess a pair of Jimmy Choo kitten heels in which to skip lightly across the floor, but these ones are from Marks & Spencer's Particularly Expensive Range, or something, and do the job just fine.

In the shop, Christian looks vaguely uncomfortable. It must have been quite an effort for him to come here. I pause at the doorway to watch him. He is fingering some of the fabrics—the ones that are £180 per meter—and if he were Elliott, I'd tell him off. I hope he hasn't got charcoaly hands.

"Hi," I say, and Christian spins round. Just his smile is enough to do very weird things to me. This is ridiculous! I am old. I am a mother. I am a wife. I am a sensible suburban woman. How can he do this to me?

"Sorry," he whispers. "I didn't know what else to do."

"You shouldn't be here," I whisper back, even though he's as much as told me he knows that. I wonder if Kath Brown has a glass pressed to the wall. I would, in her situation.

"I was missing you," he says, as if that's explanation enough.

"Christian!"

"What?"

"How did you know where to find me?"

"I went in all the designer shops until I found someone who didn't look at me as if I was mad."

"I should be cross with you."

"But you're not." His mouth curls in a smile. Such is the naiveté and the confidence of youth.

"I am."

"I wanted to see you. You haven't been in the piazza at all."

"I've been trying to avoid you."

"Why?" I can't believe how hurt he looks. "Don't you like me?"

I check that Kath Brown isn't right behind me, eyes popping with apoplexy. "It isn't that simple."

"So you do like me?"

"Of course I like you."

"Then why are you avoiding me?"

"I think it's for the best."

"For whom?"

We are still speaking in stage whispers, and I'm looking round me, checking over my shoulders, like some sort of third-rate spy. "For both of us. I have commitments, Christian."

He looks affronted. "So do I."

"You don't."

Christian does that charming smile that makes my insides go watery. "I don't, do I?"

"You don't even know the meaning of the word." I am teasing and we both laugh. Quietly.

"I miss you," he says candidly. "I haven't seen you for days. I just want to talk to you."

"We can't talk here," I warn him. "This puts me in a difficult position."

"I didn't mean to."

"Christian…" I try to sound rational and stern and instead sound faintly desperate. "I have to think of my family."

"Don't they let you have friends?"

"Yes, but…"

"Then say you'll see me." He grins because he thinks he's winning.

"No. I can't."

"You can," he insists. "Just once."

"Christian. No."

"Spend the day with me."

"How can I?"

"Just one day. Not even the whole day. Just a bit of the day. Say you will."

"No. No. Definitely no."

The doorbell chimes and two customers saunter in. They look very well-heeled, dripping with designer labels, and probably want some understated brocade fabrics for a little pied-à-terre in town. They definitely look like a £180 per meter pair. He is much older than her. I notice these things now. Christian starts to back away toward the door, incongruous in his black jeans and trainers, clutching his sketchpad. Any minute now Kath will breeze out to greet her clients. Christian lowers his voice, so I have to lean closer to him. "Say you'll meet me or I'll embarrass you."

"Don't you dare!"

"Say you'll meet me."

"Christian!" I hiss in the most threatening tone I can manage without anyone else hearing.

He grins. "Friday. Meet me on Friday."

"I'm working."

"Be reckless, take a day off."

Doesn't he know that all my days off are accounted for during school holidays? If you don't book up from one year to the next, you haven't a hope in hell of going anywhere decent. I have to grovel for weeks if I want to attend Thomas's sports day. Thankfully, Tanya's school sold off the playing fields for a housing estate during the Tories' reign and are content to let their charges become couch potatoes.

"I'll be waiting outside Kew Gardens. The main entrance at ten o'clock."

I haven't been to Kew in years, even though we live just down the road. It's so beautiful there. You'd think you were a million miles from London. We took Tanya when she was much younger, but now she'd die of boredom, it would be so uncool. Although the fresh air might kill her first though. "No."

"Don't be late," he warns. He checks that the well-heeled couple are turned away and blows me a kiss. Before I can hiss anything else, Christian backs out of the shop looking triumphant.

I smile cheesily at the couple just as Kath Brown appears. She gives me a suspicious look and then turns her attention to her paying customers, holding out her hand to greet them effusively. I slope off into the office, grateful for the chance to get back behind my desk, and I wonder what I'm going to tell Kath Brown when she asks who my visitor was. And to think, two weeks ago my major problem was coming up with a nutritious alternative to chicken nuggets. I breathe the gusty sigh of the terminally confused and open a file of invoices on my desk despite the fact I have one open already.

The afternoon is a complete waste of time. My smoking fingers are extinguished beyond re-ignition, and I shuffle paper about aimlessly until Kath Brown finally cracks under the strain.

"Is everything all right?" she asks in a way that tells me she wants to know but only if it's not too mucky.

"I think so."

"Tanya's not in trouble, is she?" My God, she thinks Christian has got my daughter pregnant! If only she knew it's me who's in trouble.

"If you need time off for anything, anything at all, you only have to say."

"Thanks." This is possibly the last thing I need to hear. I want her to tell me that we are about to be inundated by an avalanche of work as the well-heeled couple have seventeen houses that want tarting up and that she can't spare me for a minute and, in fact, would I like to work some overtime? Something that hasn't happened since I've been here. But I can live in hope.

"You can go home early, if it will help," she says kindly, and then I realize she's probably noticed that I've been staring at the same invoice for the past two hours.

"I think I will, if that's okay." I try to look pathetic and worried, which isn't all that difficult.

"Sure." Kath Brown can be very sweet. "Take it easy. I'll see you tomorrow, Ali."

"Yes." I really am beginning to feel awful now.

I fuss my papers away hurriedly to escape from her unbearably sympathetic gaze and rush out.

Standing outside the shop, I linger in the doorway. The air is heavy, close, carrying the scent of rain. I breathe deeply, glad to be out of my cupboard. I step out onto the pavement and stop in my tracks. Heedless of the taxis whizzing by, I stand back in the gutter and stare speechlessly. In bright red chalk, there is a message for me scrawled on the concrete.

DON'T BE LATE, ALI KINGSTON!!

Christian has drawn a smiley face underneath it. And two kisses. I check to see that Kath Brown is safely ensconced in her shop and try to rub it away with my shoe, starting with the kisses. Red chalk is impossible to get off pavement. Did you know that? I do. I look at the sky, and the black clouds have drifted away harmlessly. I check the pavement, and the message is still there. I hope the clouds come back and it will rain soon and wash away my embarrassment. And certainly before Kath Brown comes out. I don't know quite what she'd make of this.

I walk down the street, lighthearted in my non-Jimmy Choo's and smile to myself with exasperation when I think of Christian and his bare-faced cheek. Don't be late! No, I won't be late, Christian Winter, because I won't be there!

CHAPTER 10

Neil was puffing. He stopped running around and put his hands on his hips, bending forward to ease the stitch in his side. "Edward. You seem to be hitting that little ball with rather more venom than is absolutely necessary."

Ed stopped running about too. His face was set with determination. "What?"

"You're thrashing me already. Can't we just ease up into knockabout mode, like normal? I'll let you win *and* buy the beers if that helps."

Ed wiped the sweat from his forehead with his T-shirt. "I don't know what you mean."

"You seem to be on a mission to launch that rather inoffensive little squash ball into outer space. You're no fun to play with when you're like this. What's wrong?"

"Nothing." Ed bounced around on his toes a bit and eased his shoulders in an attempt to loosen them up. Squash courts always stank of sweaty trainers, and it was grating on his nerves. "Let's get on with it, shall we?"

Neil held up his hands. "I give in. No more. I've got a cramp in everything. It all hurts. I can't run another step. If I had a white flag, I'd get down on my knees and wave it."

Ed was getting agitated. He'd been like it all day. "Just hit the ball, Neil."

"Did the bird in the bikini saw one of her legs off?"

Ed stopped and stared at his brother. "What?"

"In the Performing Power thing advert?"

"No. She did not."

Neil snorted. "Well, it must have been something pretty catastrophic."

"It's nothing, okay? Now, hit the ball."

Neil shook his head. "I've had enough. You hit it." He threw the ball to his brother. Ed caught it on the fly and slammed it hard into the back wall, grunting with the effort. The ball, reluctant to take any more abuse, rebounded faster than a speeding bullet and hit Ed squarely in the eye.

Much, much later, Neil came ambling into the bar fingering his damp hair. Ed was clutching a bag of Sizzling Steak Ranch Fries to his injured eye. "I don't think Sizzling Steak Ranch Fries will work in the same way," Neil advised as he sat on the stool next to his brother. "You need raw meat for swelling."

"You're a bloody photographer," Ed growled, "what do you know about first aid?"

"More than you, it seems."

"It was all they had and I've got an ice cube under them, clever dick."

"Oh."

"You could hose down three elephants in the time it's taken you to have a shower."

"Are you ready to talk about what's wrong now, or do you want me to put the other eye out for you first?"

Ed scowled in what would have been a menacing way if his face hadn't been half-obscured by a packet of crisps. Neil sat in silence. Eventually, Ed sighed and said, "Orla's offered me a job. A good job. Back in films."

Neil shrugged. "Great."

"In the States."

"Less great."

"Ali won't even consider it."

"Have you talked to her about it?"

Ed glared at Neil again, but it hurt his cheek. "No, I transmitted it to her telepathically while she was asleep." He nursed his beer sullenly.

"And?"

"And I should let it go. But I can't." Ed adjusted his crisps. "I feel like someone is dangling a big juicy carrot in front of me."

"I hate carrots."

Ed ignored him. "It's so close I can smell it, but it's just out of reach and I can't bear the thought that it might always be."

"Orla?"

"Orla what?"

"Orla's holding the carrot?"

"I suppose so."

"And is that part of the problem?"

"I don't think so."

"So Ali doesn't know about Orla?"

"There's nothing to know." He had waited all day to talk to Orla, but she was busy. Busy analyzing this and reviewing that. He'd tried to bump into her over lunch and in the little kitchen where they all made coffee, but there were too many people around. She had smiled noncommittally at him in the way that people do when they have shared secret knowledge, and it churned his stomach so much that he couldn't drink the coffee he hadn't wanted to make in the first place. Ed was desperate to talk more to her about the job, what it entailed, who were the movers and shakers these days, he wanted to hear it all even though he knew it would torture him, because eventually he would have to tell her that he couldn't take it. All his dreams snuffed out in one little sentence.

Neil frowned vacantly. "I don't know what to say, bro."

"Now do you see why it was pointless even discussing it?" Ed took his crisps away from his eye and prodded the area gingerly before putting them back. "I've lived my life nursing this regret and I didn't even know it. And now I've got a chance to put it right. What if you had one thing stopping you from achieving your big break, your lifetime's ambition?"

"I have."

Ed looked at his brother. "What?"

Neil wiped his mouth with his sleeve. "Lack of talent."

"Lack of motivation more like," Ed snorted. "You're just an idle bastard."

"And maybe you're too driven," Neil said. "Stop and look at what you've got. Count your blessings. You're healthy, wealthy and sometimes, on rare occasions, wise. You could spend your life chasing rainbows and never find a pot of gold. Believe me, the only thing at the end of most rainbows is a crock of shit."

Ed started to laugh. "You're going to start singing 'Always Look on the Bright Side' in a minute, aren't you?"

"I might."

Ed took his bag of Sizzling Steak Ranch Fries from his eye and dropped the sliver of melted ice cube that remained into the ashtray on the bar. Then he tore the bag open and offered it to Neil. "Want a crisp?"

"No thanks." Neil grimaced. "It'd be like eating a surgical dressing." He jumped down from his bar stool. "Come on, let's get you home. Do you think you need to pop into Casualty on the way back just to get your eye checked out?"

"No." Ed shook his head. "It'll be fine. I can see things quite clearly."

Neil picked up his car keys and stared at Ed. "I hope so, bro. I sincerely hope so."

CHAPTER 11

"Ooooh." Ed lies down in the bed with his hand over his eye.

"Let me look at that," I say, and try to prize his fingers off.

"It's okay, Ali. It's just a bruise. I don't want you messing around with it."

"I'll get you some arnica."

"What's that?"

"It's for bruising."

"I don't want any. I've put ice on it. It's fine. Neil looked at it."

"What does Neil know about anything?"

"He knows quite a bit about getting hit with squash balls."

"You'll have a black eye in the morning."

"Will I?" Ed sits up and looks alarmed.

"Let me look at it."

Ed leans forward. "Don't poke it around."

"I won't." Wearing my serious face, I examine Ed and try not to poke around as instructed. I have inherited a lot of things from my mother, and my inability to be gentle when faced with another's pain is one of them. I use the bully-them-back-to-health method of nursing. It worked perfectly well for me as a child, and I've suffered no lasting harm from not being mollycoddled.

Ed's eye is a bit bloodshot and puffed up, but there's no cut, and I think he's been quite lucky to escape with a bit of bruising from what Neil said about the force with which Ed hit the ball.

I smooth my finger over Ed's eyebrow. "Oooh," he says again. "It hurts."

"Shall I kiss it better?"

"Mmm," Ed murmurs and tilts his face toward mine.

I stroke his fringe away, which like the lawn needs cutting again, and move my lips lightly against his eyebrow.

"Oooh," Ed moans, a mixture of pain and pleasure.

I kiss gently along his eyebrow and over his eyelid, barely touching him, caressing his skin with my breath. "Does it hurt anywhere else?"

Ed pouts his lips and points to them with his finger. "Here," he says. I kiss his lips tenderly. Ed points to his throat. "Here hurts too." And I obligingly kiss his neck.

"And here?" I ask as I slide down his body. Ed has dark, curled hair on his chest. It is soft and warm and would be fabulous for stuffing a duvet. I love lying against him on cold winter nights with the warmth of his skin and his soft down snuggled against my back.

"Mmm." Ed relaxes back against the pillow. "Are the bratlets in bed?"

"Yes," I murmur, continuing my tender assault. "Ages ago." I press my face against his soft skin. I love the scent of him. Even after all these years. He smells of musk and vanilla and manliness. I could drown in that aroma, which is better than newly mown grass or creosote or freshly baked bread.

Ed strokes my hair and I let my kisses linger over his stomach, which is burning hot, a comforting fire. I lift my head and smile at him. "Does this hurt?"

"Oh yes," he says, and closes his eyes, the pain clearly forgotten.

It is some ungodly hour and I try not to look at the clock and worry about getting up in the morning, because I am contented. We are curled together in post-coital bliss. "God, Ed," I sigh. "Midweek passion? When did we last do that?"

"When was the last lunar landing?"

I poke him in the ribs. "It wasn't that long ago."

"It's been a while."

"Too long," I agree, and Ed wraps his arms round me and we

lie comfortably in that delicious state between waking and sleeping. "Ed?"

"Mmm." Ed sounds like he has tipped over the edge into sleep and is dozing.

"Ed. Did Neil say anything about Jemma last week?"

"No."

"Oh." I snuggle farther into his arms. "Are you sure?"

"Yes."

"What—nothing at all?"

"Ali." His tone is warning.

"Do you think we should invite them both round for dinner sometime?"

"No."

"Why?"

"Because you're trying to pair them off and they're not suited."

"I think they'd make a lovely couple."

"That's because you're desperate to get your sister married off."

"I'm not." I prop myself up on my elbow and Ed opens his good eye. "I think they have a lot to offer each other."

"Like what?" Ed lies there, looking like he's winking at me. "Your sister's got more miles on her than a clapped out Volvo and my brother's got a great collection of take-away cartons. And that's another thing. She's your sister and he's my brother. How could we do that to them? Let them make their own mistakes. I do not want to be responsible for my brother's happiness."

"They might make each other happy."

"Jemma is a go-getter. Neil is so laid-back he's horizontal."

"Perhaps Jemma would encourage him to do a bit more with his life. He's always going on about how he'd like to have more exciting assignments. She might give him the motivation he needs. Get him out of his cozy rut."

Ed turns toward me. "Do you think a woman should encourage her partner to achieve his dreams?"

"Of course I do." I smile sleepily at Ed. "Haven't I always supported you?"

"Ali..."

"I think I will invite them round for dinner. It'll be fun."

"Ali..."

I stretch my neck and stifle a yawn. "I'm so sleepy." I turn to Ed and kiss his nose. "Are you sleepy?"

"Yes, but…"

"Shall we turn the light off and settle down?"

"Yes."

I turn off the lamp and the cool white light of the moon streams in through the window, picking out the white cotton cover on the bed. My house hasn't had the Kath Brown treatment and is pale and uncluttered, except when the children are awake. I lie back against the pillow and pull the duvet up to nuzzle my neck; my body is heavy and sinking dreamily into sleep. The last thing I notice is that Ed has both of his eyes open and is staring at the ceiling, but I am too far gone in my surrender to deep, deep slumber to ask why.

CHAPTER 12

I am trying to clear the breakfast dishes away and finish my own toast at the same time. I think I've drunk my tea or, if not, I can't find it amid the debris. "Have you got your gym things, Thomas?"

"Yes." Thomas is still sitting at the table playing with two plastic wotsits that came out of the Rice Krispies. His gym things are nowhere in sight. They could still be in the ironing basket for all I know.

"Have you done your homework?"

"Yes." There is more of a growl in Tanya's answer. This is mainly because I'm monitoring her homework timetable with all the fanaticism of a Gestapo officer, and she is becoming desperate for her *Buffy* fix, which she's not allowed for another week.

"Are you sure?"

"Yes."

"Even the German?"

"Yes." She looks at me as if I am some lowlife clinging to her shoe. I hear about these wonderful mother-daughter relationships all the time. Women who can talk to each other about anything, who are the best of friends and who share their emotions openly to the supreme benefit of both parties. Sometimes they even wear matching clothes. I wouldn't be seen dead in the things Tanya wears and vice versa. I nag my daughter constantly and she scowls at me. Perhaps this is something else I've inherited from my mother. We were exactly the same. All through my teenage years we fought like cat and dog, as if I was the daughter from hell, when in actual fact I was a little angel who just had a minor bit of wing slippage from time to time. It was only when I was in my twenties that I appreciated what a wonderful woman my mother was. I can only hope that Tanya has a similar revelation. But I would prefer it to happen next week.

"Elliott, have you got your lunch?" I know he has because I saw him eat the Penguin biscuit out of it as soon as he'd finished his Coco Pops, even though he tried to eat it under the table. By the time he is twenty-one, that boy's veins will flow with pure chocolate.

"Yes," he says.

"You haven't eaten the chocolate biscuit out of it, have you?"

"I only tasted it a little bit," he confesses. "With my teeth. I thought I might not be hungry enough to eat it at lunchtime," he adds with a logic that defies further investigation.

"How's the eye?" I ask Ed, who is sitting silently amid the mayhem with his cup of coffee hovering at his lips, staring serenely into middle distance, as he does every morning.

"Fine," he says, lifting a finger to test it. The skin is only slightly pink, not the shiner I expected. Even though I failed in my quest to pump him full of arnica, he appears to have suffered no ill effects. Still, he seems a bit subdued. It could be shock.

"You're going to be late," I warn him, glancing for the millionth time at the clock. I've looked at it so often I'm starting to annoy myself. Why does its hands always move faster when you're pushed for time?

He picks up the newspaper and opens it. "I'm not in a rush today."

"Why?"

Ed shrugs. "No reason. We could travel in together, if you like."

I stop my tidying up. "We never travel in together."

Ed reaches for the cafetière and tops up his coffee. "We could today."

"I've got to walk Elliott to school."

"I'll wait. There's no hurry."

"There is. I've got a thousand things to do."

"It would give us a chance to talk."

"About what?"

Ed frowns. "I don't know."

I carry on tidying up. "Neither do I."

I'm all flustered and feel like throwing the cereal bowls into the air just to see how much noise they'll make when they land. "You could walk Elliott to school for me, if you're not in a rush."

"Fine." Ed downs his coffee and folds his newspaper. "Come on, Elliott," he says, and our son for once obeys without turning it into a three-act drama. "I'll see you later," he says and gazes across the kitchen. He doesn't come to kiss me and it could be his eye or my paranoia, but it seems to me that Ed gives me a very strange look.

I am meeting Christian. But you know that already, don't you? It's only my family who are blissfully unaware of my duplicity. Now that Ed and Elliott are out of the way, I rush Tanya and Thomas out the door with hurried kisses and threats and then fly upstairs two steps at a time. I am wearing the same black trouser suit I had on yesterday, and I change into something a bit more casual that will do for Kew and for work. But you see, I'm not going to spend the day with Christian—I'm merely going to meet him, tell him I can't spend the day with him, at the very, very most have a quick coffee and then skedaddle back to work.

I have tried phoning the mobile number he gave me to tell him that I wouldn't be going anywhere near Kew Gardens today, but the wretched thing is always turned off and I haven't been brave enough to leave word on his answering service. And I don't trust those things anyway. They're like teenagers. You can never be quite sure that they're going to pass the message on.

I was just not going to go at all. Just not turn up. But then, he is a lovely boy, and I couldn't stand him up without an explanation. Have you ever been stood up? It's dreadful. I had a crush on the school heartthrob, Gary Eccleston, when I was sixteen, and I worshiped him from afar for months and months and months. He was going out with Caroline Gregory, the first sex kitten I ever came across. She was petite and girly and the most outrageous flirt, and she dumped him in spectacular style for a down-market boy from the local comprehensive. A week later he asked me out. I was gobsmacked. So was everyone else. The school heartthrob and Ginger Nut. Ha!

He arranged to take me to the school disco, and I waited for him at the end of my road, so that my mother, who was in nagging harridan mode, wouldn't see him. I looked gorgeous. Really, I did. I'd spent hours doing my makeup. I'd tamed my hair with Jemma's help, using every potion under the sun we could find in Superdrug. I'd borrowed a groovy outfit from my best friend, Andrea Thornton. And I stood there feeling on top of the world, bursting with pride. And he didn't come.

I waited for hours. Hours and hours. I couldn't believe that anyone could be cruel enough just to leave me standing there on my own. Apparently, the school disco was great. Andrea told me all about it. She got off with Joseph Simpson, to whom she is now happily married and has two children with. Gary Eccleston went on his own and got back with Caroline Gregory, who dumped him again the very next day. I cried in my bedroom all night, letting my mascara run on the pillow and wondering just where I'd gone wrong. So, you see, I could never ever do that to anyone else. Especially not Christian.

I take the Tube to Kew and, far from being late, I am ridiculously early. I walk up and down outside the curly iron gates feeling conspicuous. Ten o'clock comes and goes. I have a very weird feeling about this. This is Gary Eccleston all over again. I've only come to tell Christian I'm not coming, for goodness' sake, and now *he* hasn't come. I'm standing here with my self-confidence ebbing and one nibble away from chewing my fingernails. The thing about being stood up is that in the back of your mind you know you've been stood up but there's always that nagging doubt that your stander-upper might have had an accident and that they are not there with you through no fault of their own. I couldn't bear for anything to have happened to Christian. I hope he has bumped into some twenty-year-old Caroline Gregory look-alike last night in some trendy bar and has decided not to come. Perhaps he's sitting in a café somewhere laughing about it to her. Perhaps it's for the best.

I walk up and down again and kick the pavement meaningfully. He could have let me know he wasn't going to come. But then again, how could he? He doesn't know my phone number. He doesn't know where I live. He only knows where I work by default. It's nearly twenty past ten. Well, ten-sixteen. I'm never sure whether this watch is fast or slow. I can feel tears prickling behind my eyes and feel utterly, utterly ridiculous. This is madness. How can I have let this man, this boy, into my life like this? How dare he sketch me and turn my life and my internal organs upside down and then leave me like this, wandering up and down on my own, being watched by visiting tourists who know, they just *know* that I've been stood up. I'll give him two more minutes then I'm off. Back to the safety of Kath Brown and her frilly curtains.

CHAPTER 13

"Veggie, fruit, fruit! Veggie, veggie, fruit, fruit..."

Ed held up his hand. "Okay, okay, okay!" All the dancing fruit and vegetables stopped, bumping into each other as they did so. "Let's just take five."

He motioned to the lead tomato, who waddled over to him from the oversize kitchen that was the background to the Kitchen Kapers video—a ready-made sauce for less than discerning vegetarians.

"Could you possibly just run through your lyrics one more time and see if you can't commit them to memory before the next take?" Ed smiled pleasantly at the tomato, but naturally couldn't see if he smiled back, although from the way the tomato stomped off, it was evident that there wasn't a lot of hilarity going on beneath his lurid red costume.

Ed tried to crack his interlinked fingers by stretching them and failed. Why was this taking so long? The set was built yesterday, and the ingredients had spent all day rehearsing their big moment. It should have been a piece of precipitation. Dead easy. The advert should take five minutes to record, plus a bit of post-editing, and yet they'd been here for more than an hour already, to no good purpose. They were supposed to be a lean, mean, budget-conscious production team, and the vegetables were supposed to be actors.

Trevor looked at Ed, who said sarcastically, "I thought it was supposed to be children and animals that are difficult to work with? I don't remember anyone ever mentioning organic produce."

"Will it help if I tell you that eventually the…er…fruits of your efforts will be screened in every supermarket and in post offices all over the country?"

"Not a lot."

"What about if I tell you that it'll make the advert for diarrhea tablets they're going to show before it look like a heap of crap?"

"Shut up, Trevor."

Trevor put his camera down. "You can tell one of your Harrison stories if it will make you feel better."

"I don't think even Harrison can help me today. It's not every day one has to deal with a vegetable who can't hold a note or remember four words."

"Technically, a tomato is a fruit," Trevor pointed out.

"Yes, of course," Ed said. "How stupid of me."

"Go easy, Ed. It must be difficult being a grown man in a tomato suit."

"You're right." Ed picked up the white plastic cup next to him, but his tea had gone cold. "He'd probably rather be playing King Lear."

"He'd probably rather be playing anything other than a tomato. We all have to pay the bills."

"Some of us more than others," Ed agreed.

"Do I take it we're still not finding the exciting world of corporate videos any more enthralling?"

Ed rubbed his hands over his face. "And I thought I was hiding it so well."

"If you do decide to go back to Hollywood," Trevor said, "take me with you."

Ed looked defensive. "Who said anything about Hollywood?"

Trevor shrugged. "It's the only place to be if you want to work at the cutting edge. And I'm not sure how much longer you can stand this."

Ed turned away before he was tempted to answer. He could see the juicy carrot right there just in front of him. Only this one was sitting on a six-foot polystyrene frying pan with its foam head peeled down, eating a Mars bar. "Shall we see if the vegetables are ready? Otherwise we could both be doing this for the rest of our lives."

Ed clapped his hands. "Ladies and gentlemen! Are we ready?"

A door opened behind him, and Orla came onto the set. She walked up until she was close behind him and he could feel her breath on his neck. She always smelled good. A blend of fresh, clean soap and some ferociously expensive perfume that lured him to drink it in even if he didn't want to. "Nice," Orla said, and he wasn't entirely sure what she was talking about.

"Hi," he said, distracted by the tomatoes falling over each other to get back in line.

"This is a bad time, right?"

"You could say that."

Orla lowered her voice. "I need to talk to you some more."

Ed looked round to check that they weren't being overheard, but as soon as Orla arrived, Trevor had faded into the background. "Right."

"Did you manage to discuss this with Alicia?"

Ed made an apologetic noise. "The timing hasn't been quite right yet."

"Things are moving on. Can we set up a meeting?"

"Sure."

"Tonight. What about dinner?"

"Er…" Ed scoured his brain for any remnants of conversations with Ali about parents' evenings, dentists' appointments, concerts, dinners with friends, but none came. "Dinner should be fine."

Orla parted with one of her rare smiles. "I'll look forward to it."

Ed's mobile rang.

"Damn," he said as he checked all his pockets before finding it. He noticed that the vegetables were getting restless. "Ed Kingston." He bit his lip while he listened and then spoke again. "Have you contacted my wife? Fine. Fine. I'll be there right away." Ed snapped his phone shut, wiping his damp palms on his trousers. His face had blanched and his forehead was creased in a frown. "Orla, I have to go. Can you do me a favor and take over here?"

Orla spread her hands. "Sure."

"Find Trevor. He'll give you the lowdown."

"Is everything okay?"

"No, not really." Ed was shrugging on his coat. "I'll talk to you later."

"Are we still on for dinner?"

Ed was heading toward the door. "I'll see you at the Groucho at eight." He turned on his heels, came back and kissed Orla on the mouth. "Thanks," he said. "You're a pal."

Orla watched him rush out of the door before she ran her tongue over her lips. "You're welcome," she said under her breath.

CHAPTER 14

Christian is jogging up the road. I want to wring my hands with relief, but stand there looking unconcerned instead. I was on the verge of leaving. Really, I was. Another few seconds and I'd have been gone. Perhaps I'll look back on this very moment in years to come and wonder how things would have been different if I'd walked away, got on the Tube, gone back to work and chalked this whole thing up to experience.

I was coming down with a cold the night I met Ed and nearly didn't go to the rugby club do of indistinct origin. What would have happened if instead I'd retired to my bed with a hot water bottle and a good dose of Benylin Expectorant? Would I be married to Ed now or would he have met someone else that night, and the chance for our paths to cross would have been lost forever? As it was, we met, danced all night, had a tentative snog, during which I gave him my cold, resulting in me going through agonies wondering why he didn't ring me for over a week to arrange our next date.

Things happen all the time that can change our lives, don't they? It's like a perilous journey across shifting sands. Small, seemingly innocent incidents that suck us away from our intended life course, altering our emotional landscape forever. And I know that this is one of those moments, not yet consciously, but somewhere down deep inside round one of the corners of my psyche in a place I'm choosing to ignore. I didn't know I did denial so well. But then it isn't only love that is blind. Guilt, inertia and lust can all be pretty shortsighted too.

This is a beautiful road. Leafy and green. It is lined with magnificent trees, and all the houses are grand and rambling. Their gardens are overflowing with flowers and spring bulbs and are a fitting precursor to the glory of Kew. I turn my eyes and study them rather than watching Christian, because I feel so exposed out here, waiting. It's as if everyone who sees me knows that I really shouldn't be here.

Christian arrives in front of me breathless and smiling. "Hi," he says.

"Hi."

"I'm sorry I'm late," he rushes on cheerfully. "The Tube was delayed. Jumper."

"Oh," I say, and brush aside the thought that he might be lying. There was no mention of a delay on my line or anyone jumping on the track. But I do wonder what awful thing can happen in someone's life that they want to stop it by launching themselves into thin air in front of a moving Tube train?

"I thought you might have gone," he says, and clearly hasn't even considered that I might not have been here in the first place. He is so sure of himself, whereas I am sure of nothing anymore.

Christian grabs my hand with a familiarity that momentarily stuns me, and he pulls me toward the grand gates and the waiting kiosk.

I stop. "Christian." He turns and stops too. "I can't do this."

His face is the epitome of disappointment. He looks like Elliott did when Barney the perky purple dinosaur parted company with his ear.

"I came to tell you that I can't spend the day with you."

"Why not?" He is genuine in his disregard for anything else in my life.

"I have a family."

"I know."

"I'm deceiving them."

"Only a little bit," he reassures me. And I wonder if there is a scale to grade deception, like the Richter scale for earthquakes. Is there one that can measure how much damage this will do?

"You wouldn't believe how difficult it was for me to get away," I plead.

"You're here now," he says, and his face softens and I can see how pleased he is that we are together.

"I know."

"It seems stupid to come so far and then just leave."

I say nothing, because that's the thought that's going through my mind.

"What are you so frightened of?"

Oh, to be young and fearless again and not realize the dangers that wait ahead for us, round the next corner, just out of sight. "I'm frightened that it will go too far."

Christian grins mischievously. "Do you think I'll try to seduce you behind the palm fronds in the Temperate House?"

I laugh and say, "Don't be silly!" But it's exactly what I'm frightened of, and I'm even more frightened of what I will do.

"I've taken the day off work," Christian adds, twisting his sugar-coated knife.

"So have I." And I remember that I haven't phoned Kath Brown to tell her that I won't be there, because it was my intention to be there all along.

"Come on, Alicia, Ali Kingston. Live dangerously. You can be home hours before you've got to give your brood and your husband their supper and do your ironing and all the other wild things you've got planned."

"You're mocking me."

"No," he says with a shake of his dark blond hair. "Never."

Christian curls his fingers round mine and tugs gently. "Let's have some fun, Ali. Just for today. No one will ever know. I promise you."

CHAPTER 15

Ed was stopped at the traffic lights. He quickly grabbed his phone, punched the redial button and tried Ali's mobile again. "The Vodaphone you have called may be switched off," a charming woman's voice informed him.

"No," Ed said sarcastically.

"Please try again later," she continued, robotically unabashed.

"I've been trying solidly for over an hour, you stupid woman," he shouted at the phone. "Where the fuck is she!" Ed banged the steering wheel in frustration and the lights turned green. He tossed the phone back onto the passenger seat and slammed his foot on the accelerator. His wife wasn't at work where she should be, that much he knew.

Kath Brown had been beside herself with concern when he'd phoned up looking for Ali, only to be told that Alicia, for whatever reason, hadn't shown up at the studio that morning. This was all he needed. Had she said she was going somewhere else today? Was this Parents' Evening Syndrome all over again? Had they had a perfectly pleasant conversation about some change in Alicia's plans that had completely bypassed his memory banks?

Ed zipped past a speed camera and could have sworn it flashed. He should slow down. This was a time when he needed to be calm and in control. He knew he was panicking. Alicia normally dealt with this sort of thing, not him. Ed tried to take deep breaths. He was sure the traffic was going slower in direct proportion to the speed his heart was racing.

He took the opportunity of a traffic jam to ring Jemma's shop, but it wasn't his sister-in-law's voice that answered.

"You Must Remember This… vintage clothing."

"Is Jemma there?"

"No, sorry," a Sloaney voice replied. "Can I take a message?"

"Do you know when she's due back?"

"No, sorry."

"Do you know where she's gone?"

"No, sorry."

"Has she gone with her sister?"

"I didn't know she had a sister."

"Can you tell her Ed called. If she's seen Ali, can she get her to call me. It's urgent."

"Ali?"

"Her sister."

"She should call Ed."

"Yes."

"Okay."

"Thanks." Ed hung up, more frustrated than he had been before. Was Ali supposed to be going somewhere today with Jemma? He didn't think so. Damn, damn, damn. How could Alicia do this? Just disappear off the face of the earth. It wasn't like her at all. Some phenomenal number of people went missing every year. Just like that. There were all sorts of stories in the paper about people who woke up one morning and, for whatever reason, walked out on their lives and loved ones, never to be seen again. The next thing you knew, their faces were adorning milk cartons with HAVE YOU SEEN THIS PERSON? in ominously bold letters above a grainy black-and-white photograph which could be any one of a million people. Ali would never do that. Would she?

The traffic inched forward, and at the head of the queue was a policeman, waving on the cars which rubbernecked their way past an accident. Two cars had shunted each other in what looked like a fairly terminal way, and Ed was relieved to see that neither of the cars was Ali's, even though he knew her battered red Renault was safely ensconced on their drive where she had left it this morning. He'd gone back to the house to pick up his own car, and there was no note, no message, nothing untoward to give a clue as to where Alicia might possibly be.

There was an ambulance parked by the roadside, and one of the drivers was being helped inside. Ed hoped Alicia hadn't had some other kind of accident. A cold dread dried his mouth. Something wasn't quite right, he could feel it.

He wasn't a man given to great bouts of intuition, but this was giving him a tingly feeling, as if there were thousands of those little black thunder flies in the hairs on the back of his neck. The speed of the traffic picked up, and Ed put the car into gear and followed it. Get a grip, Edward, he told himself. There was bound to be some reasonable explanation. No need to make a drama out of a crisis.

Finally, with a sigh of relief he swung into the car park, fumbling through his pockets for change for the Pay and Display meter at the same time as pulling on the hand brake. He left the car at an alarming angle, bought a ticket with all the loose change he could muster and, forgetting to put the ticket in the windscreen, raced across the road. Breathless, he rushed through the automatic doors and into Accident and Emergency, where he found a very tearful and unhappy Elliott being tenderly nursed and comforted by Nicola Jones, the sunny, smiling owner of the Sunny Smiles nursery school.

CHAPTER 16

You can tell how old I am. I like my trainers laced right up to the top so that I can walk properly and not shuffle around dragging my feet. I do not, and will never have, a bolt pierced through my belly button, my tongue, my bottom lip or either of my eyebrows. I do not possess any clothing from Kookai. On the rare occasions I venture into a pub, I like to sit down. I know who Craig David is. He's the one with the voice of an angel and the hair of a sheep. But I still can't understand a single word he's singing. I have no desire to watch *Big Brother,* let alone care whether Sada, Andrew, Caroline or Craig, or any other of the seemingly vacuous individuals who inhabit the house, get evicted. I do, however, watch *Castaway 2000,* which in comparison could almost be considered the social experiment the BBC would have us believe it is. I think Liam Gallagher is a loudmouthed lout and am beginning to understand why women of a certain age see Alan Titchmarsh as a sex symbol. Even though he's a gardener, albeit a celebrity one, you'd never catch him with grubby old compost under his fingernails, would you? Would he ever say an extra-naughty four-letter word if he inadvertently bashed himself with a trowel? I think not.

I look at Christian and feel that he may not share similar views. (Particularly the Alan Titchmarsh theory.) Christian definitely looks like a potential *Big Brother* watcher. I have a brief, shuddering vision of him sprawled on the sofa with a beer and a take-away on a Friday night in front of Davinia McCall yelling to have Nasty Nick ousted. Christian probably also thinks that Gail Porter is a babe, whereas I see her as someone who could do with a few good meals inside her. Some people would call it getting old and staid. Some people would call it maturing. Fine wine matures. But then again, so does cheese.

It is a glorious spring day with just a slight hint of chilliness adding a sharpness and clarity to the air. I have been persuaded against my better judgment to spend the day with Christian, after all. You might have guessed. And I wonder what he thinks of this. I cannot imagine that Kew is really his bag. Has he brought me here because he thinks it's what older people like to do? I don't know. If he starts to offer me tea and cake on the hour every hour, I'll be seriously worried about his motives. This is what we do on outings with my parents—ply them with calories and Twinings to keep them happy (i.e., quiet). Christian looks cheerful enough. We are walking along side by side, grinning inanely at each other. My brain cells seem to go all haywire when I'm with him. I'll swear they do. He makes me think one thing and then do completely the opposite.

There's a huge Ginkgo biloba tree at Kew, not far from the main entrance. It's one of the oldest trees here, or something like that, and the leaves look like a million bright green butterflies. If you touch it, the bark will give you a bolt of energy so strong that you can feel it all the way down to your socks. Honestly. I'd like to show Christian this, but today, I'm going to give it a wide berth. My energy is whizzing round my body, making everything feel tingly and sensitized already. I feel very weird. On the one hand, I'm relaxed and happy to be here—the sun is shining, the birds are singing, I've bunked a day off work—on the other hand, I've never felt so tense in all my life. I ought to have phoned Kath Brown, but I've never lied to her before and can't face it now. It's Friday and I've got two whole days to think of an excuse before I have to go to work again on Monday. I've turned my mobile off and stuffed it in the bottom of my handbag so she can't contact me, coward that I am.

We've wandered all over the gardens—through the angular, ultra-modern Princess of Wales Conservatory, through the Japanese bit with its reconstructed temple gate, and have made suitably impressed-type noises at the towering pagoda which dominates the skyline at the head of an avenue of soaring trees dwarfed by its splendor. I adore trees and flowers and nature in general. Christian seems to as well. Perhaps he sees things through more artistic eyes than the average twenty-three-year-old; people of that age aren't usually known for their appreciation of trees, are they? What did my life revolve around when I was the tender age of twenty-three? I seem to recall it was gearing up for potty training. My children's, not mine.

We are lying on the grass by the Temperate House and I feel as if I'm dressed all wrong. Despite my attempts at casual, I've come in a ballgown to a bring-a-bottle party. I should be wearing trainers, and instead I have on smart imitation snakeskin broguey things that were really trendy when I bought them yonks ago. They would have made my feet sweat like a pig in the office—had I have gone there—and yet they aren't comfortable enough for clonking round gardens in. My jeans are Calvin Klein and have been pressed so much they've formed a white crease down the front, which is very eighties. And, if I admit it, even my sweatshirt's a bit glittery. I feel overdone and tied up. My daughter throws anything on and looks fabulous. That's because she has firm, high breasts that do not even entertain drooping toward the floor and slender, unblemished legs that go on for miles. Christian is clearly of the same mold. He has no hips and a flat stomach and probably doesn't even know what the word "sit-up" means. His clothes hang on him like a catwalk model. He is lying with his arms above his head and his short khaki T-shirt has ridden up, exposing his stomach. He has a great belly button. Neat and round. I'm obsessed with navels after mine went all teardrop-shaped and horrid after my first pregnancy. I try not to stare at it and fail, but fortunately Christian has his eyes shut against the sun. A fine line of blond down disappears beneath his waistband, and then I catch myself wondering whether he has any hair on his chest and blush.

I sit up and hug my knees, turning away from him. It's impossible to buy clothes once you are over thirty-five. You fall into a big hole somewhere between Top Shop and Debenhams. I never want to look like mutton dressed as lamb and spurn crop-tops and Capri pants, which look good on no one over sixteen anyway. But I'm twenty years away from A-line skirts and flatties. My dress sense is all at sea, and I buy safe middle-of-the-road clothing that will last from Marks & Spencer to anchor myself and, consequently, spend my life feeling beige. Jemma has a wonderful dress sense and combines Karen Millen with drapey bits and pieces from the 1930s that she borrows from her shop and would make me look like a bag lady.

"Do you watch *Big Brother,* Christian?"

He sits up and shuffles forward so that he is right behind me at my shoulder. *"Big Brother?"*

"Mmmm."

"Sometimes. Why?"

"I just wondered." We've had tea and cake just the once, and I'm taking this as a good sign. In fact, the day has been brilliant. Christian is very attentive and good company. And if it wasn't for the fact that I'm married and do in the odd moment feel like his mother, then I'd probably be in seventh heaven.

We haven't touched. Not really. Just the occasional lingering of fingers on fabric. The hint of a hand in the small of my back. We are self-conscious in our needs. But it's there between us all the time. The desire to is palpable. I want him to touch me and am scared that he might. I want to touch him and daren't. I want to caress his cheek, his skin which looks soft and strong and has no wrinkles. Not one. I want to trace the outline of his pouting lips. I want to know what he feels like and dread what that knowledge will mean.

"I'll say it before you do." Christian smiles sadly at me. "You should be going home."

I look at my watch. "Oh, my good God," I say. "I should. I have to collect Elliott." He knows all about my children now, and their trials and tribulations. I tried not to go on and on about them and Christian tried to look interested. But it's clear that we're about a million miles apart in our respective lifestyles.

He stands up and holds out his hands. I take them and he pulls me to my feet. "Let's walk through the Temperate House," he says. "It'll warm us up."

As if I need it! Christian takes my hand and leads the way and this time he doesn't let go.

The Temperate House is a huge building, a light, airy framework of white filigree ironwork banding a spider's web of delicate glass panes. Inside it is dense, crowded, a jungle of rampant greenery all crowding, living, thrusting and vying for space. The overwhelming smell in the Temperate House is damp, musky and earthy. It's too heavy to inhale, its weight envelops you and seeps into you, hot teasing fingers of humid air easing inside your clothes. D. H. Lawrence would call it "fecund," if I remember any of my A-level coursework correctly. How can foliage feel so sexual? Perhaps it's all that sap rising. Perhaps it's just me. Perhaps it's that Alan Titchmarsh thing again.

"There's a platform at the top," Christian informs me. "We can walk all the way round." And he leads me up a narrow winding wrought-iron staircase until we are high above the plants, in among the tops of the trees on a vertiginous ledge. If you look down, you can see patterns and whorls in the fronds of the ferns and you can reach out and touch the bark of trees that really would be more at home in a rain forest. There is no one else here as intrepid as us and, as a consequence, we are totally alone suspended high above the greenery.

We are leaning over the rail, and Christian has his arm around my shoulders, pointing out flowers and fruits lurking between the leaves.

"Christian." My voice sounds heavy even to my ears. "I've really enjoyed today."

"That doesn't sound like, 'I've really enjoyed today and let's do it again as soon as possible, Christian.'"

I turn toward him and his eyes lock on to mine, searching.

"You do want to do it again?" He strokes my wild hair, which is spiraling madly in the humid air, brushing my cheek as he does so.

"I don't know."

"'I don't know, but yes I want to'?" He is so lovely and young and hunky and I still don't know what he sees in me.

I shake my head. "It makes life terribly complicated." And at this moment I wish I were a different person, in a different life, who could just say yes without thinking.

Christian leans forward and kisses me on the lips, and it is so light and soft and forbidden, I could faint with the rush of emotion that floods through me.

He holds me and I try not to hold him back, but I can feel the heat of his skin through the thin fabric of his shirt and my hands are trembling.

"Is this so wrong?" Christian asks as he breaks away from me.

"Yes," I say. And it is. I know that. We both do.

We wind our way down the rickety staircase in silence, still holding hands, and wander out of the Temperate House, slowly following the trickle of tourists who are also heading for home. When we reach the main gate, we stand and look at each other in a forlorn and pathetic way; our hands dangle between us limply, barely touching. I am terrified that Christian will kiss me again, here in the street for everyone to see. But he doesn't.

"Can I at least ring you?" His smile has gone for the first time today and he is fiddling with my fingers.

"No." I sound as if I mean it.

He makes a sad little tutting sound that sort of sums up everything we need to say. "Oh, Ali." He brushes my hair away from my shoulders and touches his hot, moist lips to my cheek. I squeeze his hand and then let it go.

"Goodbye," he says, and then turns and walks away.

I stand and watch him, pressing my lips together, savoring the sweet young taste of him, and wonder how I will manage without it for the rest of my life.

CHAPTER 17

Elliott sucked his thumb, curled up on Ed's knee. He still looked very unhappy, but at least the tears had stopped, and all that remained were two gray tracks over his cheeks where they had dried. His eyes were rolling under the onslaught of emotionally drained sleep.

"Not long now, sweetheart." Nicola smiled at him, crinkling her eyes as she did.

Nicola was deeply optimistic. It would be a long time. Ed had never been more sure of anything in his life. You only had to look at the people ahead of them in various states of dismemberment who had the resigned air of people for whom time was passing very slowly. Michelangelo could probably have given the Sistine Chapel another lick of paint in the time it took to get any action in hospital casualty departments these days. Elliott was way down the pecking order, as he wasn't in any imminent danger of dropping dead, not that this seemed to worry the harried staff overly, and they'd been sitting here for hours already.

"It hurts," Elliott complained. His arm was swollen to twice its normal size and was an alarming shade of scarlet.

"I know. Ssh, ssh." Ed cuddled Elliott to him and kissed the top of his head. "I'm sorry about this, Nicola."

"That's okay. He took quite a tumble. I thought it best to bring him down here and let them X-ray it. I can't tell whether it's broken or not."

They'd never been required to partake of the National Health Service, or lack of it, for Thomas or Tanya. Both had been remarkably accident-free zones. They even still had their appendix and tonsils. Elliott had broken the mold and was making up for it with all the fervor of a zealot. In his few short years he had fallen over, into or through every conceivable man-made or naturally occurring obstacle that he could find.

"It could just be badly sprained," Ed said, aware that Elliott, despite his desire to be the most accident-prone person in the household, had not yet broken anything. Other than the things he fell over, into or through. "Thanks for bringing him down."

"That's okay. Really."

Nicola was the sort of person you would want running your son's nursery school, Ed decided. She was feminine and floaty in a wholesome way. Everything about her was gentle: Her eyes were soft gray and kind; she was slim, petite and delicate; her lips were pale seashell pink and she licked a tiny tip of her pink kitten tongue over them frequently. Her hair was white-blond with crinkly curls that might or might not have been natural and it hung below her shoulders in fine wisps. She had a cut-glass accent overlaid with sultry tones and a slightly breathy way of speaking as if she were about to gasp with pleasure. And you could never, ever imagine her lifting heavy weights or swearing or doing anything quite as sweaty as having sex. But then, Ed thought, you never could tell—she was probably the type who would wear Agent Provocateur frillies under her long floral dresses. All things considered and despite being a wonder with the children, Nicola Jones was definitely wasted on a bunch of four-year-olds. Elliott adored her, and Ed thought that even at his age he was showing rather good taste.

"I'm fine waiting here," Ed said, breaking his fantasizing. "Do you need to be getting back?"

"No." Nicola shook her mass of curls. "Barbara can lock up at the school. I'll wait with you." She smiled a sweet little smile, showing a row of pearly teeth. "If that's okay with you, Mr. Kingston?"

"Ed, please."

Nicola looked bashful. "Ed." She swept her hair away from her face. Not in an irritated way, like Ali did, but in a slow and sensual movement which exposed her long, slender neck. "Did you manage to get hold of your wife?"

"No," Ed said brusquely. He glanced at the red No Mobile Phones sign on the wall and eschewed the thought of going outside to try Alicia again and risk the ensuing wailing from a dislodged Elliott. "I can't imagine where she's got to." Ed mentally acknowledged that Alicia would normally deal with whatever minor crises arose and that this was, in fact, the first time he'd been left, literally, holding the baby.

"I'm sure there's a simple explanation," Nicola reassured him. "Mrs. Kingston is normally so reliable."

"Yes," Ed said vaguely. Which was why her disappearance was even more worrying.

They both looked down at Elliott, who had fallen into an exhausted sleep, a frown creasing his brow.

"Elliott is a lovely child," Nicola said.

Ed ruffled his son's curls gently. "He has his moments."

"He's a pleasure to teach. I have quite a soft spot for him."

"Do you have children of your own?" Ed asked.

"No." Nicola swished her hair about, and there was the suggestion of a smile at her lips when she looked at him again. "Not yet. Mr. Right seems to be proving rather elusive."

"Ah," Ed said sympathetically.

"All the nice men seem to be married," she continued, and a faint pink blush stained her cheeks. "It's not very fashionable to adore children these days, is it?"

"Probably not," Ed agreed. "Perhaps you shouldn't mention it on a first date."

Nicola laughed and it was as soft and gentle as the rest of her. "You're very lucky."

A lot of people had been pointing that out to him recently and, for some reason, it was starting to rankle.

"Having children must be so rewarding."

"Financially draining is the predominant emotion," Ed said with a smile. "But yes, it is on occasions, rewarding."

He wondered whether he was one of those people who, given the chance to do it over again, would choose not to go down the fatherhood route. But then it was usually the woman who made all the choices in that area, and the men just went along. He'd never known any man to be governed by the same urges to procreate as women had. In their case all three children had been "accidents," showing a carelessness in the contraceptive department that bordered on recklessness. Perhaps that's where Elliott inherited his accident-prone nature from. Maybe it was just coming out in his genes in a different way. Ed wouldn't be without any of them now. Of course not. Not even when Tanya was being the most obnoxious teenager on the planet. But sometimes he couldn't help thinking, as much as he loved Ali, that he would be better off like Neil. Free, unfettered. Chasing bridesmaids to his heart's content. But then Neil was looking to find a gorgeous, sexy bombshell who was ready to settle down and have babies. Why is it that we always want the exact opposite of what we've got?

Ed looked across at Nicola, who was gazing at Elliott in an adoring and concerned sort of way and stroking his chubby little leg as he slept. She was a soft, squishy petal in a world full of nasty, catchy thorns. Perhaps he should introduce Miss Nicola Jones to his brother. Ed pressed his lips together thoughtfully and rubbed absently at his chin. He'd had worse ideas.

CHAPTER 18

I'm standing outside Elliott's school, and there are five minutes to go before they all fizz out of the door with the exuberance of champagne bubbles, chattering and giggling and all looking like they've been every which way through a hedge. The Sunny Smiles Pre-School Nursery provides a lovely introduction to the rigors of education in a huge white-painted house in another pretty leafy lane full, as the advertising brochure states, of sunny smiles. The inside is currently adorned with Pokémon characters, which I'm not sure I agree with. Try as I might, I can't understand the attraction, and I'm just hoping they'll pass quickly and the next trend will be more wholesome. Will my children remember this inarticulate, pointless gaggle of monsters with the fondness I hold for Stingray or Andy Pandy (who, when you come to think of it, wasn't all that bright). I've heard the BBC are bringing back Basil Brush and Bill and Ben the Flower-Pot Men, which is a jolly good step in the right direction, if you ask me.

I'm taking this time to try to refocus my thoughts. For refocus, read, drag them screaming. As you might have gathered, I'm trying to stop thinking about Christian and concentrate instead on the choice between pizza or the ubiquitous chicken nuggets. Currently, it isn't working. A clutch of other mothers arrive, issuing forth from BMWs and soft-top Mercedes in Gucci loafers, well-cut trousers and navy blazers—the standard uniform for ladies-who-do-lunch. They nod and smile and I nod and smile back, but I don't want to be drawn into conversation today. I feel conspicuous in my glittery sweatshirt, and I want to be alone with my thoughts for the few moments I have left before I'm sucked back down into the crazy whirlpool that forms my life.

The crowd of knee-high hooligans are sprung from school and rush in all directions to their waiting parents. Elliott is always last. That child can talk for England. I thought it was mothers who were always chatting, leaving their offspring hanging around bored waiting for them to finish. With Elliott it is the other way round. His teacher, and owner of Sunny Smiles, Miss Jones, whom he adores, will probably be deaf by the time she's forty, and it will be mainly down to Elliott.

The doors of the BMWs and the Mercs clunk expensively, shutting out the noise of the children inside. There's still no sign of Elliott, so I wander toward the school with the hope of chivvying him up, otherwise Thomas and Tanya will be back at the house before us and even though they are older and have their own keys, I still like to be there when they come home. Call me old-fashioned, but that's how it is.

Inside the school it is cool and airy. There's always a sense of peace here, even when it's crammed with children. Miss Jones runs a very tight ship, although we do pay handsomely for it. Barbara, her assistant, is tidying away some pencils, placing them methodically back into a box with all the colored tips facing the same way. Miss Jones doesn't appear to be around, and neither does Elliott.

Barbara turns around when she hears me, and the smile of greeting on her face changes to an expression of concern. Instantly, I feel my insides turn cold.

"Mrs. Kingston." Barbara puts down the pencils. "We've been trying to contact you all day." They're the words all mothers dread, aren't they? And I think guiltily of the phone turned off and stuffed in the bottom of my handbag beneath a pile of snotty tissues. "Elliott's had a little accident."

Elliott's always having accidents and I'm always there to look after him. I should be used to it by now, but this one grips me with the hand of terror. Barbara sees my shell-shocked face.

"Accident? What sort of accident?"

"He's all right. Really," she reassures me. "He fell off the climbing frame and landed badly on his arm. Nicola didn't think he'd broken it, but she wanted to be sure. She took him down to the hospital."

My hands are shaking, and Barbara clearly thinks I'm overreacting, which I probably am, but she doesn't know the whole picture, does she? She doesn't know what I've been doing. Not like you and I.

I start to back away toward the door.

Barbara follows me, now very concerned. "They'll probably be back at home by now, I shouldn't wonder. It'll be all right, Mrs. Kingston."

"I have to go," I say, and my voice sounds like the voice of a madwoman. "I have to see my baby."

"We managed to get hold of Mr. Kingston." Barbara reaches out to touch my arm and thinks better of it.

"Ed?"

"He came out of work. He'll be with Elliott and Nicola." Now she clearly thinks I'm mad, because she's speaking slowly at me. "At the hospital."

Ed! Ed's hopeless, I want to tell her. He can't cope with any body fluids apart from his own, and even that's debatable. One spot of blood and he passes out. He's changed one nappy in his entire life, and he gagged so much that he was sick. I had more clearing up to do after my husband than the baby. I should be there, not Ed. Elliott will be howling the place down and Ed won't have a clue what to do. He might be a whiz with cameras and videotape and techno stuff, but he goes completely to pieces when faced with a wailing child.

I back out of the room, leaving a bemused Barbara to return to her pencils, and I run, panting breathlessly, because the last time I did any running was at Thomas's sports day last year in the mothers' egg and spoon race. I run as fast as I can toward home to find out what disasters await me, and I know I am being punished for being the worst mother on the planet who, instead of knowing instinctively when my child needed me, had her head full of young boys with flat bellies and beautiful blond hair. This is payback time for my illicit pleasure, and I know that I will never, ever forgive myself for this.

CHAPTER 19

Christian was sitting with his feet on the kitchen table when Robbie came home from his shift at HMV. He was nursing a bottle of Budweiser and staring glumly into the garden.

Robbie threw his backpack on the table. "We haven't been cut off, have we?"

Christian shook his head and drank deeply from his bottle.

His friend got a beer from the fridge and sat down in the chair opposite him. "What then?"

"Not now, Robbie."

Robbie tipped his beer to his lips. "I've seen that face before."

"You haven't."

Robbie held his bottle like a microphone and crooned, *"No one knows the way you feel, when you're young and so in love."*

"Fuck off," Christian said. "The tune goes nothing like that, but you're right—no one does know the way I feel."

"Problems with Miss Beautiful Soul Mate?"

Christian sniffed and pouted miserably at the garden.

"The course of true love never runs smoothly," Robbie said sympathetically.

"Not for me, it doesn't," Christian agreed.

Robbie pulled a packet of cigarettes from his pocket and offered one to Christian, who refused. "I thought you'd blown out the tourists at the market so you could spend the day together?" he said as he lit up.

"I did."

"And?"

"We went to Kew Gardens."

Robbie pulled a puzzled face. "Nice."

"I thought it would be."

"Why Kew Gardens?"

"I thought it would be romantic."

"And was it?"

"Yes." Christian fixed Robbie with a thoughtful stare. "It was perfect."

"I feel at this point there must be a 'but' coming on..."

"But..." Christian sighed heavily. "There are complications."

Robbie laughed. "There always are with you, mate."

"No. This time there are real complications."

Robbie blew out a stream of smoke. "Do you want to tell Uncle Robert?"

"Only if you promise not to laugh and not to breathe a word to Becs. She'd only take the piss, and I can't cope with that now."

"Promise." Robbie held his hand to his heart.

Christian swigged his beer and then folded his arms across his chest, staring resolutely ahead. "For a start, she's a lot older than me."

Robbie pursed his lips. "Not an unusual concept these days. Quite the thing, in fact. There's a lot to be said for older birds." He sat upright. "She's not sixty or anything, is she?"

Christian glared at him. "No. She's thirty-something. But you wouldn't think so. Really you wouldn't."

"So she's old?"

"And she's married."

Robbie dragged on his cigarette. "Now this *is* starting to sound complicated, Christian."

"And she has three children."

"Fuck," Robbie said. "Haven't they got a television?"

"And she doesn't want to see me again."

Robbie ground out his cigarette. "That sounds like a very sensible conclusion to me."

"I can't handle it, Robbie. This is the first time I've felt like this. I can't just let her go. I'm crazy about her."

"You're crazy to get involved with her."

"I know. I know. Logically I can work that all out. But she does weird things to me."

Robbie's eyes widened and he sat up. "Tell me more…."

Christian scowled. "Emotionally weird, not plastic toys weird."

Robbie slumped down. "Oh."

Christian bit his lower lip and looked up at his friend. "I don't know what to do."

Robbie shook his head. "Drop it, mate. You're way out of your depth."

"I don't know if I can," Christian admitted. "How can I make her love me?"

"You normally have trouble getting rid of them, Christian, not making them fall for you."

"Bollocks."

"We had three months of tearful telephone calls from that Tara Wotsit. You had to change your mobile phone number in the end. She was in a terrible state. And you wouldn't even talk to her."

"This is different. That was just a fling, and she knew it. This is love. For the first time. Real love."

"You are in very dangerous territory, Christian."

"I can't help it. You can't govern who you fall in love with."

"Yes, you can." Robbie wagged his beer bottle at him. "You can stop it now and walk away. Forget her. In a few weeks, a few days, maybe even a few hours, she'll be history. A pleasant memory of what might have been if only she hadn't been old, married and with three kids."

"I don't think so."

Robbie finished his beer and put the bottle on the table with a decisive thunk. "Do you know what I think?"

"What?"

"I think we should go and get ourselves very laid."

Christian shook his head. "I don't feel like it."

"You always feel like it." Robbie puckered his lips and made thrusting movements with his hips. "Come on, let's hit the clubs."

Christian smiled reluctantly. "Do you think it will work?"

"I don't know," Robbie admitted cheerfully. "But I think it's a very worthwhile theory to put to the test."

A grin spread across Christian's face. He stood up and grabbed

Robbie's hand in a fist. "Cheers, mate," he said with a nod. "I feel better already."

The front door opened and Rebecca came into the kitchen, laden down with shopping bags. She stopped and stared at them both. "Why are you two looking so smug?"

"No reason." Christian peeped in her carrier bag as he pushed past her and she snatched it away.

Rebecca frowned. "Why do I think you're up to something?"

Christian kissed her cheek. "Because you have a naturally suspicious nature."

Rebecca slapped at his hand. "Where are you going to?"

Christian winked at Robbie. "To put my lucky pulling underpants on!"

CHAPTER 20

Thomas is sitting at the table doing his homework. Bless him! Tanya, on the other hand, is watching television on the little portable and snaps it off guiltily the minute I walk through the door.

"Where's Elliott?" I gasp.

Thomas looks up. "He's been at the hospital. Daddy phoned when we came in to say they're on their way home."

"Is he all right?"

"It's just a bad sprain," Thomas says, clearly disappointed that Elliott won't have the street credibility of a plaster cast. I'm too wound up to feel the relief I should. "Daddy says they're going to stop at McDonald's to buy tea." Thomas smiles broadly at this prospect rather than the fact his younger brother is safe and relatively unharmed.

"Fine."

I feel like weeping, and as soon as I sit down opposite Thomas, there is the sound of a key in the front door and Elliott comes in carrying a Happy Meal under his good arm, and he does, despite his ordeal, look remarkably happy. His other arm is swathed in a support bandage, and he is clutching a cuddly dog Beanie Baby, the joy of which seems to be distracting him from his pain. I make a note to thank Ed for the inspiration of these small psychological tactics. It's pathetic, but they work every time.

Ed, bearing the remainder of our McDonald's offering in a large brown paper bag, does not look so happy. His face is white and there are gray rings round his eyes, but most noticeable is the black storm cloud sitting just above his eyebrows. He puts the McDonald's bag down. "We've been at the hospital," he says in a tight voice.

"I know." I sound weary. "Barbara told me when I went to pick Elliott up." I smile at my son. "Come here, darling." He runs over to my side and I give him a big hug. "Were you brave?"

"No," Elliott says. "I screamed blue murder."

I can imagine it. Kissing him on the head, I hide a smile and reach over and pull out a chair for him. "Don't let your chips get cold."

Ed goes to the cupboard and pulls out some plates, on top of which he plonks the McDonald's cartons. It is possibly the last thing in the world I feel like eating, but he has had to suffer my burnt offerings more than once, so I'll say nothing and be grateful. Tanya comes to the table.

She opens a burger box and examines the contents with disdain. "I'm thinking of becoming a vegetarian," she announces.

"Not now, Tanya," I say.

"I've been trying to call you all day," Ed says. "So has Nicola. They needed you at the school. We were right in the middle of filming for a very important client. I had to come out of work."

"I would have had to," I say. The accusation is out of my mouth before I can stop it, and I know that I sound too defensive. This is the first time ever that Ed has had to deal with anything like this. Honestly. He'd tell you so himself.

But the main reason I snap is because I'm cross. Cross with myself for not being there. Cross that I've failed Elliott when he needed me. Cross that I've been caught out in the one minor indiscretion I've ever dared indulge in. Cross that I went in the first place! And I'm cross that Ed can't handle one tiny crisis without resorting to emotional blackmail.

Ed looks at me over his polystyrene box. His voice is level, but his eyes are hard. "Except that you weren't at work today, Ali."

You'll hardly believe this, but until now I didn't even consider that I might be called to account for where I was today. Where was I? What am I going to say? I can hardly tell Ed the truth in these circumstances. First I'm going to have to lie to Kath Brown and now Ed. My face reddens. One of the other joys of having red hair is having a complexion that would be no good for a poker player. I hate blushing and do it frequently. Sometimes you could fry an egg on my cheeks, they sizzle so much. I suspect you could now. I bite my burger, stuffing a huge mouthful in so that I cannot speak even if I knew what to say, and I lower my eyes to stare at the shreds of transparent, taste-free iceberg lettuce that are in my carton. The kids are concentrating on their burgers and studiously ignore us.

"The school couldn't get hold of you. I couldn't get hold of you. Your mobile was turned off. Kath was worried sick," he continued. "And so was I."

I can hardly chew. My mouth has gone dry and there's bile rushing up to meet the contents, which are struggling to go down.

"Where have you been?"

I can hardly meet his eyes. "With Jemma," I lie and, my God, the words nearly choke me.

"With Jemma?"

"We'd arranged to go shopping."

"Shopping?"

"I thought I'd told you."

"Not that I remember," Ed says.

"Well, you did forget the parents' evening," I counter, and I sound weak and feeble even to my own ears.

"So I did." Ed gives me a relenting smile, which makes me feel a hundred and ten times worse. He bites into his burger.

I try to control the pounding of my heart and the feeling that I have a lightbulb flashing above my head with LIAR written on it.

"What did you buy?" Ed mumbles through a chip.

"What?"

"Shopping," he reminds me. "What did you buy?"

"Er..." My mind is a complete bank. Clearly my supply of lies is exhausted already. "Nothing."

"You went shopping with Jemma and bought nothing?"

"Yes."

"Well, that's a first," he snorts, and gives me a strange look even though there's now nothing at all wrong with his eye.

CHAPTER 21

There's an atmosphere. I can't really define it for you, but you know the sort of thing I mean. We're both trying to talk normally and it isn't quite working. Ed's voice is more clipped than it should be, and I'm working far too hard at being relaxed. We've all done it. It's just that I've never done it for this reason before.

"Can I watch telly?" Tanya asks.

"Yes," I say without thinking, and she is gone before I can change my mind. If she rushes she might just catch the opening credits of *Coronation Street.* She is fifteen going on thirty—aren't they all? Her ability to spot a situation which she can manipulate to her benefit is uncanny.

Ed looks up from the newspaper, which he has buried himself in since tea time. "I thought she was banned from watching television?"

"So did I," I reply, but refrain from telling him that I haven't the strength to argue with her.

The phone rings and I nearly shoot through the ceiling.

Ed notices. "I'll get it," he mutters, and stands up and strides across the lounge before I can suggest otherwise.

I'm in a quandary. I'm trying to repair a rip in Thomas's school trousers and keep stitching through the wrong bit of material, which means he won't be able to put his hands, or anything else for that matter, in his pockets. This is because I'm not concentrating, at all. I unpick the stitches and let the trousers fall into my lap before I make a fresh attempt at getting it right. I'm trying to decide whether to tell Ed where I really was today. Should I come clean and risk his wrath? He's not in the best of moods after being dragged out of work and a four-hour wait in Casualty for a bit of bandage. I think I should tell him, but this is not the right time. But then, should I keep quiet about Christian? Is ignorance sometimes bliss? And it's over before it even started. It was a one-off. A momentary madness. A minor indiscretion. That's all. And now it's done. I won't see him again. Or if I do bump into him, it'll just be for a coffee. As friends. Nothing more. Not that it was anything more, anyway. Not really.

"Oh, hi," Ed says into the mouthpiece. I look up and he's staring at me, pulling at his bottom lip with his teeth. "Yes. Yes. She did." His eyes meet mine. "I think so," he says very slowly and deliberately.

My mouth has gone dry again, and I rush out to the kitchen and put the kettle on. Both of the boys are in their bedrooms, probably doing unspeakable things, and I can't be bothered to find out if they need a drink or a biscuit. Instead, I just make a cup of tea for myself and Ed.

When I return to the lounge, he is sitting back in his chair.

"I thought you might fancy a cuppa," I say, putting it down next to him.

"Thanks." He ignores the tea, and his hands are trembling when he tries to pick up his newspaper.

"Who was that?" I venture.

"Jemma."

All the hairs on the back of my neck are on full alert, as well they might be. "Oh."

"She wanted to know if everything was all right."

"Oh."

"I told her it was, Alicia." Ed looks up and I can't read his eyes at all. "But I'm not so sure that it is."

There's a whoosh of blood filling my ears and I can hear my pulse pounding through my body.

"Jemma's been in Prague all day." Ed pauses, watching my face as it colors once again. "On a buying trip for the shop. Antique lace. Jemma might have been shopping today," he says, "but there's one thing for certain, Alicia. You weren't with her."

I'm not sure if I sit here for hours saying nothing, or if I answer straight away. I can hear the cogs whirring in my brain, but when I speak, the most trite of statements comes out. "I can explain," is all I offer my husband.

"Does it have anything to do with this?" Ed holds up a map of Kew Gardens and an admission ticket, no doubt stamped with today's date. He has been through my handbag while I was making tea, and even that minute betrayal hurts and I wonder how he must feel about me.

"Yes."

"Did you go there alone?"

And I think about lying again, even now. I can't believe my own capacity for deceit, but in a moment of clarity I realize that if Ed has an admission ticket, it is more than likely to be for two. "I went with a friend," I admit.

"I take it this 'friend' is a man."

"Yes." How can I explain this so that it doesn't sound as bad as it does? Would Ed believe me if I told him I was swept away on a rush of undivided attention and lust, but I'd returned to my senses just in time? Would you believe that? Do *I* believe it? "He's just a friend," I say again.

"Then why couldn't you tell me about him? Why couldn't you tell me where you were?"

"I don't know."

"Because you didn't think I'd find out?" I suppose so, I want to say. But it wasn't like that. I didn't even think of the consequences.

"How long has it been going on?"

"There's nothing going on. I've only known him a few weeks."

"Have you slept with him?" Ed's mouth trembles and he presses his lips together to regain control, and I'm not sure whether it's anger or tears he's suppressing, because I've never seen him like this before.

"Of course not!" I'm handling this so badly, but that's because I can't even think of the words I need to put it right.

"Has he kissed you?"

"I…er…"

"Oh, Alicia." Ed stands up and paces the lounge. "Don't even answer. It's written all over your face."

"Today is the first time I've seen him. Alone," I say. This is the first time it was cold, calculated premeditated deceit, I mean. "Nothing happened."

"Is this him?" He tosses the business card of La Place Velma onto my lap from my purse, and Christian's address and telephone number are written on the back.

"Yes." I look at Ed and I want to hug him and kiss him and tell him that he's got it all wrong, but his face is set like stone and he has put a barrier between us as impenetrable as steel. I stuff the card in my back pocket, not knowing what else to do with it. "Just let me have a minute to think, Ed," I say. "I want to talk to you about this. We need to sort it out."

"I don't want to talk to you, Alicia. You're lying to me."

"I'm not," I protest, even though I am. "It's a misunderstanding."

"Is he anything to do with the sketch that's pushed to the back of the wardrobe?"

"Yes." I knew I should have put that wretched thing in the bin, but vanity is a strong emotion, and Christian had made me look so, so beautiful. I wanted to keep it until I was ninety and wrinkled like a walnut, to look back on a time when I was young and admired. "He drew me."

Ed gives a half-laugh and it's cold and empty. "Then you must be very much in love with him, Alicia." He turns his back as if he is unable to bear the sight of me. "I have never seen you looking quite so radiant," he says.

CHAPTER 22

The music was thumping so loudly Christian could feel his brain shaking. It pulsated from the inside out, making his muscles throb and his chest vibrate. He twitched vaguely in time with it as he leaned on a wrought-iron balcony overlooking the dance floor. To say it was crowded was an understatement of the highest order. Sardine tins would be roomy compared to this. Christian felt himself sigh inwardly.

Robbie was gyrating next to him, beer bottle in hand, eyeing the talent. Christian couldn't remember where they were, only that it was their third nightclub in succession and they'd paid an extortionate amount to get into each one. Robbie assured him this was *the* place to be seen, but to Christian they all looked pretty much the same. Black, smoke, foam, dry ice, strobes, everyone pretty much off their face.

He looked down at the bottle he was drinking from. It was some vodka concoction recommended by Robbie. It was mixed with fruit juice and herbs, as yet unspecified. It tasted like pop and had a kick like several mules. He'd had more than an adequate sufficiency, and the swirling emotions he'd felt earlier were settling down to a benign numbness. He looked at his watch, the night was still young and already he wanted to slide into bed and sleep, preferably alone. But the consuming of vast quantities of alcohol was only Phase One of his friend's rehabilitation plan for him. Robbie nudged him in the ribs, with an excess of effort often employed by drunks. Phase Two, it appeared, was about to begin.

"What about those two?" Robbie shouted above the music, waving his beer around in the direction of the dance floor.

There were lots of "those two's"—girls out for a night on the town—and Christian wasn't sure which particular "those two" he meant. There were two girls who appeared to be smiling back at Robbie's leering face with affected coyness. They were both pert and perky with long black hair parted in the middle. They wore black crop-tops, black Lycra shorts and black knee-high boots, in between which they both exposed acres of fake-tanned flesh. They clutched identical purses and bottles of beer. No doubt they would giggle like schoolgirls if asked if they were twins.

"Eh?" Robbie prompted.

Christian shrugged. "Fine."

Phase Two was to chat up two women who didn't look too fussy. Phase Three was to get them back to the flat for a night of fun and frolics. The music picked up a beat, and the two women thrust themselves about with considerably more verve now that they knew they were being watched.

Christian's heart wasn't in this. He'd been game at first, but now his enthusiasm was waning. The major flaw in Robbie's plan was due mainly to the success of Phase One, and he now felt totally incapable of proceeding to Phase Three without first having a nice little nap. Perhaps he could go into one of the chill-out rooms and have a lie down.

Robbie downed his beer and threw the bottle on the floor. "Come on, mate!"

Christian still had half a bottle left, but he swallowed it nevertheless. They made their way down the stairs, pushing through the crowd on the dance floor until they found their prey. Robbie made a beeline for the prettier of the two, and Christian stood in front of the other one and started to dance. She wasn't bad-looking, but she didn't have incandescent gold hair or translucent skin as delicate as mother-of-pearl or enigmatic feline eyes the rich, dark color of emeralds. And it was a shame that he felt like that, because up until now he'd hardly thought of Ali all evening.

Robbie was right. He should just drop the whole thing. Ali was too sincere, too honest ever to go for just a fling. Stick to loose women that you meet in nightclubs and you won't go far wrong.

"Hi," said his dancing partner. "I'm Sharon." Christian was caught slightly off guard when she thrust her thigh between his and rubbed salaciously against his groin. The girls were clearly here with the same intentions as he and Robbie. Get drunk, get laid. Phase Two, it seemed, had been an unnecessary preliminary to copulation. Christian resisted the urge to pull away, and instead, lifted his arms above his head and gyrated himself back. Sharon smiled as if she had made some sort of conquest. Robbie already had his hands full of the other girl's breasts and was grinning triumphantly as they writhed together. He stuck out his tongue and wiggled it like a lizard toward Christian before securing his face onto hers and disappearing into the crush. Sharon started to move her hands all over Christian, his chest, his groin, his buttocks—and he wondered how women could do things like this with strangers whose names they didn't even know or care to know. It had taken him weeks to cajole Ali into a chaste kiss, and there was something rather nice and unexpected about that.

There was a time, a very short time ago, when he would have taken the opportunity to slide his hands inside this girl's ridiculously short shorts and grabbed whatever was on offer. Sharon smiled and snaked her hand round his testicles, squeezing them gently. Perhaps he was getting old, but he suddenly found the whole thing very depressing.

CHAPTER 23

"The children are all in bed," I say as I shut the door to our bedroom. It isn't strictly true. Tanya is in her room with the television blaring out, and this late on a Friday night she's probably seeing all manner of things she shouldn't, but at this point in time, I don't care.

Ed has a small case open on the bed.

"What are you doing?" I ask, even though it's quite obvious. "You can't leave."

"I'm not leaving, Alicia." He is making a mess of folding some trousers. "You are."

"What?"

"I want you out of here. Now."

"Why?" My mouth wants to keep opening and closing even when it's not saying anything. Ed doesn't answer. "Why? This is ridiculous."

"You might think so." Ed looks up and his face is pinched with anger. "But I don't."

"Don't be like this. You know what I mean."

"I don't know what you mean, Alicia. I have no idea who you are anymore."

"Ed, we need to talk this through. Rationally. We can go back to the point where you brought Elliott home from the hospital and I'll tell you exactly what happened."

"I thought you said nothing happened."

"Ed, this isn't a courtroom. Don't twist everything I say."

He stops stuffing my clothes in the bag. "I think you've got a nerve, Alicia."

"You're overreacting," I say calmly. "I know you're hurt…."

"You can't even begin to know how hurt I am." His teeth are gritted and he hisses the words out between them.

I hug myself. Where has this come from? Ed and I have always been able to talk. Admittedly, our conversations of late have generally been over nothing more taxing than the choice of wallpaper, although we did have a major spat over whether or not we should have the all-singing, all-dancing, Georgian-style conservatory built. We didn't speak for three days over that, and I won in the end when Ed capitulated and we had it built. We're still paying it off on the mortgage, and now he spends more time in there than I do, but I wouldn't dream of mentioning that it's been a waste of money. "Ed, I have made a huge mistake."

"On that we're agreed," he snaps.

"I want to put it right." I advance on my suitcase and go to take the clothes back out and Ed slaps me. *He slaps me.* He slaps my hands away and they are stinging and I too am stung.

"It isn't that simple, is it?"

I am speechless with shock and can only stare at the back of my hands, which bear bright beetroot-colored marks.

"I want you out of here, Alicia. Out of my house. I need to think about this, and I don't want you near me. Or the children."

"What!" I don't know whether to cry or shout. "You're throwing me out?"

"Don't be so dramatic."

"Permanently?"

"I want some time alone. I think you might benefit from some too. You can reassess the situation in light of recent developments." Ed sounds like he is giving a presentation at work to a room full of suits, not threatening to end our marriage.

"And where am I supposed to go?"

"That is entirely up to you," Ed replies, and closes my case.

"Can't I sleep on the sofa?"

He pushes the case across the bed toward me without a word.

I pick it up and its weight drags me down. What's left of my energy seeps out of me into the bedroom carpet. "Now you're the one who's making a big mistake," I say quietly.

"Just go, Alicia."

And I do. I'm not going to be able to talk any sense into Ed while he's in this mood, and I can't believe we've come to this situation so quickly. I'm shell-shocked at his lack of compassion, and it hasn't even occurred to him to ask what might have led me to strike up a friendship, albeit unwise, with another man. Perhaps when he's slept on it for a night, he'll be ready to talk.

I walk down the stairs, not really knowing what I'm doing. My coat is on the end of the banister rail, and I don't remember putting it there. I stop, put my case down and shrug it onto my shoulders. Ed is standing at the top of the stairs and I look up at him, ready to plead my innocence again, but he turns away from me, goes into the bedroom, our bedroom, and firmly shuts the door.

I pick up my case again, and now my stubborn streak kicks in even though I'm feeling pathetic. Let Ed stew for the night, and when he's good and ready to listen then I'll give him my explanation. I don't have red hair for nothing. In a whoosh of unbridled ire, I am out the door and slam it so soundly behind me that its hinges reverberate and its glass shakes fearfully. I don't care. I pull my collar up and, chin held high, stamp out into the cold, dark night.

CHAPTER 24

It's raining. Lashing down. It's also pitch-black and I'm standing outside Jemma's flat, which is above her shop. The flat is also pitch-black, which is not generally considered a good sign if you're looking for a warm welcome. No one is keeping my sister's home fire burning.

In my temper, I have walked out without my handbag. In my handbag is my spare key to Jemma's front door. And I have only just realized the enormity of this slight technical omission. In my coat pocket, I had exactly two pounds and seventy-five pence, which was change from the sandwiches that Christian and I bought for lunch at Kew. (And doesn't that seem like a different lifetime?) I spent two pounds and fifty pence on my Tube ticket to get here because my car keys are also in my handbag, and I dropped twenty pence on the floor while I was searching for my money, which was picked up by a tramp whom I hadn't the nerve to challenge for its return. So now I have the princely sum of five pence, no checkbook, no credit card, no mobile phone, no keys. In a fit of pique, I hurl my five-pence piece down the street, rendering myself totally penniless. Great job, Alicia.

Jemma's shop is in Ladbroke Road, in quite a villagey bit just away from the main bustle of Notting Hill Gate. You Must Remember This… (great name, I know!) is in the middle of a small, select row. There are a couple of café bistro places, one looking distinctly more salubrious than the other, a Majestic wine outlet and two antique galleries, one selling gorgeous Chinese artifacts, which I daren't go into because I'd come out several hundred pounds poorer. The parade also has one of those quaint old-fashioned cab ranks complete with a British racing green hut and a queue of shiny idle cabs parked outside, and I can't begin to imagine what might go on inside. The only thing that spoils the vista is a huge concrete tower block of flats looming over the top of it.

Jemma's is one of a rash of nostalgic and retro clothes shops in the area. It's a strange place, full of stuff that my mother still has in her wardrobe. Oxfam tat with Harvey Nichols price tags as far as I'm concerned. So what if they're 1960s designer labels? They're horrible! And why, oh why, would anyone want to wear cast-offs from the 1970s? Even if it does bear a Halston or an Ossie Clark moniker? For me, that was the time that taste forgot and it's best that we forget it too. My daughter has just bought her first pair of hot pants, which, twenty-five years later, are back in fashion for the third, or probably the fourth, time, and I shudder to think that I ever went out dressed like that. Jemma says I have no soul, but clearly her customers do, because she makes a small fortune despite her astronomical rent. To give Jemma her due, the bulk of her stock is pure vintage—there are very few wide lapels and flared trousers on view. Her chic, crowded rooms groan with rails of elegant beaded gowns from the 1930s and 1940s, which, in terms of style, I'm much happier to relate to. She says her customers want to look individual and creative in their dress, but that sounds suspiciously like sales-speak to me. Who would know, apart from another hip and enlightened "classic" clothing fan, that you weren't just wearing something you'd dragged out of a charity shop for a fiver? I would rather look new, but perhaps it's me that's missing the point. And there's no doubting my sister's commitment, as she devotes every waking moment into making it a success. If only she were as attentive to her relationships. But then, standing here in the pissing-down rain because my husband's thrown me out, I'm a fine one to talk.

I rap at Jemma's door once more, and the thought that I'm getting nowhere fast flashes through my brain again. I huddle into her strip of doorway so that I'm getting merely drenched rather than totally drowned. I thought Ed said my sister had come back from Prague, but maybe she was phoning from there? There isn't a single sign of life. This place definitely has the look of its owner being terminally out.

I consider breaking in, but due to the value of the stock the shop has more alarms than a nuclear-power plant and, no doubt, half of the Metropolitan Police force would descend upon me, because policemen are never around when you want one and arrive in droves when you don't.

I can feel my hair tightening into ringlets, and I'm probably sporting the same hairstyle as Lenny Kravitz by now. I have to do something! I could go to my parents' house. They live miles away in Harpenden, but I could hail a cab and get them to fork out for it and then ask Ed to pay them back. It would cost a small fortune and serve him right! But they would worry terribly if I turned up in the middle of the night, as they'll have had their Horlicks hours ago and will be well into the land of Nod by now. They're that sort of people. Also, turning up there would make this whole stupid disagreement seem so much worse than it is. My mother would then spend the rest of her life thinking that we have a shaky marriage. My heart sinks to my sodden shoes. Perhaps we do.

I search my pockets again for any sign of cash, noting ruefully that my emergency ten-pound note is safely secreted in the little pocket of my handbag, which is also safely in my kitchen at home. Perhaps I need to put an emergency ten-pound note underneath the inner soles of all my shoes if I plan on being stupid on a regular basis. I would agree with you, at this juncture, that my emergency situation procedures could do with an extensive review.

I cannot in any event return home. That would be just too humiliating for words. I would rather huddle down in Jemma's doorway for the night. Lots of people sleep rough these days, and it's only for one night. I could head toward…er…somewhere that has arches and look for a spare cardboard box. I look at the torrential rain and wonder how on earth these poor unfortunate people manage. I feel on the verge of tears. I have a beautiful home and a soft, comfy bed. Ed cannot be so cruel as to leave me out on the streets. I won't let him do this to me, however much I have to beg.

Just as I am about to give up hope and slink back to the marital home, penitent, my icy fingers fold around a business card. La Place Velma. It has Christian's address on the back, and it shines in my hand like a beacon under the streetlight. God, he lives just around the corner. If I had a stone, I could throw it there. I could be there in five minutes. Less. I wish I had my phone, then I could ring him. I know, I know, I know. I know what you're thinking. I'm thinking it too. He's the last person in the world I should contact. But what else am I to do? At the very least, he might give me a corner of his floor, or a cup of tea, or be able to lend me some money so that I can get a room for the night. And didn't he say that I should drop in any time I was in the area? I sigh as a big splat of rain splashes onto the address and smears the ink. I just don't expect he thought that it would be at one o'clock in the morning.

CHAPTER 25

Ed lay on the bed staring at the ceiling. His clothes were scattered on the floor in the way Ali hated most, and he was wearing just his boxer shorts. He had his arms crossed behind his head on the pillow and to the untrained eye he looked relaxed, but wasn't. There was a knot of tension in his stomach as if he'd had a bad curry, and the crick in his neck was reaching osteopath-visiting proportions. Every beat of his heart thundered through his body.

He'd been meaning to decorate this bedroom for ages, but as with a million other nonessential domestic duties, had never got round to it. The favorite excuse was time, but the overriding factor was lack of inclination. It would have been far easier to pay someone and keep Ali happy, but his motto was always: If you're going to make a mess of doing something, you might as well do it yourself rather than pay someone else to make a mess of it for you. And making a mess seemed to be his speciality at the moment.

Ed moved his gaze from the ceiling to the alarm clock, which blinked digitally at him in a very accusing way. Ali had been gone for ages. Real ages. Not storm-round-the-block-in-a-fit-of-temper ages. But gone-a-long-way-and-doesn't-appear-to-be-coming-back ages.

What an arse he'd been, ranting on like some sulking schoolboy when there could be some perfectly good explanation.

Why hadn't he listened? At least he should have extended his wife that little courtesy as she protested her innocence. There was no way Ali could be having an affair. Even if she had the inclination. There was no way she had the time. She was either at work or doing something with the kids. It didn't leave many opportunities for romping round sordid hotels or whatever one did these days in pursuit of extramarital excitement. Ed looked at the Kew Gardens ticket for two. That didn't sound like the perfect venue for a clandestine romp. But then, there *were* a lot of bushes.

He wished Ali would come back and they could talk about it. Ed was sure that she'd gone to her sister's flat, but he'd tried Jemma's number and it had been switched, intractably, to answerphone. He could imagine it now—they'd be halfway through their second bottle of wine and having a good old whinge about men. Him in particular. They were like two peas in a pod at times like these. Except all the previous "times like these" had been when her sister's boyfriends—in various states of marital entanglement—had left and Ali had rushed to the rescue. Undoubtedly, her sister was now reciprocating.

Ed looked at the phone. She could at least ring so that he wouldn't worry, but then Ali knew that he wouldn't sleep until she rang, so she was probably exacting some minuscule revenge by making him sweat. And sweating he was. It was a muggy night. The rain was still heavy, but it was bringing no freshness with it. He'd had to close the bedroom window, because the curtains were starting to get wet and he knew Ali would give him an ear-bashing if she came home to damp drapery. This was all the fault of Harrison Ford and the National Health Service, both of whom had left him feeling, in their own way, unsettled, restless and disgruntled. If he hadn't had his mind filled with fantasy longings of life in Hollywood, then perhaps he wouldn't have been so brackish with Ali when she'd stepped out of her allotted box to find a little fun.

The phone rang and he snatched it up.

"Hello?"

"Is there any particular reason you left me sitting at the Groucho for three hours like a lemon?"

Ed let out the breath he hadn't been aware he was holding. "Orla."

"That's me."

Ed rubbed his face as he clamped the phone to his ear with his shoulder. "I forgot. I'm so, so sorry."

"You forgot?" Her voice was tense. "That's not awfully flattering, Ed."

"Believe me, if you knew what'd been going on here today, you'd forgive me." Ed suddenly felt very weary, the weight of a thousand tons of responsibility crushing down on his shoulders, and he wanted to weep, howl into the wind, rent his soul and purge his lungs of anguish with a plaintive, primal scream. Instead, he sighed a meaningful sigh.

Her voice softened. "Are you okay?"

"No," he admitted. "I'm having a domestic crisis."

"Is this a bad time?"

"In my life or for ringing?"

"Both," Orla said, failing to recognize his attempt at humor.

"Yes to the first. Not particularly to the second."

There was a weighty pause before Orla spoke again. "Do you want me to come over?"

"I don't think so."

Again an uncomfortable silence. "You know I'm always here for you, Ed."

He did now. "Thanks," he replied.

"Will you call me tomorrow?"

"Yes," Ed said, without really knowing why.

"Look." Orla paused again, and all Ed wanted to do was hang up, curl up and try to go to sleep. "You only have to ask and I'd do anything," she said. "I care deeply for you. You know that, don't you?"

He hadn't previously but, again, he did now. "Yes," he said. "And thanks, Orla. I'm really sorry about tonight. It went straight out of my head." And despite being on the phone, he made a straight-out-of-my-head type gesture. "I'll make it up to you," he promised.

"I might just hold you to that," she said, laughing slightly. "Good night, Ed."

"Good night, Orla."

She hung up, and before Ed could contemplate just what making it up to Orla might conceivably involve, there was a heart-stopping, ear-piercing, gut-wrenching scream coming from the bathroom, and he shot off his bed and raced at full pelt across the landing.

Elliott was standing in the bathroom in the dim glow of the shaving light which they always left on because both boys were afraid of the dark. Why was that? They were two perfectly healthy, nurtured middle-class children. Why did they imagine unseen terrors that waited for them just around each darkened corner? What had happened to cause that? And why was it that the things that lurked in darkened corners of your adult psyche were the ones that you were able to ignore the best of all?

Elliott let out another unearthly shriek. Ed burst through the door like some boxer-shorted superhero. "What's the matter?"

Elliott howled again. "I want Mummy!"

Ed crouched down next to him and put his arms round him. "Mummy's out."

Elliott screamed louder. "I want Mummy!"

"Darling. Mummy's out. Daddy's here. What's wrong? Are you hurt?"

"I want Mummy!"

"Is it your arm?" Ed felt his heart jump to his mouth for about the twenty-seventh time that day. "What's wrong?"

Elliott turned to him tearfully. His face was wet and shining in the light. Racking sobs shook his body. "I weed up my nose!"

"What?"

Elliott sobbed again. "I weed up my nose!" He looked horrified at himself. "I couldn't point my willy properly with my sore arm," he wailed. "And my wee went up my nose!"

Ed stifled a smile. "It's not the end of the world, Elliott."

But the small boy remained unconvinced and cried louder.

"It's just a little accident." Ed went to pull his youngest son toward him and then remembered the wee dripping down Elliott's face.

Elliott's sobs subsided from hysterical to heartfelt. "I want Mummy."

Ed swallowed hard. "She's not here."

"Where is she?"

"She's gone to Aunty Jemma's."

"When will she be back?"

Ed felt his eyes prickle. "I'm not sure." He scooped Elliott up and, holding him at arm's length, maneuvered him to the sink. "Come on, let's wash your face and get you some clean pajamas." If he could remember where Ali kept the clean pajamas.

Elliott offered his face while Ed got to work with the flannel and soap. He took Elliott's pajama top off. Tanya appeared at the bathroom door, yawning. "What's wrong?"

"Elliott's had an accident."

"Another one?"

"I weed up my nose," her little brother said miserably.

Tanya looked impressed. "Great party trick."

Elliott smiled proudly.

"Do you know where Mummy puts your clean pajamas?"

Tanya nodded. "Of course I do."

"Be an angel and get Elliott another pair."

Tanya ambled off and banged around in the big chest of drawers at the top of the stairs. At this rate, Elliott's accident was going to wake the entire street up. They'd remind him of it at drinks parties when he was twenty-one. They'd probably ask him to do it at drinks parties when he was twenty-one!

Thomas came sleepily into the bathroom. He was rubbing his eyes and looked deathly white. "Daddy," he said. "I don't feel well." And he promptly threw up over Elliott's pajama trousers, causing his brother to scream and indulge in a Navajo-style war dance round the bathroom, spreading the sick nicely round the vinyl flooring. "I want Mummy! I want Mummy!"

"I want Mummy too," Thomas said politely, his pallid face merging nicely with the white bathroom tiles.

"I'm sorry. You'll have to make do with me. Tanya!" Ed shouted. "Clean pajamas for two!"

With much shushing, Ed manhandled both of his sons into the shower and turned it on full. It smelled like some foul torture chamber from the Japanese game show *Endurance*. Ali always dealt with this sort of stuff. She had cream for everything. Vomit and blood did not faze her. She just waded in and mopped it up while making comforting cooing sounds. Whereas if he saw anyone being sick, he just wanted to join in. Ed yanked the boys out of the shower and toweled them down.

"That's because he ate my burger as well as his own," Tanya informed Ed, tossing the pajamas to him.

"Thanks," he said. "You don't want to part with any of your body fluids, do you?"

"Don't be gross!"

"Just checking," Ed said.

"Where's Mum?"

"At Aunty Jemma's."

"Uh. What's happened now?" Tanya said.

Ed paused. "Mummy will tell you when she gets back."

"Will she, hell," Tanya said. "She never tells me anything juicy."

"Go to bed," her father said.

Tanya wandered off, muttering.

Ed stuffed Elliott in his pajamas and buttoned up his jacket, amazed that this former screeching wreck could now look so angelic. Thomas quietly changed in the corner. "If Mummy's not here," Elliott mused, "can I get in bed with you?"

"Just this once," Ed said wearily. "Don't make a habit of it."

"Can I too?" Thomas asked.

Ed smiled. "Of course you can, darling." And firmly pushed the thought of his son throwing up in the bed to the back of his mind.

He gave the bathroom floor a quick once-over, vowed to do it properly in the morning and then shoved the dirty clothes in the linen basket, also to be dealt with the next day.

Ed guided his sons back to his bedroom, and Elliott bounded across the double bed heedless of his sprained, bandaged arm and bounced under the duvet. Tiredly, Ed got in beside him. Thomas slid in next, making a tight sandwich of Ed. "Don't fidget, Elliott," he warned. "Or you're back in your own bed."

Ed turned off the light, and Elliott and Thomas curled against him. It felt strange having these tiny, bony bodies nuzzled in next to him instead of Ali. It had been a long time since Elliott had slept in their bed. Even longer since Thomas had done it. And it had been a long time since he had shared a bed with anyone other than Alicia. She'd always hated their periods of enforced separation when he was away working on a film—it turned her cranky or whiney. He'd never minded too much because he was always totally exhausted or totally drunk by the time he fell into his bed on location, and everything else revolved around work, work and more work. There was only one night when he'd gone to bed with another woman, a production assistant or makeup girl, he couldn't even remember now. She was cute, young, available. They'd both been very drunk and he'd had a row with Ali about something or nothing. The girl had probably tried to pick up Harrison Ford and had failed. Whichever way, they'd spent the night together and it was great fun. Until the morning. And then he'd felt wretched and stupid and she'd felt sober and stupid. They inched round each other on the set until the movie was in the can, and he'd never done anything like it since. It wasn't that there hadn't been the opportunity, but he felt the whole casual-sex thing wasn't really worth the effort. He was happy with Alicia. He was in love with Alicia.

Elliott wriggled against him. "You smell nice, Daddy."

Ed inhaled. Elliott smelled of wee. Thomas stank of puke. He would have to improve his nursing and washing skills.

Elliott sucked gently at his thumb as he drifted off into sleep. "I don't like it when Mummy's not here," he mumbled.

"Me neither," Thomas agreed.

"Ssh," Ed said and stroked his sons' soft downy hair. He stared at the ceiling in the dark even though he could no longer see the tiny cracks where it badly needed painting over. Ed didn't like it when Ali wasn't here either, and he fervently hoped it wasn't something that he or his sons would have to get used to.

CHAPTER 26

The street Christian lives in is very posh. Which sort of surprises me. I don't know why. I suppose I expected scruffy, student-style digs, but this is no such thing. You'd be pushed to find anywhere to live in this area unless you had about half a million quid sitting in your back pocket. Particularly since the area shot to fame in the film *Notting Hill.* Hugh Grant has made a lot of property owners round here very happy.

It's a quiet, narrow street just behind Notting Hill Gate Tube station, lined with tall copper beech trees which will soon outgrow their limited space. The houses are mostly well-kept chichi terraces painted in hopeful Mediterranean shades of pink, yellow and cloudless-sky blue. In this tungsten-lit downpour they look as I feel, a little washed out and pasty. They all have iron railings, ornate wrought-iron porches and window boxes overflowing with daffodils and spring bulbs. Some of the houses have roof terraces, a desirable commodity in any London street. Their exotic blooms reach toward the moon and are buffeted by the rain against the skyline for their pains. On the street are parked the type of cars that little boys dream of. Don't ask me what they are. I only care if my car starts in the morning and, at a push, what color it is. But you know the sort I mean. Flashy red things and long silver ones and soft tops that purr along and turn impressionable heads.

I marry the number on the card, which is now more than a little soggy at the edges, with the number on the front door. And double-check the address just to make sure this really is where Christian lives. I feel a knot of apprehension tightening within me and sigh out my breath like they told us to do at prenatal classes, which was just as useless during childbirth as it is now.

Christian's house is a little shabbier than the rest, and that makes me feel slightly relieved. The window box seems to be bearing the remnants of last year's geraniums, and they're probably the only things round here grateful for the deluge of water. There are two bicycles chained to the railings, and the bin at the bottom of the basement steps is overflowing with rubbish. One of the neighborhood cats is enjoying what appears to be the remains of Chicken Chow Mein from a foil carton. The front door is purple and ornately carved, but on close inspection the paint is cracked and peeling.

A slight frisson of fear creeps over my scalp as I wonder if Christian lives here with his parents and hasn't dared to confess, knowing how uncool that is? Before I can turn and run away, I press the doorbell, but hear no comforting ring on the other side.

I wait and get wetter and realize that this could probably be considered the worst night of my life to date. I'm clutching my pathetic little suitcase like some overgrown version of Paddington Bear and seething quietly. Like Jemma's, there doesn't appear to be a light on in the house, and it seems reasonable to assume that Christian has gone to bed. I'm sure if the doorbell worked, he'd be here by now. I press it again and stand a bit nearer to the door under the inadequate but attractive shelter of the overhanging porch. A few minutes pass, and I resort to twanging the letter box, convinced that the doorbell has died.

As I do, a girl opens the door, rubbing sleep from her eyes. She's wearing a silky slip and nothing else. Do you remember me telling you about Caroline Gregory? She of the Gary Eccleston saga? Bitch sex kitten of Our Lady of Perpetual Succour High School? Remember? Well, her doppelganger is standing right in front of me.

I quickly check the address, fearing that the splat of rain might have impaired my reading (my glasses are also in my handbag) and that I've got some totally unconnected sex kitten out of bed in the middle of the night. She looks blankly at me. As well she might.

"Hi," I say and push back my flat, wet, corkscrew hair so that I might appear marginally less like a madwoman. "I'm looking for Christian Winter."

Her eyes widen, despite her sleepy state. "Chris?"

"Yes."

"He's out."

There's a lengthy pause in which one of us ought to say something, but neither of us does. She, possibly because she is half-asleep and dazed. Me, because by this point I'm totally brain dead. The girl yawns and stretches, and I feel I must say something before she's tempted to close the door.

"I wonder if I could possibly wait for him?" I say. "If it's not inconvenient."

Her look says, *Of course it's inconvenient, it's one o'clock in the fucking morning!* She comes out of her sleepy state, folds her arms across her chest and eyes me suspiciously.

Well, would you let me into your house in the dead of night looking like this? "It's important."

"Are you his mother?"

"No." I look bad, but not that bad! "I'm a friend. He may not have mentioned me," I say with studied patience. Why should he? "My name's Ali. Alicia."

The sex kitten looks horrorstruck, and her eyes travel from my hair to my shoes and back again in slow motion. "*You're* Ali?"

"Yes."

"Shit," she mutters, and stands aside. "You'd better come in."

I do. I step inside this rather grand house in this rather posh street and, as I follow her through to the hall, try not to drip on what looks like expensive carpet. The sex kitten pads in her bare feet through to a huge kitchen, which in my disorientated state looks the size of ten football pitches. And I wonder who on earth she might be.

I put my case down on the tiles, which won't matter too much if they get wet, and sidle self-consciously across to the kitchen table. I can't believe I'm sitting here. I know so little about Christian. Who is this? She can't be his sister, even if he has one, because she'd have recognized her own mother on her doorstep even in the dead of the night. Does he share the house with other people? Why hadn't I considered that? What on earth did we talk about all day? Did I slip into typical doting mother mode and rattle on about my kids for hours?

"Tea?" she asks, picking up the kettle.

"If it's not too much trouble."

She says nothing, but I gather that it is rather a lot of trouble and that her hospitality is somewhat forced. But I try to put myself in her position. She'll probably kill Christian tomorrow. I sit in silence while the kettle takes an age to boil and she makes just one mug of tea.

The girl puts the steaming hot mug on the stripped pine table in front of me, seemingly unaware or uncaring of the fact that it will leave a white scorch mark in the wood. "Thank you."

Never in all my life have I been so grateful to see a cup of tea. I nurse my hands round it and realize that they're as cold as ice. A towel would be nice to dry myself down, but I'm not offered one, and as I've already intruded so much, I wouldn't dare to ask.

"I'm Rebecca," the girl says. "Christian and I share this place." She looks dismissively at the grand kitchen. "We're...old friends."

It's a loaded statement and contains a warning. And if I hadn't left my sense of humor back at home in my handbag too, I might have found it amusing that this perfectly formed sylph could feel threatened by someone who currently looks like something the cat dragged in.

Rebecca doesn't sit down with me, but leans against the Aga and scrutinizes me. "You're not what I expected."

How am I supposed to answer that? I have no idea what, if anything, Christian has said about me, but presumably, from the look on her face, she expected some little glamour puss, not someone she'd consider ready to collect her bus pass. I have a horrible thought. I was probably at the very peak of my groovy hot-pants phase somewhere around the time that Christian and this young miss were born. I say nothing and concern myself with the job of drinking tea in an effort to thaw out my frozen insides.

"What are you doing here?" she asks, glancing at the clock to make sure I'm aware what time it is.

"I'm not really sure," I answer, truthfully. I don't want to tell this stranger about my row with Ed and how I've been tramping the streets because he's being childish and unreasonable. Mainly due to the fact I'm about to cry.

She rubs her bare arms against the chill of the night air, and I can feel myself start to shiver inside.

"What time do you think Christian will be home?" I ask timidly.

Rebecca snorts. "Who knows? Christian is a law unto himself—but then I expect you know that." I see a slight smile curl on her lips when my face clearly registers that I don't. "He's gone out on the razz with Robbie, the other guy who lives here. They may not come back at all." There is a challenge in her eyes. My mother would call her a "little madam."

"I'll drink this and be out of your way," I say, swallowing the tea without tasting it.

"Stay," she says with a shrug. "If that's what you want. If you're not in a rush to get home."

"Would you mind?" Again the indifferent shrug.

"I'm off to bed." She stifles a yawn. "You can have Chris's bed, I guess. Or camp down on the sofa. It's up to you."

"I'll just wait here," I say.

"Suit yourself."

"Thanks, Rebecca." I smile at her. "You've been very kind." And she has, in her own way. She has taken me into her home despite not knowing me from Adam, and obviously convinced I'm far too old and gnarled for Christian. And I'm inside in the dry and the warm, although the atmosphere has a decidedly chilly edge. If this is the alternative to a cardboard box, I'll take it.

"If you decide to leave," she adds as she walks out of the room, "don't bang the door. I'm a light sleeper."

I smile at her retreating back, her rigidly set shoulders and her pert little bottom. Wriggling down in the hard-backed chair, I try to make myself more comfortable for what could be a long wait.

She glances back one more time. "I hear everything."

And I'm quite sure she makes it her job to.

CHAPTER 27

The hammering at the front door took several minutes to permeate through the fug of Ed's subconscious and rouse him into waking. He sat bolt upright and realized that Elliott had long since departed the bed. Thomas, still pale and interesting, slept on. Pulling on his dressing gown, Ed briefly entertained the thought that the insistent pounding might be Ali come home without her key, but he would recognize the thud of that fist anywhere. Ed peered out of the window and, sure enough, Neil's motorbike was haphazardly abandoned in the drive in the style that his brother termed "parking."

"Oh shit," Ed mumbled, and headed downstairs.

Elliott was sitting in the lounge watching *Postman Pat* with the headphones on. "Uncle Neil's been hammering at the door for the last ten minutes!" Ed reproached him.

Elliott raised his headphones. "What?"

"Never mind." Ed yanked open the front door.

Neil stood there grinning, with his crash helmet tucked under his arms. His smile faded. "You look like rancid dog shit, bro."

"Thank you," Ed said, standing aside while he walked past. "I also feel like it."

Ed followed his brother, who looked like a funky young dude in leather, into the kitchen. Neil put down his helmet and was already filling the kettle. "You need coffee," he said. "Strong and black."

Tanya leant on the door frame.

"Who is this gorgeous creature?" Neil asked.

Tanya blushed. The gorgeous creature was a foot deep in foundation and floating in a cloud of Ali's perfume, Ed noted. She fluttered her eyelids. "Hi, Uncle Neil." She turned to Ed and the flutter froze. "You look like you've been drinking, Dad," she accused.

"I haven't," Ed said. But I wish I had, he added silently.

"Where's Mum?"

Ed avoided looking at anyone. "She's still at Jemma's."

"The sickie clothes need to go in the wash."

"Can't you do it?"

"I'm spending the day with Hannah Cooper. We're going to Brighton. *Now.* Mum was supposed to make me sandwiches."

"I don't suppose she had the time," Ed reasoned. "And you're fifteen years old and perfectly capable of making your own sandwiches."

Tanya opened the fridge and stared sulkily at its contents. "I don't like anything we've got in. I'm a vegetarian."

"Since when?"

"Since today."

Ed sighed. "Neil. Have you got a tenner?" Neil searched in his leathers and produced a ten-pound note. He gave it to Ed who gave it to Tanya. "Buy yourself a soya burger."

Tanya smiled and kissed him. "Thanks, Dad. I don't know when I'll be back."

"It's a recurring theme in this house," Ed muttered, and his daughter slammed the front door.

Neil put a strong black coffee that looked like it could eat through the mug in front of him. "I owe you ten quid, mate," Ed said.

"I'll put it on the slate with all the others," Neil remarked as he tentatively tasted his coffee. "Has Jemma got another man crisis then?"

"No."

Neil pursed his lips. "Girlie night out?"

"No."

"Anything you're likely to share with me?"

Ed folded his arms and leaned on the counter. "She's left me."

"Who?"

"Catherine Zeta Jones. She said she preferred Michael Douglas all along."

"What?" Neil looked very puzzled.

Ed huffed in a way that showed extreme exasperation. "Alicia. Who do you think? Alicia has left me!"

"No, no, no. Bro, bro, bro!"

"She has."

"Never."

Ed indicated the otherwise-empty kitchen.

"When?"

"Last night."

"Why?"

"What is this, Twenty Questions?" Ed snapped.

"You can't just casually announce that your wife of blah, blah years has left you and expect me not to want to know the nitty-gritty. Ed, if this is true, it's serious."

"I don't really think you need to remind me of that."

"So…"

"So she packed a case and left."

"Why?"

"Because I asked her to."

"She's left you because you asked her to?"

"That about sums it up," Ed said.

"Are you mad?"

It was something he had considered in the last twelve hours. "She's seeing someone else."

"Ali?" Neil grimaced. "When?"

"I don't know."

"Ali doesn't have the time. She's too busy looking after you lot."

It was also something that had crossed his mind.

"How long has it been going on?"

"I don't know."

"Who is it?"

"I don't know that either," Ed admitted.

Neil frowned. "Oh, I see you've discussed this very thoroughly."

"They've been to Kew Gardens together."

"Oh, that old hotbed of lust!"

"You're my brother, you're supposed to be on my side!"

"I would be if you hadn't developed bollocks for brains!" Neil strode across the kitchen and leaned in front of Ed. "You think she's having an affair, but you don't know quite how she manages to find time for it, you don't know how long it's been going on and you don't know who with. But you think that's sufficient reason to ask her to leave. So she's packed a bag and gone to Jemma's."

Ed nibbled his thumbnail. "Do you think I was a bit hasty?"

"Oh, for fuck's sake," Neil said.

"I'd had a really bad day, mate."

"And they'll get a lot worse if you don't apologize soon." Neil ushered him toward the door. "Get dressed. Go on—get dressed. With a bit of luck I might be able to get you round there before they get up and have hatched a cunning plan to exact their revenge on you. This could cost you dear, bro. We are talking Caribbean cruise here, mate."

"New bedroom furniture and the decorators in," Ed countered, but he looked more cheerful.

"Whatever," Neil said. "Now. Get dressed. Get your checkbook and let's get round there, before she decides you're a complete twat and refuses to come back."

CHAPTER 28

"Do you know if you've got any bread?" I have no idea whose voice this is, and I can only risk opening one eye. I sort of know where I am, but my brain is refusing to get cracking on all cylinders so that I don't realize the full enormity of it all at once.

When I do manage to focus on who's speaking, it is very definitely a shock. I am surrounded by half-dressed, undernourished gorgeous creatures in this place, and my already low self-esteem is digging a hole to Australia.

"Bread?" she repeats.

"I don't know," I mumble. Somehow I've ended up curled up on the worn Chesterfield sofa in Christian's kitchen when the last thing I remember was sitting at the kitchen table. I'm freezing cold and my bones have solidified into one inert mass. One arm is dead so that I can't push myself up, and I daren't even look if there's a pool of dribble because really it's a foregone conclusion, isn't it? "I don't live here," I say.

"Me neither," the girl replies.

This one has less clothes on than Rebecca did. She's wearing just a bra and pants, and trendy ones at that. See-through animal-print gauzy numbers that wouldn't do anything to keep out a stiff wind. Or even a gentle breeze. Her slender body is lightly tanned, but her face bears the ghostly pall of the incredibly hung over. She's hopping about on the terra-cotta floor, opening all the cupboards, presumably in her search for bread, and waiting for the kettle to boil. "I need toast," she says as she shivers.

I can quite categorically state that toast ranks as a fairly low priority on my list of needs at the moment. Although a hot bath would be up there at the top somewhere. Some feeling has tingled its way back into my arm, and I push myself upright, massaging my lifeless muscles as I do. Upright feels worse than I remember it, and I let my head sag back against the sofa.

The girl is looking at me with concern. "Are you okay?"

I try a weak smile. "I'm fine."

"I'll make you some tea," she says.

"Thank you." I am still wearing my coat, so I obviously didn't plan on staying when I retired to the sofa. I feel ridiculously overdressed for the occasion, given the attire of my companion.

"I'm Sharon," she says with a smile.

"Ali." At least I think I am. "Are you a friend of Christian's?" I ask.

She wrinkles her nose. "Not really. Well, sort of. I only met him at Exodus last night." I have no idea what or where Exodus is and no wish to appear ignorant, so I nod and smile and say nothing. Sharon finds some bread and waves it triumphantly in my direction. "I came back here and spent the night with..."

Sharon looks up and I follow her gaze. Christian is slouching in the doorway. He is wearing slouch pants and they are, appropriately, slouching on his hips. I get the answer to one of my musings. His flat, muscular chest is as bare as Elliott's bottom. He looks squarely at his houseguest and she blushes.

"Hi," he says, his lips hovering somewhere between a wry smile and disinterest.

Sharon looks coquettish. I love that word. Coquettish. This is mainly because I could never, ever be coquettish, no matter how hard I tried. I'm too old, too experienced and far too bad-tempered to be bothered to learn to use such a beguiling technique to my advantage. Men fall for it every time though. Christian has certainly brightened. Sharon folds her bare arms across her midriff, which, far from hiding anything on display, only succeeds in plumping her cleavage up further. How is she managing to look coy while wearing nothing but see-through leopard-skin drawers?

I am too world-weary to feel cross, but I do feel like an intruder. "Am I interrupting?" I venture into the flirty silence.

Christian looks at me for the first time. I don't know quite who he thought this madwoman camping on his sofa was, but he clearly didn't recognize her as me. "Ali?"

He is visibly shaken and so is Sharon, but doesn't seem to know why she should be. "What on earth are you doing here?"

It's a question I'm going to have to find an answer to at some point. "I... I... I..." I can't bring myself to say I had nowhere else to go. There's a torrent of tears backing up behind my eyes and I daren't let them go or I might not stop.

"How long have you been here?"

I sniff. "Most of the night."

"Oh, shit." Christian crosses the room and kneels by my feet. "Did you hear us come in?"

"No. Nothing. I don't know what time I fell asleep."

He searches my face with a flicker of anxiety in his eyes. "This is serious, isn't it?"

I nod, unable to speak. "I can leave if it's a bad time."

"Of course it isn't." He and Sharon exchange a look that I can't decipher, but she smiles sympathetically at me.

Christian touches my coat and then looks at his hand as if it is covered in blood. "You're soaking," he says.

I nod again. It's not often my powers of speech desert me—ask any of my close friends. But they always do when you need them most, don't they?

"Let's get you out of those things and into a nice hot bath."

I could weep with relief. Christian is being so kind. He eases me up from the sofa as if I have just discovered I have a terminal disease.

"I'll bring you both some tea," Sharon says, and they nod at each other earnestly.

Christian takes my hand and leads me out of the room. He squeezes it reassuringly, and I follow him up the stairs. Did you ever see the first moonwalk where the astronauts were shuffling around awkwardly, dragging lead-weighted boots one painful step at a time? That's what my legs feel like now. Perhaps it's due to spending the night on a rock-hard Chesterfield, or I may have a cold coming due to sitting in wet clothes. All the times I laughed at my mother for saying that, and it turns out she may well be right. Or it could just be the weight of emotional fatigue. I'm sure my blood has the consistency of Primula cheese spread—you know, that stuff that's a nightmare to squirt out of the tube. It's romping round my veins with all the exuberance of a lethargic snail on Valium. Christian looks like he might carry me, but thinks better of it. I struggle on manfully to the top, unaided.

"We're here." Christian flings open the bathroom door.

"Wow," I gasp.

The bathroom is amazing. It's huge and so breathtaking it momentarily takes my mind off my troubles. The fittings are white and vaguely Victorian, but the rest of the room is painted with the most stunning mural I've ever seen. Neptune with his trident dominates the far wall, surrounded by sea nymphs and shells and gargantuan fish that look like they've taken a swim straight out of mythology. The colors are vivid ocean hues of turquoise, aquamarine and coral pink. Dolphins play across the ceiling attended by mermaids with gold-spun hair and impossibly iridescent tails.

"This is fabulous." I am shaking my red ringlets in disbelief.

"I did it," Christian says.

"You did?"

He nods. "As a present to the owners."

"I bet they love it." I try to get my mouth to shut.

He shrugs noncommittally. "They haven't seen it yet. They're away," he says. "We're sort of minding this place for them."

I slide off my coat and let it plop in a wet heap on the black-and-white marble floor.

"I'll run the bath," Christian says, and he leans over and flicks the taps on, while I tentatively start to undo my blouse, which is stuck to my skin, which is in turn clammy and goose-pimply.

Sharon pops her head round the door and proffers two mugs of tea and a plate of toast precariously balanced on a tray that's too small. Christian takes it from her.

Sharon bobs nervously. "I'll be off now," she says. "I'll say goodbye to er…"

"Robbie," Christian supplies.

"Yeah. And…thanks." She smiles at me. "See you around sometime."

I smile back, because Christian has already lost interest. He is simultaneously munching toast and pouring lashings of bubble bath into the steaming water.

"She's nice," I say.

"She seems okay," he answers over his shoulder. "Though I'd doubt the sanity of anyone who'd want to spend the night with Robbie."

"Oh." I'm relieved that she spent the night with Robbie, whoever that is, rather than Christian, because I did have my suspicions. I also have a grudging admiration for the current attitude of the young toward having sex with strangers. Despite all the risks involved, it doesn't seem to deter them. You could end up with AIDS, a nutter or at the very least damaged self-respect, but they do it with reckless abandon and no heed of the potential consequences. How can they do this without recoiling in horror in the morning? I have no idea. Will Tanya stomp heavily through this minefield? I wonder. Will she lose her innocence to someone whose name she doesn't know after a night out at a club? God, I hope not. I want her to wait—preferably for several years—and be seduced by an older man who knows what he's doing, in some lavish country retreat complete with champagne and four-poster bed, so that her first time will be a wonderful occasion that she can look back on with fond memories. I don't, however, think she'd thank me for telling her my view of her entry into womanhood.

I lost my virginity laughably late in life, even for my era, and by today's standards I was positively past it. Tanya, my little girl, can go and get the morning-after pill from the school nurse without me ever finding out, which is a terrifying thought. Is that really progress for a supposedly civilized society and a Labour government? I think not. What's the going rate now? Thirteen? Fourteen? Fifteen? Much less if that bastion of knowledge, *Seventeen,* is to be believed. I hope Tanya has the sense to wait until she's twenty-seven, at least, for this vastly overrated pleasure in life. But who knows? She may already be vastly more experienced than her mother. It wouldn't be hard. If things continue like this, by the time Tanya herself is a mother with a teenage daughter, they'll be fitting Pampers with condom pockets. And then she'll know what it feels like to worry!

I think alcohol is the main problem. When I was fifteen, booze tasted like booze. It was something you had to acclimatize yourself to—gradually increasing your intake in direct proportion to the amount you were prepared to be sick. Now booze tastes as blandly inoffensive as fruit juice. You can drink three Bacardi Bombshells, or whatever, and have no ill-effects until you're flat on your back. Perhaps this is why this generation lose their inhibitions so quickly. Or perhaps they are desensitized to everything. There isn't a night of the week when you can't watch someone having sex on the telly, so where's the mystery in it when it comes to your turn?

My bath is run and the glorious bathroom is filled with strawberry-scented steam. I am getting warmer by the minute.

Christian sits on the loo and watches me. Which I can tell you is a deeply disconcerting experience. How do you get naked in front of someone you barely know? His eyes never leave my body. Not in a lascivious way, but nevertheless it feels like I'm performing a striptease. I want to huddle into myself and protect my imperfections from the intensity of his study. No one has looked at me like this before, and I'm stripped bare before him in more ways than one. This is definitely a moment when three Barcardi Bombshells would come in useful, even though it's barely ten o'clock in the morning. I let my clothes fall to the floor, brazening it out, although I can't bring myself to look at Christian.

I step into the bath with as much grace as I can muster and feel my feet sizzle in the heat of the water. Lowering myself into the bubbles, I enjoy their light caress on my weary skin and let out a sigh as the blissful relief of the warmth starts to soothe my frazzled nerves. I squeeze my eyes shut, and the tears thread themselves through the barrier of my lashes and start to make silent tracks over my burning cheeks.

Christian slides onto the floor beside the bath, and I open my eyes as he dabs the tears away with a Pooh Bear flannel. He hands me my tea and holds out a piece of toast while I bite it gratefully, then leans his hand on his elbow and studies me some more.

"Want to tell me why you're here?"

Not really, I think. This is too soon. Too complicated. And far too painful. I take a deep breath, which shudders from my lungs. "Ed found out about us," I say as calmly as I can. "He found out about us and he threw me out."

I recount the story of Elliott and the climbing frame, the visit to Casualty, the Kew Gardens ticket, et cetera, et cetera. You know it all. And by the time I've finished, so does Christian.

"Shit," is all he says by way of acknowledgment, and I know exactly what he means. "What are you going to do?"

"Get dressed, go home and grovel, I guess."

"But we haven't done anything."

"That's what I'm going to try to explain."

Christian tugs at his fringe in agitation. "This is all my fault."

"I don't think so. You didn't exactly drag me screaming into it."

"You still love your husband?"

I don't even need to think about it. "Yes."

His face is sad, and I can't bear to see the corners of his smiling mouth downturned. "And what about us?"

"I think 'us' has to end here."

"I was hoping you wouldn't say that."

"I can't do anything else," I reason. "This isn't just about me. I have three children to consider. I came here because I didn't know what else to do."

Christian traces my cheek with the back of his hand. He takes my cup from me even though I've hardly touched my tea and puts it on the floor. "I'm glad you came here," he says, and his fingers twine in my hair at the nape of my neck.

"So am I." I lean toward him and nuzzle into his neck, which smells of stale smoke and booze, and his stubble grazes against me. He presses his face into my hair and kisses it with tender, featherweight brushes of his lips.

"Oh, Ali," he murmurs. "I am so very much in love with you."

"Christian…" I start to say, but his mouth is on mine, hot and damp and soft. My breasts are wet against the warmth of his chest and he draws me into him, whispering my name. I am gone. As easily as that. Softening, swooning, melting away under the heat of his touch. Could anyone feel the fire of this passion and not willingly surrender themselves to the flames?

Our lips are still molded together as he sloughs off his slouch pants, and his naked body makes me want to gasp out loud. His youthful curves and hollows are as beautiful as any classical sculpture, and his muscles show the definition that will blossom soon to full manhood. He steps into the bath and is above me, covering me with eager kisses. His face colors with lust. Have I ever before aroused such open desire in a man? I don't think so. It is such a powerful feeling that any ideas of inhibition I might have harbored, fly away in the bold, bold face of it. His eyes and his body are hungry for me. Ravenous. And I too want to devour him. We twist and turn until I am astride him and we make love. We undulate together, his hands urging my hips in their frenzy until we cry out together that our ecstasy is spent. And I don't even think about whether the bathroom door is locked, or about the water lapping over the side onto the plate of toast, or whether Sharon or Robbie or the keen-eared Rebecca might hear us or the fact that I've never made love in the bath before. I don't think of any of these things until much, much later, and then I can't stop.

I lean on Christian's chest, and we are breathing heavily and grinning inanely at each other.

"Remember the day I drew you?" he says, brushing my hair from my face.

I nod and he bites his lip, smirking. "I said your hair was beautiful."

I nod again, and Christian stifles a giggle as he tugs at one of my sodden dreadlocks. "Well, now you look just like Lenny Kravitz," he splutters.

I splash against the bathwater, drowning him, when he is already too wet to care. We kiss again, laughing and struggling together in the bath until the tears run down my cheeks once more.

CHAPTER 29

"So where is she then?" Ed massaged his unshaven beard and his face hurt.

"I was rather hoping you'd tell me," Jemma snapped. She was stomping about her flat and was unnaturally purple in the face.

Ed hung his head farther. "I thought she was here."

"Well, she isn't. So now what?"

Neil fidgeted uncomfortably, his leather biker's trousers squeaking inappropriately against Jemma's Conran leather chair. Ed noted his brother's sneaky looks at his sister-in-law's own bottom, clad in 1960s leather hipsters.

"What about ringing your parents?" Ed suggested.

"To say what? That you've temporarily misplaced their daughter?"

"She might be there," he reasoned.

"And she might be under a bus, for all you care!" Jemma ranted. "Ed, how could you be so callous? She is the mother of your children."

"I know, I know," he pleaded. "And if I could find her, I'd make it up to her."

"You let her walk out into the night, into the rain, without her handbag, without her phone. She could be anywhere."

"I know."

"She could have drowned in the canal."

Ed looked alarmed. "What canal?"

"Any canal!"

Ed gnawed the skin at the side of his finger. "I'm sure she'll be fine."

"Are you mad?" Jemma said. "London is full of lunatics." She gave him a searing look. "Bits of her could be in a bin bag in some seedy backstreet."

He could feel his blood turning to one of those Slush Puppies that Elliott was so fond of. "And she definitely didn't come here?"

Jemma shook her head. "I was here all night. Not a peep."

"She can't just have vanished," Ed said. "Do you think I ought to call the hospitals or police? Isn't that what you do when someone goes missing?"

"She didn't 'go missing,' Edward, she was thrown out after a domestic argument. The first thing the police will do is dig up your patio."

"Oh shit."

"Oh shit, indeed," echoed Jemma.

"Did she tell you anything about this bloke? This…Christian?"

"Of course she did. I'm her sister." Jemma held her hand to her heart. "She tells me everything."

"And…?"

"And, nothing! It was a silly flirtation. A bit of fun. Lord knows, she needs it." Jemma looked accusingly at Ed, and he wondered what else Ali had told her. "He's a boy," she added. "A child."

"Is he?"

"If you'd taken the time to talk to her instead of going off at her like a bear with a sore bum, you would have known too. He has a crush on Ali. A silly schoolboy crush. You'd have probably had a good laugh about it."

Ed somehow doubted it. The image of a schoolboy drooling over his wife didn't strike him, on any level, as rib-ticklingly amusing.

"Shall I put the kettle on?" Neil said brightly.

"I think that's a splendid idea, Neil," Jemma said, as if he'd just announced that he'd solved the riddle of the meaning of life rather than resorting to the usual lame British answer to a difficult situation. A nice cup of tea. Ed tutted to himself. Jemma turned off her scowl and smiled widely at his brother. "I'll show you where everything is."

Jemma breezed out toward the kitchen, which was all chrome and steel and white tiles and looked like a trendy morgue with tea-making facilities. Neil followed with a leery wink at Ed, his clonky motorcycle boots at odds with the streamlined elegance of the rest of the flat. This wasn't a home, this was a house. A show house, with nothing out of place. It was small, compact to the point of being cupboardlike and the epitome of style. There were no sticky fingermarks on the wall, no curled-up drawings stuck to the fridge produced via a cunningly shaped potato dipped in paint; there were no toys, Rollerblades or skateboards booby-trapping the floor. The atmosphere that Jemma had tried to create meant that it lacked any form of atmosphere at all as far as Ed could tell. But then, he'd lived in a house that resembled Laura Ashley crossed with Hamley's toy store for so long that he'd forgotten what life was like pre-clutter. He hoped the boys were all right. Perhaps he should give them a quick ring and check, but then that would clog up his mobile and there might be a remote chance that Ali could ring just at that second.

He'd sworn them both to good behavior. Thomas was no problem. Ed had left him sitting wanly in a warm bath with instructions to go straight back to bed. His twelve-year-old son was the epitome of good behavior and would, no doubt, grow into a model citizen whose only attempt at rebellion would be to join the Freemasons when he reached forty. Elliott, at the tender age of four, was a lost cause, however. Ed was already dreading the time he'd turn seventeen and would be let loose on cars. Real cars. The things he managed to do with his toy ones defied description—he'd had to have bits of them surgically extracted from virtually every orifice of his body so far, and the nearside tire of an Aston Martin DB7 proved particularly tricky. Ed had thought of tying Elliott to a chair while he was out, but Social Services are funny about that sort of thing these days. Instead, he had warned his youngest child not to move, touch or jump over anything in his sternest possible voice, promised not to be too long, then had left for Jemma's on the back of Neil's bike in a shower of gravel.

Fat lot of good it had done him, Ed thought, while he waited for tea he didn't want. There was a lot of hilarity coming from the kitchen, which Ed didn't feel that the circumstances warranted, but he appreciated that he was sulking and it wasn't acceptable to expect everyone else to sulk with him. It was the old adage—smile and the whole world smiles with you. Sulk and everyone thinks you're a sad, old git.

So when Neil and Jemma came back in with the tea, Ed took it and smiled, although he didn't want to be here now. He wanted to be at home and waiting for Ali to come back. Surely she would? Wouldn't she?

CHAPTER 30

"I don't want you to go." Christian has his arms round my waist and is fixing me with those deep brown puppy eyes.

I am dressed in an eclectic mixture of clothing courtesy of my husband, Ed. He would never make a personal shopper if he ever decides to stop hankering after a life in films and change careers. In the small case that my husband so kindly packed for me are three shades of nothing remotely useful. There were no knickers, so I'm bare-arsed under my itchy wool trousers—something that's keeping Christian amused, but not me. This sweater hasn't seen the light of day for about ten years because it goes with nothing else I possess. But then I don't think Ed was paying much attention to color coordinating when packing my clothing for my impromptu trip.

"I have to." My little case is waiting patiently at my feet and I'm ready to leave.

"It was good though, wasn't it?" He puts his nose against mine.

"Yes." I have had sex with a stranger despite all those things I said not two chapters ago. And I can tell you, I feel very weird. And not just because none of my clothes match. I have slept with only one other person apart from Ed and that was a teenage fumbling, and as far as I was concerned a complete waste of time. I defy anyone to say that their first experience of sex wasn't a total disappointment. You're bombarded with images of waves crashing and loud, resonant music like the Old Spice advert and exploding fireworks and shooting stars, and reality isn't like that. Is it? Reality is—that can't be all there is to it! I can't have waited all these years for that! That's reality. Not a single wave crashed when I surrendered my virginity to David Chatham after months of saying no. It wasn't even as powerful as a dripping tap. There wasn't a single note of classical music to be heard. Not anywhere. Not one firecracker cracked. Not one star shot. It was after a party and I'd had too many Cherry B's and cider, which I think puts it into context. See? Booze again. Disappointment reigned and we split up shortly afterward. Three days afterward, to be exact.

With Ed it was different. It was good. It was exciting. It still wasn't long before we slipped into the Comfort Zone though. Sex for people who worry about having to get up in the morning for work or whether their contraception will work. Sex where you can't have fireworks because loud bangs wake the children. Sex where you don't have to worry if you pull a funny face when you come or if bits wobble like unset blancmange. And I've got used to that. Nay, even liked it. I thought that's all there was.

Christian, on the other hand, has blown my mind. I have never smoked pot, but I can imagine what it feels like. I'm sort of drifty and smiley and squishy inside. And I should be anxious—you know my situation. After "The Bath" incident we made love again on Christian's bed and...well, I don't think I'm even going to attempt to tell you about it, because you'll go green, tear the page out and eat it out of sheer frustration. It has opened my eyes—no, really it has. That boy has been taking lessons, he must have, because no one gets born so sensual. I have had crashing waves, I have had the full rendition of Carl Orff's *Carmina Burana O Fortuna* (Old Spice advert again...). I have had exploding fireworks. Stars shot about all over the place. And I am going to have to do some serious reevaluation, because I don't know whether comfort sex will be enough when I get home. I didn't think I was discontented, but maybe I am. Ed and I are going to have to nip down to the porny video shop and rent *The Lover's Guide* or something not too seedy, because I sincerely believe we need help when I didn't two hours ago.

"I still don't want you to go." Christian nuzzles my ear. I have erotic zones that I didn't know I had and I'm in complete turmoil.

"Don't." I ease myself away from him, using my best schoolteacher's voice.

"There's loads of room here," he says. "The others wouldn't mind."

I think Ms. Rebecca Pert Bottom would definitely have something to say.

"I'll phone you," I say.

"Promise."

"We can have coffee sometime."

"It isn't enough, Ali. It isn't enough for me and it isn't enough for you."

"It'll have to be," I say, and I really sound like I mean it this time. "I really appreciate this." I gesture at the house. "And I'm really, really glad we had this morning together."

"But…"

"There are too many buts, Christian." I look at my watch. "And four of them will, no doubt, be waiting for me to give them lunch."

Christian smiles sadly. He rummages in his pocket and pulls out ten pounds. "You won't get far without this." He hesitates before he hands it over. "I could hold you captive," he threatens.

He wraps his arms around me and holds me so tightly that it hurts. How do I tell him that already I am completely captivated and it will take all my strength to walk away?

CHAPTER 31

Ed's car is in the drive, but there's no sign of life when I open the kitchen door. "Hello!"

Nothing. I have been missing and could have been presumed dead for a whole night, and no one has batted an eyelid. Me and my stupid suitcase have bounced all the way back on the rickety, rattly Tube dreading this moment, and now there's no one here with a shred of interest in my well-being. My traitorous handbag is sitting on the work surface looking suitably shame-faced. I poke it belligerently and vow to buy a new one just to spite it—one that sets off an ear-piercing alarm if you stray more than five feet from it.

The breakfast dishes are abandoned on the table, and I gather I am still the only person in this household who doesn't need to look at *Auto Route Express* to find the dishwasher.

The post is still unopened. Although it looks like nothing but bills, I start to leaf through it, and as I do there is a quiet, but disturbing whimpering coming from the lounge. It's a horrid noise. The sort of noise you hear on scary movies when the crazed Slasher has recently departed from a crazed slashing spree.

I drop the post and rush across the kitchen and, pausing only to check my heart is still beating, fling open the lounge door. A truly terrifying sight greets me.

Our next-door neighbors, the Beresfords, have a dog called

Harry. He is a black Labrador, fat and intrinsically stupid. Aren't they all? The Beresfords say he isn't fat, but has a muscular physique. Harry spends a lot of time in our house because the biscuits are better and in more plentiful supply than at home. I rest my case. For years it was suspected that Harry had some deadly form of undetectable brain tumor because he used to weave alarmingly rather than walk in a straight line as most dogs do. Then they found he was drinking Mr. Beresford's homemade pear wine straight from the demi-johns kept under the stairs and discovered that Harry didn't have a brain tumor at all, but that he was a drunk. The word "bite" has never entered his soft, canine brain.

Harry is lying inert on the floor, his big pink tongue lolling stupidly out of his mouth. Elliott takes a huge safety pin and finishes off his handiwork. Harry whimpers a bit more.

Elliott looks up and smiles. "Look what I did, Mummy."

"Elliott," I say through clenched teeth. "What have you done?"

"I've made him better," he says, as if it's the most obvious thing in the world.

Harry is covered from head to toe in surgical bandages. Elliott has wound them round his head, over one eye and in an elaborate crisscross pattern round his body. I didn't even know we possessed so many of the damn things. Harry's legs, front and back, are bound together, and his tail, though thickly bandaged, is wagging ferociously. He would probably bark a friendly welcome as he usually does—if he could. Elliott has also bandaged his muzzle, which is neatly polished off with a bow that is tidier than anything my son has ever managed on his shoelaces.

"Elliott!" I yell, and kneel down beside the beleaguered dog. "That is so naughty!" Harry is trying to lick me despite the confines of his bandage.

"I thought he might have broken something," my youngest son protests.

"He might have now, you silly boy," I say, and I smack Elliott on the bottom. Hard. I don't believe in smacking children. Only when they deserve it. Or when I have completely come to the end of my tether and my sense of reason has departed. Both of which are implicated in the current situation.

It is a very long time since Elliott has felt the force of my hand and he's clearly in a state of shock. He sucks in all his breath, stands rigid as a statue until he is a livid shade of puce and then issues forth an earsplitting scream at the top of his lungs. Harry starts to howl with him.

"Elliott! Shut up!"

But he only screeches louder. I tug at Harry's bandages, trying to loosen them, which makes him howl too, like the Hound of the Baskervilles. If the Beresfords hear him, he'll never be allowed in here for Tunnock's Caramel Wafers ever again.

At this juncture, Ed walks in.

Elliott runs to him and clings to his legs. "Mummy's hitting me!"

Ed's face blackens. "What?"

"Look what he's done to this poor dog!"

"I was only being a doctor," Elliott snivelled.

Ed curled his son into him. "He was only being a doctor."

"Doctors don't drag healthy dogs off the street and try to mummify them!" I untangle Harry's legs, and he yelps gratefully as he staggers to his feet.

"There's no harm done," Ed snarls helpfully.

"And where have you been?" I ask coldly. "Why was Elliott left alone? You know what he's like."

"I've been at Jemma's." Ed stares directly at me. "Looking for you."

I'm breathing heavily already, and it goes up a gear. I snatch the biscuit tin. "Elliott, give that poor dog a Wagon Wheel and take him home."

My son does as he's told amid dramatic sniffles and leads Harry, who of course is none the worse for his amateur animal husbandry, out of the door.

Elliott is so angelic, even though I'm sure he has 666 tattooed in his hair somewhere, that it's impossible to stay mad at him. At this point Ed and I would normally break down into fits of giggles. Today it doesn't happen. We stay, horns locked, staring angrily at each other.

"You weren't at Jemma's," Ed says.

"I went there and knocked for ages. She was out," I state.

"Jemma says she was in all night. You never went there."

"That isn't true."

"What is, these days, Alicia?" Ed laughs, but it's clear he finds nothing amusing and there's a bitter edge to his tone. "So, where did you go?"

What can I say? Whatever I am charged with now, I'm guilty. Yesterday, I could justify being filled with righteous indignation at being so unfairly accused. But now? Images of my wanton watery romp swim by and, viewed from this distance, it isn't a very pretty sight. I've slept with another man and my innocence has gone.

"Did you go to *his* house?"

"Yes."

Ed folds his arms across his chest and lets out a steady stream of breath. "And are you still insisting that there's nothing going on?"

How can I? I have been making love with Christian with no thought of my husband or my children or anyone but myself and...what does that make Christian now? My lover? What does it make me? A pretty crap wife, for one thing.

But I don't know that having gone this far, I can never see him again, never want him again, never hold him again. What on earth has happened? Why do I feel like this? Has my brain been scrambled because I'm thirty-eight and enormously grateful that someone so young and so beautiful could fall in love with me?

I love Ed. I always have. But suddenly *we* are the strangers. I look at him, and the connection between us has somehow been broken and I don't know what I can do to put it right. There are miles stretching out between us across a dozen dusty kitchen floor tiles. This has happened so quickly. One minute I'd told a teeny-weeny fib, and now I'm flailing about in the Grand Canyon of lies with no idea how to find my way out.

I try to move toward Ed, but I can't, the chasm is too big for me to cross. I catch sight of myself in one of the glass-fronted kitchen cabinets which I hate, because, hey, who wants to show off their tins of baked beans. And I don't recognize myself at all. I have no idea who I am. I swallow hard. "I'm sorry."

Ed doesn't move either. "So am I," is all he says.

CHAPTER 32

Robbie and Rebecca were waiting in the kitchen. Christian closed the door and leaned against it. "She's unpacking her case."

Rebecca tucked her knees in tighter to her on the Chesterfield. "Great."

"I said she could stay if she needed to." Christian looked at them both apologetically. "I just didn't expect her to be back so soon. I hope that's okay."

Robbie shrugged. "Suits me, mate."

"She looked like she was here for the duration." Rebecca sucked her finger petulantly. "Exactly how long is she going to be our houseguest?"

"I don't know," Christian admitted. "Until she gets sorted, I guess."

"Why here?" Rebecca whined. "I thought we'd got enough problems."

"She had nowhere else to go, Becs. The situation is difficult. Complicated." Robbie and Christian exchanged a glance.

"I'm missing something, aren't I?" Rebecca insisted.

"You'd better tell her," Robbie said.

Christian sighed. He left the door and came and sat down next to her on the sofa.

Rebecca frowned. "Why don't I like the sound of this?"

Christian picked up a cushion and fiddled with it, unpicking the tassel from the corner. "Ali's married," he said. "Or was. She's left her husband. And I'm sort of involved."

"Oh, this is a classic, Christian. Even for you."

"I love her, Becs."

"You don't know the meaning of the word," Rebecca replied. "This woman has turned her life upside down for you, and your idea of commitment would be baby-sitting a goldfish for a week while its owner was on holiday."

"That's not true."

"You forget that I know from bitter, personal experience."

Christian laid his head back on the sofa and hugged the cushion to his chest. "How can I forget? You'd never let me."

Rebecca stood up. "Well, good luck to you. And good luck to her. My God, she's going to need it."

And then she flounced out the door, slamming it behind her.

Christian put his hands behind his head and stared at the ceiling.

"Dotty totty," Robbie declared. "She's probably premenstrual."

"It would be nice if it were that simple."

Robbie twisted round in his chair. "Look, mate. It can't be that easy for Becs. She's still got it bad for you, and yet since you broke up, you've paraded a different bird through here every week. And now this?"

"I know."

"She would seem perfectly entitled to one small tantrum."

"I don't want her making things difficult for Ali."

"You know Becs. It's not going to be easy for her."

"She could move out," Christian pointed out.

"To where? Where is she going to find a gaff like this at the price we do, or don't, pay?" Robbie looked at the crystal chandelier that hung incongruously from the kitchen ceiling. It was covered in dust and cobwebs but still managed to retain its splendor. "And let's face it, Chris, if it were a young bit of fluff—as per usual—she might not feel so bad. But a bird that's twice your age with three kids? That's a bit like being slapped about the face with a wet kipper."

"You're right," Christian said. "I'll try to be more sensitive."

"Yeah, and Sylvester Stallone's going to take up embroidery."

Christian threw the cushion at him and Robbie ducked, laughing. Christian chuckled too.

Robbie folded his arms on the table and looked earnestly at his friend. "I take it Ali doesn't know about your wild night of passion with the lovely Sharon?"

Christian groaned and ran his hands through his hair. "It was a close thing. Very close." He looked up at Robbie, appealing. "I don't want anything to spoil this, mate. It's too important."

"Better keep certain parts of your anatomy under control then."

"It was you who persuaded me!" Christian protested.

"As if you've ever needed any encouragement." Robbie swung his legs round and put them on the table.

Christian grinned. "I told her *you'd* spent the night with Sharon."

"Oh, thanks a bunch! That's a bit rich. I was flying solo listening to you two through the wall due to the fact that, Uncle Robert, despite his best attempts, didn't get so much as a whiff of willing knickers."

"That's because whatever her name was passed out in the taxi."

"I am fully aware of that."

Christian walked over to the table and clapped Robbie on the back. "I owe you one, mate."

"You owe me several," Robbie reminded him. "I'm counting."

"I'd do the same for you."

"Yeah, right," Robbie moaned. "Chance would be a fine thing."

"Beer?"

Robbie brightened. "Why not?"

Christian went to the fridge and pulled out two beers and opened them.

"Tell me," Robbie said, "as I was supposed to be there, was she any good?"

Christian put the beers on the table. He twitched his eyebrows at his friend and lowered his voice. "She was sen-*fucking*-sational!"

"Oh God! I knew she would be. I should have gone for her instead of whatshername." Robbie slumped forward on the table. "You're such a bastard, Winter!"

Christian smiled and kissed his friend on the top of his head. "That's why you love me," he said.

CHAPTER 33

We are sitting in a trendy bar called Black and Blue. And that's pretty much how I feel—bruised and sad. I am on my third glass of Chardonnay, and it has made not the slightest impression on me yet. The doors are pulled back so that we are almost on the pavement and exposed to the full hurly-burly of Kensington Church Street. Intermittently, red double-decker buses rumble past and shake the glass.

Christian is eating some sort of goat's cheese concoction that sounded revolting but looks okay. He is quiet and probably as shocked as I am—if not more so. I won't bore you with the details, but I am back at Christian's house with a larger suitcase than before and a feeling of impending permanency about it. Ed and I parted dry-eyed and angry. This is a trial separation—whatever that is when it's at home. I thought only pop stars and sports personalities announced that they were having trial separations, which always seemed to me to be publicity-speak for, "I've run off with someone else younger and sexier." Actually, I don't think I'll dwell on that too much….

Ed and I are supposed to be having time to think. At the moment I would rather not think, but I can't help it. I have so many different emotions swirling around inside of me and yet feel utterly, utterly numb. Maybe we just can't face saying to each other that it's over and this "trial separation" is a less brutal way of letting go. I don't know.

Christian has been marvelous. He's been clucking round me like a mother hen and has even promised to change the sheets on his bed later—which I have to say do look like they've seen a bit of action. Robbie seems very nice even though he's a little more pierced than I normally find appealing in a man. Rebecca banged out of the front door not long after I arrived, so I think you can probably ascertain from that what her view is on the subject.

"Okay?" Christian asks from the depths of his lettuce.

I nod, but I'm not. Of course I'm not. Ed took the boys out while I left, and Tanya will come home from a great day out in Brighton with Hannah Cooper and find her mother gone. That is just so tragic, I can only bear it on the fringes of my consciousness. How will they manage without me? I slog back some more wine before I become so maudlin that I want to leap in front of the next double-decker.

I've phoned Jemma and given her a brief rundown of the situation. The conversation swung giddily between relief that I'd been found and anger at what she saw as running away again. She's coming down here after work, when she's sold her last silk smoking jacket to a soap starlet or whatever. She shouldn't be long now.

I couldn't stay with my sister. Partly because she lives in a shoe box—albeit a shoe box that's been decorated by Heal's. And partly because we'd kill each other within twenty-four hours. I adore Jemma—she is my baby sister and I would lay down my life for her. I would not, however, willingly share a bathroom with her. I wouldn't call her maniacally tidy, but she'd fall in a dead faint if there was even a millimeter of toothpaste left sticking out of the tube when she came to use it. I consider myself supremely lucky if any of my family actually manage to get it in their mouths, as their aim invariably seems to involve going via the bathroom mirror. God help you if you actually *used* any of Jemma's Egyptian cotton towels for wiping *dirty* hands! If she saw a pubic hair on the soap, she'd probably slit her wrists—if it wasn't for the mess. I couldn't cope with that now. I need to be loved and mollycoddled, not gasped at every time I put a teacup in the wrong place. Christian's sheets might be crumpled, but that's easier to deal with right now. And at least I helped to get them that way.

"Do you want me to leave when your sister comes?" Christian says.

"I think so," I sigh. "She'll probably want to bollock me, and I wouldn't want her to feel inhibited." Not that Jemma ever does when it comes to voicing her opinion. I would just rather Christian's first encounter with my family be on slightly more convivial terms than this.

"I love you, Ali," he says, and his young, beautiful eyes are earnest. Christian clearly thinks that love is enough, and I don't want to quench that inside him. Have you noticed that I haven't said I love him? I can't. It seems too huge a thing to voice. I feel an overwhelming rush when I see him, and perhaps I'm besotted to the point of insanity or at least major irrationality. But is that the same as love? Perhaps if I were twenty years younger and didn't remember having a crush on both Starsky *and* Hutch, then I'd be less analytical. What do you think? Is there such a thing as love at first sight? Doesn't love start when lust is spent and you've got a joint mortgage, equitable pension funds and other knee-high, helpless people who rely on you to make it work?

I never wanted "a Sewage Worker marriage." One of Jemma's phrases. Day after day of going through the motions. Staying together because it's expected of you, the done thing. Apparently, most of my sister's menfriends have them, and I wonder if this is what Ed says to other people when he is talking about me. I wanted us to have a strong, deep, abiding love that would grow more secure through all of life's inevitable adversities. Sounds like the start of a hymn, doesn't it? Did Ed and I stay together, muddling along, purely for the sake of the kids? I wouldn't have said so. A few weeks ago I would have said that I adored him and that I'd never look at another man. But here I am, holding hands across the table with one, having parted from my husband. If you ask me, there must have been a lot of undetected, smelly effluence floating about just below the surface for us to have come to this point so quickly.

"I'll get a job," Christian says. "A proper job."

I smile at his sincerity and squeeze his fingers, but before I can answer, I see my sister swing round the corner at the top of the road. She looks fabulous. Her hair shines in the sun as if it's been buffed by a ton of beeswax. "Here's Jemma," I say, and I notice Christian sit up a little straighter. And so do I.

As she approaches us, she's staring at Christian in a faintly mesmerized way. She kisses me on both cheeks and sits down with us.

"Jemma, this is Christian," I say. "Christian, Jemma."

"Pleased to meet you." Christian turns on his best smile. Jemma nods speechlessly. "Can I get you a drink before I leave?"

"Wine. White. Dry," Jemma manages.

Christian disappears self-consciously into the back of Black and Blue.

"Shit, Ali," Jemma hisses. "He's gorgeous!"

"Is he?" I say. "I hadn't noticed."

She glares at me. "There are, however, copies of *Country Life* in my doctor's waiting room that are older than him!"

"Meaning?"

"Exactly how old is he?"

"Twenty-three."

Jemma snorts. "He looks a lot younger!" My sister leans toward me. "He wasn't even born when 'Dancing Queen' was in the charts, Ali. How scary is that?"

Quite scary, I'll admit.

Christian returns and puts a glass of wine in front of both Jemma and me. "Thanks." I look up, and his face is the picture of worry and I don't think it's because Abba at the height of their fame passed him by.

"I'll go back to the house," he says. "And wait for you there."

It's clear in his eyes that he thinks Jemma will persuade me to do otherwise. I nod and Christian kisses the top of my head, threading his fingers through the back of my hair out of the range of Jemma's stare. We both watch him walk away, and several other heads turn as he passes.

"Well," Jemma says as we switch our attention back to each other. "I wish I'd got to him first."

"So do I," I comment. "Then perhaps I wouldn't be in this mess."

"It is a mess, Alicia," she says, like I need reminding. "Why didn't you tell me about this? I'm your sister and yet you've said nothing."

"I didn't think there was anything to say."

"What about Ed? What about the children? How can you risk breaking up your home? All you've strived for?"

How can I answer her? This is the kick side of what Jemma

does. But clearly it doesn't register on her conscience that all the men she's loved have wives, children, lives they too have strived to build. I decide it isn't a good time to bring it up. She is here to save me from my fate for once, not the other way round.

Jemma snatches sips of her wine. "Do you really know what you're doing?"

"Of course I don't. I have no idea how we came to this point."

"Is this…this…boy really worth leaving your husband for?"

"Ed won't discuss it," I say. "He's acting very strangely."

"Ed is!"

"I didn't leave Ed," I explain patiently. "He asked me to go."

"I can't believe it. He was so worried when you weren't at my place. Why didn't you come to me first?"

"I did. I spent half an hour trying to hammer your door down. I thought you were still in Prague."

Jemma looks horrified. "When?"

"Late," I say. "Very late."

"Shit." Jemma looks mortified. "I took a Temazepam at about eleven and went to bed with my earplugs in."

"Thanks. I wish you'd told my husband."

"How did I know you'd be trying to break down my door?"

"Christian lives around the corner. I had nowhere else to go. Ed thought I was lying and had gone straight to 'my boyfriend.'"

"Oh bugger, buggeration," Jemma sighs.

I glug my wine, and by now it's starting to make me feel considerably more mellow. "My thoughts exactly."

"Come to me now," she offers.

"And stay where? There's loads of room at Christian's. It's a temporary measure until we sort things out."

"Do you think you and Ed will get back together?"

"I don't know," I say, and at this moment I really have no idea. I feel like I've been torn into a million shreds and it's going to take one of those funky new magicians like David Blane or someone to come along and reassemble me.

Jemma twirls her wineglass by the stem, deep in thought. "Do you think you'll divorce?"

Divorce? What a truly horrible, final word. I hadn't realized how harsh it sounded until now. Divorce. Fracture. Detach. Disintegrate. Divorce. I divorce. You divorce. He, she or it divorces. They divorce. We divorce.

"I don't know," I stammer.

Jemma is suddenly tearful, and it was easier when she was lecturing me. "I don't think I could bear to think of you two no longer being a couple," she sniffs.

A double-decker thunders past, giving the windows a good rattle, and the ground vibrates beneath me, shaking me to the core. Right at this moment, neither can I.

CHAPTER 34

Ed threw the tea towel over his shoulder and opened the front door. He stood back in surprise. "Oh, hi."

Nicola Jones looked very bashful. "Is this an inconvenient time?"

"No. Yes. No. Well, sort of." Ed stood aside. "Come in. Come in."

Nicola smiled and walked past him into the hall. "I've come to see how Elliott's arm is."

"Oh, right. It's fine. Fine," Ed said. "Well, no. It's not really. It's giving him a bit of pain. And he can't play computer games or football, which also makes him cranky."

Nicola laughed. Ed stopped and turned to her. "Nicola," he said, pausing to bite his lower lip. "This is a bit difficult."

Elliott's teacher looked suitably concerned.

"You see..." He chewed his lip a bit more. "You see...my wife has left me. Us. Only yesterday. And, you see..."

"Ed." Nicola touched his arm. "I'm so sorry."

"Me too." He tried to smile chirpily. "These things have a habit of happening, don't they?"

"All too often." Nicola's mouth turned downward, and she looked incredibly cute when she was sad, Ed thought, and then was astonished he could think such a thing while still knee-deep in the aftermath of his separation. "How are the children handling it?"

Ed shrugged. "Remarkably well, but I don't think it's sunk in yet."

"Is there anything I can do to help?" Nicola asked.

"I don't know," Ed said. "I'm not even sure what there is to do. I'm your typical hopeless, undomesticated male."

"Oh, I don't believe that for one minute!"

Neither did he. Not really. It would be difficult coping without Ali—after all, she did run a very tight ship—but he could manage. How many mysteries could there be to Bold Automatic washing powder?

"I could mind Elliott after school for you," Nicola offered, "if that would help."

"That would be fantastic!" He resisted the urge to kiss her. Even out of gratitude it would be unseemly. "Come through. He's in the kitchen. I'm just about to increase their cholesterol levels with egg and chips."

Nicola held his eyes. "You're very brave," she breathed.

Ed shook his head. "I don't think so." Stubborn. Foolhardy. Stunned. These were all adjectives which were more appropriate under the circumstances.

"And modest," Nicola continued. "I like that in a man."

Elliott appeared at the doorway, Buzz Lightyear's arm dangling from the corner of his mouth like a lime-green roll-up. "My mummy's gone, Miss Jones," Elliott mumbled.

Nicola crouched down next to him and wrapped her arms round Elliott, hugging him to her. "I know. I know. Poor, poor lamb." Elliott adjusted his Buzz cigarette. "I'll help daddy to look after you." She smiled up at Ed.

"Will you?" Elliott brightened considerably.

Nicola ruffled his hair. "Of course I will."

"Will you stay for tea, Miss Jones?"

"Elliott!" Ed warned.

"I'd love to," she said, standing up. "But I can't. Not tonight. I'm having an old friend for dinner."

"We're having egg and chips," Elliott informed her.

"Elliott!" Ed said. "Miss Jones has got better things to do than entertain us."

"It's just a friend," she protested. "An old friend."

"Daddy says we're never having chicken nuggets in this house ever again," Elliott piped up.

"Ali's speciality," Ed explained wanly. When Elliott was better, Ed thought, he would remind himself to kill him.

"That seems very sensible," Nicola said to Elliott, who, given his chicken-nugget addiction, amazingly looked as if he agreed. "I came to see how your arm is."

"It hurts," Elliott said with a pitiful grimace. "But I think it will be better enough to go on the climbing frame again tomorrow."

"Elliott!"

Nicola laughed. She laughed a lot, but it was sincere and not all girly and giggly, which would have driven Ed mad. "We'll see," she promised and whisked back her hair. "I won't keep you from your supper. I just wanted to…well…"

"Yes," Ed nodded. "Thanks for popping by," he said as he showed her to the door.

"I meant what I said," she reiterated. "I want you to call on me whenever you need help."

"Thanks," Ed said. "I appreciate that."

"That's what friends are for," Nicola Jones added and, with a coy smile, she turned and walked away.

Elliott was picking at his chips with his fingers.

"Use your knife and fork," Ed instructed.

Elliott picked up his cutlery. "It hurts my arm," he complained.

"Nonsense. Just eat them, Elliott."

Tanya was cutting burnt bits off her egg white, and Ed noted that in her one day as a vegetarian she had become very picky. She had been extraordinarily quiet since she'd returned home from Brighton to face possibly the most devastating news of her short and relatively pain-free fifteen years. She had retreated into her bedroom, put on her headphones and had ventured out precious little since then. He would talk to her. Properly. Father to daughter. Later. Tomorrow. Soon. He hadn't imagined telling the children would be so hard. Why? What was he—some sort of emotional vacuum? Of course they'd be devastated. *He* was devastated.

"Why did Mummy leave?" Elliott asked for the seventeenth time since they had returned from the Häagen-Dazs café at the front of the Odeon cinema in Hill Street and he had the unenviable task of informing them Ali had gone.

Ed sighed and put down his knife and fork. "Sometimes grown-ups fall out of love with each other."

"That doesn't sound very grown up," his son observed.

"I know."

"Is falling out of love like falling out of a tree?"

"Yes," Ed said. "It is. Exactly like falling out of a tree."

"It must hurt."

"Yes," Ed said. "It does."

"More than my arm?"

"Even more than your arm."

Elliott looked suitably impressed. He toyed with another chip. "Are you in love with Miss Jones?"

"No." Ed was taken aback. "Whatever makes you think that?"

"I love her," Elliott said plainly.

"Eat your egg, Elliott."

The little boy pushed his plate away from him. "Daddy. Do you know how you can tell when you're in love with someone?"

"No."

"You get an erection."

Thomas spat a half-chewed chip out onto his plate and started to cough. "Thank you for sharing that with us, Elliott," Ed said.

Ed passed Thomas a glass of Coke, which he gulped gratefully. Out of all of them, he was most worried about his quiet, thoughtful son. Elliott would jabber his way through a crisis. Tanya would go all moody. But he never knew what went on in Thomas's studious little head. "Okay?" Ed inquired with a concerned smile.

Thomas nodded.

"Do you get an erection when you see Miss Jones?"

"No." Ed sighed. "Elliott, I'll only tell you one more time. Eat your tea before it goes cold."

"Do you get an erection when you see Mummy?"

"Look, Elliott, can we have this conversation when you're about thirty-five? Or preferably never."

"I only wanted to know," his youngest son said huffily.

I used to get erections, Ed thought. I used to get them all the time. At one time his penis had a mind of its own. Never matter whether he was in a board meeting or on a shoot filming a commercial about a glass of milk, his old fella would be popping up all over the place. The word "inopportune" never troubled it. Even a stiff breeze would have it standing to attention. Now erections sort of had to be coaxed out of it. He needed time to be cajoled and caressed. The epitome of his sexual virility could be said to be having a bit of a sulk. He wondered whether that was what had made Ali develop wandering eyes, wandering hands and, ultimately, wandering feet. He wasn't impotent—not by a long chalk. But there was, he admitted, a certain sluggishness in the trouser-snake department. It had, somewhere along the line without him realizing it, semi-retired into more of a trouser slug. You could buy all the conservatories you liked and call it caring, but deep down women liked nothing better than some well-aimed passion and ardor. And his ardor had, he admitted, been sadly lacking. It was only Harrison Ford who had moved him to any kind of passion recently, and even that was only in the movie sense rather than the biblical interpretation.

He'd like to bet that Ali was bouncing round the bedroom like a space hopper on speed with her new man. You did, didn't you, in that first flush of euphoria? The "new man" wouldn't be put off by the fact it was a weeknight and he'd be required to go to work knackered in the morning. Oh, no. When sex was new, it was energizing, liberating, it put a spring in even the most tired of steps. When you'd been making love to the same woman for a third of your life, it made you utterly, utterly shagged. The next morning your balls developed a dull ache and your briefcase dragged along the ground. Jemma had said this Christian was a boy—nay, a *child!* Ed remembered what he had been like at the tender age of nineteen. If he'd had a pound for every lustful thought and every errant erection, he would have been living in a swimming-pooled mansion in Bel Air by now.

These thoughts were not good for the digestion. Ed put down his knife and fork and stared at his cold, congealing egg. When he looked up, all three of his sorrowful, doe-eyed children were staring back at him, food abandoned. Thomas looked as if he was about to cry. How could he have been so foolish! He needed to get hold of Ali and talk to her sensibly about all this before too much damage was done. He had neglected her—and not just in bed. But that's where the rot started, didn't it? They would have a few days' cooling-off period in the best-honored tradition of time-share. Perhaps Ali would get this fling out of her system and would come back and be prepared to carry on her uneventful life once the dust had settled. All Ed knew was that he wanted her back in his life, his bed, his kitchen—chicken nuggets and all.

CHAPTER 35

"Can everyone stand still, please!" Neil shouted. It was clear they couldn't. He was facing his fourteenth lot of mini-monsters that day, all decked out in matching maroon sweaters and all fidgeting more than a sack full of fidgety ferrets for the sole purpose of taking the time-honored "class photo."

He didn't know what was worse, trying to snap bunch after bunch of motley urchins or the mammoth task of getting a whole school to smile and stand still both at once. Neil tugged at his tie, which seemed to be getting tighter by the minute. It was a hot, muggy day, one of the few that punctuate the blossoming days of spring, the ones that are usually welcome unless you happen to be standing outside on a shadeless school playing field trying to take photographs of hot, bored and petulant pupils dripping in their unnecessary sweaters.

The children had all been sorted according to descending order of height so that when he eventually managed to record this for posterity on film, it would make a wonderful photograph that would, no doubt, then spend the next thirty years gathering dust in someone's loft until it was thrown in the bin by an overzealous spouse on a spring-cleaning mission. Life was constantly cruel.

"Tallest two in the middle, please!" The teachers herded the chosen pair forward and into place standing on the benches that had been purloined, as they were every year, from the gym equipment corner—a ragtag of broken sports gear hidden behind a 1970s psychedelic curtain in the far reaches of the assembly hall. "Next two! One on either side."

Daylight, his patience and his life were rapidly running out while Neil tried to capture this snapshot moment in the lives of years One, Two and Three of The Bleeding Heart of Bernadette Lower School. And it wasn't just Bernadette's heart that was bleeding. His own heart was being put through the mangle day after day, doing this. It wasn't what he wanted. He knew that. He wanted to take photographs of women draped seductively over chaise longues deep in chenille throws, wearing skimpy designer frocks that didn't cover their bottoms. He wanted to capture on film similarly semi-clad females running through the edge of the surf on some secluded Seychelles beach. He wanted to be snapping starlets as they arrived at film premières in Leicester Square or, preferably, LA. What he did not want was snot-nosed brats in Bermondsey, Balham or Brixton.

During his reverie, the children had been filing in a disorderly manner onto the benches. "Back row, stand up. Nice and tall," Neil instructed. "Middle row. Sit up. Come on—sit up. Nice and straight now. Fingers out of noses. Good. Good." He looked through his camera. "Front row, cross legs. All the same way. Right foot over left. Left. *Left.* This one. This one. Like this." Neil crossed his legs. "Good. Good. Stay like that. *Fingers out of noses.*" He checked the setup again. "Those of you with no front teeth, remember to try to keep your lips together when you smile. You don't want to look back at this when you're sixty and see nothing but a big hole in your face." Neil emulated a smile with his lips closed together. The class giggled.

"Are we all ready? Sir! The gentleman at the back in the middle. Tongue inside your head where it belongs, please!" The tongue was duly retracted. "Back row, stand up straight. Hands behind backs not in noses." Neil looked up and attempted a grin, which, at this stage in the day, probably came out as a snarl. Fingers were also hastily retracted. "Middle row, sit up. Gentleman at the end! You can find what's in your ear later. Front row. *Listen to me.* Listen to me. Arms folded, like this." Neil folded his arms. "One on top of the other. Like this." The front row, it seemed, were not blessed with lightning dexterity or coordination. "Like *this*. See?" He folded his arms again. It was better, he'd learned through bitter experience, to give them something to do with their hands. That way they were less likely to explore bodily orifices with them—either their own or their neighbor's. "Good. Good. Are we ready?"

It was on days like these when he wondered why on earth he wanted to settle down and produce more of these little horrors of his own. What was the attraction of children anyway? Every school he went to they all looked absolutely identical—scruffy, bad-mannered, and with hair that needed combing. Only the color of the sweaters changed or the design of the school badge. There was always a class clown, always a bully and always the poorly dressed little boy or girl with a patch over one side of their glasses and an unhealthily pale complexion who tugged at his heartstrings.

He had been doing this for more years than he cared to admit, and in that time he had watched the children grow year by year. It was strange watching them race through life from a distance. You could tell the girls who would break hearts and the ones who would get their hearts broken. You could tell the ones who would be pregnant and out of school by the time they were sixteen. You could spot which boys would be accountants and which would turn out to be criminals. You could even tell the ones which would be criminally inclined accountants. And despite all the downsides, he did want a family of his own, and it wasn't just because he was keen on the conception part. He'd always envied Ed and Alicia. They seemed to be the perfect family, and it was gut-wrenching to see how quickly it had all disappeared.

He'd been to see his brother yesterday after Ed had phoned to say that Ali had gone again. It seemed that her fling with this Christian guy was more serious than Ed had first thought. His brother looked stretched and white-faced and suitably distraught, but Neil couldn't help feeling that there was a certain family trait of stubbornness in Ed's demeanor that wasn't exactly helping the situation. It was ridiculous to stand by and watch them both destroy all they'd built up. Their kids were fantastic. Didn't they deserve more than having two supposedly intelligent adults with locked horns damage their lives? Neil sighed to himself and realized that Year Two were getting restless. Perhaps he was better off single after all.

He held his hand aloft. "Everyone ready then? Stand up tall. Sit up straight. Nice smiles. After me! S-m-e-l-l-y-s-a-u-s-a-g-e-s!"

All of Year Two leaned forward. "SMELLY SAUSAGES!"

Before he could take the photo, his mobile rang. "Fuck," he said, wishing he'd turned it off and ignoring the echoing chorus of *fuckfuckfuck* that had started in the front row who no longer had their arms folded.

"Neil Kingston."

"Hi, Neil. It's Jemma."

Neil turned away from the children and tried to look suave down the phone. "Hi, Jemma."

"Neil. Is this a bad time?"

"No. No. No. Not at all." He glanced back at the children. "I was just doing a cover shoot for a magazine. Take five," he said nonchalantly to the class of perplexed pupils, who had momentarily been replaced by a vision of Liz Hurley, chenille throws and a chaise longue. "What can I do for you?"

"Neil, I'm worried about Ed and Ali."

"Me too," he agreed sympathetically.

"This is a stupid, stupid situation."

"I know. I told Ed exactly that yesterday."

"And I told Alicia."

"Good. Good."

"What do you think they'll do?"

"I don't know. Only the pair of them can sort it out."

"We can't just sit back and watch them make such a mess of things."

"We can't?" Neil paused. "No. No. We can't."

"We must do something," Jemma urged.

"You're right. We must."

"Let's have dinner tomorrow night and decide what," she said.

It had taken him several expensive dinners and months and months of smooth-talking to persuade one of the pretty bridesmaids he'd met at an unseasonal winter wedding to pose topless for him. He knew she'd be brilliant because when she was shivering in the cold outside the church, her nipples had stood out like champagne corks beneath her bridesmaid's dress. It had taken all his concentration to even worry about getting the bride in the photographs. This was going to be the start of his burgeoning glamour portfolio and hers. His big chance. The appointed time she was going to get her bra off was tomorrow night at eight o'clock.

"You hadn't got anything else arranged, had you?"

"N-n-o," Neil stammered. "Dinner would be nice."

"We're not doing it to be nice, Neil. We're doing it to save the marriage of your brainless brother and my stupid sister because they haven't the sense to do it themselves."

"Yes," Neil said.

"Come to the shop at six o'clock. We can go across the road to Calzone's or somewhere."

"Right," he agreed, entertaining the thought that if he really, really bolted down his food he might be able to have one bird in the hand and another one in the bush of his photographic studio. But then the bird in his hand would definitely be worth two in the bush, and his photographic career could go to hell for yet another night. Would Patrick Lichfield be so easily bought? Possibly not. Nevertheless, he would phone the accommodating bridesmaid, citing family crisis of the most extreme emergency, and hope she would understand and agree to get her bra off next week instead. Yeah, right.

"Thanks, Neil," Jemma said. "You're a darling." And she blew a kiss down the phone just before she hung up.

Every cloud has a silver lining, they say. And Jemma might just be his. God, she was a wonderful woman. Vibrant, dynamic, successful and more than a little horny to boot. Every so often something surprising would occur, right out of the blue, that would lift you out of the mundane and ordinary and onto a slightly higher, more pleasant plane. He might be having dinner with Jemma to try to stop his brother and sister-in-law divorcing, but he was having dinner with Jemma, and that could only be embraced as a positive thing.

With a silly grin still plastered to his face, Neil turned round. Year Two had disintegrated into some sort of after-hours street brawl—the sort that usually happened on a Saturday night outside bars called The Shamrock or McLafferty's. The boys on the back row were kicking the shit out of each other. The girls in the middle row were tearing each other's hair out in handfuls. And the front row were all crying loudly due to misdemeanors that had been perpetrated while his back was turned. The headmistress, meanwhile, was heading across the playground to see what all the noise was about. And he'd still got this to go through with Year Three.

Neil closed his eyes and wished with all his being that he were somewhere else. When he opened them, he was still on a school playing field, camera poised and knee-deep in howling children. Just then, the sun went behind a particularly big, black cloud and it started to rain.

"Smellyfartingflippingfuckingsausages," Neil muttered to himself.

CHAPTER 36

Christian has very strange CDs. They are stacked up in a Pisa-esque tower on the floor by his bed. They include: *The Friends of Rachel Worth* by The Go Betweens, *Art & Life* by Beenie Man, *Tourist* by Saint Germain, *In the Mode,* Ronnie Size & Reprazent and *The Marshall Mathers LP* by Eminem. I have never heard of any of these except Eminem, and I've only heard of him because the *Daily Mail* said he should be banned—or was it hung, drawn and quartered? Anyway, I dutifully banned Tanya from buying any of his records. She told me I was pathetic and that all her friends had them anyway because her friends' parents weren't neurotic fascists. I'm going to stop buying that bloody newspaper.

I do hope that you haven't heard of any of them either—otherwise I will feel totally uncool and lacking in hip. The last CD I bought was *White Ladder* by David Gray. This is the CD that all thirty-something people have in their collections at the moment. Much like *Brothers in Arms* by Dire Straits was the 1980s must-have album, which was there to be displayed rather than played. We also possess, along with 99 percent of my age group, Nigel Kennedy's *The Four Seasons* and *Songs from the Blue Turtle* (which I always thought was a ridiculous title) by Sting. I'd never heard *White Ladder* when I bought it, but someone said I should get it. Probably the *Daily Mail.* So I did. I'm still not sure if I like it. Tanya said it's sad, old gits' music. I think she might be right.

This is not the normal bedroom of a young man, I would suspect, apart from the cheese-fragrance sheets, which we've now removed for fumigation. The furniture is heavy, ornately carved mahogany, massive pieces that sit easily in the vast space of the room. The new duvet is best described as army combat camouflage in design—muted shades of khaki, beige and sludge green. It looks ill at ease on the four-poster bed, but then there is a commando bursting forth on the ceiling only marginally hampered by the Edwardian plaster ceiling rose, which doesn't look like a polystyrene replica from B&Q. You could say it picks it out quite nicely. There is a Sly Stallone–type figure lurking on the wall near the tallboy of sturdy drawers, bare-chested, bandanna-ed and brandishing a machete. I feel like I'm going to be stabbed every time I reach for a pair of knickers. The words *aaargh, eeeeow,* et cetera, drawn in bloodred, are plastered all over what looks to be ferociously expensive Farrow & Ball paints in traditional country house colors—magnolia with a hefty price tag. Despite being a designer, I imagine Kath Brown's corsets would ping at the sight of Christian's creation. I can feel my own stretching at their constraints. Only an artistic mind could see this "working." I must make more attempts to quash Elliott's desire for drama or he'll be wanting to do this to his bedroom, and I'm happier for him to stick with his Bob the Builder motif just now. Despite the shock of it all and the fact it isn't the most relaxed color scheme I've ever seen in a bedroom, it's fantastically painted and it's clear that Christian truly does have talent—or is completely warped.

The most disconcerting thing about the room, though, is that there is a drawing of Rebecca hung above the bed. At least I think it's Rebecca—I daren't look too close and I haven't the nerve to ask Christian. She's nude, in the drawing. Not soft nude like Rubens's nudes, all round-bottomed and rosy pink, coyly smiling out from the canvas. No, this is a legs splayed, belly in, breasts thrusting, head thrown back sort of pose more commonly associated with magazines of the top-shelf variety. It's raunchy, rude and raucous, and I'm pretty sure it *is* Rebecca. This confirms my suspicion that she and Christian were more than just old friends, and I don't know if I'm happy about sleeping beneath it. I'll let you know.

I should have thought to bring the sketch that Christian did of me in my hastily packed suitcase, lest Ed should decide to pin it up and throw darts at it. I could have propped it up on the mantelpiece so that, at least, I have some sort of presence in this room. I might consider getting it framed so that Christian can hang it up next to Rebecca as a sort of mini-gallery of conquests—it would save him cutting notches in his bedpost, I suppose.

My new roommate has budged up all his stuff in his wardrobe and mine is hanging cozily next to it. God, even that feels weird. The only closet I've ever shared before has been Ed's, and it takes some getting used to opening a cupboard and seeing your blouses next to strange trousers.

I feel very uncomfortable here, generally. This morning I couldn't go down to start breakfast without my makeup on because I'd have looked about three hundred years older than anyone else. The boys both sat in nothing but boxer shorts while they ate their toast, and I tell you, when you've reached a certain age, that is a very unsettling way to start the day. Rebecca was, thankfully, fully clothed and came complete with a black cloud. I wonder if Tanya will grow up to be like her—she is definitely showing the potential. I had a terrible stomachache by the time I'd forced down two rounds of toast, and it's still growling like a demented wolf even now. I've no appetite and I feel like throwing up, but other than that I'm great.

Rebecca is something in advertising. I think it must be something pretty lowly, because she spends an awful lot of time saying how important she is. And important people don't do that, do they? Important people just bask in it. Robbie has gone off to his shift at an HMV record store, and he gets quite good staff discounts, so maybe that's why Christian has so many weird CDs. That leaves us here alone. I have a terrible confession to make—yes, another one. I phoned Kath Brown this morning…well, I phoned the studio before I knew she'd be in, and left a message on the answerphone saying I was sick and would be off work for a few days. This is the first time I've done this, ever, ever, ever. I feel absolutely dreadful, to the point of nausea, so perhaps I am sick after all. Life has a funny sense of humor sometimes.

Christian has arranged for an artist friend to take over his pitch in Covent Garden for the week so that we can spend some quality time together. So here we are, doing just that. I'm lying on Christian's army combat bed and he is snuggled in behind me. We've been here for hours downloading each other's lives and backgrounds, and from this silly shaky start I can feel myself falling more deeply for him. He has such a verve for life and an enthusiasm for so many things that I'm sure I didn't when I was twenty-three. I'm not sure that I do now.

I've taken my wedding, engagement and eternity rings off, because it just didn't feel right wearing them while I'm in bed with another man. They're sitting in a little ceramic dish perched on the bedside table, staring accusingly at me.

Christian twirls my hair round his finger. "How were the kids when you phoned last night?"

"Not great," I say. "Elliott's missing me desperately. Tanya's sulking and Thomas is hardly saying anything. He's the one that worries me most."

"They'll survive," Christian says reassuringly. "Kids are hardy little beggars."

I nod, but I don't really agree with him. The only knocks Elliott has had to deal with are the ones where he constantly walks into things. "I'm seeing them on Saturday."

"That's nice."

I prop myself up on my elbow and turn to Christian. "Would you like to come with me?"

"Where?"

"To meet the kids. Would you like to come?"

Christian backs away from me slightly and holds up his hand. "Whoa!"

I laugh. "You don't have to! I thought it would be nice. But you're right, it's probably too soon anyway. They'd be happier with just me there. It was a silly suggestion."

"No. No," Christian protests. "You're right. I should meet them. I just hadn't thought this through. I mean, it stands to reason that if you're going to be part of my life, then they will be too."

This sounds far too complicated and I wish I'd never started this discussion. I've been part of a family for so long that it never occurred to me that it would be a big deal for someone who hasn't.

"There's one thing I ought to tell you, Ali." Christian grimaces. "I hate kids."

"How can you hate kids?" I say. "You are one!"

Christian looks hurt. "That's not fair, Ali."

"I'm sorry." I kiss his lips. "You're a big kid!"

We have a tickle fight for ten minutes just to prove it, but he forgets I'm a mother of three children and can, therefore, tickle anyone under the table, and Christian eventually concedes defeat. We both lie spent and breathing heavily.

"My kids are different," I say. "They're lovely. They're the best kids in the world." And a lump the size of Birmingham lodges in my throat.

Christian holds me to him. "I'll come and see them."

"You don't have to."

He smiles that knee-trembling smile that can make you believe anything. "I want to."

"Are you sure?"

"Positive. There's just one condition."

"Name it," I say.

"On no account must we go near a McDonald's."

"I can assure you, the last place on earth my children will want to go if there's a free meal on offer is McDonald's."

Christian snuggles behind me again and starts to kiss my neck. I have a very good feeling about Saturday. Thousands of single-parent families do this every week, and it doesn't do them any harm. Does it? I shake any negative thoughts away. The sun will shine, the kids will be adorable, they'll *love* Christian and we'll all have a great time together. And there won't be a hamburger in sight.

CHAPTER 37

Orla was bossing everyone around as Ed jogged as fast as he could down the uneven towpath without falling into the Grand Union Canal. She was tapping her foot and pointing her pen at Trevor, who was looking very hangdog. The rest of the crew were lurking by the canal gates with polystyrene cups of coffee, cigarettes and cowed expressions. It looked as though they had all been troubled by what had become known in the company as Orla's Disease—fleas in the ear.

"Damndamndamndamn," Ed muttered, banging his best aluminum briefcase against his knees as he ran.

Wavelength were making a video about safety for the British Waterways Authority, with the enthralling title *Walking the Inland Waterways in Safety* and he should have been here an hour ago. It was set just north of Watford, where the canal meandered through a landscape that was pleasantly rural rather than the grimy, grubby urban backdrop that London provided. It was a promotional feature that had taken a disproportionate amount of time to set up in comparison with their meager budget, and Ed wanted to get it finished as soon as possible and pack up. This was also due to the fact that for the past week his days had been governed by the need to get home in time to collect Elliott.

That he was late was also largely due to his son. Recently, Elliott had decided that he should make some sort of clothing statement about his personality every morning in the manner of Quentin Crisp and spent an inordinate amount of time in front of the bathroom mirror selecting which particular one of his seventeen Pokémon T-shirts he would wear to suit his mood. Ed's chosen color would have been black. Deep, dark, potentially homicidal black. No amount of cajoling could persuade Elliott to grab the first one that came to hand and just wear it whatever like real men did.

To top it all, when the clock had swallowed twenty minutes and Elliott was finally happy with his choice of dress for the day, Nicola Jones was invariably waiting for them at the school entrance as he deposited the fashion-conscious Elliott to her care. She seemed intent, presumably out of sympathy for Elliott's plight, on keeping Ed talking for ages. It had taken him ten minutes to edge away from her today and that was good going, because what with her fluffy hair, her breathy voice and her singsong laugh, she was quite a difficult person to leave. Subsequently, Ed had been late for work every day this week.

He was going to have to do something about it—the first thing being to sort out this silly mess with Ali. Orla looked up as he stumbled toward her, breathless. Her face was as dark as her suit, her lips pinched as if she'd been kissing a lemon. Correction, the first thing he needed to do was get back on track with Orla. Alicia and his marriage, at this moment, came a very close second.

His colleague, and newly acquired confidante, had been very busy this week, rushing in and out of the office at breakneck speed. They'd only managed to snatch snippets of conversation together, which had been restricted to purely work matters because there had always been other people around to overhear and he'd never found discussing his personal life in public very easy. Ed had apologized for standing Orla up, but he hadn't really had the chance to tell her the full story. And he'd been meaning to phone her every night, but somehow the evenings were eaten away by cooking, washing, ironing, homework and eventual exhaustion.

Orla pushed back her crisp, buttoned cuff and looked at her watch pointedly. "You don't mind that we've started without you? I thought we might lose the light." It was ten-thirty in the morning. Orla might not have much of a sense of humor, but she gave great sarcasm.

"Sorry." Ed puffed and tried to look pathetic and helpless in a masterful, in-control way. "I'll explain everything later."

"Yes," Orla said. "You will." She turned back to continue hounding Trevor.

Ed dumped his briefcase on the ground. There was nothing remotely useful in it, unless you counted yesterday's copy of the *Independent,* but he thought it made a good impression and, in a week where the rest of his life was happily falling apart of its own volition, it suddenly was very important to him to make a good impression. He wanted Orla to know that her trust in him was not misplaced and that her judgment of his sublime, but so far concealed professional talents had been totally sound. And it wasn't just because he was frightened of her, as was everyone else, but now he had good reason to want to impress her. If his aim to get back to Harrison Ford territory was ever going to be achieved, Orla was the one shining light on the horizon who could illuminate the tiny crack in the door he so much needed.

The man from the British Waterways Authority was big, bellowing and bearded. Appropriately named Mr. Rivers, he was standing on the canal bank posturing and wringing his hands with pent-up impatience while Trevor was struggling to fit him with a radio mike. Ed's heart sank as he realized they were in for a long and painful morning trying to make a video with a man whose previous acting experience was probably restricted to small roles in his local amateur dramatics group. He also looked like the type who would be first in the queue to volunteer for pantomime dame come *Cinderella* time. Ed was always deeply suspicious of these butch, bristled types who whipped on women's clothing given the slightest excuse. He let a sigh escape into the fresh morning air. Come back, singing tomatoes—all is forgiven!

"I'd like to go through the Waterways Code part," Orla said, and Mr. Rivers nodded forcibly in agreement, being pleasant, as they all were, at this stage in the day. Len the cameraman and Mike the sound technician shuffled reluctantly away from the sanctuary of the canal lock gate, where they had been quietly helping two Nike-clad boys to let a battered, but brightly painted narrowboat through, and took up position. Mr. Rivers straightened his tie. Ed hovered because there was nothing really for him to do now that Orla had taken charge and he wasn't really feeling manly enough to wrest control from her. So he fidgeted about behind everyone and got in the way.

"From the top," Orla suggested.

Mr. Rivers straightened his tie again.

"And—*action!*" Orla walked backward along the towpath, following the script on her clipboard and smiling widely in an attempt to make Mr. Rivers feel comfortable and relaxed as he launched into his speech about the joys of water. Mike and Len shuffled along next to Orla with the videocam rolling and the sound boom being buffeted by the wind, avoiding the outcrops of brambles and stinging nettles while simultaneously trying not to step in dog poo. Ed trailed behind her, trying to look usefully decorative.

Mr. Rivers went into David Bellamy overdrive. "Waterways are beautiful things." Orla smiled widely. Mr. Rivers grimaced tightly back. Ed studied the green slime frothing delicately with what might be chemical waste that formed the Grand Union Canal. "But take care and watch out for hidden danger." Orla grinned. Mr. Rivers, encouraged, pointed at an imaginary but potentially dangerous thing with a suitably serious expression. "Not all towpaths afford easy, carefree walking."

Orla smiled sympathetically. Rivers was really getting into his stride now. Ed noticed that the narrowboat had cleared the lock and was chugging serenely toward them. On its side in yellow lettering he saw for the first time the words ESCAPE! CANAL HOLIDAYS FOR YOUNG OFFENDERS. Someone had painted out YOUNG OFFENDERS and graffitied-in, YOBBOS! On the roof of the narrowboat several young men, presumably the aforementioned offenders and certainly yobbos, had gathered. Most of them looked like they had very recently escaped. Ed's nostrils filled with the scent of trouble. Orla and Mr. Rivers carried on, oblivious.

"Keep noise to a minimum. Be courteous and considerate to all other canal-users," advised Mr. Rivers earnestly.

At this moment, the young men on top of the narrowboat dropped their trousers and waved their bottoms in the air. "You're a bunch of fucking arseholes!" they shouted in unison to the tune of the conga. "A bunch of fucking arseholes! Da, da, da, da. Da, da, da, *da!*" A beer can was jettisoned from the barge, hitting Mr. Rivers squarely on the head and showering him with a sprinkling of froth—not unlike that floating on his canal. Then the bared bottoms sailed on by, captured on film for the authorities by Mike.

"And—*cut!*" Orla said, showing one of her fingers to the jeering teenagers as they departed and shouting, "Assholes yourself!" after them.

She mopped the dazed and trembling Mr. Rivers down with a pristine white handkerchief and straightened his tie. "Let's start again from the top. Everyone ready?" Everyone nodded. "And—*action.*"

"Waterways are places of beauty..." he said with a tremulous voice.

"Cut, cut!" Orla waved her arms. "Let's skip that bit and pick it up further down. Take it from... 'Watch out for...'"

Mr. Rivers composed himself and straightened his tie. He bared his teeth, jaw locked, at the camera. "Watch out for concealed mooring pins, ropes or other discarded objects that may lie dangerously across your path."

Orla smiled and some of the tension sagged out of Mr. Rivers, the pain of being bombed with a beer can receding in the face of Orla's urgings. His voice grew stronger. "If a person accidentally falls in the water, don't automatically jump in after them. Lie down and try to reach them with a stick. Or throw them a rope." Mr. Rivers demonstrated both maneuvers admirably to the back of the stalls. "Crouch down, so that you are not pulled in yourself, and find something inflatable to keep them afloat until help arrives."

Orla was nodding and smiling.

Mr. Rivers smiled back. "In any emergency situation always stay calm. Think before you act."

This was going well now. The sun was shining, the birds were tweeting, the yobbos had yobbed off. Ed stretched his neck with relief. A heron landed majestically on the far bank. Waterways were, indeed, places of beauty. Orla smiled benignly at Mr. Rivers again—just before she tripped over Ed's briefcase, which he had abandoned earlier right in the middle of the towpath.

"Orla!" he shouted in warning, scaring the heron away.

But before Ed could reach out to her, she had stumbled forward and cannoned into Mike and Len, knocking both them and their recording equipment into the murky depths of the canal. Orla followed shortly with a loud splash and an earsplitting scream.

Mr. Rivers rushed forward to help and she grabbed at his hand, pulling him in after her.

Trevor ran up and down the bank, tearing at his hair and screaming, "They're all going to drown! They're all going to drown!"

This was clearly a state of emergency. Ed, fixed rigid, deep in his state of shock, tried to keep calm and think before he acted. He crouched down and looked round him for a stick or a piece of rope. As he saw Orla struggling to the bank of the canal, coughing up green water and with slime plastering her hair to her head, he realized that he had nothing remotely inflatable about his person and that any help that was going to arrive had better be bloody quick.

CHAPTER 38

Neil pulled up outside Jemma's shop and cut the engine on his motorbike. He'd thought about coming in the nacky old Citroën and decided it would do his image no good whatsoever. It was six o'clock and the traffic had ground to a standstill as the commuters started their nightly battle home, giving Neil a warm glow and a feeling of superiority about the sense of riding a bike in London.

Parking the bike on the vast expanse of pavement outside You Must Remember This… he checked his reflection in the window as he walked toward the door and tugged nervously at his neck scarf. He'd worn his best crash helmet and plain black leathers with red detail stitching that coordinated with the color of his motorbike. These things mattered to women, he knew that. He'd once had a red Honda FireBlade CBR900 RR with Andes Blue and Winning Red farings with a capacity of 929cc, upside-down front forks, computer-controlled fuel injection and a Variable Intake Exhaust. He had also had a state-of-the-art, safety supreme, green crash helmet with a blue hexagonal pattern on it, a purple-and-pink striped Kevlar overall, yellow gloves with orange knuckle protectors, funky silver-gray boots and a girlfriend who nagged him continuously about looking a mess. The fact that the bike could single-handedly blow anything else on the road into the weeds had not impressed her. Was it an icon of modern motorcycle technology? Yes, it was. Was it faster than a Porsche Boxster? Yes, it was. Was it faster than a speeding bullet? Yes, it was. Did it matter one iota to Samantha? No, it did not. She'd never go on the back of it—or within fifty feet of it—so he sold it, bought a bike that would match his outfit and she'd left anyway. Women! Now he was the biker's version of *Color Me Beautiful.* The last thing he wanted was to turn up in seriously mismatched biker gear and give Jemma an excuse to phone the style police. He took his helmet off as he reached the door, just in case she mistook him for a well-turned-out armed robber.

As he entered the sophistication of the shop, Neil smoothed his hair, wishing his helmet didn't crush it to the point where he looked like a leftover punk rocker. Jemma glanced up when he walked in, and it was a second or two before recognition dawned.

"Come in, Neil," she said with a bright smile. "I'll be with you in a few minutes. Have a look around."

Neil shuffled a bit farther into the distinctly feminine emporium and started to sift aimlessly among the rails while Jemma attended to her customers. It all felt nice and silky, but he didn't have a clue what was what or why they warranted some of the seriously loaded price tags. Why should something forty years old and covered in *Come Dancing* sequins be worth more than four hundred quid? But then shopping wasn't a bloke thing, was it?

He watched Jemma from the corner of his eye. Two tiny Japanese women hugged each other with delight as she handed them two hefty carrier bags and an even heftier bill. The pair tottered out tittering gleefully under the weight of their packages.

"Two happy customers," Neil observed.

Jemma shrugged. "Regulars. If you can call twice yearly visitors regular. They take bags of the stuff back to Japan. Retro couture goes down a storm over there."

Neil let the hem of the silk evening gown he was fingering fall. "You've got some nice stuff," he said, realizing there were probably more technical terms.

"Thanks." They stood for a moment, smiling wordlessly. Jemma closed the till and frowned. "Can't you make dinner?"

Neil looked behind him. "Yes."

"Oh." Jemma twiddled her hair round her finger. "Shall we have a quick coffee in the flat?" she asked. "Or do you want to get changed in the back?" She flicked a glance to a curtained cubicle.

"Into what?"

"Well, you can't go to dinner dressed like that."

Neil surveyed the outfit he considered the epitome of biker style. It all matched. He looked back at Jemma. "Can't I?"

"No."

"Oh."

It had never occurred to Neil that someone who spent their days selling retro couture would object to his taste in dress. But then Jemma should perhaps have appreciated that someone who spent their days shouting "Donkey Burgers" and "Cheesy Toenails" to entice five-year-olds to smile probably wouldn't have any taste. A suit and tie would have been wasted on Year Three. He was a chinos and polo shirt man—and at this moment he wished he'd thought to bring them.

Jemma folded her arms. "You've brought a change of clothes along, haven't you?"

Neil decided to try sheepish and bemused. "No."

She tutted. "God, Neil, you're as bad as that dunderheaded brother of yours." She pointed at his leathers. "They might look very nice and sexy, in a tight kind of way, but those are the sort of clothes you wear when you're having an early night in."

Neil looked at himself again. "Are they?" His voice was higher than it should be. He lowered it. "Are they?"

"Or for riding a motorbike," she added as a dismissive afterthought. "You're not taking me out looking like a part-time Hell's Angel. Let's go through to the back and see what I can do for you!"

Neil allowed himself a quiet smirk.

What she did was find him some men's retro couture. Or, as he himself would have put it, old clothes. Sometime later, Neil emerged from the cubicle minus his smirk and wearing a velvety, horribly 1940s yucky, pouffy jacket, some sensible trousers from an indeterminate period and some suede brogues two sizes too small. He stood clutching his motorbike helmet like a security blanket.

Jemma smiled contentedly. "That looks better," she trilled.

Well, he certainly didn't look like a Hell's Angel anymore. "Wanker" was the first term that immediately came to mind.

She pointed at his motorbike helmet. "Leave that there."

Neil reluctantly deposited his pride and joy on Jemma's glass display counter next to some rather exclusive 1920s beaded Flapper cloche hats.

"Come on, let's go," she instructed, grabbing her handbag and heading for the door.

And, feeling rather more like Noël Coward than he would have wished, Neil trailed in her wake to the restaurant across the street.

CHAPTER 39

Orla was coming to dinner. And Marks & Spencer were providing the fare. Ed was ripping bags open as if his life depended on it. He slugged down some wine and checked the clock. She'd be here any minute.

She'd had to come here because Tanya was going to a school disco and he didn't want to get a baby-sitter for the boys in case it got back to Ali that he couldn't even manage alone for one week.

Elliott looked up from the table and waved a picture of what appeared to be a short, fat purple man with a mustache. "I'm drawing Miss Jones," he informed Ed.

His father studied the artwork. "And this was *before* her sex change?"

"What does that mean?" Elliott asked.

"Nothing," Ed said, sticking his finger in a carton of red-currant sauce to taste it. St. Michael was also providing lamb noisettes, which were in the oven on their way to burning, and a variety of other pre-prepared delights. "It was a joke."

"About what?"

"If I have to explain it, then it's not a joke anymore."

"Do you like this lady more than you like Miss Jones?"

"Elliott, I do not want to have any more of your 'erection'-type conversations. Orla is a colleague. Someone I work with. She is coming to discuss business. I want you to be very, very good tonight. In fact, I want you to be more than good, I don't want you to say anything. Nothing at all." Ed waved a red-curranty finger. "In fact, if you speak even once when you're not spoken to, I'll cut your tongue out and give it to the cat."

"We haven't got a cat."

"Next door's cat."

"Which side?"

"Elliott, have I made myself clear?"

"Perfectly."

The doorbell rang and Ed whipped off Ali's ancient and threadbare *Country Diary of an Edwardian Lady* apron and rushed to open it. Orla stood there smiling shyly and had clearly dressed for the occasion. Ed hadn't had time to change since he got home because there had been a ten-mile queue at the till in Marks & Sparks. She was wearing a cashmere dress and high-heeled boots and her hair fell loose to her shoulders. Ed brushed his own hair out of his eyes. "Wow!"

"Thank you," she said, proffering a bottle of wine.

Ed took it from her. "Come in. Come in."

Elliott was putting the finishing touches to Miss Jones. Red hobnail boots. "Orla, this is Elliott. Our youngest and most troublesome son."

Orla tried to look winning. "Hi, Elliott."

Elliott pressed his lips together. "Mmm, mmm."

"Elliott. Say hello."

Elliott picked his nose with his felt pen. "How am I supposed to say hello, when I'm not supposed to speak?"

"Cat. Elliott. Cat," Ed warned.

"Hello," his son muttered.

"Orla, can I get you a drink? Wine? Is red okay? Or white?"

Orla nodded. "Red's fine."

Ed poured a glass and handed it to her. This was ridiculous—he felt as nervous as a kitten. Perhaps it was because he hadn't seen Orla in such intimate circumstances before. It was the first time he'd seen her out of work clothes and it was a strange experience. When Orla did casual she did it in a very glamorous way, but she somehow looked softer, gentler, almost nervous herself. It was disconcerting having her here in the kitchen, and yet it had seemed such a good idea at the time.

Orla held the glass to her lips. They were slicked with scarlet lipstick like an overripe cherry, full and pouty. "Cheers," she said. "To us."

"Are you in love with my daddy?" Elliott employed his felt pen in a nasal capacity again while scrutinizing their guest.

Orla spat the wine back into her glass with a cough.

"Elliott!"

"My schoolteacher is," he informed her. "I've drawn her." Elliott held up Miss Jones's questionable likeness for inspection.

Orla cast her eyes over the image. "I'm sure your daddy's very flattered." She fixed Ed with a wry smile.

"It's time for bed, young man."

"Oh, not yet," Elliott pleaded. "I just have to do some more drawing." He gathered his felt pens to him hastily, smearing the snot from the top of one onto his sweater, and whipped out a clean sheet of paper.

"It's late," Ed said. "Bed."

Thomas peered round the door frame. "Can I go to bed? I want to read."

"Don't you want to have a small sip of wine with us?"

Thomas shook his head. His son had been unusually quiet all week, even for Thomas. Ed wanted to hold him and tell him that everything would turn out all right, but it felt like tempting fate.

"It's only early," Ed said lightly.

"You said it was late!" Elliott protested.

"Elliott, shut up and go to bed."

The small boy got down from the table and wagged his finger at Orla. "Be very careful what you say. Daddy's being very strange about pussies at the moment."

Orla blinked.

"Good night," Elliott said huffily and stalked to the door.

"'Night." Thomas turned and ran after him.

Ed tried an apologetic laugh. "Sorry about that."

Tanya appeared at the door. "I'm off."

Ed blinked. "You're not going out like that?" His daughter was wearing next-to-nothing and a full face of makeup to match it.

"I am. Bye. Don't wait up."

"Don't wait up!" Ed yelled.

The front door slammed.

When he laughed again, it sounded flat. "Sorry, sorry, sorry."

"I think I like this new, domesticated you," Orla said. She slid herself onto one of the stools at the worktop.

"I'm not sure that I do," he admitted.

They both lapsed into an extended silence.

"Fully recovered from the canal thing?" Ed inquired politely.

"I'm on antibiotics," Orla said.

"Oh. Good. Right." Ed topped her wineglass up, deciding not to point out that she shouldn't be mixing alcohol with antibiotics. If the tablets didn't kill the bugs, the booze might. The conversation sagged again. "I'll serve dinner if you don't mind," he said, resisting the urge to put his apron back on. "Otherwise it might well be burnt offerings."

He lifted the lamb out of the oven.

She was studying him closely. Too closely. He could feel her eyes following his every movement and it was making them all jerky.

"It smells divine." Orla sniffed the air.

"It's lamb," Ed said pointlessly.

"My favorite."

"I didn't know if you ate meat." Although most of the crew voiced the opinion that she probably ate it raw. For breakfast. "It's all bought. I take no credit for the preparation and accept no blame if it's not to Madam's liking."

"I'm sure it will be fine," she said.

Ed served the meal and took the plates to the kitchen table, sticking Miss Jones to the fridge lest she get red-currant sauce splashed on her orange triangular skirt and ruin the rest of Elliott's life. He hadn't bothered to put on a tablecloth, primarily because he wasn't sure where Ali kept them, and he thought candles might have given the wrong impression. He didn't want Orla to think he was making romantic overtures. Now he wished he'd made a bit more effort. It was hardly relaxing to be sitting at the kitchen table eating convenience food under halogen spotlights, trendy though they were. Candles would have been a good idea. Orla sat at the table, and Ed joined her with a heartfelt sigh.

"Sorry this is so rushed," he said. "This week's been a nightmare."

Orla held out her glass. "Shall we toast again?"

Ed clinked his to it. "Cheers."

"To the future," Orla suggested.

"Yes. The future," Ed echoed. He cut into his lamb and was relieved to find that it wasn't like shoe leather and was, in fact, fashionably pink.

"So," Orla said, tasting hers. "Want to tell me what's been going on?"

Ed sucked against his lip. "Alicia has left me."

Orla sat back. "No."

"She's gone off with a young, penniless artist." Ed gestured the full extent of his hopelessness.

"Oh my God," she said. "How romantic!"

It was Ed's turn to sit back. "No, Orla. Not romantic. Tragic."

"Oh, of course. Tragic. Tragic." She sipped her wine. "But in different circumstances and with a different woman, romantic." Orla licked her lips, smacking them together thoughtfully. "*Very* romantic."

Ed was tempted to glare at Orla. "Apparently he's a dish," he continued miserably.

"Of what?"

"Dishy. Handsome. You know."

Orla shrugged. "I guess he must be."

"Would you be tempted to turn your back on seventeen years of marriage just to sleep with someone who looked younger than Leonardo Di Caprio?"

"You bet your sweet ass…." Orla looked up and stopped. "I wouldn't even consider it."

"I don't know what's made her do it." Ed shook his head, nonplussed. "I thought we were happy."

"Did you?"

"Well, yes. Although sometimes it might have been a married-for-more-years-than-I-care-to-remember type of happy. We never had anything much to worry about. Very few people can say that, these days."

Orla studied him. "From the first time I met you, I saw a man who was sacrificing himself for others."

"Me?"

"Yes. You, Ed," she said earnestly while helping herself to microwaved mange-tout. "You are a man trapped by duty."

"Am I?" It was something he'd considered once or twice. Particularly after a few beers.

"Well, you were," Orla observed.

"Yes."

She slid her fingers across the table and reached for Ed's hand, holding it with a firm but comforting grip. "We have a lot to discuss, Ed. About the future. If Alicia was your only obstacle to accepting my job offer in the States, then that obstacle has just very conveniently removed itself."

Ed wanted a glug of his wine but didn't dare extract his fingers from beneath Orla's touch. His mouth had gone very dry. This was an angle that he hadn't really thought about at all. His wife leaving him for someone else wasn't something he felt able to embrace with glee.

"You are now free to make your own decisions about your life," she said.

It was a paralyzing, scary thought. Ali had walked away to pursue her own life without a backward glance. Could he possibly do the same thing?

Orla's eyes were soft and determined at the same time, seductive, sultry and strong. "Every cloud has a silver lining, Ed," she said as she slid her finger slowly round the rim of her wineglass. "And I might just be yours."

Ed licked his lips nervously. Perhaps candles wouldn't have been a good option after all.

CHAPTER 40

Jemma snapped one of those pointless, pencil-thin and tasteless breadsticks in half and risked her very fine sparkly white teeth by biting it. "My sister and your brother are driving me potty," she said with an exasperated huff. "They are both so bloody stupid."

It was seven o'clock and Calzone's was already comfortably busy. The pesto sauce and Chardonnay brigade were out in force, and their laughter crackled in the air above the soft jazz. Neil had taken off the yucky jacket before he noticed the £1,700 price tag, and now he didn't know what to do with it. He had hung it on the back of his chair and couldn't stop checking that it hadn't inadvertently fallen on the floor.

He had phoned the potentially topless bridesmaid yesterday to attempt to postpone their "session" until another time and had been met with a stream of invective casting aspersions on his parentage, himself and photographers in general. This made Neil think that she wasn't quite the blushing bridesmaid she had portrayed herself to be. But then again, neither was he the suave, sophisticated society photographer that he'd made himself out to be.

That was the trouble with dating these days—or trying to. You couldn't really be yourself or the chances were no one would want to go out with you. All the women he knew wanted to find themselves dynamic, urbane multimillionaires, or wanted to become dynamic, urbane multimillionaires themselves. It seemed as if the qualities of kindness, reliability, contented slothfulness and scruffiness were just not appreciated by the new millennium daters. And he was trying very hard to become dynamic, urbane and even just a minor millionaire, but it was all such a lot of effort.

Ed had never suffered from the family trait of lethargy. No sacrifice was too great to make Wavelength the successful, growing company that it was. But no matter what he did, his brother always seemed to harbor the overriding feeling that it was never quite enough. Whereas Neil blamed their father for his in-built apathy where everything was more than enough. Daddy Kingston had been a company director for most of his life—stressed, successful and totally selfish in his pursuit of that success. Then one day he decided he was going to die of an early coronary if he carried on and he resigned. Just like that. He banked his golden handshake, downsized to a smaller, cozier house, somehow discovered a previously untapped altruistic streak and took up a part-time job helping ex-prisoners to rehabilitate by starting their own businesses and, when they weren't away on lavish exotic holidays, he and his wife played golf every afternoon. It was an idyllic existence, and he continually said how he wished he had got out of the rat race earlier. Neil aspired to the same thing—but without the striving, success and ensuing stress in the middle. Ed, however, was definitely taking after his father in his working life. Neil just wished his brother would put a bit more effort into trying to save his marriage.

Alicia was wonderful, Neil mused. He only wished he could find someone just like her. He stared up at Jemma, who was sucking the end of her breadstick and returned quickly to his dish of linguine. There was a certain desperation creeping into his dating habits, he had noted. After all, he had just turned thirty-six, and suddenly from somewhere had unexpectedly sprung the desire to be married and spend his weekend shopping at Ikea and Baby Gap as all his other friends did. Maybe the taste of takeaway food was starting to pale. Whatever it was had driven him to join Snappy Setups, and he should have known from the name that it was likely to be a disaster.

Snappy Setups was a dating agency that "specialized" in finding partners for "busy, beautiful, professional people" who were presumably too tied up in being busy, beautiful or professional to have a life or bother finding people to love for themselves. And the odd photographer. Who was neither busy, beautiful or particularly professional, but was, by his own admission, too lazy.

The concept was sold on the simple idea of why should you need to spend an entire evening deciding if the woman for whom you'd just bought a gin and tonic was Miss Right, when you could get through half a dozen said women in one night. Speed dating. The fast-food version of good old-fashioned courting. It took Neil back to his days of extended adolescence in Scamps disco. Had that been any different? Only financially, he decided. This was an expensive cattle market and, therefore, trendily acceptable.

For the paltry sum of one hundred pounds, Snappy Setups made sure you were herded round a swishy wine bar for the evening by a "fixer"—his had been, inevitably, blond, bubbly and called Felicity—who was intent on finding you the "date of your dreams." You were allowed half an hour to suss out each prospective soul mate before Felicity appeared to whisk you away to meet the next victim—or predator, depending on your viewpoint. Half an hour to decide whether you could hear wedding bells or the waste bin calling—at which point you were supposed to mark a little white card accordingly to allow Felicity to do further "fixing" and move on without a backward glance. There had been some very attractive women present, but the whole thing had been terribly depressing, and by the end of the evening Neil had lost the will to live and was ready to admit defeat and string a rope up round the beams.

The women seemed even more desperate than he was, and explaining why you were still single at the tender age of thirty-six to the fourth person in a row was enough to bring on a panic attack. The only person he really and truly fancied was Felicity and, when he found the nerve to voice this opinion, she informed him that she'd been with the same man for five years and there was no way she'd ever sign up for this sort of stupid stunt. At least he thought she said stupid stunt. The music was very loud.

There was something very demeaning about hoping to select a woman as if you were going round Sainsbury's looking for a nice bit of rump steak. He wasn't the most romantic soul on the planet—in fact, one or two of his girlfriends had, in the past, felt moved to remark on it. But even Neil would rather spend Friday nights in with a take-away and an old James Bond film than find a relationship with all the verve and glamour of doing the National Lottery.

"You're not listening to a word I'm saying," Jemma said.

Neil snapped his head up, and she was glaring at him. "I was thinking."

"About what?"

He tried to look as if he'd been concentrating. "About what you were saying."

"And?"

"And, I think you're right."

"About what?"

"Everything," Neil said with conviction. "Absolutely everything."

Jemma smiled. "Good."

Neil smiled back. "Good."

"That's what I like about you, Neil. You're so easy to talk to."

He gave a self-effacing shrug. "Thanks."

"So you think we should meet regularly to discuss tactics?"

"Yes," Neil agreed. "Regularly." This was as easy as falling off a log, and the bill at Calzone's was easily going to be less than one hundred of our fine English pounds.

"Good."

"Good."

"God, is that the time?" Jemma drained her wine. "I don't want to beat about the bush. I need to get you out of that outfit right now."

Neil's smile widened. He loved women who were upfront about what they wanted.

"I've got a date," she said as she stood and slipped on her coat. Jemma winked at him. "Hot stuff."

And Neil had that awful sinking sensation in his stomach that indicated she wasn't necessarily referring to him.

CHAPTER 41

Elliott is clinging to the wooden post which supports our rather elegant, honeysuckle-clad porch and he's screaming.

"I want Daddy to come!"

I look pathetically at Ed for assistance, and he gives me a look-what-you've-brought-us-to glare. I am collecting my children at my predetermined appointed time, and it's a hundred times more agonizing than I ever could have imagined.

When I got up this morning, the sun wasn't shining as my vivid imagination had hoped. Neither were the birds tweeting. The sky was weighed down with grubby clouds and the roads were wet with rain. Christian had a hangover from too much Diamond White last night and was stomping round the bathroom, and I couldn't wait to leave the house. I was so excited about seeing my children, and I thought, hoped, that they would rush into my arms, relieved that I was back in their midst. But, like the weather, they are all being gray, grizzly and depressing.

"I want Daddy to come," Elliott repeats at full volume, bracing his legs into the gravel.

"Daddy can't come," I say in my best pleasant and reasonable voice. "Daddy's busy."

Ed leans on the doorpost, looking like a man who has hours and hours of leisure time stretching far ahead of him. Buckled and belted into the back seat of the car, Tanya and Thomas hang their heads and try to ignore the rest of us.

"Elliott, please don't be naughty."

"I'm not being naughty! I'm being upset!"

"Elliott, please!"

"I want you and Daddy to be my mummy and daddy again!"

"We *are* your mummy and daddy. That's a silly thing to say."

"I'm four. I'm allowed to say silly things. You're the ones who're grown up," he howls. "You're the ones who should stop being silly!"

I hate the logic of children, which is heartbreaking in its simplicity.

I try the reassuring tack. "Whatever happens, we will always be your mummy and daddy."

"Daddy says you're not. He says you're like shits that pass in the night."

"*Ships,* Elliott. We're like *ships* that pass in the night." I glance up at Ed, and his features are frozen. Perhaps we are shits after all, to be able to do this to our trusting children who don't deserve it at all.

"What if Mummy takes you somewhere nice and then we can talk about it a bit more?"

Elliott releases his death grip on the honeysuckle. His face loses its Jim Carrey contortions, and he shows grudging interest. "Where?"

I smile softly. I absolutely adore my son in between wanting to throttle him, and I've missed him so much this week it's given me stomachache. I've missed all of them. Ed included. "Anywhere you like."

"McDonald's," Elliott announces.

My heart shudders. "We can go anywhere," I state again, hoping that Elliott will get the hint that this is not a good choice. "Anywhere."

"McDonald's." He is absolute in his finality. If I am ever going to get him to part with the foliage and his father, McDonald's it must be.

"Okay," I say with a resigned sigh.

Ed gives a disdainful snort which says, "First day out as a single parent and you can't think of anywhere better to take them than McDonald's?" And he's right.

"I'll bring them back later," I say, humbled. "About five."

"Fine," he answers tightly and closes the door.

"I'd like a Happy Meal," Elliott trills, and I herd him into the car before he can change his mind.

McDonald's is packed. I'll swear that there are children hanging from the light fittings. There are certainly plenty crawling round under the tables. I move my knees for yet another ketchup-smeared three-year-old and note that the place is heaped with the remains of long-dead hamburgers and clearly the McDonald's policy of trying to keep their outlets ultra-tidy has gone somewhat to pot today. We are all sitting round a little red table on the most uncomfortable chairs in the universe in a sectioned-off part of the restaurant that's designed as Ronald McDonald's car. It is painted in the migraine-inducing colors of orange and pink, and I might as well be in hell.

I tried to keep up a cheerful little patter in the car while we drove here and was largely ignored and now I've sort of run out of steam, so I'm doing an impersonation of a hyperactive *Playschool* presenter on speed. Christian comes through the door, and I can sense him recoil in horror. I rang him on the mobile to say don't come, but he insisted. He's trying very hard to force himself to take an interest in the kids, but I can tell it isn't easy. And why should it be? The last time he had anything to do with kids was when he was at school and was one himself. Which, by now, you'll realize wasn't all that long ago.

He approaches the table and, even in my stressed state, I'm overwhelmed by feelings of love and lust for him. I need him desperately, and not in the more usual places, but I need him behind my eyelids and in the crook of my elbow and in the hairs on my neck. I'm far, far too old to be having a crush on someone so young, but I haven't got time to discuss it at length with you now. This is an important meeting, and I want it to go so well.

"Hi," he says with a feigned casual wave, and all my children stare at him agog. Tanya is the most agog of all. To her it is probably the equivalent of seeing her mother with one of Boyzone. He looks very trendy today in a hungover, pallid way.

"I wanted you to meet someone," I say in my overbright singsong voice. "This is Christian."

Christian folds himself awkwardly into a chair that is too small for his long legs.

"Are you our new daddy?" Elliott has always liked getting straight to the point.

Christian looks horrified. "No." He looks to me for backup.

"He's just a friend," I say.

"Have you done it yet?" Elliott asks.

"Elliott!"

Christian has blanched. "What?"

"Have you kissed my mummy?"

Christian looks relieved. "Oh..."

"Elliott!"

My son retreats into sulk mode. "I was only asking!"

"Well, don't," I warn him.

"I thought *he* was my new daddy because we've already got a new mummy," Elliott informs me brightly.

I'm glad I haven't yet ordered the hamburgers because I probably would have spat mine out. "Have you?" I think my voice comes out.

"She's called Orville."

"Orla, you limpet," Tanya snarls. "She's called Orla. Orville was a green duck."

"Does everyone want a Happy Meal?" I am shrieking and can't stop.

"There's nothing here for vegetarians," Tanya complains.

"Have a Chicken McWotsit," I suggest.

"That's got chicken in it." You can't pull the wool over that girl's eyes.

"Chicken is considered a vegetable in certain parts of the world," I insist through clenched teeth. Even Elliott looks up at that one, and he is convinced that tinned Spaghetti Hoops count as vegetables.

"Right," Tanya says, even though she means all adults are liars.

"If you're going to be a vegetarian, Tanya, you'll have to do a bit more research on your subject."

"I'll compromise my principles," she states loftily. "Just for today. I'll have the fish thing."

"Good," I say. "Thomas? Happy Meal?"

Thomas nods. He is the only one here who realizes that it would be a really bad idea to contradict me. "What do you want, Christian?"

He seems surprised that I'm speaking to him like a five-year-old, but he shouldn't be, because I've gone into bossy, overbearing mother mode and he just happens to be in the way. "A Big Mac," he says, somewhat bemused. "I'll come with you."

"No," I say, or shriek. "You wait here. Get to know the children. I'll be back in a minute."

His face is horror-struck, but I can't help it. He'll have to cope. My nerves are shredding. I can feel them coming apart from my muscles and the little fibers are ripping away from each other, fraying like an overstretched rope. I need Valium. Lots of it. Not fucking hamburgers and synthetic milk shakes! I also need five minutes alone while I'm queuing up to get our food to think about the fact that even though I've only been gone a week, Ed has apparently managed to find someone else to take my place.

I tap my foot as I wait for the spotty teenager who is serving me to get our order right on the third attempt. Do they all have spots because they eat too many free hamburgers? My insides are seething quietly, and there is probably smoke exuding in comely drifts from my ears. No wonder my husband was standing there so smugly at our front door. I should have taken a bit more notice of this Orla-Orville woman. Perhaps I would then have realized just how many times Ed casually dropped her name into the conversation. Orla this. Orla that. And now Orla the other! My God, and he is trying to make out that *I'm* the villain of the piece. That I, alone, am responsible for this family's breakdown when he too has been quietly contributing to it without my knowing. And I had been feeling terrible. Truly terrible. I was seriously thinking that this whole thing was just one big victory for the fuck-up fairy and was really, really going to sit down and decide what was the best thing to do. For me, for Ed, for the kids. And now I find I wasn't in possession of all of the facts. Well, they say the wife is always the last to know. And I know that I shouldn't feel righteous in my indignation, but I do. Despite the fact that I too have little dark sins lurking on my soul.

I hand over a second mortgage to the spotty young man, hoping that Thomas will be blessed with clear skin, take my tray of Happy Meals, fish burgers and Big Macs and turn to head back toward my family. They have another woman in their lives now, my children, and it occurs to me that they may well like her more than me. Will she be funnier, kinder, more tolerant than I am? For some reason, I feel as if I'm being edged out of my own life. I wonder if this Orla is young and beautiful too, and realize, with a pang of sharp emerald-green jealousy, that age as well as size really does matter.

An uneasy silence descends on us while we eat, and I'm trying not to be too aware that we're all bunched together in a cartoon car. Why, oh why, did I think this had any hope of being a success? Christian smiles at me. He is trying to be understanding, but I can tell from the rod that appears to be holding his shoulders up that he's not what you might term classically relaxed. I feel his hand squeeze my thigh under the child-size table.

"So," Christian says confidently, "what do you want to be when you grow up, Thomas?"

Thomas looks vaguely surprised at being addressed like this, but is too polite to be dumbstruck. "A paleontologist," he says quietly and disappears into his Happy Meal box again.

"Thomas loves dinosaurs, don't you?" I say.

Thomas nods.

"And what about you, Elliott?" Christian is clearly feeling emboldened. "What do you want to be when you grow up?"

"A burglar," Elliott says with conviction, which pretty much ends the conversation. Christian returns shame-faced to his chips.

"I need to go to the toilet," Elliott says through his burger.

"No, you do not, Elliott," I say patiently. "You went for a wee five minutes ago. Eat your burger."

Elliott wriggles pointedly in his chair.

"Sit. Still."

"I need to go to the toilet," he insists.

"You do not!"

"I do!" Elliott shouts. "I'm doing a poo! It's peeping out of my bottom!"

The whole of McDonald's turns round to look at us.

Elliott is now purple. "I'm having to try really hard to hold it all in!"

I know just how he feels. Christian puts down his hamburger. "Go to the toilet, Elliott," I mumble. "Be quick."

Elliott shoots off at breakneck speed. A steady hum of noise descends on McDonald's again. We are all sitting in silence.

"Well," I say cheerfully. "This is going well, isn't it?"

Christian, Tanya and even Thomas look at me as if I am completely and utterly barking mad. I stare at my Happy Meal and want to weep. And I seriously contemplate whether it is possible to slit one's wrists with the sharp edge of a chip.

CHAPTER 42

I am sitting in Jemma's flat and we are both crying. Jemma is issuing tissues and chocolates, and I am consuming both in equal measure.

"You look dreadful, Ali," she says. "Are you getting enough sleep?"

"I'm living with a sexually rampant twenty-three-year-old whose hormones are currently on lust overdrive and who is constantly, for some inexplicable reason, mad for my body," I sniff. "Of course I'm not getting enough sleep."

"Bitch," Jemma hisses, and we laugh through our tears. "And you've lost weight." She passes me another chocolate and I oblige. "Cow."

"I'm not eating," I say, stuffing a chocolate into my mouth. I wipe my snot away again and drag my hair back from my forehead, which feels hot and feverish. "The children were all so horrid today. They were like…like…like…"

"Children," Jemma supplies.

"Christian hated them. They hated him. They were deliberately obnoxious."

"Elliott is always obnoxious. With a modicum of training, he could be the next Macaulay Culkin."

"Except for Thomas, who sat there quietly like he was dying

from the inside out." I start to cry again. "I don't know what to do."

"I hate to see you so unhappy," Jemma sniffed. "Can't you just go back to Ed and sort this all out?"

"He's got someone else," I point out. "That's why I'm sitting here sniveling."

"At least you still have feelings for him."

"You can't just turn your back on years of marriage. Of course I still l-love him." I stutter slightly on the word "love," as if it's something that's now an alien concept to me. And I must say that my traditional perception of that giddy state we loosely term love has shifted somewhat recently.

"And he still loves you. He can't have found someone else."

"My children are a fairly reliable source of information."

"They are not. You give them far too much credit. You should know what children are like. They put two and two together and come up with four million."

"I should have had my suspicions about this Orville woman. Ed's been talking about her a lot recently. That's a sure sign of adultery."

"He's probably doing it deliberately to make you jealous," Jemma says.

That makes me brighten considerably. "Do you think so?"

"Oh, Alicia," Jemma sighs. "You are such a fucking idiot."

That's what I like about my sister. She is so supportive.

"It may have escaped your attention, but you've just run off with a hunky young toy boy. How do you think that will make Ed feel?"

I can feel my lip pouting involuntarily. "I don't know."

"Then try, Alicia. Try. Try thinking about someone other than yourself for once."

I think that's very unfair. That's what I think. It is a little-known fact that solicitors can charge clients for "thinking time" on a case. Two hundred pounds an hour for just thinking. Great work if you can get it. Those of us who have to think on our own time probably do considerably less of it. No one thinks about anything anymore. I don't. I don't have time. I don't have the time to think whether my bum looks big in anything or whether I'm getting the right balance of vitamins in my diet. I don't have time to think if I'm too tired and emotionally weary to go on. I don't have time to think about what to wear in the morning, I just open the wardrobe and grab what's nearest to hand and fling it on. I didn't even think about this. "This" being my life. And "this" is a fairly big thing to go through without giving it due thinking time.

I think if I did have time to think, there might not actually be anything there that's remotely useful to think about anymore, and that frightens me more than you'd care to know. I think it's because all my good thoughts fall off the back of my brain like lemmings as I fill up the space in the front with shopping lists and borderline nutritious menus. I think my brain is frozen. All that is between my ears is Ben & Jerry's Phish Food. I am taking the lurch-about-from-one-crisis-to-another approach to my life, and there's no need for you, my sister or anyone else to point it out to me, I know that it isn't working. What shall I do? I'll have to think about it. When I get time.

"I reckon this is all down to the fact that you've always suffered from unrequited-love syndrome," says Jemma, who clearly has more time to think than is good for her. This is because she dates married men and spends most of her time alone waiting for them to sprinkle their company on her, but I don't feel anywhere near brave enough to voice this thought. You wouldn't think I was the older, wiser sister who has suffered the pain of three children and has a bag full of worldly experiences to her name, would you? "You've always had crushes on younger, unattainable men," she continues blithely, unaware that my jaw is setting. "Now that you've actually attained one, you're not quite sure how to handle it."

"Lots of women have younger men these days," I protest.

"Who?"

"Joan Collins, Tina Turner. Probably Ivana Trump. And undoubtedly Cher. They all have younger men."

Jemma tuts.

So I'm at the cutting edge as far as soap stars, aging rockers and has-been film stars are concerned. Great. And it is a mixed blessing going to bed with someone as acutely young and beautiful as Christian. It makes me feel utterly powerful and sexy and much more aware that my body is falling to bits.

My sister is right, in some ways, although it grieves me to admit it. And, anyway, she prefers the fat stomach and even fatter wallet look in a man, so there's really no need to throw stones. But I have always mooned over pop stars and movie stars, although not in the bare-bottom "moon" sense. And I'm not talking about the clammy-handed crushes that saw me through my teens either. I'm talking about now. I still do it. Perhaps this is really why I have no time to think about serious things. Set me off musing on what might be up Russell Crowe's little leather skirt and I am lost in an entirely adult clammy-handed reverie. Am I alone in hoping that Brad and Jennifer won't last? Robbie Williams has a lot to answer for with his chubby romper suit, biteable bottom and "Angels." At least I have the pretense of buying teen CDs and magazines with free glitter nail varnish taped to the front for my daughter, who is, for some reason, uninterested in any of Robbie Williams's anatomy. I hope she's not a lesbian.

Perhaps there is something deeply unfulfilling about my life that makes me desire these elusive men. I have no idea. Add it to the list of things to think about. Eventually.

"God," Jemma says. "I'm going to open some fizz—otherwise we'll both be depressed. Bubbles are just as good in times of crisis as they are for celebrations. In fact, they're probably better."

"I have to be getting back." I think I want to cry again. "I've got to face Christian," I say weakly and reach for my handbag.

"Not yet," she says. "Not until you're happy again. Or, at least, drunk." And she snatches the bag from my reach.

My copy of *How To Be a Sex Kitten at Any Age* falls to the white ash laminate floor with an embarrassed clonk. I can feel a rash coming up on my neck. Jemma picks my book up and scowls at the title. "Oh, Alicia!"

I sit on my hands and lower my head.

My sister waves the book at me. "Since when have you been reading this brain mush?"

"I've only flicked through it."

"And what useful advice, if any, does it contain?"

"It says I should scatter frozen rose petals on the bed every night to create a sensual ambience," I mutter into my chest.

"Oh, that'll make a world of difference!"

She could be right. I have to say that when I pictured rose petals scattered on Christian's combat camouflage duvet beneath the warring, bleeding soldiers, I thought better of it.

Jemma has opened the book. "'Drape an item of perfumed lingerie over the table during an intimate lunch.'" Her eyes are wide with horror. "Ali!"

"I wasn't going to do it!" McDonald's was hardly the right setting for Estée Lauder–soaked knickers.

"You are not the sister I know and love," she says sternly.

I wish Jemma's sofa would eat me.

"Would you be reading this sort of crap if you were still with Ed?"

"No," I mumble guiltily. Jemma would have made a great headmistress.

"You are clearly not confident in this new relationship," she pronounces. "It is damaging your self-esteem. I can't understand you, Alicia. You and Ed are so perfectly suited. I was saying to Neil..."

"Neil?" I look up. Jemma has blushed. Which is a very rare sight, as nothing makes my sister shame-faced. She buries her face in *How To Be a Sex Kitten at Any Age.* "Ed's Neil? My brother-in-law Neil?"

"Yes."

"What were you doing with Neil?"

"We had supper together."

"Why?"

"Because he's nice."

"Did he ask you?"

"No. I asked him. It's not unusual these days."

I look at her suspiciously. "Did you have a good time?"

"Yes," she says. "And we're going to do it again."

"When?"

"I don't know."

"Oh." This is all very interesting. "So. What were you saying to Neil?"

"Nothing," she says, and her pink-tinged face deepens to strawberries, beetroot and tomato ketchup mashed together.

I think I like the sound of this. Or do I?

CHAPTER 43

Robbie dumped his backpack on the table. "You are looking particularly ragged, my friend." He opened the fridge door and grabbed a beer. The fridge now smelled of Mr. Muscle rather than fungi and rotting vegetation because Ali was cleaning up for them, but it still contained nothing remotely healthy, unless you counted Budweiser and Toblerone. Oh, and one corner reserved for Rebecca's fat-free yogurt that was strictly out of bounds to them. Robbie flopped down next to Christian on the sofa.

Christian half opened his eyes and regarded himself critically. He seemed to have ketchup in places that shouldn't necessarily be smeared with condiments.

"I have spent the afternoon in that popular version of Armageddon they call McDonald's."

"Ah."

"And I am utterly, utterly exhausted."

"You look it."

"That is because I have just met the children from hell." Christian clinked his bottle against Robbie's and downed a mouthful.

"Ali's brood?"

Christian nodded.

Rebecca opened the door and strode into the room. "She's got children?"

Christian and Robbie exchanged glances.

"Why did no one tell me?"

Christian and Robbie exchanged glances again.

"I wasn't snooping," Rebecca snapped. "You two don't realize how loudly you talk. Or do anything else." She looked pointedly at Christian.

"If you didn't walk out of the room every time Ali came in, then you might have had a conversation with her about them."

Rebecca grunted in a way that said "fat chance." She crossed to the sink and busied herself making a cup of tea. "So, how many kids has she got?"

"Three."

"*Three?* Isn't that a bit excessive?"

Robbie laughed. "You've got none, then suddenly, three come along at once. Like buses."

"And women," Rebecca added. Robbie sniggered.

She brought her tea to the table and sat down opposite them. "What flavor are they?"

"Two footballers and a shopper."

"Ages?"

"Fifteen, twelve and the little one's four, but he could easily be a hundred and four. He's like Yoda. He misses nothing."

"Do they call you Uncle Christian?"

"Leave it, Becs," he warned. "I'm just going to have to try harder. They made it pretty clear they didn't want me around."

"Of course they don't. You're stealing their mother."

"I'm not stealing her."

"Oh." Rebecca raised her eyebrows. "Are you going to give her back when you're finished with her?"

"I want her in my life, Becs. Permanently. If that means I have to make compromises, then it has to be that way."

"You won't even compromise about which side of the bed you sleep on, Christian. Speaking of which…" Rebecca pulled a piece of paper from her pocket. "That girl Sharon phoned today."

The boys looked blankly at her.

"You know, the one that spent the night with Robbie just before Mother Earth moved in." She gave them both a knowing look. "Funnily enough, she phoned for you, Christian."

Robbie and Christian avoided looking at each other.

"What did she want?" Christian asked.

"Oh, for heaven's sake. What do you think she wants?"

"A repeat shag would be my bet," Robbie said.

His friend glared at him.

Robbie looked vacant. "What?"

Rebecca held out the slip of paper and Christian took it. He scrunched it up and put it in his pocket without looking at it. "I'm in a committed relationship now," he said. "Things are different."

"Plus ça change, plus c'est la même chose."

"And what's that supposed to mean?"

"It means you talk out of your arse, Christian," Rebecca said. And she left the room, taking her tea with her and banging the door behind her.

Christian and Robbie looked at each other. "Dotty totty," they said in unison, and clinked their beer bottles together.

Robbie settled into the sofa. "So you think you'll stay with this bird?"

Christian nodded. "She gives my heart wings."

"Have you been at the wacky baccy again, mate?"

"No." Christian's eyes twinkled. "Why? Have you got any?"

Robbie smiled. "Is the Pope a very fine upstanding Catholic gentleman?"

"I think you'll find he is," Christian said.

"Then I will be back momentarily," Robbie said, springing to his feet. "I think we are both deserving of a little chemical-induced relaxation at the end of a particularly stressful day."

Christian tried to blow a smoke ring and failed. The spliff had taken the tension from his shoulders and had made the room blur at the edges. He was at one with the soft furnishings and the cushions folded around him like fluffy clouds. He narrowed his eyes and peered through the fug.

"I want to do this right," he said sleepily.

"Right," Robbie echoed. His legs were stretched across Christian's lap and his feet were on the arm of the sofa next to him. Robbie's feet weren't fragrant and lovely, but he was Christian's best, best mate in the whole world, and he wasn't about to ask Robbie to move them. And, besides, Robbie was balancing the ashtray between his knees.

"Right," Christian agreed.

"What?"

"This whole commitment thing."

"Right."

Christian took a long, soothing toke. "I want to get a job."

"No, no, no."

"I do," Christian insisted. "I do. I do."

"No, no, no."

"A nice little nine-to-five job that pays a shit-load of cash."

"No, no, no!"

"I want to look after Ali. I want to look after her children."

"No, no, no!"

"I do. Everyone loves children." Christian waved his hands expansively.

"I don't," Robbie said.

"I don't either. But I will."

"Becca doesn't."

"Okay. Well, not everyone. But *nearly* everyone."

Taking another long, lingering toke, Christian, with wavering fingers, passed the spliff back to his friend.

Robbie took it as if it were a china vase. "Do you think we should give Becca some puff?"

Christian shook his head vigorously.

"She's a bit uptight," Robbie observed.

"I don't think she likes Ali," Christian ventured.

"I like her."

"I like her too." Christian sighed. "I love her."

Robbie grinned inanely. "Awww."

"I want to go away with her."

"Awww."

"I want to take her on a big, nice cuddly holiday with lots of sun and sea and sex."

"Awww."

"Awww," Christian beamed.

"And run up and down the beach without your togs on?"

"Mmm..." they both agreed.

Robbie's legs hit the floor with a thump as Christian pushed them from his lap. "I'm bloody well going to do it," he said.

Robbie tried to focus his eyes. "Get a job?"

"What job?"

"I don't know. I thought you were going to get a job."

"No, no, no. I'm going on holiday!"

"But you haven't got any money."

Christian stood up, weaving slightly like a drunk. He tapped the side of his nose and then giggled into his hand. "But I know exactly where I can get some!"

Robbie licked his lips and waved the spliff toward Christian. "What are you up to, Winter, you bastard?"

"You wait and see," Christian wandered toward the door, taking the scenic route.

"What was it Rebecca said about talking out of your arse?" Robbie teased

"The more things change, the more they stay the same."

"Is that the same as a leopard never changing its spots?"

"I think it might well be," Christian said. And, accompanied by his friend, he burst out laughing.

CHAPTER 44

The phone was ringing, and Ed smoothed down his hair, fidgeting on his kitchen stool. He must get it cut. Ali normally made his appointments and he just trotted along at the allotted time. He'd found the business card for the salon, but hadn't yet found time to get there. Elliott's hair was looking a bit more like a windswept sheep than normal, so he probably ought to drag him along too.

At the other end of the line, Nicola Jones picked up the phone. "Hello." Her soft, breathy voice caressed his ear.

Ed adjusted the collar of his polo shirt. "Hi. Nicola. It's Ed. Ed Kingston." As in: James. James Bond. Smooth. Ed smiled down the phone.

"Ed. Lovely to hear from you."

"I know this is a bit short notice, but well…" This was the tricky bit. Ed's heart was doing a salsa rhythm. "Well… I wondered if you were doing anything tonight?"

"Tonight? Er…no. No, I'm not."

"Good. Good. Well, no, not good that you're not doing anything. Well, yes. Good."

Elliott walked past. "Daddy, you're wittering."

Ed folded his hand over the mouthpiece. "Shut up, Elliott!"

Elliott helped himself to a Mars bar and left.

"Elliott, you'll ruin your appetite!" But his son had already gone. Ed returned to his phone call. "Sorry."

"That's okay. How are you coping?"

"Badly," Ed admitted. "But that wasn't why I was ringing. I wondered if, well, if you'd like to come over for a bite of supper tonight."

"That would be lovely."

"Would it? Yes, yes. Of course, it would." Ed could feel his brow perspiring. This was ridiculous. He'd asked women out before. Hadn't he? He must have done. How did he end up with Ali otherwise? It was just that he was out of practice. "About eight?"

"Eight would be fine."

Eight would be fine, he hoped, because then all the children would be out of the way. It was rather strange having to conduct your entire social life from between four walls, but needs must. "I'll see you later," he said.

"I'll look forward to it," Nicola replied.

Ed hung up. Elliott put his head round the door. He had Mars bar smeared round his mouth. "Can I stay up?"

"No," Ed said. "And wipe your mouth before you put chocolate all over the sofa." He dialed another number. "Neil!"

"Bro!"

"What's happening?"

"Nothing much."

"Fancy coming round for some supper tonight? Nothing fancy."

"Since when have you done fancy?"

"I'm a new man." He wasn't really, but at least he was trying to make an effort and not go to pieces or hit the bottle like some sad sacks would. The Groucho Club had seen precious little of his custom in recent weeks, and there was no fun to be had in drinking Jacob's Creek in front of *Law & Order* alone. So, essentially, it was boredom that had brought him to meddle in his brother's love life. "About seven-thirty?" Neil was always "fashionably" late and he didn't want to be sitting around with Nicola like a pair of bookends waiting for him to arrive.

"Yeah. Okay."

"Great." Ed grinned to himself and rubbed his hands together with satisfaction. This was easy-peasy lemon-squeezy.

* * *

Ed had found a tablecloth and some candles and was currently going to great trouble to arrange them in an aesthetically pleasing manner. He stood back and admired his handiwork.

"Matchmaker, matchmaker…la, la, la, la…la, la, la, la."

And then the song went on about making a match and finding a find or catching a catch. Or something. The big Hollywood musicals had never really been his thing, that was Ali's forte. He was more of a Bach or Bruce Springsteen bloke.

Elliott leaned on the door frame in his pajamas chewing Barney's ear. "Come here," Ed said, and Elliott rushed to him for a hug. Ed felt a surge of love for his son even though at times he could gleefully choke him.

"Are you going to snog Miss Jones?"

This was one of those times. "Elliott, if you want to live to see your eighteenth birthday, I suggest you start behaving yourself."

"So you *are* going to snog her."

"No. No. I'm not going to snog anyone." Although I might thrash you within an inch of your life! "What's this obsession with snogging?"

"I'm worried," Elliott confided, eyes brimming with tears. "We seem to have an awful lot of mummies these days."

Ed crouched down and cuddled his son. "You don't," he said. "You only have one mummy and no one can take her place." And suddenly there was a searing, burning feeling through his guts that gripped him as if he'd swallowed ammonia. Yesterday, when said mummy had brought the children home, he had wanted to tell her that this had all been a terrible, terrible mistake and that he wanted her back. On her terms. He'd do anything as long as he didn't have to deal with any more real life. It was too exhausting and empty without her. He would eat chicken nuggets daily until he died, if that's what it took. And he was going to tell her this. All of this. But she rushed in white-faced, drawn and distressed, and had rushed back out again, back to her toy-boy lover, before he'd had the chance to say a word. He missed Ali. He missed her so much it kept him wide-eyed until three o'clock every morning, when he fell into an exhausted sleep. But she didn't seem to be missing him. Ed pushed the thought away. "I've invited Miss Jones, Nicola, so that she can meet Uncle Neil."

"Why?"

"Because I think she'll like him."

"Doesn't she like you?"

"I think she does."

"Do you like her?"

"I do. She's very nice."

"And does Uncle Neil like her?"

"I hope he will." Ed put his finger to his lips. "But that's to be our little secret. We mustn't tell Uncle Neil."

"Why?"

"Er…" Ed racked his brains. "I'll explain it to you when you're older."

"Explain it now."

"Go and do something useful, Elliott."

"Like what?"

"I don't know."

His son stomped to the kitchen door. "Why do grown-ups always have to mix things up?" he said with an exasperated sigh.

Why indeed? Ed wondered.

Neil and Miss Nicola Jones were laughing at each other's jokes, which was always a good sign. Neil was in excellent form, sparkling, happy and looked more laid-back than he usually did—which was saying something. And, flying in the face of convention, he'd been early for once, which meant they'd managed to get conversations which contained the word "Alicia" out of the way before Nicola arrived.

Ed, too, felt more relaxed than he had done in days, which was nice and was probably attributable to the amount of wine he'd glugged; now he was tidying up around them, imagining himself in the role of mother hen. He'd cooked a proper dinner. Well—only salmon fillets, salad and wild rice, but at least it was better than the dehydrated gloop out of a packet which is what they ate most evenings. Gloop that still looked like all the manky bits that had been scraped from the floor under the cooker no matter how much water you added to it and for how long you simmered it.

Nicola Jones was looking particularly gorgeous tonight. Her cheeks had taken on a pink blush from the wine, and her eyes were shining brightly. Her laugh was soft and genuine, and you just couldn't help but smile along with her. And although, initially, she'd looked slightly taken aback that his brother had been there at all, she was now giggling heartily at another of Neil's outrageous tales. Ed smirked to himself. This was all going rather well.

"Dessert?" Ed ventured. He had cheated here. Fazed by the plethora of Alicia's cookery books and the endless lists of ingredients and garbled instructions they contained just for knocking up a pud, he'd dashed out and bought the last thing they had left in the little patisserie in the High Street. It was a chocolate and cherry calorie-mountain thing and looked good enough to eat. Which was a bit of luck.

Nicola nodded. "Mmm."

Neil sat back and massaged his tummy. "Would love to, bro, but I can't stay."

Ed nearly dropped the stack of plates he was holding. "What?"

"Gotta go."

Miss Nicola Jones tilted her head to one side. "Oh."

"Busy, busy," Neil apologized.

Ed could feel that his face had blanched. "You're never busy."

Neil looked hurt. "I resent that remark." He stood up and pushed his chair back from the table. "Tonight, I really am busy."

"You can't be," Ed said.

"Look—I am. Okay?" Neil repeated tightly.

"But you haven't had dessert."

Neil patted Ed's stomach. "A few more calories won't hurt. You'll have to eat it for me." He smiled at Nicola. "It's been lovely meeting you, Nicola."

"You too."

"Have coffee," Ed pleaded. "Brandy? Choccy mint sticks?"

"Bye!" Neil waved at Nicola and headed for the door.

Ed put down the plates. "I'll see you out."

Neil frowned. "I haven't stolen the silver."

Ed forced a smile. "Back in a minute," he said to Nicola.

He bustled Neil into the hall and closed the door behind them. "What do you think you're doing?" he hissed.

"Leaving," Neil hissed back.

"Why?"

"Is there a problem?"

"You can't just walk out on Nicola like that."

"She doesn't mind."

The blood rushed back to Ed's face. "Well, I do."

"Am I missing something here, bro? I'm sure you don't need me as a chaperone." Neil winked. "It all seems to be going rather well."

"I thought so too!" Ed realized he'd hissed rather loudly and checked the door behind him. He took Neil's elbow and moved him toward the front door. "Nicola is a lovely woman."

"I don't disagree," Neil said. "Nice hair. Great tits."

"Is that all that matters to you?"

"No. But it's a good start."

"I've organized this especially for you."

"For me?"

"I wanted you to meet Nicola."

"You don't need my approval. You're a free agent."

"I'm a married man."

"It pains me to point this out, but you've got one vital factor missing at the moment. A wife."

"She'll be back," Ed snapped.

"Look, if you want something more than a hot-water bottle to keep your bed warm at night, who am I to judge?"

Ed looked astounded. "Is that what you think this is about?"

"Isn't it?"

"No. Can't you stay?"

"No. I've got things to do."

"Like what?"

Neil shifted cagily, jingling his car keys. "It's none of your business."

"I'm your brother."

"Since when has that given you the right to unlimited access to my personal life?"

Ed wanted to take his tea towel and wring it round his brother's neck. "I thought you and Nicola would well…get on well together, hit it off, whatever the bloody hell you call it these days."

"You're trying to fix me up with her?" Light dawned on Neil.

"Put crudely, I suppose that's about it."

"Do I strike you as desperate?" he asked sternly.

"On occasions."

"Well, I'm not!"

"You have an unhealthy obsession with Britney Spears."

"That does not make me desperate. A little sad perhaps, but not desperate," Neil huffed.

"You said you were going to join a dating agency."

Neil lowered his voice further. "I said I was *thinking* about it!"

Ed looked shifty. "I was trying to save you the bother."

"I can look after myself." Neil dropped his car keys, bent to pick them up and knocked a dragon plant in a Chinese pot off a china ornamental stand with his head. Ed caught the pot before it hit the floor. Neil scowled. "And, anyway, Miss Nicola Jones seemed to have eyes for only one person, and it certainly wasn't me."

"I don't know what you mean."

Neil put his arm round his brother's shoulders. "Edward, go back in there, get drunk and get laid."

"Get laid!" Ed lowered his voice. *"Get laid?"*

"She's gagging for it."

Ed looked shocked and hugged his pot plant to him. "That's Elliott's nursery-school teacher we're talking about."

"I only wish I was his age again. She sure as hell beats Mrs. 'Warty' Warburton, doesn't she?" Neil winked.

"Don't leave me," Ed pleaded.

"Relax and go with the flow," Neil advised.

"I don't know how to."

"It's like riding a bike," Neil told him. "It'll all come rushing back to you once you jump up in the saddle." And with a reassuring pat on Ed's arm, he walked out of the front door, leaving his brother openmouthed with shock.

Nicola Jones had slipped her shoes off when Ed finally divested himself of his plant and plucked up the courage to go back into the kitchen. Her strap had slipped from her shoulder, highlighting the sheer white translucency of her skin, and he was sure she looked a bit more…tousled, than when he'd left. She licked her lips round her pretty pink mouth and pouted over the rim of her wineglass, teasing it with her tongue.

Ed's body seemed to have frozen into short, jerky Frankenstein movements, and it took a great deal of effort to slide nonchalantly back into his seat without giving the impression that he had just received 50,000 volts up his bottom. "Sorry Neil had to leave," Ed said. There was definitely a squeak in there.

"Never mind," Nicola Jones purred. Ed was sure she hadn't

purred before. He would have noticed. Surely. "That means we can get a little more cozy."

Cozy. The candlelight danced mischievously in her cool gray eyes, which seemed to have gone all soft and misty and warm. Fire and ice.

"I think I'd better pop upstairs for a minute just to check on the children." Ed twitched his body out of his chair again.

Nicola's lips parted. They were moist with wine. "Should I come with you?"

"No. No," Ed said. "I'll go by myself. Thanks. Thanks all the same."

"Did I ever tell you that I absolutely adore children?" Nicola said.

"I think you might have mentioned it," Ed said, backing out of the door and thinking that "cozy" suddenly sounded very scary indeed.

CHAPTER 45

Did you know that you can measure the passing of your life by how many *Now That's What I Call Music...* albums there've been? Well, you can. I'll give you a hint. My first ten were bought on shiny black vinyl before CDs were even a twinkle in a record company executive's eye. I think we're up to *Now That's What I Call Music...52*. Except that you can't call any of it music anymore. It's just an incessant thumping noise with no attempt at coherent lyrics. Am I sounding like my mother? I vowed I never would.

Age is such a terribly depressing thing. And so subjective. I don't feel as if I've aged at all. Women of fifty, sixty, ninety, will all tell you the same. Your body may become decrepit, but inside you're convinced you're forever young. And although your brain may suffer from severe memory lapses which we laughingly term "senior pauses," you put it down to anything other than the fact it's slowly but steadily wearing out—like the rest of you.

I don't feel as if I'm any older than twenty-five, but occasionally I catch glimpses of this woman who looks remarkably like my mother in full-length mirrors in Marks & Spencer, and I know without a shadow of a doubt that I am older.

I want my children to think I'm a very funky and hip mother, but they don't. They think I'm pathetic. And old. Sometimes I get the same feeling with Christian too, and that's very unnerving. Try as I might, I cannot distinguish between jungle, underground and drum'n' bass music. Nor do I care to. He says he's never heard of Donny Osmond, but I hope he's just trying to wind me up. I used to do the same to my mother when she mentioned Roy Orbison.

I, on the other hand, clearly remember Brutus jeans, when George Michael wasn't gay even though he sported long blond curly hair and looked it, and when people on council estates didn't call their children Nike. I also remember when being "lush" meant you were an alcoholic and was not a desirable thing. And if you're convinced Limp Bizkit is a chocolate digestive that's been left out on a plate for too long, then you're not as hip as you'd like to think either.

I have time to dwell on these things because I am back at work—if I may use the term loosely. I've been sitting here all morning bashing through invoices that have mounted into a pile as high as during the period of my unauthorized leave. I phoned Kath Brown and groveled before I dared to show my face, and promised her solemnly that I would never, ever go AWOL again. She was very cool and made me beg. A lot. But now I see the size of the backlog I can see why she relented. Despite her unassuming name, she must be raking it in.

However, she hardly greeted me like the Prodigal Son. More like a leper whose thumb had just dropped in her soup. She's keeping up the chilliness theme. There is so much frostiness in the atmosphere that icicles are hanging from the fabric swatches. Really, there are. Frosty the Snowman would feel right at home here. And she keeps looking at me with a snarl about her lips. She's twice made herself a cup of herbal tea and not offered me one. That alone speaks volumes, doesn't it?

My fingers have got keyboard basher's cramp, and I say I'm going into the showroom to check a price when I'm not really. I'm going to look in the mirror to make sure I haven't turned into my mother yet. If Carol Vorderman can reinvent herself from Brain of Britain to vacuous sex kitten, then I'm sure it isn't beyond the realms of possibility for me either. And she's got to be forty if she's a day.

I'm just approaching the £180 rack of soft furnishings and the front door tings itself open exuberantly. Christian pops his head round and my heart sinks. Not because of seeing Christian, but suddenly the opening bars of "There May Be Trouble Ahead" drift unbidden into my mind. Christian is grinning broadly. He's wearing clothes so baggy that someone else could get inside too—preferably me. He hasn't shaved and is sporting a bristly little smattering of goatee à la Brad Pitt. Kojak, the bald Yorkshire terrier that had been abandoned outside a rescue home and was pictured on page three of the *Daily Mail* this morning, is the only thing I have ever seen look cuter.

"Hi," he whispers loudly. "Coast clear?"

"No. Get lost," I say, shushing him out of the shop. "I'm in deep doo-doo already because of you! Go—go on. Shush. I'm going to see you at lunchtime." I glance nervously back toward the office. "If I can get away." I feel it may be pushing it.

"I can't wait," he says. "I have to show you these!" He waves an envelope at me and goes, "Da, da!"

It could be a gas bill for all I know. "What?"

"Da, da!" he says again. Kath Brown will be out any minute. He gives me the envelope. "Tickets!"

"What for?"

Christian is so excited he can barely stand still. "Look."

I open the envelope, and there are two plane tickets inside and a hefty bill. "Where the hell are the Maldives?"

"In the Indian Ocean," Christian says triumphantly. "We're going on holiday!"

"I can't go on holiday," I say. "I've had to grovel to get my job back as it is. Kath Brown will blow a major fuse."

Christian is unshaken by this revelation. "It's booked."

"Christian, you should have checked with me."

Now he folds his arms and tries to look stern. "You would have said you couldn't go."

"I can't!"

"Of course you can! She won't mind." He is childlike in his assumption that he will always get his own way. My sister would say immature. "You need to get away."

With that I would not argue. "But two weeks, Christian?"

"It'll do you good."

I can't fault that argument either. I look at the final total and gulp. "Where did you get the money to pay for it?"

His face darkens momentarily. "Let me worry about that," he says.

"Did you borrow it?"

Christian kicks at Kath Brown's designer carpet. "Sort of." He stuffs his hands in his pockets and, for a moment, he reminds me of Elliott. "I'll pay it back."

"Oh, Christian." I sigh and smile.

His face lights up again. "So you'll come."

"Of course I will. It's booked," I remind him.

He comes to me and wraps his arms round me. "I love you, Alicia, Ali Kingston," he murmurs in my ear just as Kath Brown appears at the office door. I knew she would.

Christian lets go of me and I straighten my skirt and fuss with my hair, which never really looks any different whether I've been ravished or not. "I'll see you at lunchtime," I mutter to Christian, and he disappears out of the door quicker than you can say caught-in-the-act.

I turn back to Kath Brown, who, as designers go, is not looking happy.

I lick my lips and hope I look suitably penitent. "I need to ask you another favor."

Kath Brown folds her arms and braces her bosom. "Ask away."

"Christian has booked us a holiday," I say, realizing that I'm sounding more and more feeble. "Would it be all right if I took another two weeks off?"

"That's fine," Kath Brown says.

I smile with relief. I wouldn't have blamed her if she'd been a complete cow about it.

"You can have as long as you want, Alicia." Kath Brown shows me her teeth. They look like little icicles. "You're fired."

CHAPTER 46

The viewing suite in the 1970s concrete block that Wavelength called its offices housed a dozen chairs in varying states of dilapidation, a coffee machine that was usually full of warm black syrup and the biggest television that money could buy. The offices themselves cost a seriously ridiculous amount of money to rent and were sandwiched between a sex shop and an Italian deli. One of which Ed frequented most days. In the summer, unbelievable smells came out of both of them. Wavelength was one of a dozen or more small film companies squashed in between delis and sex shops in the same road and, if you didn't actually see the offices, it gave them a very trendy address on letterheads.

Next to him Orla sat primly in her black leather club chair, legs crossed neatly at the ankles. She was sniffling slightly following her unfortunate interlude in the canal and had a vaguely consumptive cough. She did, however, also have one too many buttons open on her blouse, and beneath it there was a black lacy bra. It could have been because she was feeling feverish, but whichever way, it had been giving Ed dry lips and a certain difficulty in concentrating on the finished promotional video he had previously made for Auto-Choppers, a gadget no overloaded, low-tech kitchen should be without. It had a variety of different interchangeable blades, which could be used for a wide range of slicing, chopping and general pulverizing of unsuspecting kitchen comestibles into certain oblivion. If he weren't a cynical, hard-bitten video producer, he would have sworn it was a millennium replica of that scourge of the kitchen, the K-Tel Chop-o-matic, an orange plastic device designed to bludgeon vegetables to certain death and your Formica work surface along with it. If you didn't keep a close eye on it, it would have your fingers too. Like the offices, also a product of the 1970s.

The company had poured a suitably large amount of cash into paying for a minor soap star to promote it, and she was doing a grand job for them, perkily dissecting a red pepper with all the skill of a would-be pop star. Orla was making appreciative noises. At least Ed hoped she was—the room was very dark and stuffy, and there was an outside chance she could have been snoring. The closing title music signaled the end of the film, jingling away chirpily until the video clicked and automatically started to rewind itself. Ed got up and turned on the lights. He drew back the curtains, jerked open a reluctant window and let the traffic noise and fumes of London backstreets pour in. Orla stretched, arching her arms above her head and testing the breaking point of her blouse with her breasts. "Great work, Ed," she said when he sat down again.

Ed shrugged. "The client will be pleased."

"So should you be," she said. "It's neat, tidy, professional."

"Yes," he said with a nod. "But not pushing the boundaries of creativity."

"Er…no," Orla conceded. "I guess not."

Ed huffed.

"Don't brood on it, Ed," she advised, touching his arm with a deft, light stroke. "Things are happening. This isn't how it will always be. There's a way out."

"I know," Ed replied. Orla and he had chatted more about her schemes and plans when she'd been over to his house for dinner, but, as yet, she hadn't pushed him for a decision. Nor had she opened her checkbook to him and told him how much the deal would be worth. No doubt, crunch time would be coming for both.

"How are things at home?" Orla hadn't moved her hand.

Ed's lips tightened. "Not great," he said. It wasn't simply the fact that the Auto-Chopper promo was never going to be the advertising world's equivalent of a Guy Ritchie movie that was making him brood, it was more the fact that Ali had announced she was going on two weeks' holiday. Ed picked his fingernail and looked up at his colleague. "Alicia is going to the Maldives—"

"It's a great place," Orla gushed.

Ed's face clouded over "—with love's young dream."

"Great if you like sand," she said hurriedly. "And sea. And fish..." Her voice trailed off weakly.

Ed puffed meaningfully.

"I thought he was supposed to be a starving artist?"

"So did I. Or perhaps I just hoped he was."

"That's understandable," Orla said sympathetically. "Maybe he'll dash off a few more masterpieces."

"He's not bloody David Hockney. He does drawings of middle-aged women with nothing better to do than hang around in Covent Garden. Passably good drawings. It's hardly art."

"Saatchi paid thousands of pounds for a run-down beach hut because Tracey Emin had stuck a note to the door. The same woman wheels a disgusting unmade bed into your Tate Gallery and it's hailed as a triumph. So what's the definition of art?"

"If you can masturbate to it, it's pornography. If you can't, it's art."

Orla gave him a patronizing smile. "You have a lot of bitterness inside you, Ed."

"You know what I'd like to do?" he replied with a world-weary sigh. "I'd like to take one of those little plastic Auto-Choppers and grate Lover Boy's dick off for him."

Orla looked at him, brow furrowed with concern. "You must move on, Ed," she told him earnestly.

Yes, I must, thought Ed. I must move on to inserting a strange and interesting range of Performing Power Tools into a selection of his bodily orifices.

"This could hold you back in life. Living with anger stifles the creative process," she lectured.

"Yes," Ed said wearily. As if he hadn't got enough to worry about.

"She's showing no sign of wanting to return?"

"No." But then, as Neil had pointed out, he hadn't exactly asked her to. He had, however, made several visits to lurk outside Christian's house. And he wasn't sure whom he wanted to catch a glimpse of more—Ali or Christian. Thankfully, he had seen neither.

Ed had noted the address and telephone number down when he had found the card in Ali's handbag. It was a stupid thing to do and he wasn't proud of it, and he'd tortured himself with it ever since. He'd phoned Christian's mobile a dozen times, maybe more. And he'd always remembered to dial 141 beforehand so his call couldn't be traced. Sometimes he'd listened to Christian's irritatingly chirpy and hip message: "Hey, man! Whassup? Leave a message!" and wanted to punch him on the nose even more. Sometimes Christian had answered the phone himself, and he sounded so young, so sure and so lacking in responsibilities that it made Ed's tired, burdened, middle-aged heart want to bleed.

"You know what you should do?" Orla broke into his thoughts.

"No."

"Give her a taste of her own medicine."

"Great idea." Ed brightened. "I just don't know any obliging twenty-three-year-olds."

"How about an obliging thirty-something?"

If it was a honey trap Orla had set, he had a feeling he'd just walked straight into it.

"Where would we go?"

"Budleigh Salterton," she joked.

"What about the kids?"

"Let Ali look after them for the weekend." It seemed a reasonable suggestion, but then that would mean Christian Trendy Bastard having them for the weekend too.

"If we're going to be partners, it would help to get to know each other better. Away from the work environment."

Partners? This hadn't cropped up before. Ed had assumed that Orla would be the boss and that he'd be the hired help. This put a whole new slant on things.

"Yes," he said hesitantly.

Orla leaned on the back of her chair, her hand cupping her face. One black eyebrow arched imperceptibly. "After all, what's good for the goose is surely good enough for the gander...."

And in the absence of a better suggestion, Ed decided it probably was.

CHAPTER 47

I put the phone down and turn to face Christian. "Ed wants us to have the children for the weekend."

"All weekend?" Christian's voice has gone up an octave. He is lying on the sofa in the kitchen and immediately swings his feet round and sits up in the manner of a man who's just had an awful shock.

"Yes. Isn't that great?"

"Oh no," Christian wails. "That's terrible."

"No, no," I try to reassure him. "That's good. It means that Ed is starting to accept things." I'm not sure about this even as I say it.

"Why can't he have them?"

"He's going away," I say absently. "On business."

"Where to?"

"I didn't ask," I admit.

"But the whole weekend, Ali?" Christian tosses aside his music magazine. "Two hours in McDonald's was bad enough."

"You don't have to come," I say breezily and put on my face that says, "If you loved me, you'd damn well come!"

"Where will we take them? What will we do?"

"Let me worry about that," I say airily, thinking: Where will we take them? What will we do?

"We've got packing and stuff to do."

"How long can it take to throw a few pairs of shorts in a case? There's nothing there but sand, you said so yourself. My holidays are usually like military operations," I say. "You forget I'm used to packing for five."

"But it's Friday, already. We might have had things planned."

"Like what?"

"I don't know." Christian spread his hands. "Couldn't he have let us know earlier?"

"So that you could have planned to flee the country?"

We both laugh. "You're a hard woman, Ali Kingston," Christian says and pulls me down onto the sofa next to him, spanking me playfully on my bottom as he does.

I pout my best soft, pouty pout. "I want you to like them," I say. "I want them to like you."

"I'll try," Christian promises, and that's all I want.

"I know this isn't easy." I kiss the tip of his nose. "But they're part of the deal."

"Maybe I should have read the small print first before I signed up?" he says with a smile that barely reaches his mouth, let alone his eyes. The hairs on the back of my neck stand up. He kisses me, and any doubts I feel for the future or for spending a weekend with my own children are quelled by the passion of his embrace.

"You're going away with another woman!" Neil shrieked in surprise, spraying the froth from the top of his beer.

"Sssh!" Ed looked round. The barmaid had inched closer. It was lunchtime and the Groucho Club was crowded. "It's business."

"Bollocks," Neil said.

"It is."

"Monkey business."

"Orla thought it would be a good idea," Ed said.

"I bet she did!"

"Look, Neil," Ed reasoned, "you said yourself that I was a free agent."

Neil frowned. "Edward. Since when have you ever listened to a word I've said?"

"I'm taking your advice. I'm going with the flow."

"That was to go with the flow when it involved the soft, nice, squishy stream of Miss Nicola nursery-school teacher Jones, not the torrential battering of Ms. Ball-breaker Orla the 'Orrible."

"It's no good telling me that now," Ed said. "And, anyway, Orla's okay once you get to know her."

"Which you no doubt will if you're going to be ensconced with her for the weekend." Neil frowned at his beer. "And what does Ali think of this new departure?"

"She doesn't know," Ed admitted. "I told her it was a business trip. But then I hardly feel I have to take Alicia's feelings into account after she announced that she's going to the other side of the world with the toy boy." He gulped at his beer.

"Is she?"

Ed wiped the froth from his lip. "Maldives."

"Really? It's supposed to be very romantic…."

"Don't think about going there, Neil," Ed warned.

"…in a sandy sort of way," his brother added quickly.

"Alicia hates sand," Ed said thoughtfully.

"Well, there you go, mate." Neil clapped his brother on the back cheerfully. "She'll have a crap time."

Ed looked rueful. "And me?"

"Cancel it, Ed."

"I can't."

"She'll understand."

"She won't. She's only just about forgiven me for making her fall in the canal."

"It's your marriage that's at stake here."

"I'm not sure that it's in Orla's interests for it to continue."

"And yours?"

If things didn't work out with Alicia and, at the moment, that looked somewhere between slim and remote, then Orla was his lifeline, his escape route, his tunnel out to better things. He could put all this behind him, start afresh in a different, more glamorous life. A life where the sun would shine every day and people wouldn't take the piss out of him for talking about Harrison Ford.

"This is so unfair, Edward. I can't get hold of a decent woman and here you are, still technically married, and you've got them stacking up like junk mail." Neil tipped some peanuts into his hand and tossed them into his mouth, snapping it shut. "Life is constantly cruel," he moaned.

It was, Ed agreed. The one woman he wanted was about to pack her bucket and spade and increase the distance between them even further.

CHAPTER 48

I'm standing in the kitchen of my own home, feeling like a stranger. A stranger who's just made a bad smell. The kids are sitting quietly at the table—even Elliott—and my kids just don't do quiet. Ed is fidgeting, and I can feel my irritation rising. He is wearing his coat already and his weekend bag is at his feet, and I resist the temptation to ask him if he's sure he's got everything. He's chewing his fingernails, which drives me barmy, and he's been doing it for fifteen minutes.

"I thought I'd be gone by the time you got here," he says for the millionth time.

"It doesn't matter," I say. "Does it?"

Ed glances out of the window. He seems very agitated.

"It's not like you to work at the weekends."

"No," Ed says and doesn't meet my glance.

"Shall I make a cup of tea?"

"I might not have time to drink it."

"Oh," I say. I'm trying to be bright and chirpy, but no one is helping me and the whole kitchen feels like an elastic band stretching to twanging point. "Do you mind if I make one?"

"No. No. Go ahead."

This is my home. My kitchen. My kettle. My tea bags. And I'm asking if I can make a cup of tea! Except that it isn't really my home anymore. It's more grimy than it was when I left it, and there are things left out on the work surfaces that should have been put away. I don't seem to feel comfortable anywhere anymore. I feel as if I'm in limbo, which is the outskirts of hell according to the Bible—which I would agree with, but I have no idea why it should produce such a strange breed of dancers.

Christian is concerned that I don't feel at home at his house. But then none of them seem to be particularly at home there either. They don't know how anything works—or care to. They don't clean it. They don't cosset it. Robbie doesn't really move from the sofa in the kitchen, and Rebecca, during the fleeting time she is there, never comes out of her bedroom. I mentioned to Christian that it might be the decoration—as every room, apart from the two which Christian has customized, has a sad, unloved air about it. The dining room is never used. It has cobwebs all over it, like something out of *Great Expectations,* but I haven't had the strength to tackle it yet. It takes me all my time to tidy up after the boys—so some things are exactly like home.

Christian's kitchen has neglect stamped all over it. When I went back there yesterday, he'd painted a six-foot mural of Lara Croft on the kitchen wall and was glowing with pride through his covering of emulsion. It is stunning. Though quite why he thought a gun-toting, large-breasted, scantily clad cartoon goddess would make it feel more homely is beyond me. He was anxious that I adore it and I do. I just have this thing about making spaghetti bolognese with a machine gun aimed at the back of my head and, no matter how hard I try, I can't help feeling somewhat attached to floral prints and pastel shades. I blame Kath Brown.

I fill the kettle and take a mug from the cupboard, mainly because it gives me something to do rather than out of a burning desire for the delights of PG Tips. "Why aren't you taking your car?" I ask Ed, again for something to say more than anything else.

"I…er…" he says and then stops and looks vacant.

"Who's collecting you?"

"I…er…" he says again and, at that moment, a large shiny car pulls into the drive.

An utterly, utterly gorgeous woman gets out and stands on my gravel. She is as sleek as her car and as slender as a reed. A reed that's been on the Vanessa Feltz *Let's Get Svelte* diet. For her entire life. She's wearing black jeans and a tan leather jacket that shrieks expensive and a cream silk roll neck underneath. Her hair is piled up on her head and she's wearing trendy *Men in Black* sunglasses. She is doing casual like she's on a catwalk. When I do casual, I do it like I've just fallen out of bed.

Ed doesn't move. No one does. Only Elliott. He looks up and out of the window at the approaching woman. "That's Orville," he informs me.

"Orla!" everyone else says.

Ed and I exchange glances. Orla taps at the back door and then walks straight in—which even I didn't feel comfortable about doing. She takes off her sunglasses, and her eyes are gorgeous too. They're like the blacked-out windows of a swanky limousine. They let the occupant see out, but are far too dark to let people on the outside know what's going on behind them. I hate her already and she hasn't even opened her mouth.

I look at Ed. Ed looks at Orla. Orla looks at me. I look back at Orla. Who looks at Ed. Ed blushes. "This is Alicia," he mutters.

"Hi," she says and folds her arms across her cleavage.

"What time does your conference start?" I ask, looking at Ed.

Ed looks at Orla. Orla looks at me. I look back at Orla. Who looks at Ed. Ed blushes even more. He could well burst a blood vessel at this rate. I hope. "I…er…"

"You don't want to be late," I say.

I look at Ed. He looks at me. I look back at him. We don't need to speak—we've been married far too long for that. My eyes can convey every message I'll ever need and now they say, Business? Bollocks!

"No." He snatches up his case.

"I take it you won't mind if Christian comes round here while you're away? On business," I add.

"No," he says with a look that translates as, Of course I bloody mind!

"Good." I smile magnanimously and nurse my tea. "Nice to meet you, Orville," I say.

"Orla," Ed hisses.

He kisses the children hastily and rushes to Orla's side, taking her elbow, steering her to the back door.

"What shall I tell Nicola if she calls while you're away?" I ask as he leaves. His face is dark and stormy.

"Tell her I'll be back tomorrow."

Before the door closes, I hear Orla saying, "Who the hell is Nicola?"

I cover my smirk, knowing I'm being childish. How is Orla to know that the only love interest Miss Jones has in this house is Elliott? It might give her something to think about while they're doing their "business."

I sit down with my tea and my children. I don't know whether I want to laugh at our situation or cry. "It's nice to be home," I say, and my voice sounds wobblier than Jell-O.

"There was an awful lot of looking going on," Elliott observes.

"Was there?" I say.

"I can't wait until I get older and can do looks." He smiles at the thought.

"You won't need to do 'looks' when you're older, Elliott," I say. "I'll have killed you by then."

"You're the one who's going to get Daddy into trouble," he advises me.

"Really?" I say. "Why?"

He leans toward me conspiratorially and lowers his voice. "I think Miss Jones stayed here all night." Elliott puts his hand across his mouth and giggles. "In Daddy's bed."

Tanya's head snaps up from her magazine. "Elliott, you little snitch. We don't know that for sure!"

The one good thing about having a son with a big mouth and no idea of discretion is that I get to hear everything. Eventually.

"But she might have done?" My voice isn't at all steady.

Tanya shrugs and retreats behind her glossy pages.

"I don't think Orville knows," Elliott says. "And I don't think she'd like it."

My hands have turned to ice, despite the warmth of my tea permeating through the cup. "She's not the only one," I reply.

CHAPTER 49

We have decided to take the children to a fairground, Christian and I. And it seemed like a really good idea at the time. But let's face it, a day that starts with you poking yourself in the eye with a mascara brush just isn't going to get better, is it?

And I couldn't find my rings this morning. Not that I wanted to wear them, but they were conspicuous by their absence, and the dusty ceramic dish on the bedside table was empty. I don't know where they are, and neither does Christian. But then men never know where anything is, do they? I expect I've put them in a safe place and as with all safe places, have totally, utterly and completely forgotten where.

Then, to top all that, I find out that my husband, even though he might almost be considered my ex-husband, has not one, but two young, pretty gorgeous women on the go which is a bit more than anyone could reasonably be expected to bear. And it's going to take a lot more than a bit of limp pink candy floss to sort my mood out, I can tell you.

I used to love fairgrounds when I was a child. Everything about them. I loved the smells and the noise and the flashing lights. They were places of excitement and daring, exotic and glamorous. I'm sure they were. Memory seems to have a very cruel way of playing tricks.

It's been raining for the past few days—when isn't it? Which means that the once green and pleasant playing field upon which the fairground has disgorged itself is now a sea of sticky brown mud with the odd tuft of flattened grass struggling through. It's a very small playing field, and all the stalls are cramped together, so that you can't help but walk on the mud. The skies are dark and moody, a bit like me, and the clouds roll across them like waves the color of tar. The cheery colors of the fairground, red, yellows and flashing neon struggle bravely against it, but prove themselves unequal to the task. It's the sort of day when you should stay indoors with sheepskin slippers, a glass of mulled wine and a weepy film. With three children? What a laugh. I think I last did that in about 1980, when I had a bad bout of the flu and the mulled wine had been Lemsip. I can dream though, can't I?

Although the full-blown rain has died down, there's a sort of gray drizzle running from the conical rooftops, so that if you stop to look at any of the stalls it manages to drip directly down the back of your neck. Surly, scruffy people man the stalls and everything is so expensive. If you want to win one of the poor, half-dead goldfish it could end up costing you about twenty-seven quid! But you do get a "free" poster of some greased-up WWF wrestling hero to go with it, which might be some consolation when the fish dies, as they usually do, a few days later.

There are half a dozen white-knuckle rides, some of which I remember from my youth, some of which are clearly newfangled inventions and spend far too much time upside down for my liking. The children—well, the boys—are so excited and hyper. Tanya is far too cool to be hyper about anything. She is tottering over the mud in her four-inch platform shoes, pretending that it isn't a problem. Have you ever tried to find anything to do that will keep both a fifteen-year-old girl and a four-year-old boy entertained? Don't. It's impossible. Totally impossible. Tanya would rather be with her friends, and she's made that patently clear, but if I don't insist on her coming with us, then I won't see her at all. It's something we'll have to address. But not today. Not after the mascara, the rings, Orville and everything else. Not today.

I wonder if children have a capacity to ignore the peeling paint, the fixed shotguns on the rifle range, the bent, blunt darts that haven't a hope in hell of connecting with any of the playing cards and hoops that are too small to fit over the glass bowls of the fish who have lost the will to live.

Thomas is smiling broadly, and I'm so relieved because he has seemed so down recently. And it's hardly surprising, I know. I hug him to me. "Okay?" I say.

He nods. I miss the children so much, I can't tell you. When I'm not with them, there's a gaping hole inside me that, try as he might, Christian just isn't able to fill. No one else can.

Elliott is beside himself with joy. Anything that has the potential to be life-threatening, extremely dirty and involves spending lots of other people's money hits the spot in Elliott's book. Every single thing we have passed so far Elliott has wanted to have a go on, whether it turns him the wrong way up, shoots him sideways or just simply tries to terrify him. My son is indiscriminate in his desire to be shaken about every which way. As you'll probably guess, that's exactly how I'm feeling without the need to part with a pound for a fairground ride.

"Let's go on the dodgems," Christian suggests. He's entering into the spirit of this very gamely, and I love him all the more for it. "Elliott," he says, "come with me." And before I can say anything, he snatches my youngest son's hand and they race to the dodgems, which are idling in between bouts.

"Come on, Tom!" Thomas and I chase after them, and Tanya paddles in our wake. Thomas grabs a dodgem, easing himself into the driver's seat, and exchanges the pound I've given him for a token with the grubby man who's jumping between the cars with the ease of someone who has done it for too many years. "Want to go on with Tom?" I ask my daughter. She shakes her head and lurks at the side of the rink, leaning insolently against one of the brightly painted supports, arms hugging her leather jacket around her.

I jump in beside Thomas, and a man with all the clarity of diction of a British Rail announcer mutters that *"We're off!"* And we are, shrieking and screaming at the other cars as I direct Thomas to smash into as many dodgems as we can hunt down. Never has being a back-seat driver been so much fun. For a moment I forget where I am and who I am, caring about nothing but bracing myself against the pain of another bump. Smashing legitimately into other cars is very therapeutic. And then I see Tanya out of the corner of my eye. She is watching Christian with a strange expression on her face and it jolts me as surely as my lover's dodgem hitting us squarely in the side does, that Tanya, in her own teenage way, feels the same about Christian as I do. The man collecting money on the dodgems is watching Tanya, but she is oblivious to him. Her eyes are following one face. A face that is laughing and smiling and shouting encouragement to Elliott, roaring in triumph, and is completely unaware of her. And I can't express the emotion I feel when I realize that Christian is closer to her age than he is to mine. How would I feel if she brought someone like Christian home? It isn't beyond the bounds of possibility, let's face it.

The dodgems grind to an abrupt halt, and we unfurl ourselves from the cramped cars unscathed. Physically, at least. My back is aching and so is my head, and we've only been here ten minutes.

"Let's go on the Ghost Train," Elliott yells, and we splash across the mud to some cracked plastic ghosts that glow yellow in the gloomy light. "Coming, Tanya?" I shout as we all leap into one of the rickety carts shaped like a coffin.

"I'll wait here," she says. And I hope it is fear of being seen by her friends at somewhere so tragically uncool that is making her hang back. We trundle into a tunnel lined with lime-green fur fabric and what appear to be old sheets, and Elliott starts to vent forth earsplitting screams before anything has happened. And I try to push down the feeling that this cheap and tacky ghost train, with its lurking Lurex phantoms and macabre, staged shocks, holds infinitely less terror for me than my daily life.

I am broke. Utterly and absolutely. And I suppose it wouldn't have mattered so much if I hadn't just rendered myself gainfully unemployed. We have eaten toffee apples, candy floss and hot dogs. In that order. We have been on the dodgems, the Ghost Train, the Twister, the Sky Rocket, the Wild Mouse and the Thunder Racer. Tanya is clutching a pile of moth-eaten soft toys, a WWF poster featuring an extremely dubious greased-up orange wrestler called The Rock and a goldfish, yet to be christened, which is not looking well already.

I am clinging on to a cup of warm, hairy-chested tea in a polystyrene cup and trying to get my center of gravity to agree to go back to where it belongs. The boys are drinking Coke and are pink-cheeked and grinning. And the rain has held off. Mostly. I think, with one notable exception, you could count this as a fairly successful day.

"Let's go on the Waltzer!" Elliott shouts.

"You've been on enough," I remind him, ever the voice of reason.

"Oh. Just one more." My son pouts like Marilyn Monroe.

"Elliott, you'll be sick."

"I won't."

"You will. You've just had Coke and hot dogs."

"Just one last thing," he begs.

"I'll take him," Christian ventures.

"You'll be sick too," I warn.

He grins. "I promise I won't."

"Okay." Elliott takes hold of Christian's hand and they exchange smiles, and you won't believe how much that means to me. "Do you want to go too, Thomas?" But my older son shakes his head. Thomas has more sense than the rest of us put together.

"One go!" I say sternly, trying too late to reassert some sort of authority in the face of being viewed as a pushover.

"We won't be long," Christian assures me, and they head off to be twirled and whirled again.

"Shall we go and watch?" We follow them, and by the time we reach the Waltzer, Christian and Elliott are trapped in one of the cars by a big metal bar and are meandering slowly round the track as the ride picks up speed. Elliott's knuckles are white from gripping. Christian has his arm round him, and my son is tucked into his side with a look on his face approaching ecstasy. We lean on the rails round the side and can feel the vibrations beneath our feet. Everything is clanking and rattling more than the chains in the Ghost Train, and I wonder how often any of these rides are checked for safety.

The ride picks up speed. Thudding music is pumping at some hideous volume out of the speakers above us. When I was a girl, Waltzer music always blared out "All Right Now" by Free, which still seems to have a certain melodious charm compared to this stuff. Sorry, I'm doing my mother again. "DO YOU WANT TO GO FASTER!" the man in the central control box shouts. The lights flash on and off, faster and faster. I hear Elliott scream, "Yes!" above everyone else. Their car comes round and they are a blur, huddled into one corner, hanging on for dear life and my stomach joins the lurching. "DO YOU WANT TO GO FASTER!" Elliott is virtually lying on the seat now, the car trying to vest itself of the insubstantial weight of his body. Christian has hold of him by his jacket. *"Yeeeeeesssssss!"* he shouts as he passes us. The ride seems endless, and just as I think I can bear it no longer, the lights cease flickering madly, the insane rattling slows to a series of worrying clonks and the cars instead of whirling like dervishes, spin as gracefully as ballerinas to a halt.

They stop just in front of us. Thomas rushes to open the bar. Christian is laughing and sitting Elliott upright. My little boy gets out of the car, gripping its sides as it starts to whirl again, and staggers toward me, his legs trembling like Slinkies and his face chalk white. His eyes appear to be rotating in his head. *"That,"* he says, "was absolutely brilliant!"

Christian gets out and comes up behind him grinning from ear to ear. I smile at him and want him to know that I really do appreciate how much effort he is putting into trying to get to know my children. Christian answers my smile—he knows how much this means to me. And I know that somehow this is all going to work out all right. At that very moment, Elliott also turns round, smiling cheesily, and is promptly and heartily sick all over Christian's trousers.

CHAPTER 50

Ed and Orla didn't go to Budleigh Salterton. Mainly because neither of them were quite sure where it was. Instead, they went to Bath. Ed had this notion that Orla would enjoy it, being American and all that. If they didn't get on, then surely there were plenty of Roman bits and pieces and ornate buildings to keep her happy? And Ali always said the shopping was great—which was something he never felt qualified to comment on. But it probably didn't matter which side of the Atlantic a woman was born on to appreciate great shops.

They stayed in a hotel just on the outskirts. A comfortable thirteenth-century manor house in pale gold Bath stone set in its own grounds. Orla had nearly fainted with delight when they swooped into the gravel drive and wound their way up through a field full of miserable-looking cows huddling together in the rain, past a brimming duck pond to the iron-studded front door. She had nearly fainted with shock when they had been forced to walk on planks from the car park to the house because everywhere was so flooded. But then this had been the wettest winter on record and the records went back a fairly long way. This was not going to be a weekend for tramping through the countryside, and it was a shame because Ed hadn't tramped anywhere for a while and had started to look forward to it. Or, at least, he'd started to look forward to it once he was out of Ali's radar gaze. She had sussed straight away that this was no business trip, try to fool her, and himself, as he might. And he had felt so guilty, which was a bit rich, all things considered.

Ed had stayed here once before years ago when he'd been filming a promotional extravaganza for dog biscuits, of all things, to be screened in premier pet shops across the nation. So some things never change. The hotel had, though. Beyond recognition. It had been subjected to extensive refurbishment, and everything that had been faded with age and elegantly worn on his previous visit seemed to have been replaced with brand spanking new antique replicas.

They checked in and climbed the lurid carpet to the first floor and their room. Deciding that everyone in the thirteenth century must have been midgets, Ed ducked down through the low door that led to their bedroom. Carpet aside, the rooms were a definite improvement. A roaring log fire greeted them, and beyond that a four-poster bed complete with heavy silk drapes adorned the center of the room. The only small snag that Ed could see was that the bed was most definitely a double and not the twin beds he had requested when booking. Although, on reflection, it seemed a very stupid thing to do, to assume that two fully grown, emotionally stable and commitment-free adults were going to spend the night divided by a bedside table and a yard of carpet, ghastly patterned or not. But it was a daunting thought. How do you spend the night with someone, particularly in the carnal sense, that you've never even held hands with, let alone seen naked? This presumably was just another one of the taxing puzzles of our times. And one he'd only had to face once before, and that had been aided and abetted by copious amounts of local hooch, which had all but blotted out the memory of it. Ed's mouth was suddenly dry. He could do with a drink now, come to think of it.

His one and only one-night stand had been a lesson to him in many ways, although Ali might not appreciate the educational value of it if he were to confess to her now or had done then. He'd seen too many of his friends and colleagues strike out to grasp the alluring flower of adultery only to have it turn to a stinging nettle in their hands. And a very expensive stinging nettle too.

He wondered if this little liaison was helping him one step further along to the divorce courts, and questioned his wisdom in agreeing to it. Perhaps he should have viewed Ali's indiscretion as an educational jaunt, and then they might not have been in this situation.

He'd narrowly avoided seeing the lovely Nicola Jones naked too. She'd been rather more keen to disrobe herself in the kitchen than he'd thought appropriate for a nursery-school teacher. Not that he hadn't wanted to see her minus her Laura Ashley, but he was so totally unprepared for it. Spontaneity and sex were definitely out of bounds since the children had arrived and it was hard getting his mind, and other parts of his body, back into leaping-around mode. And that was another thing. If it was difficult enough to find the opportunity to have sexual relations with your wife because of being interrupted by one or more bored and/or weeping children, just think how much the odds went up when you added a stranger to the equation. The kitchen table had just not been an option for him. He had tried to explain his predicament nicely, but Nicola had left in the early hours of the morning clearly feeling rejected at having had to chase him round the chairs. At least this setup—i.e., no children—was more conducive to a little adult fun should it be on offer.

Ed's eyes traveled round the room. In lieu of a separate bathroom there was a Victorian enameled claw-foot bath in a corner of the room and a matching washstand complete with water pitcher and the added modern accoutrement of skillfully concealed Ideal Standard new millennium taps, for which Ed was truly grateful. There was no screen to separate it or hide behind—it just stood there sturdily slap bang in front of them. It looked like he was going to be seeing Orla naked long before bedtime. Thank God for small mercies that, at least, the loo wasn't an open-plan affair too!

His companion dropped her small holdall to the floor. "This is just so English," she said. Which Ed wasn't awfully sure was a compliment these days. "I love it!"

Orla swept past him into the room, throwing herself onto the bed, which responded by enveloping her in its lacy coverlet. "It's so romantic," she breathed.

There was a bottle of champagne in a bucket of ice on the coffee table, rapidly getting warm in the face of the inferno of the log fire. Ed hadn't had the forethought to order it, but he was glad that someone had.

"Champagne?" he suggested.

Orla propped herself up on an embankment of small, silky cushions stacked on the bed. "You are a wonderful man, Ed," she breathed. "I'd love some."

Ed set the two flutes on the tray beside them. He wondered what had happened in the intervening twenty years since he had last been on the dating scene. No one had ever shown the slightest bit of interest in dirty dancing with him then.

Orla kicked off her shoes.

Ed lifted the champagne from the bucket, wiped the ice water away with a cloth and a flourish. Perhaps a few gray hairs and a certain air of suave maturity was what women wanted these days? He smiled a sultry Roger Moore smile across the room.

Orla stripped off her coat and threw it to the floor. With her red lips pouting, she started to unbutton her blouse. "Bring it to bed," she instructed throatily.

Ed's nimble fingers froze on the bottle as his cork popped prematurely and shot straight across the room, knocking a grinning pot dog off the mantelpiece with one fell swoop.

They'd gone down to dinner late, the delights of Roman Bath in torrential rain having been forsaken for torrid pleasures of the flesh in a four-poster bed.

The dining room was filled with lovey-dovey couples holding hands across tables set for two. The restaurant was Egon Ronay–recommended and the food was sublime, but no one seemed to be doing much eating. The subdued lighting had been taken to coal-mine proportions—there were candles on the tables, candles in the alcoves, candles competing with the light from log fires at either end of the room. An azure-blue swimming pool housed in a tropical oasis of a conservatory adjoined the dining area, and candles shaped like lotus flowers floated serenely across its untroubled surface.

Orla smiled up at him. She looked lovely. And not a little flickery.

"You told Alicia this was a business trip?" she said.

"Not really. I just didn't tell her it wasn't." Ed savored his wine. "Besides," he admitted, "I wasn't entirely sure myself."

Orla slid her fingers into his. "But you're sure now?"

"Yes," he said. Well, it seemed churlish not to, but the truth was he still wasn't sure. Orla was beautiful. She was clever, looked great in a business suit and was very organized. What more could a man want in a woman?

Ed didn't know, but he knew there was no buzz in his stomach like there should be. No stirring in his loins. Although he was wearing a slight smirk. But then he had just had sex—and pretty good sex—for the first time in weeks, and he was only human after all. He'd felt that with Nicola Jones too, but then the only woman who had ever made his stomach churn was Ali—and that wasn't just with some of the meals she produced. Ed turned his attention back to his Dover sole.

"Are you going to tell her that we're an item?"

Ed choked and sloshed down a gulp of mineral water. The other diners stopped to glare at him. "Bone," he croaked, smiling weakly at the other tables.

"She needs to know."

"Does she?" he said, dabbing his mouth with his napkin. "I don't want to rush this."

"She'll find out soon enough," Orla reasoned.

"Elliott will probably tell her."

"I mean when you come to the States with me."

Ed felt moved to choke again, but knew he couldn't get away with blaming it on a fishbone twice.

"You are coming, aren't you?"

Was this part of the deal? he wondered. Had it always been? And if it was, did that have to be a bad thing? Was there any reason why he and Orla couldn't go on from here to make a great relationship? But then was it wise to rush into the first shoe shop you came to and buy the first pair you could grab without trying any others on?

"Harrison Ford is waiting, Ed," she said. "And so am I."

Making a mental note to kill Trevor, Ed raised his glass and clinked it to hers. Orla's eyes flashed and blazed in the candlelight. A triumphant smile curled the corners of her mouth.

"To Harrison Ford," he said. "And to us."

CHAPTER 51

If you could be any woman in the world, who would you be? Right now, I'd be Andrea Corr. Permanently. She's petite, extraordinarily pretty, can belt out a tune and looks like she doesn't get involved in any way, whatsoever, with vomiting children. What more could you want?

Next to her, the other two Corr sisters look like regurgitated Nolans and the brother, poor old Jim Corr, looks like a bit of a gonk. But then lined up against such beauty, it would be hard not to. I used to be content being myself, but now I've got all sorts of bits that make me dissatisfied. I examine my face every morning to see if any of my myriad wrinkles have dared to edge another millimeter into my face. When I find another job—thanks again, Kath Brown—I'm going to set up a face-lift fund for when I'm fifty. Or maybe even forty. Depending on how bad things get.

They say that stress is aging, in which case my insides feel about ninety-four. I have almost continual stomachache and a crick in my neck like Ed always used to. My periods are completely up the spout, and I'm terrified of becoming pregnant. Ed, after much persuasion, had the chop—mainly because I'd threatened him with two house bricks in the garden shed if he didn't. We never really got the hang of condoms—something for which Elliott should be eternally grateful. You wouldn't think there was too much to go wrong, but we always managed to cock it up. No comments, thank you!

Christian and I also exhibit a certain carelessness in the condom department, which surprises me, considering how much he goes on about not being able to stand children. Hasn't anyone told him the cabbage patch is a myth? And I worry about AIDS, but I haven't said anything, because it seems to make a statement about not trusting your partner, which I know is stupid, but I can't help it. I just hope Christian's short past isn't as colorful as his paintings.

I'm sitting here stressing about all this in my lounge and watching *The National Lottery Show,* hoping for a miracle. And a miracle it would have to be, because I never have time to buy a ticket. I have a drink in my hand and my feet on a footstool. And you will not believe this…brace yourself for it…despite his protestation of being a no-go zone as far as ankle biters are concerned, Christian is upstairs bathing Elliott. I think that's worth repeating. *Christian* is *bathing* Elliott! As much a miracle as me winning the lottery without a ticket, I think you'll agree.

This is mainly because I wept in the car all the way home, which, incidentally, made it an interesting drive. Elliott continued to produce vomit the color of candy floss and chopped-up sausage, and Christian, finding a strength of stomach from somewhere that was truly admirable, nursed him all the way home.

I don't know how Social Services or even Ed would feel about the political correctness of a strange man bathing our four-year-old son, but at the moment I don't care. There's a lot of laughter drifting down the stairs, and that suits me fine. I have had enough of real life, really I have. Downing some more gin, I ponder on the day's events. I wanted it to be so great. And, once again, Elliott steals the show. I think I'm going to sell that child for organ donation, starting with his head. The other two are no trouble at all. Or perhaps their version of trouble simply pales into insignificance when faced with a brother who is the world expert on trouble. I think he studied under Bart Simpson.

I have no sympathy for his illness, at all. It is entirely self-inflicted and, therefore, deserving of utmost contempt. If I'd bathed him, I'd have scrubbed him all over with a loofah just to make sure he remembered it. This gin is going down very quickly.

There is a thunder of feet down the stairs, and two faces appear at the door. Christian is clearly a man of his word. He promised not to be sick, and he, at least, has kept all his junk food safely inside him. He is, however, soaked, quite literally, through to the skin. "I've someone here to say good-night," he says, and pushes Elliott into the room.

Elliott is scrubbed and gorgeous and his damp hair is curling round his face, framing it like a lovely little angel. Christian has dressed him in his cutest pajamas, and what's left of Barney is on parade. Elliott comes up and throws his arms round my neck, cuddling me. "I'm sorry about being sick, Mummy," he says, and I feel so awful that I've not looked after him properly that I'm going to have to drink some more gin to get over it.

"That's all right, darling," I coo—yes, I do. "It wasn't your fault."

"I think it was mine," Christian says guiltily.

"Christian's going to read me a story," my beautiful, wide-eyed child says.

"Are you sure he didn't say he was going to bludgeon you over the head with a book?"

"No." Elliott slithers off my knee. "Christian likes me."

Christian smiles indulgently. Elliott cups his hand to his mouth to whisper, and in a voice that could wake anyone unfortunate enough to be in one of the several cemeteries in the vicinity says, "And I like Christian!"

Much later when Christian must have worked his way through Elliott's entire stash of storybooks, plus a few that he'd nicked from Thomas, my lover finally appears. It's nine o'clock, and I look up from *Parkinson,* the only talk show I know where the host can actually string two sentences together. Parky is trying to get some sense out of the gorgeous, if slightly wrinkled, Welsh crooner Tom Jones and is failing. Christian flops down next to me. I pass him the gin bottle and a glass. He puts the glass to one side and swigs it straight from the bottle. I don't blame him.

"You survived," I say.

Christian turns his eyes to me. "It's hard work, isn't it?"

"Try doing it every day." I raise my eyebrows in the very superior way that those with children do. "And it's years before we can force Elliott to leave home."

Christian takes my hand and fiddles with my nails. "I can see why you miss them so much."

"Can you?" I didn't mean to sound quite so incredulous.

"Of course I can. Elliott's wonderful. He's his own little person," he says.

"Bastard child from hell, you mean."

"You'd be lost without him."

And perhaps it's the gin, but my throat closes up and my eyes start to water.

"Don't cry." Christian pulls me to him. "I could get used to this parenting lark yet," he says chirpily.

I sniff. "One clearing up of vomit does not a parent make."

"I am trying though." And even though he is nineteen years older than Elliott, he is every bit as cute.

"You did brilliantly," I say and squeeze his hand. "You're a hit with Thomas too."

Christian screws up his nose. "I don't think Tanya likes me."

What can I say? I can hardly voice my fear that my daughter might like him just a tad too much. As it is, I have to compete for her affection with Ed. This is a situation I don't even want to confront.

"She'll come round," I mutter.

Parky moves on to David Beckham, who I know is a footballer and, although he's possibly not the sharpest pencil in the box, he is very sweet and uncomplicated. Or perhaps I just have a greater understanding of younger men now.

"Shall I stay here the night?" Christian asks.

I shake my head. "I don't think I could cope with that. Even though it's my house too, I feel very strange being here. It's going to be weird enough to be back in my own bed. I don't think I can face sharing it," I confess. "Even though I'd like to."

"We'll have a quick drink," he says, tipping some more gin into my glass and his mouth. "And then I'll go home."

"You'll come back tomorrow?"

"I promised Elliott I'd teach him how to use a skateboard."

"I'll pencil in a visit to Casualty then...."

Christian laughs. He clearly thinks I'm joking.

CHAPTER 52

Christian was sitting in front of the television with a cup of hot chocolate snuggled in his lap, flicking through the TV channels trying to find some late-night viewing that might involve gratuitous sex or football. Currently both were eluding him. He was missing Ali and feeling distinctly uneasy about the thought of her spending the night back in her own bed in the bosom of her family, and him banished to the outside of this cozy enclave with his nose pressed against the cold glass. The hot chocolate and a Channel 4 documentary about the life and times of Benny Hill were not providing the comfort he sought.

Rebecca came in wearing a minimalist skirt and a top that looked like two Dairylea Cheese triangle wrappers joined together by a piece of glittery dental floss. She stopped in midstride.

"You are not staying in on a Saturday night," she tutted, grabbing some money from her handbag on the table.

"So what if I am?" Christian tried to look engrossed in *Heroes of Comedy*. "I'm waiting for *Match of the Day* to start."

There was an outpouring of the most forced, empty canned laughter he'd ever heard.

Rebecca put her hand on her tiny, jutty-out hip. "Who's playing?"

"Er…"

Rebecca wagged her finger at him. "She is turning you into a boring old git," she said.

"Just because I don't want to get off my face every weekend anymore? It's called growing up, Becs. You ought to try it."

"So where is Lady Bountiful tonight?"

"At home. With her children."

"And your presence wasn't required?"

Christian wished he'd got a bottle of Vodka Absolut in his hand—you couldn't do mean and moody with hot chocolate.

"It must feel very different for you to be at someone else's beck and call," Rebecca continued when he didn't answer. "I have to hand it to her, she's certainly got you where she wants you."

Christian sank lower into the sofa.

"Come out with us," Rebecca said.

"I haven't got any money."

"It's never stopped you before." Rebecca sat on the arm of the sofa and twisted one of Christian's curls through her fingers. "Raid piggy."

"Piggy helped us out of our last predicament, remember?"

Rebecca tutted again. "I'll sub you," she said. "In fact, I'll treat you. Call it my way of saying that I forgive you for dumping me because you couldn't stand commitment and then shacking up with someone old enough to be my mother with three brats in tow."

"You're all heart, Becs," Christian sighed.

"Come on. I'm only going to The Rat to meet Robbie and a few mates."

"Why are you dressed like that?"

"Because I live in the vain hope that there might be someone there worth pulling," she said. "Come on. We'll just get there in time for last orders. It'll cheer you up."

"I'm not depressed."

"Yeah, right." They both looked at Benny Hill. "It's ages since the three of us have been out on the town together. As mates."

"Since Ali arrived," Christian said pointedly.

"Well, now that you come to mention it…" Rebecca risked a smile.

Christian put down his hot chocolate. "I'll have to come out to keep you quiet, won't I?"

"There is one other way, Chris," she said. "Kiss me." She

leaned forward, threatening to burst free of her triangles, and covered his mouth with hers. The kiss was long and searching and pleasantly familiar.

Rebecca broke away from him and pressed her lips together, tracing round them with her tongue. She looked at him ruefully. "But I guess that's not on the agenda."

Christian stood up. "Let's go to The Rat," he said.

The Rat was the pub that closing time forgot. Christian remembered his last drink. Or at least he thought he did. Robbie bought it for him, and possibly the ten previous ones. It was a Tequila Stuntman, Robbie's invention, which was a sadistic progression from a Tequila Slammer that had seemed like a really good idea at the time. Instead of licking the salt from the back of his hand, downing the tequila in one and then squirting the lime juice in his mouth, his "friend"—and it was pertinent to use the word in quotation marks—had persuaded him to snort the salt, down two shots of tequila and then squirt himself in the eye with the lime juice. In hindsight, it was probably that which made him fall off the table.

Now it was some ungodly hour in the morning and he was propping up the wall by the front door of the house, with no idea how the journey back from the pub had been accomplished. His eyes were still smarting from their lime-juice assault and the salt had dried out the inside of his nose so that he was having to breathe through his mouth. Robbie stood in the road singing "Land of Hope and Glory" at the top of his voice, sucking, still, at a wedge of well-chewed lime. A window opened farther down the street and a voice shouted, "Shut the fuck up!" And, perhaps surprisingly, Robbie did.

Rebecca was searching all her pockets for her key, while Robbie took the opportunity to urinate loudly on the black plastic bin bag next door had left unwisely on their path.

When Rebecca finally opened the door, they all fell inside, sprawling on the welcome mat and the black and white Victorian tiles of the porch. Christian was giggling loudly.

"Toast," Robbie croaked. "I need toast." And he staggered off toward the kitchen, feeling along the wall for support as he went.

"Count me out, mate," Christian slurred. "I need my bed."

"Me too," Rebecca said. Christian put his arm round her and

somehow managed to haul her up without falling over himself again. They stumbled up the stairs, tripping over each other, laughing, falling down and finally crawling on all fours to the top of the landing.

Rebecca straightened herself up, leaning against the door frame in an attempt to stop swaying and pulled Christian up toward her. He stopped, arms round her waist, their breathing audible in the sudden stillness. Her hair smelt of cigarettes and her mouth of booze and cheese-and-onion crisps. The triangles of her top were very skewed. She rolled her eyes slightly as she tried to maintain a steady focus.

Rebecca traced her finger across his cheek in a line that wasn't altogether straight. "Tonight was just like old times," she said, smiling lopsidedly, a mixture of drunkenness and sadness. Coy, girlish, bold.

"Yeah," Christian said. He should have taken his hands off her waist, but he had forgotten how he could almost touch the tips of his fingers together in the small of her back and the urge to see how far they could go was gluing them there.

The stubborn remains of Rebecca's lipstick had stained her lips red. The black smear of her eyeliner had given her dark shadows under her eyes, making her look like a heroin addict, vulnerable and vaguely unhealthy. Her fingers grasped for Christian's T-shirt at his shoulder. They were tiny, slender, like the rest of her, the nails painted scarlet. Temptation. "Do you still have that drawing of me over your bed?"

"Huh, huh."

"What does Ali think of it?"

Christian shrugged. "She's never said."

Rebecca wet her lips, and her eyes fixed in a steady stare on his. "Can I come in and look at it?"

"You want to see my etchings?" Christian looked solemn. If he could have found a laugh from somewhere, it might have broken the moment, but like the canned laughter on the television, he couldn't make the right sound. "It's a very old line, Becs."

"It's the best one I can think of," she said, and taking Christian's hand followed him into the bedroom.

CHAPTER 53

Neil parked his aging Citroën half on and half off the curb outside Jemma's shop in the vain hope that if there was a late-night clamping service, they would give him the benefit of the doubt and pass by without troubling him with a yellow boot. Also, Citroëns were bastards to clamp. It had been the main reason he bought one. That and the fact that he couldn't afford a Ferrari.

He had tried to phone Jemma all day yesterday, but had been distracted by Years Five to Eight of St. Apsley's Middle School. The agenda had been sports photos—football, hockey and netball. It was a nightmare taking team photos. Despite the fact that each child had been sent home with a letter duly requesting that parents equip them with their appropriate team garments, invariably half of them turned up without kits. Consequently, on the team photos they came out looking like they'd been dressed from the Lost Property box—which they usually had.

Every time he had actually managed to call Jemma, her phone had been engaged. Or if it wasn't engaged and his heart leapt joyously as it rang, it would only be dashed again by the answerphone cutting in. Last week when he'd rushed away from Ed's and the appealing Miss Jones, he was heading for Jemma's for another "strategy" meeting in the quest to reunite Alicia and Ed. Halfway to her house, his mobile had rung, and Jemma had broken the arrangement, citing a streaming cold as the excuse. And she did sniff convincingly. Since then, he had heard nothing.

It was ridiculous, but Neil seriously felt like he was halfway toward being in love with her. He had missed her so much this week, and he'd found himself looking dewy-eyed at St. Apsley's netball team and not for the reasons you might think. Was it only women whose biological clocks ticked? He had a feeling his might be winding itself up for a chime or two.

He hadn't been able to call today because the wedding season, it seemed, had begun in earnest, and from now until September he would be spending his Saturdays knee-deep in brides draped in satin and raw silk every conceivable color of the rainbow and grumbling wedding parties. It was late and he was on his way back from a particularly boisterous bash in Bermondsey, where the bride had looked big enough to give birth before the priest had pronounced the couple husband and wife and the best man was wearing his tails with an intimidating scowl. It had been a long and busy day, and Neil rubbed the tiredness from his eyes.

Notting Hill was not what you'd call especially "en route" to Camden. But then, where is? In fact, if he'd decided to go through Nottingham, it might have been a less circuitous route, but Jemma wasn't to know that, and he could casually say that he'd dropped in on the off chance, such was his concern over the state of his brother's marriage. Which wasn't actually a million miles from the truth.

The light in her upstairs flat was on and the curtains open, which boded well. Jemma was a girl-about-town, and he had realized as he turned the ignition off that, given it was a Saturday night, she might well have been out on it.

Neil checked his hair in the rearview mirror, spat on his hand and plastered it over his hair to no good effect. He tutted at his image, got out of the car and rubbed his fingers in the chill night air. He should have thought to bring a jacket, but then again he didn't plan on standing out in the cold for too long. Striding across the pavement with his hands in his pockets, he shivered against the freshness of the night. He rang Jemma's bell and lounged against the wall, waiting for her to come. The lights were bright in Calzone's restaurant across the street, and the windows were misting with condensation. He should have tried to phone her before he set off, and then they might have been able to go out to dinner again. Neil glanced at his watch. Maybe it wasn't too late. When there was still no sound of encouraging footsteps, Neil rang the doorbell again. It was freezing out here.

He was torn between ringing the bell again and giving it up as a bad job. Neil backed away from the door and looked up at the window. Jemma was peeping out, trying to see who was downstairs. He waved up at her helpfully, and he thought he saw her frown. A minute later the patter of her feet came down the stairs and she opened the door.

God, she looked fabulous. She was wearing a cream silk kimono, short, with precious little else. Her feet were bare and her tiny toes were painted with pearly peachy polish, which did very strange things to his insides. And her hair was all tangled, although she was trying to smooth it, and she looked even more like Alicia than she normally did.

"Hi," he said.

Jemma pulled her kimono round her. Neil could tell she was cold too. "What are you doing here?"

"Did I get you out of bed?"

Jemma looked round. "Sort of."

"Still got your cold then?"

"What?"

"Your cold."

"Oh, yes," Jemma said, and she sniffed.

"I wanted to talk some more about Ed and Alicia."

"Now?"

"No time like the present," Neil said hopefully.

Jemma looked like she felt differently. More *any* time but the present.

"Ed's going away with another woman," he said. "And Ali is off to the Maldives with her schoolboy."

"She's not?" Jemma let an unhappy stream of air out of her nostrils, which curled like smoke in the cold night. "She didn't tell me."

He was getting a little chilly in his shirtsleeves. "I think this calls for a crisis meeting," he ventured.

"Not now," she said. "I can't. I don't feel up to it."

"Oh." Neil tried his Princess Diana cute eyes. "I'm so worried about them."

"Me too," she said. "But there's nothing I can do now. I'll call you."

He couldn't believe this! He was being given the brush-off. He'd driven miles through driving rain and snow—well, not really—to get here and she wasn't even going to let him in for a quick cuppa. "When?" he said pathetically.

"Soon," she promised, but he didn't like the way she looked over her shoulder when she said it.

"This is important to me, Jemma."

"And to me," she replied. "We'll get together soon. Night, Neil." And she shut the door rather too hastily for his liking. Her feet pattered away from him back up the stairs to the warmth of her flat. Neil stood looking bemused at the closed door, wind whipping round his neck.

He hunched his shoulders and shuffled back to his car. This was not how it was supposed to go. He was supposed to go inside for one thing, have a few sociable drinks and then they'd have a brief chat about what twits their respective siblings were, by which time he'd have drunk far too much to be able to drive, and where could you get a cab at this time of night, wasn't it always a problem, and Jemma was supposed to have offered to share her bed for the night. So, what was wrong with fantasizing? Nothing except that fantasies rarely came true.

That's why he was climbing back into his car with nothing to look forward to but the joy of a bag of soggy chips from the Chinese chippy at the end of his road. If it was still open. Knowing his luck, it would probably close as he drew in sight of it. He sighed as he went to start the engine. At that moment, Jemma came to the window and looked out. Perhaps she had changed her mind? Neil thought joyously. A bit of Night Nurse could work wonders. Then he noticed the shock of blond hair go past the window behind her and sucked in his breath without meaning to. There was someone else in the flat. No wonder she was looking so tousled—she'd got a bloke in there! Another bloke. A bloke who wasn't him! Had all that flirting, all that fluttering of eyelids, just been a con? He'd thought there was at least a chance that Jemma had felt the same way he did. He'd worn a suede jacket for that woman! And flared trousers. He couldn't believe that all the time she'd been playing with someone else's ball. Perhaps it was just a mate she had in there. But then, if it was a mate, why couldn't he have gone in too? Surely he wasn't so embarrassing, despite his dress sense?

There was only one way to find out whether the potential love of his life was getting jiggy with someone other than him. Stake-out time. Neil clicked on the ignition, tuned the radio into Virgin FM and hunkered down in his seat, wishing, not for the first time, that he'd brought a nice, warm coat.

There was a knocking sound going on in his head. Neil sat bolt upright and banged his knees on the steering wheel, struggling to get his eyes to focus. A breakfast presenter on the radio was chattering wildly about nothing in particular, and Neil realized with a shock that it was rather more daylight than he had expected it to be. The sun streamed through the windscreen, making him wince. The knocking came again. It wasn't in his head, it was on the window of his car. Jemma was standing in the road with a cup of tea in her hand.

Neil wound the window down.

"I brought this for you," she said.

Neil looked grateful. It felt like a canary had fallen asleep in his mouth during the night, and he was as stiff as a board. It had to be said that a Citroën wasn't quite as comfortable as a Slumberland when it came to a good night's sleep.

"Thanks," he croaked, and reached out for the cup, which Jemma didn't seem keen to relinquish.

"Why are you still here?" she asked.

"Er..." Neil said, not even sure why he was there himself. A steady stream of traffic buffeted the car as it drove by.

"Wouldn't your car start?"

"Er...yes. Er...no."

"Or were you spying on me, Neil?"

"Er...yes," he admitted sheepishly.

"Do you think you had any right to?"

"Er...probably not."

"Definitely not, I'd say."

"I can explain," Neil said.

Jemma was wearing jeans and a beaded jacket, and the color of the beads picked out the flames in her luxuriant red hair and the round red patches of anger on her cheeks. "Can you?"

"No. Not really." He smiled wanly.

"Don't ever sit outside my flat again, Neil," she said. "Not for any reason."

Jemma threw the cup of tea in his face and then handed him the cup and saucer through the window.

"Right," he said as he dripped tea into his lap. Then Jemma flounced off and got into a huge silver Mercedes parked farther down the pavement. And as it drove away, Neil felt a little light go out in his heart.

CHAPTER 54

Christian is very quiet. And white.

"Hangover?"

He nods and then looks as if he regrets it.

"Did you go out?"

"No." He forgoes a shake of the head. "Watched *Match of the Day* with Rob."

"Who was playing?"

"Er…"

I smile indulgently. "It must have been a great match."

"Er…"

"Not that it matters," I say. "I haven't a clue who any of the teams are anyway. Want some tea?"

There is an infinitesimal movement that indicates a yes. "Advil? Dark glasses?" I think that's a yes to all of them. His eyes are the cerise-pink color of pain, and every time he blinks I can tell that his eyelids are grating over his pupils like coarse-grade sandpaper. His nose is running and he is sniffing tiredly.

"Give me a minute," Christian says hoarsely. "I'll be fine."

"You must have done a lot of cheering."

Christian sinks lower toward the table. "Yeah."

Elliott comes into the kitchen and leans up against Christian's chair. "Are we going to do skateboarding?"

"In a minute." Christian is looking less than convincing. I turn away to hide my smile.

"Anything to eat? Eggs and bacon?"

Christian gives an involuntary shudder. "No. No bacon."

"Just eggs?"

"No. No eggs."

"A minute's gone," says Elliott.

I think Christian is beginning to realize that having a hangover does not preclude you from parental duties. A child who wants to be entertained cares little for any fragility in your constitution. I bet he wishes that he'd stayed at home in his cozy bed rather than rushing round here first thing this morning.

If Christian spent most of last night drinking, I lay awake most of the night worrying. Don't ask me what about. Everything is the short answer. The universe was bombarding me with worry vibes. I even got to wondering why I'd failed my maths "O" level, and that was about a hundred years ago and hasn't made the slightest difference to anything at all, nothing whatsoever, since. I tied myself in several knots over a scarf I have that belonged to my grandmother that's been kicking around since the 1950s which now has a nice hole fraying in one corner—not surprisingly. It was about three o'clock when I decided I ought to ask Jemma's advice on stopping the steady erosion of the fragile material. It's the sort of thing she would know about. She acts like she's the world expert on everything anyway. And then I worried why I hadn't thought of doing that earlier. See? I think I was avoiding worrying about the big issues really, like how are my children coping now that we are a dysfunctional family and how I'm going to pay my bills now that Kath Brown has bulleted me. I nearly, nearly rang Christian, but you know how it is. I didn't want to wake him up and then have him lying awake worrying that I was worrying.

"I'll come and watch you practice what I taught you yesterday, and then, when I'm feeling a bit better—" Christian looks remorsefully at me "—I'll show you some more. Go and put your knee-pads on." Personally, I'd be happier if my child was wearing full body armor. Elliott, placated momentarily, heads for the door.

"How much time did that buy me?" Christian asks.

"With Elliott, not much. He's far too astute to allow a mere adult to blackmail him." I am quietly pleased at how quickly my lover is learning to manipulate his way round the minefield of child care.

"I'd better go out then." Christian pushes away from the table rather unsteadily.

As he passes me, head hung low, I touch his arm. "I missed you last night," I say.

"I missed you too." And he looks so hang-dog that it makes me smile again. "I love you, Ali," he says, his misery turning to seriousness. "You do know that?"

"Yes." I nod reassuringly, but my heart starts to pound. Though at times, I do wonder why, I want to add. This can't be an easy situation for my young, beautiful boy. He takes my hands and puts them to his lips. His mouth is dry, his lips cracked and I bet his breath smells like a brewery.

"I'm sorry I got drunk."

"It doesn't matter," I say. "You're entitled to some fun. You're young. And foolish."

"I am," he says, and follows Elliott out into the sunshine. And I stand at the kitchen sink and wonder why I feel like crying. I start to prepare some food on autopilot, moving around my kitchen with a familiarity that belies the fact I haven't been a permanent resident for quite some time.

I can hear Elliott giggling, the carefree laughter of childhood, and I feel awful that in our cruel adult way we are compromising him, blighting his memories, marring the days that should be all sunshine and roses. It gives me a quiet surge of warmth to know that something as simple as a skateboard can provide temporary relief from his worries. Will I ever find the right time or the right words to tell him that we, Ed and I, never meant any of this to happen? It wasn't in our plan. Yet, all over the country fathers, and sometimes mothers too, are leaving their children. The divorce rate is so high now that I wonder it's not possible to see them streaming away in droves from their suburban houses in their Ford Mondeos—a mass exodus of confused, bewildered, displaced adults. What are the statistics now? One in three? Every minute someone is born and every minute someone dies, and in the blink-of-an-eye gap in between, someone leaves their family to the clutches of the legal system. I wonder how many of these leavings are premeditated, planned over months, years, of unhappiness and deadness? Men frustrated with their lives, their work, their softening stomachs, their receding hairlines. Women who, tired of years of picking up socks, decide to find themselves before it is too late and they are lost completely in a world of detergent adverts. And maybe for some of them it isn't like that. How many of them consider themselves happily married and then, through a series of silly and unfortunate events, find themselves outside that marriage, adrift on a raft of accusation and recriminations?

I call the boys in for lunch, and amid the vast issues of the breakdown of family life, still find the time to admonish myself for being a lousy cook.

We have finished lunch, such as it was. All that Ed has in the freezer is pizza, and I feel like offering to do a big shop at Tesco's for him to stock up, but I'm not sure how he'd take it.

Christian is struggling to force down some pizza, but I can tell his heart and his stomach aren't in it. But then, the pizza does vaguely resemble roadkill. He's looking a lot perkier though, and some blood has returned to his face. Elliott's has no blood, anywhere. And I'm truly grateful. His skateboarding lesson has again passed without incident which I feel is something of an achievement for an activity that is so potentially lethal. Elliott has decided that Christian is totally cool and they are happily bonding.

I prized Thomas away from Harry Potter to join us. I worry that Thomas is becoming quieter—along with everything else. Tanya has also graced us with her presence. She is wearing too much makeup and too little clothing. My daughter is treating Christian with an air of studied indifference that screams she also thinks he is totally cool.

"I want to pop round to Aunty Jemma's," I say. "Anyone want to come?" My children stare blankly at me. "Don't all shout at once."

"I want to stay here with Christian," Elliott announces.

"Me too," Thomas says, which is a bit surprising.

"Tanya?"

She shrugs.

"Is that a yes shrug or a no shrug?"

She shrugs again, but more emphatically.

"Shall I go on my own?"

"Yes," Elliott says, peeling a mushroom from the abandoned remains of his pizza crust and licking it. "We'll take care of Christian."

"Oh good." I look at Christian, who seems unconcerned about being abandoned in the depths of my family. "Is that okay with you?"

"Yes," he says, and I wonder if he's still a bit drunk.

"I won't be long. I just want to borrow some bikinis and bits for the holiday." I want to ask her about mending Grandma's scarf too, but don't dare confess this anxiety in public. "Are you sure you'll be okay?"

They all stare at me as if I'm mad. "Well, I'll go then," I say hesitantly. "There's ice cream if anyone wants it."

"Fine." Christian gives me a wan smile over his plate littered with pepperoni debris. "I'll sort it out." And my children look at him as if they have no doubt that he can.

I shoot over to Jemma's, all in a flap and a panic. And when I get there, she's not really in the mood to talk. She's all grunty and distant, but obviously doesn't want to tell me why. I keep looking at my watch, and that irritates her a bit more.

"I never see you these days, Alicia," she moans.

"Come back with me now," I say. "I don't want to leave Christian alone with the children for too long."

"Why? Do you think they'll scare him off?"

The thought had crossed my mind. "He isn't used to them."

"Well, he's going to have to bloody well get used to them, isn't he?"

Clearly, my sister has not put a shilling in her sympathy meter today.

I give up trying to verbalize my anxiety and trail after her into her immaculate designer boudoir with her light oak wardrobes and her snow-white linen and her church candles that are never, ever burned. Jemma's picked out some of her poshest bikinis for me, which is very thoughtful of her, but how I'm ever going to get my bum in them I'll never know. I don't feel like exposing the full glory of my bare bottom to her ridicule, and so I stuff them in my bag with mumbled thanks and think that I'll try to rush into Marks & Spencer this week and spend some more money I haven't got on a bikini that's designed to hold a sagging posterior. They might even do one with a built-in secret tummy-control panel and my tummy could do with all the secret control it can get. I am torn between not wanting to look like mutton dressed as lamb and not being mistaken for Christian's mum. A bikini feels like a fairly big danger zone.

"Will you look after the shop if I decide to go on holiday?" she says. "Seeing as you haven't got a job now."

Thanks for reminding me, Jemma. "Yes. Of course I will."

"Good."

"When are you going?"

"I don't know."

"Where are you thinking of?"

"What's this, Alicia?" she snaps. "The Spanish Inquisition?"

So, he's married and they're waiting to see when they can get rid of his wife. What's new? I make my excuses and prepare to leave, and my sister takes our grandmother's scarf as if it is an old dishrag and says she'll look at it, but I suspect it won't be this millennium.

I rush out as slowly as I can, promising to send Jem a postcard, but I expect I will exact a minor spite and won't. But then I'll probably buy her something nice when I get back to make up for it.

I fly back across London, careless of the lurking speed cameras, and can feel myself race into the gravel drive, so sit and make myself count to ten when I pull up in the drive. The gravel always heralds an entrance, but no one comes to greet me. Not even Elliott.

When I have served my patience penance, I find the kitchen is deserted, apart from the dirty pizza plates, and the ice cream is out on the table, melting. And when I go into the lounge I find out why.

Christian is fast asleep, stretched out on the sofa. Elliott is wedged along the length of his body, sucking contentedly on his thumb. Thomas is flat out on the rug in front of the fire, head resting on a cushion. And Tanya is flaked out in the armchair, showing an alarming amount of leg. I have never seen my children in this soporific state on a Sunday afternoon. Normally they are bounding around with energy like a pack of caged tigers. Some tired old film, possibly the original version of *The Thomas Crown*

Affair, is playing away to itself on the television with the sound off. I tiptoe into the room, and they are blissfully, peacefully unaware of my presence. My heart lurches, and I'm not sure if it's for the family I have lost or for the one that I have just found.

CHAPTER 55

As is fitting for a holiday, we left a bog standard British battleship-gray sky behind at the purgatory known as Gatwick Airport, and now the sun is so sharp and clear and white it hurts your eyes to look at it directly; instead you have to squint behind your sunglasses and peer at it through knitted eyelashes. I never knew the color blue could be like this; it's deep and pure and totally unbroken.

I am lying on a strip of sand twenty-five meters wide and a hundred meters long and as flat as the proverbial pancake. That's all. This is Veligandu, which means, romantically, "spit of sand." It is one of about a zillion similar spits of sand that make up the islands of the Maldives—somewhere I'd never actually heard of until Christian booked the tickets. Beyond the precarious coral reef which bounds our particular spit of sand, the ocean plunges violently to unmeasured fathoms that reach down farther than the height of our tallest mountains. So, in effect, I am lying on a spit of sand as high as a sea-locked Everest. It is a very strange feeling for a number of reasons.

One: even the slightest spitefulness from the ocean would obliterate this tiny scrap of laid-back civilization. Even a hint of a wave would cover the lot, sucking it back into the depths of the Indian Ocean forever, and it is far too beautiful for me to want that to happen. And I'm sure Airtours wouldn't be too happy either. I think the thing that hurts most is that it's a horrible reminder that something so solid, so necessary, so abiding, something that other people depend on, can be swept away in an instant by nothing more sinister than a change in the wind. But I'm not going to think about my marriage. I'm here for the sole purpose of *not* thinking about my marriage.

Two: this is the first holiday I've ever been on without my children, which means I can relax on said sand safe in the knowledge that I'm not about to be buried up to my neck in it. I've never been particularly fond of sand, but then I've really only experienced heavy, wet, orange British sand. Sand that sticks damply to your skin, dyeing it brown and working its way inside your sandwiches, doing goodness knows what to your digestive system. This sand is fine white powder, as alluring and narcotic as cocaine. It trails through your fingers leaving no trace and, despite the supreme effort of the scorching sun, holds no heat. If you didn't like sand, this would, undoubtedly, be the wrong place to be. There are no floors in the casual arrangement of thatched buildings that calls itself the hotel, just more sand. Large crabs meander aimlessly through the dining room, and no one, not even me, which is amazing, takes the slightest bit of notice.

This is not a children's holiday. Elliott would be climbing the walls, if there were any, within ten minutes. There are no chirpy T-shirted happy club leaders, no water slides, no themed swimming pools, no water sports, no Frisbees, no Ping-Pong tables, no age 10–14's disco, no hut selling overpriced Wall's ice cream. Christian is the only person here under the age of thirty. This is the sort of holiday only couples do. Couples with plenty of cash because they have no children. Happy couples. Imagine being stuck on a spit of sand for a fortnight with someone you couldn't stand.

Three: I can't believe that Christian and I are here. We have left behind the stress and strain of London, Ed, Kath Brown, my sister, the lovely pouting Rebecca, the drizzle, the fumes, the bills and absolutely everything else. We are here in a blissful little cocoon that nothing—apart from unprecedented torrential rain—could spoil. For the first time in a long time, possibly my entire life, I am relaxed down to my bones. The heat has seared its way through my skin and muscles and is turning my hard, brittle skeleton to soft, melting wax. No doubt I'll pay for it in years to come with an excess of sun-induced wrinkles, but I'll just slap on some more anti-aging cream and consider it a price worth paying. Right now the sun seems unfeasibly kind and comforting. It is baking me back to health. My stomach isn't cramped into a knot as it has been since the first time I said hello to Christian. I really had no idea quite how stretched I'd become, and now that I've got off the giddy treadmill of my life, I wonder how I will ever get back on again.

There's only a handful of people here, scattered about in wooden water bungalows that jut out into the sea beyond the confines of the sand on twiggy stilts. Some are honeymoon couples, possibly vampiric, who have not yet ventured out into the cruel light of day. Fancy coming all this way and staying indoors. Or am I missing the point?

I have brought six books with me and have read none. Jemma would be very pleased about this, and you might understand why when I share a couple of the titles with you. *How To Drive Your Man Wild in Bed.* My favorite thing when I was married was to remark to Ed how the ceiling needed painting. I can quite categorically state that that never failed to drive him wild. Well, I was usually in the right position to notice it! And that alone will tell you that we probably needed help. And, anyway, I wouldn't dare suggest to Christian that the ceiling needed painting—God only knows what we'd end up with.

Another one is called *How To Make Anyone Like You*—which I'm really struggling with, because I'm not even sure I like myself much at the moment. They should produce these books with plain brown covers. They're all a bit too relentlessly cheerful and citrus in hue, which means that anyone within a half-mile radius can read the title and know that you are a sad sack, racked with insecurities. It's not what you might call typical holiday reading matter either, is it? The urge to improve oneself shouldn't extend into holiday periods. That's the two weeks of the year when you should be happy to be a sun-lounger potato and turn yourself into a lush (old-fashioned meaning) on bright blue cocktails with matching parasols and indulge yourself heartily from the calorie and botulism buffet. I should have gone out and bought something slushy by one of these trendy young authors with names like Charlotte, Clare or Camelia.

I have given up pretending to read; the light is too bright and I've spent my time staring at the infinitesimal swell of the sea, which is making me as drowsy as about ten Valiums.

Last night we sat on the beach, alone, holding hands, and watched the sun sink down beneath the sea. Dolphins swam across the horizon, silhouetted in the golden-orange light, leaping playfully as if they hadn't a care in the world. No wonder they always look like they're smiling—they don't have mortgages or school fees or high blood pressure or cellulite or Decree Absolutes. And I wonder if they realize how hard it is for us humans just to cope with existing, and why, after the age of ten, we somehow lose the urge to leap playfully.

As the sun set, it left a warm, comforting glow that spread across the surface of the ocean, familiar and soothing, and as I looked behind me the moon was already out, sharp, crescent-shaped, a slashed sliver of silver thread in a vast expanse of mysterious, unfathomable inky blackness. The stars twinkled, tantalizing, alluring, sparkling on the water like white diamonds scattered on plush black velvet. And I was torn. I didn't know which way to turn. What drew me most—the soft safety of the setting sun or the clear, rising newness of the moon and stars? If I could only look at one for the rest of my life, which would I be most willing to sacrifice?

Propping myself up on my elbows, I cup my face in my hands and look out to the sea, which is blue, beguiling and unthreatening, and as hard as I try to decide, I still don't know which I'd choose.

Christian is snorkeling. That boy—man—has more energy than is good for him. The word "tired" just doesn't cross his brain. I can just see the silver tip of his blowpipe glinting in the join between the turquoise of the sea and the azure sky. His fins are paddling lazily in the water and he's wearing a T-shirt, because I didn't want his back to get burned. He says I speak to him like a four-year-old, but then, at times, he can be as petulant as anyone I've come across—including Elliott. And I worry about him like he's a child—is he too hot, too cold, has he had enough to eat, has he put plenty of sunscreen on his beautiful delicate skin? It's only at night when we are alone in the seething warmth of our bungalow and he is moving above me in the dark and I can't see the youthful, exuberant light on his face that he is all man to me, my lover and only my lover.

Christian pads out of the sea and flops down on the beach next to me. "The water is so warm, Ali," he says breathlessly. "It's like being in a bath."

I pass him a towel and he puts it down without using it. "Have you ever made love in the sea?"

I think I can quite safely say that I haven't, but then all our holidays have been in Cornwall or Devon, which somehow doesn't have the same appeal. And the kids might have objected to waiting on the beach. "No," I say.

Christian rolls over and kisses my feet. "I think it's something we have to correct." His eyes twinkle and in this revealing light they are an indeterminate blue-gray, the color of the horizon where the sea meets the sky. I still have trouble believing that he loves me.

Some people are naturally charismatic. Princess Diana was. So is Jeffrey Archer. I met him once. You'll just have to take my word for it. Christian is too. He has an energy that radiates into a room the minute he walks in. It flows from him and draws people to him like iron filings to a strong magnet. They cleave to him, want to spend time with him. And he's not aware of it yet—I don't think. The worst thing about charismatic people is that once they realize they're charismatic they manipulate their attraction, and I hope Christian doesn't learn to do it, because it will make him a lesser man.

He leans against my sun lounger and rests his head back on my thigh, while I stroke his hair. We are becoming very comfortable with each other. I couldn't sleep when we were first together because I didn't know how to curl round him. I don't remember if it was ever like that with Ed, because we had fitted together so well for so long. Christian's hair used to tickle my nose and his arm was too heavy across my body and the rhythm of his breathing was all wrong and there were very interesting parts of his body which didn't seem to need sleep at all. Now we sleep easily, slotted together like spoons, and I'm not sure if I should view this as progress.

"Come and swim," he murmurs.

It's a good idea. I'm probably just about done to medium rare, and the sea may well sizzle on my skin. I turn toward Christian, and he reaches up and strokes my face. His cheeks glow pink and his eyelashes are damp and dark. The sun has bleached his hair and he looks like he's just stepped out of a glossy magazine. "Do you love me?" he asks.

I do. My heart is melting, like my bones and probably my brain. "Yes," I say. "I love you."

"Good." Christian jumps up and grins. "Last one in the water's a sissy," he says and sets off down the beach.

I race after him, knocking *How To Make Anyone Like You* to the sand, and we cannon into the water, our joyous shrieking loud in the sunny silence. Christian surfaces from the sea just behind me, giggling and splashing. He wraps his arms round me and his lips, wet and salty, find mine and he pulls me down onto him; slowly, slowly we surrender to each other, sinking deep, deep beneath the waves. And I wonder at this moment, which will stay with me forever, whether it is possible to die of happiness.

CHAPTER 56

Ed was standing at the window in the study, looking out over the front garden. The rain had slicked the road until it was as shiny as PVC and had transformed their plain gravel drive into a carpet of polished semiprecious stones. The leaves of the laurel hedge were lush green and glossy and bowed their heads with the weight of the torrential water, tossing the raindrops from side to side in the steady wind.

It was a fairly ordinary family house, but it represented nearly twenty years of steady slog and it mattered an awful lot to him now he seemed about to let it all go. He wondered what would happen when he went to the States. It would be nice if he could afford to run a home here and in downtown Beverly Hills, but the practicalities of it weren't that easy. Would Ali move back in here so that the children would have somewhere to come back to during the holidays? But then, when they weren't here, she'd rattle around like a lonely little pea in a pod all by herself. And there was one thing for certain: no way was Mr. Christian Trendy Bastard ever going to set foot in here on a permanent basis—or he'd do so over Ed's dead body.

He hadn't yet told the children, or Ali come to that, of his plan to transport them to the other side of the world so that he could realize his ambition of once again being involved in big budget, box-office, blockbusting movies—but he was sure they would understand. It was just that they'd had so much upheaval recently and so much to cope with that he was trying to find the right time to introduce the subject. Nor had he discussed with Orla what the living arrangements would be. Would they live separately to start with and then move in together, or did she envisage them as one big happy family from day one? She hadn't even met the kids properly yet—supposing they didn't get on? Orla didn't strike him as particularly maternal, so perhaps it would be better if he and the kids had their own place. He didn't even know if she had somewhere to live over there, but she looked like the sort that would. Ed nodded to himself. It was something they needed to talk about. That and a shitload of other stuff too.

Their relationship, if you could call it that, had been weird since they'd got back from "the weekend" in Bath. Orla had taken it that there was a tacit acceptance that they were now a couple, doing and talking about coupley things, mixed with a shy standoff at work, where they did and talked about worky things. Orla said "we" a lot. Trevor had noticed. He hadn't mentioned anything, but Ed was aware that his colleague had stopped calling her Orla the 'Orrible, the Ogre, Cruella De Vil and "that stuck-up old cow." So Ed gathered that it was common knowledge among the staff at Wavelength that "something was going on" between them.

Ed sipped his whisky. He was celebrating his one night of freedom in the time-honored male way by getting slowly but surely drunk. He'd thought about asking Neil over and making a session of it, but solitude was such a rare commodity now that he had decided to bask in it a little before getting down to the dirty task of some serious thinking. It also crossed his mind that he should have been wanting Orla to come over, but he let the thought tiptoe through from one side to the other without stopping to examine it.

Sinking down into the sofa, Ed patted the cushions with a proprietorial air. Elliott was spending the night with his quiet friend who looked like the Milky Bar kid, and whose name Ed could never remember. Thomas was away at a swimming gala with the school and would be back tomorrow. Tanya had also taken the opportunity to go out with one of her friends, Michaela, and Ed had tried to ignore the fact they had both gone out in the pouring rain with bare legs, high heels and skirts the size of cat flaps. She wouldn't be coming home until morning, and he hoped it wasn't the start of a future trend.

Ed was on his third tumbler of whisky. They had closely followed his three glasses of particularly fine Bordeaux that he'd consumed with his Tesco frozen lasagna, microwaved jacket potato and an entire packet of Jaffa Cakes, all of which he would work off with Neil if they ever got round to playing squash this week. Ed picked the newspaper up and glanced blearily at the television pages—*Coronation Street, The Bill* and *Peak Practice*—and put it back down again. He would stick with Dvorak's *Symphony No. 9* for the time being.

The doorbell rang and Ed sighed, hoping it wasn't the Avon lady. It was horrible to keep having to explain to various women collecting or distributing catalogs that Ali wasn't here anymore. He padded to the door and flicked the outside light on. Nicola Jones was standing outside in the rain getting very wet.

Nicola sniffed a raindrop away from the end of her nose. "Can I come in?"

"Of course. Of course." Ed stood aside. She came in and dripped on the hall carpet. "You're wet," he said.

"I've been walking."

She looked upset as well as wet, Ed noticed. "Is there anything wrong?" he asked.

"Elliott," she said flatly.

Ed's heart sank. He might have guessed. "What now?"

Nicola looked up and her eyes were red-rimmed and distressed. "He told me you're seeing another woman."

"Did he." That child was going to be grounded until he was thirty-six. "You'd better come through."

Nicola slipped off her coat and hung it on the end of the banister and followed Ed through to the lounge.

"Drink?" he offered with a wave of his glass.

Nicola hugged her arms. "I'll have whatever you're having."

"This is neat scotch."

"That's fine," she said and sat herself down on the sofa.

Fighting his rising eyebrows, Ed poured her a large scotch. He handed her the glass and sat down next to her. "Thanks," Nicola said with an unhappy smile. Her mass of blond hair cascaded in sodden curls round her shoulders and her damp T-shirt clung tightly to her bra, which seemed a rather inadequate container for its voluptuous contents. Ed dragged his eyes away from them.

"So what exactly did Elliott say?"

"He said she was called Orville."

Ed laughed. "Orla. She's called Orla."

Nicola gulped her whisky. "So it's true?"

"She's a colleague," Ed said, hoping that he didn't look as hot as he felt.

"Nothing more?"

"We're working on something together," he replied, wondering what it had really got to do with Nicola and why he couldn't just tell her straight out that moving to the States and shacking up with Orla were both fairly imminent moves. "Is it a problem?" he said.

"It shouldn't be, I know," she said, glugging her whisky again. "We hardly know each other. But..." She curled her knees up on the sofa and huddled into herself. "Do you mind if I'm frank with you?"

"No," Ed said. "No. Not at all." Oh please, please be anything but frank with me!

"I really feel that there could be something special between us, Ed."

"Special?"

"I know you feel it too." Her face was imploring. "Or at least I thought you did."

Did he? Well, it was certainly true that various parts of his anatomy had perked up considerably since she'd arrived. Particularly since she'd arrived looking like a lost and bewildered entrant for a Miss Wet T-Shirt contest.

"Is it because I'm Elliott's teacher?"

"What?"

"Do you think it's a barrier between us?"

"No. No. Not at all." Realizing as he spoke that it would have been a great get-out clause. "Well, perhaps."

"I adore your children," she said earnestly. "I have a special soft spot for Elliott."

"So do I," Ed agreed. *About six feet under at the base of the cherry tree in the garden.*

"He's at Toby's tonight, isn't he?"

"Yes. And Thomas is at a swimming gala...." It was information he wasn't sure he should have volunteered.

"Is Tanya out too?" Nicola's voice had risen slightly. She knocked back the remains of her drink.

"Yes," Ed said. "She's out terrifying the local youths with Michaela Johnson."

"So we're alone?"

"Yes," Ed said uncertainly. "I think I'll just pop upstairs and get you a towel. You're still looking awfully wet."

Ed shot out of the lounge and bounded up the stairs. He leant against the airing-cupboard door and finished his own drink. What was he thinking of? He should have told her that Tanya would be back at any minute or that Neil would be calling round. How could he possibly entertain the thought of sleeping with Miss Jones? He was behaving like Julio Iglesias! Well, not quite. Julio Iglesias had bragged of bedding two thousand women, so two in a fortnight was chicken feed by comparison, but it was better than Ed had done in his previous twenty years. What would Neil do in this situation? *Oh don't even go there, Edward.* His brother would simply hurl himself into it joyously like Elliott diving into a ball pond.

Technically, he wouldn't be cheating on Ali because they were by all accounts separated, and was he in a committed enough relationship with Orla to remain absolutely one hundred percent faithful? How would he feel if she were doing the same thing? Not overly worried at this minute, he had to admit. Going back to the shoe-shop analogy, this could be the ideal opportunity to try on another pair for size. Just to make sure. Ed chewed at his fingernail. Perhaps he should phone Neil.

Ed heard a creak on the staircase and whipped open the airing-cupboard door and started searching the untidy piles for a towel that didn't look like it had bathed a hundred children. He found one and turned to see Miss Nicola Jones, Elliott's nursery-school teacher, stark naked at the top of the stairs, wearing nothing but a sexy smile.

"I thought I'd catch my death of cold," she said girlishly. "I had to get out of those wet things."

Ed gulped. "I can see," he said.

Nicola slinked toward him and took the towel from his now rather unsteady hand. She tossed it back in the airing cupboard, closed the door and, taking his hand, led him toward his own bedroom.

"What shoe size are you?" Ed murmured.

"What?" Miss Jones purred.

"Nothing," Ed sighed. "Nothing at all." And he scooped her up in his arms and kicked the door closed behind him.

CHAPTER 57

Neil was wearing his boxer shorts, eating yesterday's pizza out of the box and watching a grainy blue movie that Adam at the pub had lent him, and it was truly, truly terrible. Adam had insisted it was hot stuff, but in Neil's opinion it was marginally more lukewarm than the pizza he was reluctantly munching. Neil tilted his head and tried to work out what he was watching. There was some fat German bird involved and a bloke who looked like he'd just walked straight out of *The Village People* and they were in a lift together, or it might have been a cupboard. There was no plot, so it was hard to tell, but then there never are in these things. The German bird was starting to moan at things that were presumably going on out of camera shot, and the bloke had a very funny look on his face and his eyes screwed up.

Neil put his pizza to one side and opened another can of beer. Perhaps his brother ought to consider going into the world of pornography; the last commercial he had made for Post Office Savings Accounts had been way, way more interesting than this. It had featured the lovely Gloria Hunniford, and right now Gloria was more likely to do it for him than this German bird.

The doorbell rang, and Neil put his beer down and headed down the stairs to the front door. He had opened it, wide, before his brain computed the fact that the shapely silhouette outlined in the frosty glass belonged to his beautiful sister-in-law, Jemma. She looked immaculate and very slightly horrified. Her hair shone like polished amber in the sunshine and she was wearing flared camel leather trousers, the sort that Gwyneth Paltrow would look great in, and a soft, fluffy sweater that was probably cashmere if Neil had any idea what cashmere looked like, and a leather jacket the color of melted Mars bars. Jemma's eyes conducted a brief appraisal of his own wardrobe, and he realized that her assessment of his clothing would not require the same amount of eloquence. He was wearing boxers, black, circa 1991 of the Kmart variety. Caught by the love of his life in ten-year-old shreddies.

"Neil," Jemma said, as if she was unsure.

"Hi," Neil said, resisting the urge to cross his hands above his testicles in penalty shoot-out mode. "I wasn't expecting anyone."

Jemma gave him an ice-maiden stare. "You haven't returned my calls."

"I've been meaning to," he said, but in truth he hadn't felt much like talking to Jemma after the cup-of-tea-in-the-face incident. He was humiliated, embarrassed and not a little sulky. And he hadn't a clue what to say anyhow.

"I'm sorry about the cup-of-tea thing," she said, fiddling with her hair. "I wanted to apologize."

Neil shrugged. "That's okay. You weren't the first." Actually she was, but he didn't want to give her any sense of satisfaction or originality. "You probably won't be the last." Although he sincerely hoped she would be.

"You're not cross with me?"

"No." Yes. And he wanted to know who was the Teutonic-looking bloke with the blond hair and the big car and whether they'd laughed at him as they'd driven away. Probably. He would have.

"I don't usually do that sort of thing. I don't know what came over me." Jemma shuffled about on the pavement as the traffic of Camden High Street trundled by the end of the road. "I'm under a lot of pressure," she explained. "This thing with Ed and Ali has got me really stressed."

"Me too," Neil said. He suspected Jemma might be even more stressed if he told that his older brother was now not only shagging his work mate, but was also giving one to Elliott's nursery-school teacher. Ed had phoned him in a state of heightened anxiety to confess all to him the following morning. Neil wasn't sure how much it had helped his brother come to terms with his guilt when he had laughed like a drain and nicknamed him Edward "Two Shags" Kingston.

Jemma glanced up and down the street and then back at Neil's boxer shorts. "Can I come in?"

"Well…"

"We need to decide what to do."

"This isn't a great time…." Two could play at that game.

"We have to have something in place before Ali gets back from the Maldives," Jemma said. "It'll *have* to be now." And she pushed past Neil and started to climb the stairs to his flat. A waft of perfume teased his nostrils, it was heavy, exotic and, no doubt, hellishly expensive. He had always wanted to be the type of man who could identify perfumes by the merest hint, but he couldn't, not by a long chalk. This could have been anything—Opium, Ghost, CKOne or Jif Lemon-Scented Bathroom Cleaner even. With a sigh, Neil closed the door on the noise of the street and tramped up the stairs behind her.

Jemma's step faltered only slightly when she approached the lounge door and the sounds of an enthusiastic orgasm started to drift out. *"Yes, yes, yes,"* the German bird shouted.

Jemma flushed. "Have you got company?"

Neil adopted a vacant look. "Me? No."

"Oh do it to me, big boy!"

Jemma turned and looked questioningly at Neil, who feigned ignorance with a suitably blank expression and casual shrug of his shoulders. "Channel Five?" he offered, as if hazarding a guess.

His sister-in-law strode into the room ahead of him. On the television screen, big boy did indeed appear to be doing it to her, in rather Technicolor magnificence, as it happened.

"Channel Five," Neil confirmed with a nod.

They both stood and tilted their heads to watch, partly in wonderment, partly in horror.

"Well." Jemma sat down abruptly on the sofa, her hand resting on the video box that announced *BIG, BAD AND BOUNCY IN BERLIN* in dripping red letters two inches high with a picture of the same woman being particularly bad and bouncy on the cover. She picked up the box. "Well," she said again.

Neil snapped off the television. He thought about telling her he was trying to learn another language and this was for purely educational purposes, but then realized that the language of commercial bonking was pretty much universal. Jemma had paled and she was staring glassy-eyed at him. His eyes followed her gaze, and he realized that he had a glob of lovely red tomato sauce and cheese from his pizza sticking to his chest hair. And a bloody great hard-on.

"I can explain," Neil said.

"Save it, Neil," she said frostily. "What you do in your spare time is none of my concern."

"But…" Neil felt on the verge of spluttering.

"Needless to say, I won't mention this to either Ed or Ali. It will remain our little secret." Jemma put the box down pointedly, with the picture facing downward.

"But…"

"And that's what I'm here to discuss." Jemma sat primly, as if filth was emanating from the fibers of the carpet. Which it quite possibly was.

"Let me go and get dressed," Neil said, trying to keep the begging note from his voice. They both glanced at the small but very noticeable tent in the front of his shorts.

"Hurry up," she said briskly. And all thoughts of them being reconciled and traveling round Europe together in blissful union and Neil photographing stylish collections of her clothes in exotic locations for a four-page spread in *Vogue* vanished before his eyes in a puff of smoke. Smoke so strong that it was actually making them water. His erection deflated like a popped balloon. Deciding that saying nothing was probably the best policy, Neil slumped his shoulders and skulked from the room.

Jemma had reluctantly accepted a cup of tea and he had moved the lager cans and the pizza box and the *BIG, BAD AND BOUNCY IN BERLIN* video and she was no longer looking at him as if he was a depraved monster. He, in turn, was no longer looking at her as potential girlfriend material.

"We need to set them up," Jemma said, clutching her mug for safety.

Neil had checked all of his cups for suitable slogans, eschewing *I caught the crabs at Vic's Seafood Restaurant* and *Photographers Do It in the Dark,* featuring a naked man with a large telephoto lens, and had given her the very unsexy one for Stannah Stair Lifts that Ed had got free on a video shoot years ago. He kept a close eye on it, lest she felt moved to hurl the contents at him again. Clad in jeans and a black T-shirt, also without slogan, he had retreated to the armchair in the corner so as not to appear he was about to pounce on her in the mode of *BIG, BAD AND BOUNCY IN BERLIN.*

"They're never going to agree to meet each other to talk this through. They're both being so pigheaded. I can't understand it. You'd think they didn't want to sort it out."

"Maybe they don't," Neil ventured.

"Don't be ridiculous," Jemma said. "They're made for each other, and we've got to make them realize that."

"How will we do that?" Neil asked, trying to sound enthusiastic. It wasn't that he had lost interest in the quest to reunite Ed and Ali, since he did agree that both were being pigheaded and were made for each other—well, yes, he had in fact lost interest in the quest now that there appeared to be no perks for him involved.

"We'll arrange for them to have a surprise meal together and just leave them to their own devices." Jemma nodded confidently.

"I thought it was being left to their own devices that had got them in trouble in the first place?"

Jemma ignored him. "I thought The Ivy," she said. "Ali's always wanted to go there."

"Don't you have to book about a squillion years in advance?"

"You'll think of a way round it." She waved dismissively with her hand. "Give them a ring."

"Now?"

"Time is of the essence," Jemma said.

Huffing, Neil searched down the side of the armchair until he found his mobile phone. He punched for Directory Enquiries and got the number for The Ivy. Neil sat up in the chair when someone from the restaurant answered the phone.

"Hi," he said. "I'd like to book a table. As soon as possible. For two."

He examined his fingernails while he waited. "Three months!" He looked aghast at Jemma. "You can't do one for how long? Hold on, please." Neil whispered to Jemma. "They can't do a table for three months."

"Of course they can!" she whispered back. "Say something!"

"What?"

"I don't know."

"Can't they go somewhere else?"

"Where?"

"I don't know," Neil hissed. "You don't have to book at Pizza Express."

"Neil!" Jemma looked venomous.

"Okay, okay." Neil thought for a moment then: "Er… This is Lord Neville of Kingston," he said as if he'd got an entire bag of boiled sweets stuck in his mouth. "I wanted to bring Daddy up from the country. I hoped to do it rather sooner."

Jemma flung herself back on the sofa in disgust.

"What?" he mouthed at her.

Jemma beat herself about the head with a cushion.

Neil's face broke into a smug grin. "Two weeks?" He fixed Jemma with an I-told-you-so look. "Why, thank you. That'll be fine. Charmed, I'm sure."

Neil hung up and punched the air.

"Charmed, I'm sure," Jemma sneered. "You sounded more like a Cockney street vendor than Lord Flaming Neville of Wherever."

"They're in," Neil said sharply. "What more do you want?"

Jemma stopped and bit her lip. Tears filled her eyes. "I want them to be happy," she said softly.

Neil crossed the room and took her hand, giving it a squeeze. "Me too, Jem. Me too."

"Neil," Jemma frowned, and all her fierceness sagged out of her, "what do you think the chances are of bringing Ed and Ali back together?"

"At the moment?" Neil mused sadly. "About the same as bringing back hanging."

CHAPTER 58

Elliott, Thomas and Tanya sat on the floor in Thomas's bedroom. The Scalectrix, the Game Boys and Harry Potter had been cleared away to under the bed, and the children faced each other in a tight circle. Tanya twiddled her fingers in what she assumed to be an expert way and then licked her tongue wetly along the cigarette paper. The boys looked on in rapt awe.

"So," she asked, "which one of the new other halves do we like best? If any."

"I like them all," Elliott piped up.

"That's because you're a lamebrain," his sister snarled.

"It takes one to know one," he retorted. Tanya kicked out at him.

"We want our parents to get back together, don't we?"

"Why?" Elliott said.

"Because that's how it's supposed to be, idiot."

"All my friends' parents are divorced," Thomas said.

"Yes," Tanya sighed, "but that doesn't mean they know what's good for them. You know what adults are like. What do you think?"

Thomas shrugged. "I like Christian. He's pretty cool."

"He's an arsehole," Tanya said. "I can't stand the way he drools all over Mum."

"I thought that's what boyfriends were supposed to do," Elliott said.

Tanya narrowed her eyes. "Not when they're that age! It's revolting."

"He can't be that bad." Elliott nodded at the cigarette papers. "He showed you how to do that."

"He didn't show me," Tanya snapped. "I sort of copied him," she added more softly, admiring her handiwork from all angles.

"I like Nicola Jones too," Thomas continued, unperturbed.

"I think she might be too demanding." Elliott lay back on his Bob the Builder pillow, which adorned the floor, and wrinkled his forehead in concern. "And she has a lot of hair. It must take her ages to get ready."

"Mummy's got lots of hair too," Thomas said. "And she doesn't do anything to it."

"That's because she's a mummy, not a girlfriend," Elliott said wisely.

"Oh," Thomas said, bowing to his younger brother's greater knowledge of the female sex.

Ed let himself in the front door and tossed the *Independent* onto the phone table. The worst thing about coming home since Ali had left was that the house didn't feel like a home anymore. No one was here to greet him and ask him if he'd had a good day, even, it had to be said, if he didn't always feel like responding. When the kids were around, they barely looked up from the table or, if they were parked in front of *All My Children,* he didn't get a look in, just lots of shushing.

Dumping his briefcase, he wandered through to the kitchen and flicked on the kettle. He might have a bath before dinner, if you could call Cheddar Cheese Crispy Pancakes and a packet of Super Noodles dinner. His back hurt and his head hurt, but they were nothing compared to his heart, which hurt grievously. Ali had sent a postcard to the kids from the Maldives, which he felt was rubbing salt into wounds somewhat, and he wasn't sure whether he was piqued or pleased that his name didn't even feature on it. He might forgo the tea route and head straight for the strong drink instead.

It also might help assuage his guilt over his newly promiscuous persona, which he wasn't entirely at ease with. He'd nipped into the men's room today and examined himself several times in case he'd developed some sort of rash. Nicola Jones had been unconcerned that they had no protection when they made love, which was a bit scary considering how desperate she seemed for kids. Perhaps he should have told her that he'd had the snip and that the whole thing would be a bit of a wasted effort if she ever thought that he might be capable of procreation. It seemed so unnecessary to be using condoms if he was firing blanks, but if he was going to sleep around, as his brother laughingly termed it, he was going to have to be a bit more careful.

He wondered if Orla had been able to sense anything different about his demeanor, as he'd been trying very hard to remain normal and she usually didn't miss a trick. If she had, she didn't say anything. Ed massaged his temples. He couldn't cope with all these ifs, buts, whys and wherefores. It was all too taxing for someone as old and weary as himself.

Ed threw off his jacket. There was no television blaring out and the house was as silent as the grave, which couldn't possibly mean that by some stretch of the imagination his children were secreted away in the bedrooms doing homework, could it? Like England ever becoming a leading force again in Test cricket, it was too, too much to hope for. He would definitely have a bath. Perhaps he'd feel better for a brisk rubdown with some strong soap and a rough flannel. Ed stretched, cracked his neck and went in search of his offspring.

"Orla's scary," Thomas said, propping himself up on his elbow.

"Scarier than Scary Spice?" Elliott wanted to know.

"Scary Spice isn't scary anymore, dipstick. She's a has-been." Tanya let the smoke curl in front of her eyes and pouted her mouth to see if she could blow a smoke ring, which she couldn't.

"So why's Orville scary?" Elliott absentmindedly punched Barney the perky purple dinosaur in the face.

"Orla!" Tanya and Thomas corrected.

"Orla is a predatory female," Tanya said with a grudging touch of admiration in her voice. "She is afraid of no one and nothing. She's like Sigourney Weaver. She's independent, single-minded." Tanya pinned Elliott with her eyes. "She is a woman in control of her own destiny."

"Well, that sounds nice," Elliott said chirpily. "What's a destiny?"

Tanya rolled onto her back. "She'd make our lives hell."

Elliott frowned. "That doesn't sound so nice."

"Christian and Nicola Jones, we could control," Tanya said with a wistful look. "Orla would squish us all like flies."

"Then I don't think I want her to be our mummy," Elliott said.

"No one can replace our mother, Elliott," Tanya growled. "Don't ever forget that."

"Okay," he said with a shrug. His eyes followed Tanya's fingers longingly. "Give us a go."

"No."

Elliott pouted. "Christian said we had to share."

"Christian doesn't know what he's talking about."

"Oh, go on!"

Tanya huffed with exasperation. "How did I ever get landed with two manky brothers?"

She sat up and moved toward Elliott. "If you ever, ever tell anyone about this, Elliott, you are seriously dead meat. Get it?"

"Yes," Elliott said, eyes bright and excited.

"What are you?"

"Dead meat," he repeated obediently.

"You too, Tom."

"Dead meat," he echoed.

Tanya maneuvered her fingers. "Hold it like this," she said.

At that moment the door flew open and Ed walked in. "Hi, kids," he said, then ground to a premature halt in the doorway. His face blackened and his eyebrows met in the middle. "What the…!" he shouted.

CHAPTER 59

I am golden brown and looking gorgeous, even though I say it myself. I feel relaxed, lovely and lithe—though why the lithe bit I'm not sure, because I've eaten enough fish in the last two weeks to warrant growing gills myself and enough cake to have thighs of pure lard. I can't believe we're back from our holiday already, because it feels like we only just went. The pile of washing and ironing I'm ploughing through tells me that I am, well and truly, back.

The only strange thing about being in a sort of no-man's-land in terms of my abode, is that there wasn't the obligatory foot-high pile of bills and junk mail awaiting my return. It seems that in my absence not a single soul has missed me. However, it was two weeks of pure, unadulterated bliss, and I now feel ready to face all the flotsam and jetsam floating about in the murky sink that is my life.

With luck, Ed is also feeling fairly mellow, as I'm going to ask him if the children can come to stay at Christian's house for the entire weekend. What do you think about that? It's fairly tricky, this shared-custody thing. I don't want to put the arrangement on an official footing if I can help it because I think we're still both in denial about the actual nitty-gritty of what we're doing and we ought to be adult enough to sort it out between ourselves without running up solicitors' bills. Ed says that I can see the children at any time, but makes it clear that I am rationed just enough to make it hurt. Staying overnight moves visitation rights onto a new level, and although I'm desperate to see more of the children, I'm trying not to think how this will facilitate his relationship with that Orville woman or Nicola Jones or whoever his current squeeze is, because for some reason that starts to turn me as green as a Halloween witch. Perversity, thy name is woman!

The children can have the beds in Robbie and Rebecca's rooms. This has been made feasible by the fact that Robbie is going home to Kent for the weekend, no doubt to scrounge off his parents, and Rebecca has met a *man* who is taking her sailing on his *yacht* for the *weekend.* And if we've heard about it once, we've heard about it a thousand times. It is possible to get the word "yacht" into almost any sentence if you try really hard. I am, in truth, genuinely very pleased for her, since she might now be moved to keep the smile that has been reaching from one ear to the other all week and not snarl around the house looking like she's sucked a lemon. Both she and Robbie have been very kind and have offered to tidy their rooms, and Robbie has vowed to hide his porno mags and take down his topless picture of Pamela Anderson, which is very thoughtful.

Christian is also being very chill about this. In fact, he suggested it. I think the day we spent at the fair was a ground-breaking day for him in coming to terms with me being a mother as well as a wanna-be Sex Kitten at Any Age. He's starting to appreciate some of the things that family life can offer: closeness, sharing, caring—along with the other benefits of poverty, squabbling and total lack of privacy. And it's also time for Elliott's next skateboarding lesson, as he was deemed not to have damaged himself nearly enough on his last outing—so clearly the boy wasn't trying. You won't begin to believe how pleased I am that Christian is starting to develop good relationships with the children. He no longer seems to view them with terror and actually looks forward to seeing them. Long may it continue!

I'm about to develop ironer's elbow, so I have a break and decide to phone Ed. No one else is in the house, and I am feeling a bit lonely. There's never anyone round here during the day, and Christian has gone back to Covent Garden to reclaim his pitch from his friend. I think, despite his grumbles about leaving me, that he was looking forward to it. I dial Ed's mobile and it occurs to me that we are in that twilight zone where we no longer know each other's every movement. Our lives are becoming separated, not through any conscious effort, but by the natural passing of time. He answers after a few rings.

"Ed Kingston." His voice, although abrupt and worklike, still thrills me. It's soft, mellow, deeper for some reason on the phone than in real life, sexy.

"It's Ali," I say.

"Oh." There is an uncomfortable pause. "You're back then?"

"Yes."

"Good holiday?" It's said sharply, as if he can hardly bear to ask. But then, I shouldn't be surprised, I wasn't exactly overjoyed when he spent two days in Bath with Orville.

"Yes," I reply, trying to keep a neutral tone. What else can I say? I can hardly rattle on about the dolphins and the sunsets, can I? And I think the bit about bonking in the sea is best left out too. "Thanks."

Ed snorts.

"I wanted to talk to you about this weekend," I continue briskly. "Had you made any plans with the children?"

I can hear Ed breathing. "Why?"

"I wanted to spend the whole weekend with them." It comes out in a rush, as if I'm asking him a favor and not something that really is my right. "If that's okay with you."

"I don't think that's going to be possible," he says, and there is a harsh edge to his voice, all the mellowness gone.

"Oh?" I'm careful to moderate my own tone. "Would you like to explain why?"

"Not over the phone," Ed says.

"I could come to see you." I conjure up a relaxing vision of dolphins splashing playfully across the sunset in an attempt to curb my rising irritation. "Where are you?"

"In the office," he says and I wonder if he has realized how much space now separates us. "Meet me at the Groucho Club," Ed orders. "In an hour."

"Fine," I say. One benefit of living in Notting Hill is that it's only a handful of Tube stops into the thick of things. It's possibly the only benefit I can think of at the moment.

"Fine," Ed says.

"Ed." I suppress a sigh, an inch of my hard-earned relaxation ebbs away and my dolphins disappear beneath the waves. "We have to be sensible about these things."

"Being sensible, Alicia, is the last thing you are qualified to speak about." And, with that parting shot, the line goes dead.

The receptionist graciously allows me to wait in the bar area at the Groucho for Ed, after much persuasion. I've only been there for about two minutes, long enough to have found a sofa and sat myself down, but not much else, when Ed pushes through the door. He is looking tired and harassed. I've sort of dressed up. I'm not really at ease in these media-type surroundings. This place has such a reputation, but I'm not actually sure that it warrants it. Maybe it's just because I'm on the outside of this world, I don't know who the movers and shakers are, but to me they all look like overweight, middle-aged men drinking too much. It's just before the early evening rush and the place is relatively empty, apart from a few diehards propping up the bar. I've only been in this hallowed place a couple of times—once to the launch of a commercial for a new type of tampon which Ed did the advert for, and the only other time was for the one Christmas party where Wavelength partners were invited. It was at that party that I began to realize how often people's eyes glaze over when you tell them that you're a housewife, who stays at home all day to devote themselves to their husband and their children—which I did at the time. The whole thing was a stilted, uncomfortable disaster, and so they kept everything in-house from then on. Housewives were banned substances.

Ed sees me and does a slight double take. I hope it's because I'm looking so fabulously tanned and relaxed, but if it is he doesn't say so. He just throws himself in a heap on the sofa opposite me and sighs wearily.

"Drink?" he says by way of introduction.

"Mineral water." I want him to remember me as a good mother. "Sparkling." Like my wit.

Ed orders from a hovering waiter, and we don't say anything else until the drinks have been delivered. My husband takes a stress-relieving glug of his scotch. His eyes meet mine and I have no idea how to read them, but the expression on his face leaves me in no doubt that he's not a happy little chappie. "Let's get this over with, shall we?" he says, even though I've no idea what he's talking about.

Ed glances furtively round the bar, rather like an overacting Bond criminal. He opens his briefcase and rummages in its depths. There is a black coffee table between us, marked with the sticky residue of drinks forming Olympic rings and bits of left-over peanut from lunchtime. In the middle of it Ed methodically places a small battered silver case, a cheap plastic cigarette lighter and some Rizla papers, slowly, slowly, one at a time. He pauses dramatically, clearly waiting for some form of recognition, and when he doesn't get it, he looks away from me, does the Bond criminal routine again and opens the lid of the silver case. He holds it out to me, eyes wide and questioning.

The case contains a squashed Old Holborn wrapper and a lump of brown goo, which may or may not be the earwax of someone desperately in need of a Q-tip.

"What?" I say.

"Oh, come on, Alicia!"

I want to laugh, but Ed is clearly taking this very seriously. "Come on, what?"

"Don't play the innocent with me."

"Sorry, Ed." I bite my lip so that I don't smile. "You're going to have to draw me a diagram."

My husband scowls. "Oh, for goodness' sake!"

I examine the brown goo more closely. It could be an out-of-date bouillon cube. I pick it up and sniff it. It smells like a rancid bouillon cube.

"Put that down," Ed hisses, looking round nervously.

I do as I'm told. "Why?"

Ed's face darkens until he is blending in with the black leather sofas. "It's puff," he says. "Dope. Gear. *Shit.*"

I look at the inoffensive, if slightly grotty-looking brown earwax more closely. "Is it?"

"Oh, come on!"

"Stop saying that," I snap. "The only puff I've ever got close to is Thomas's Ventolin inhaler."

"Well, he's obviously moved on a little bit," Ed snarls. "Last week when you were in the *Maldives* with your *toy boy,* I caught *your* children—Thomas, Tanya *and* Elliott—smoking this."

"Thomas?" Now I did want to laugh.

"Yes, Thomas." Ed is stony-faced.

Tanya I could understand—if her friends were doing it, then she would be right there at the front of the queue. Elliott too, despite the fact he's only four. If it's naughty, he's in on it. But

Thomas? Thomas would only consider smoking dope if Harry Potter did. And as far as I know, the bespectacled wizard isn't known for being a pothead. I sit here bemused until my anger kicks in. What has Ed been doing that they weren't properly supervised and could get themselves involved in drugs? I bet he was off...*canoodling* with one of his Misses Pretty Knickers.

"How do you know what it is, anyway?"

"I did go to college," Ed says loftily.

"Oh." That explains everything then. "And how did they get hold of it?"

"Really, Ali." Ed snorts with disgust.

"What?" I wouldn't know where to go to buy drugs even if I wanted to, and I doubt my fifteen-year-old or my twelve-year-old—and certainly not my four-year-old—have been hanging round seedy East End pubs or talking to men in dark glasses in BMWs. And where did they get their money? Thomas and Elliott spend their pocket money on sweets, and Tanya single-handedly supports Bobbi Brown.

Ed sits back in his sofa, grim-faced. He needs a shave and his bristles are tipped with gray, making him look older than his years. "Christian gave it to them."

"Christian?" I huff disbelievingly. "*My* Christian?"

My husband grinds his teeth. "Is there any other?"

I shake my head. "You're making this up."

"Am I?" Ed looks drained.

"Who told you Christian had given it to them?"

"Thomas," Ed says.

Thomas is pathologically incapable of telling lies, and I feel the blood drain out of all of my veins, leaving my insides empty, hollow, a vacuum.

"He gave it to them 'for a laugh,'" my husband adds.

I want to say something, to reassure Ed that this is a terrible mistake, that this isn't dope or puff or *shit,* it's earth-tone Play-Doh or, indeed, a stale bouillon cube or a practical joke or something else other than cannabis resin that my children have been smoking, supplied by my lover. How would Christian have given it to them? He would have had to show them what to do, and he's never been alone with them except for the Sunday afternoon when I popped over to Jemma's.... Oh fuck.

The Sunday afternoon when I came back to find them all

stoned out of their heads and not just sleeping gently as I supposed. My stomach does a double somersault and I feel like I'm going to vomit, adding my own signature to the manky coffee table. How could Christian have done this? He wouldn't, surely? I can hardly breathe, I hurt so much. "I'll sort it out," I say tightly. "Let me speak to Christian."

Ed goes an even darker shade of black. "If I ever see him, I'm going to break his fucking neck, Alicia. You can tell him that from me. I haven't yet decided if I'm going to go to the police. I wanted to see what you had to say. But, Alicia, if it's up to me, neither you nor that bastard boyfriend of yours will be allowed within twenty miles of my children ever again. Do you understand?"

I shake my head, unable to take this in. "I'm sure there's been a mistake…." Even I don't think I sound convinced.

Ed stands up. "Are you?" he says. He snaps the silver case shut, taking his evidence with him. Case closed.

CHAPTER 60

Orla was sitting up in bed with a sheet wrapped round her waist and her breasts exposed, and Ed was trying to avoid looking at them because he really didn't want to make love again and thought discretion might be the better part of valor. He was also drinking champagne, which he didn't want either. After his meeting with Ali, something that smacked of celebration was a long way from his mind. His performance in bed had been half-hearted, quickly over and not even attempting to scale the dizzy heights of perfunctory.

They were in her dark, antique-ridden rented flat, and the sun was about to leave the sky for the night. He hated the fact that she had sheets and blankets—they pinned him to the bed with their weight, and whoever did Orla's cleaning made up wicked hospital corners, which meant you had no hope of dislodging the covers even if, unlike Ed, you did manage to be particularly athletic and amorous.

"I feel like going round there and blacking both his eyes," Ed said now.

"I can understand that." Orla nodded sympathetically.

"With a baseball bat."

"It's good to let go of your anger." Orla sipped her champagne.

"Well, it might be in America," Ed pointed out wearily, "but here you just get arrested and charged with grievous bodily harm."

Orla snuggled down next to him. She didn't do snuggly very easily. She was all pointy bits and angles. Even her curves were sharp, and there was a tension in her muscles that never quite went away. Not like Nicola Jones, who was far too snuggly for her own good. And that was another thing; he wasn't very proud that he too had turned into some kind of moral black hole, although his brother seemed to find it highly amusing.

It wasn't that difficult to avoid Nicola. He just sort of threw Elliott at her in the morning, and while his son had got her stalled with his incessant chattering, legged it to the school gate with a friendly, noncommittal wave. Nicola was a barnacle, but a barnacle with a small "b." One that could be prized away without a great deal of difficulty or overexertion. Clingy rather than stuck fast. With Orla it was more difficult. Orla was an octopus. Powerful and crushing. She had wound her tentacles around him tightly, encircling his mind, filling it with dreams of Hollywood, entwining their lives, drawing threads of them together until she had woven her version of an interlocked future for them. And it was so hard to keep his head out of the water and gasp for air that he didn't have the time to consider what it was he really wanted.

"This will all be over soon," she said. "Sooner than you think."

"Oh?" Ed dragged his attention back to her.

"I've been meaning to tell you." Orla glanced at him with black, shuttered eyes. "I had a meeting with the Board last week. My contract with Wavelength is about to be foreshortened. I've done all I can for them. For you. My report's almost finished. It's time for me to go home." Orla brushed her hair from her face. "You should think about putting your resignation in soon. In the next few days."

"How can I?" Ed sighed. "What will I do with the kids? I need to wait until the end of the summer term. Tanya's at a critical stage in her education," he said, sounding more like her headmaster than her father. "And you haven't even met them properly yet. We'll have to sort it out soon. I want them to like you. I'm sure they will. You can't be any worse than *him*...."

"Your faith in me is touching, Ed."

"And what will I do with them in the holidays? I don't want them coming back here without me to keep an eye on them."

Orla lowered her champagne and pulled up the covers. "Coming back?" The softness had disappeared from her mouth. "From where?"

"That's another good question," Ed said. "Where are we all going to live? We haven't discussed it."

"We *all...?*"

"The kids," Ed said hesitantly. "And us."

"You're thinking of bringing your *children* to the States?" Orla's lips pursed into a small tight circle.

"What did you think I was going to do with them?"

"Leave them here," she said plainly.

"Here? With Ali—and *him?*"

"Why not?"

Ed huffed. "Not on your nelly!"

Orla turned toward him in the bed, but Ed noticed that she was putting a little extra distance between them. "We are going to be extraordinarily busy setting up this new project, Ed. It means everything to me. Everything. I thought it did to you. This is your big chance to get back into the real world. A world without zero-budget promos for Easi-Lift Bath Attachments and Fresh Bottom Incontinence Pads. Who do you think's going to look after them?"

Ed looked hurt. "I thought we would."

"Not on *your* nelly!" Orla said. "Whatever a nelly is."

"Don't you like children?"

"I love children. Someday I would like children of my own. When the time is right."

"You're not getting any younger," Ed tried, pushing to the back of his mind the fact that he might be required to be the father of these proposed children.

"And neither are you," Orla snapped back.

In the same way he'd avoided the subject with Nicola Jones, he hadn't mentioned to Orla that he was firing blank ammunition either. Ed decided this possibly wasn't the best time to raise it. "I can't just abandon them. After all they've been through."

"And I can't have someone else's children thrust upon me."

"Other people manage." Ed knew he sounded pathetic.

"Well, not me."

"I thought you...you...loved me," he said, realizing that it wasn't a word that, as yet, had been spoken between them.

"So did I." Orla pulled at the sheet in frustration. She let out a puff of exasperation. "And I do," she said. "I love *you.* I want *you* to come to the States."

"But my children are a part of me."

"But they're not a part of *me,*" Orla said more softly.

Ed's mouth had gone dry, but he couldn't bear the taste of his champagne and put the glass down, half full. He wondered if this was how Ali was feeling and then realized he hadn't given a thought to how difficult it would be for her to be separated from the kids. Not until he had been forced to face it himself.

The sun had gone and Orla snapped on the bedside light, drowning them in a pool of harsh, revealing light. Ed let out a heavy, unhappy exhalation of breath. "I don't know what to say."

"Neither do I, Ed. This is something you have to work through for yourself."

"Yes."

"You have to prioritize," she said firmly.

"Yes." As if this could be sorted out with the logic of a business report. Orla was back to her "izes." Minimize, maximize, compartmentalize, finalize. Jeopardize. Now his immediate wish was to organ*ize* his departure. He wanted to be out of here. He wanted to go. He wanted to leave and rush home to his unloved, unwanted, destined never-to-be-American children, who would be coming home from their clubs and Scouts and music lessons ferried by other children's parents because he wasn't around to do it because he was in bed with a woman who didn't want them around.

"I have to get back to the children." And he sounded old and sad and worn-out.

Orla's face was impassive. "I know," she said.

CHAPTER 61

Christian hasn't yet come home, even though the hands of the clock are currently nudging midnight in the ribs. I can't relax. You know how it is. I am fully aware, on one level, that Christian is being a selfish bastard and is out somewhere enjoying himself without giving a thought to me and how concerned I might be. Somewhere, on another, entirely separate level, I am terrified that he is hurt, has been mugged, is lying in a deserted ditch or is currently on a stretcher sweating it out with the drunks in an Accident and Emergency Department somewhere waiting for some overworked doctor to find time to attend to a potentially mortal wound. And, if he isn't dead, I'll kill him when he gets here.

This is the golden age of communications. My God, it's harder to stay out of touch than it is to stay in it! I've tried phoning his mobile, but one of those bloody robotic voices keeps telling me that it's not responding. I know that! What I want to know is why? He is going to get it with both barrels when he gets back!

I am pacing up and down the kitchen floor. Robbie and Rebecca have wisely disappeared to their rooms. We have nothing to talk about when Christian isn't here as some sort of emotional Superglue. Robbie isn't so bad, he'll chat away about nothing, but with Rebecca it's all meaningful pauses, slights, covert jibes and veiled accusations. God, it's like being married to her! I don't fit in here. I know that. I'm like a fish out of water. I'm out of place. As welcome as an unsightly blob of cellulite on the lovely thighs of Liz Hurley. And now that I've found out that Christian is some sort of drug dealer, I really have no idea what I'm doing here. Other than waiting to murder him.

I hear a key in the lock and all my hackles rise—not just the ones on the back of my neck, but hackles in places that you can't even begin to imagine. Christian thumps around in the hall for a bit. Goodness only knows what he's doing. Probably taking his coat off. Whatever it is, he's making a meal of it. The lid is rattling up and down on my boiling pot of anger, and great puffs of steam are escaping. Christian opens the door and smiles the most beautiful, disarming smile. "You waited up," he says, delighted to see me.

"Waited up?" I say. "Waited up! I'll say I waited up!"

Christian looks deeply concerned, as well he might. "Is something wrong?"

"Something wrong?" I say. "Something wrong? I'll say there's something wrong!" I regret that my eloquence, like a timid young bird, has temporarily flown its nest in fright.

"Sit down, Ali. You're looking very purple. Tell me what's wrong."

"Sit down?" I say. "Sit down! I'll sit down when I'm ready!"

"Good." Christian is obviously very bemused, and I feel that I'm perhaps not putting my point across clearly enough. He looks as if he's about to make a cup of tea—in the midst of my pain he can still only think about himself.

"I'll make you a nice cup of tea," he says sweetly.

"Where the hell do you think you've been until now?" I burst out, more loudly than I'd intended.

"Pimlico," he says.

"Pimlico!"

"I was doing a talk at the Arts Club about the joys of being a street artist in Covent Garden. Nice bunch of people. It went well." Christian nods contentedly to himself. "Remember? I told you."

"Yes," I say waspishly. And I do remember, now he comes to mention it.

"I went for a swift half with them afterward. Got a couple of commissions. Birthday presents, that sort of stuff. Not life-changing, but it'll keep the bank manager from the door." He is clearly very pleased. "Then one of the guys offered to run me home, but he got chatting so I had to wait. I tried to phone you, but I'm out of talk time. I need to get a voucher tomorrow," he adds absently.

"Couldn't you have borrowed someone else's phone?"

Christian tuts. "It didn't even cross my mind, Ali. What an idiot! Tea?"

"I do not want tea!" I am going even more purple. "I saw Ed today."

Christian frowns. "Won't he let us have the children for the weekend? Is that what this is about?"

"He might not even let me see the children ever again." I can feel tears rushing up, choking my words.

Christian crosses to me and puts his arms round my waist. I don't want them round me. I don't want him touching me. "Why? Why not?"

"Because he caught them smoking dope, Christian. Dope that you gave them!"

He has gone pale and his arms drop away from me. "Shit."

"Exactly." I narrow my eyes.

Christian sits down at the table. "It was a mistake, Ali. A mistake."

I fold my arms. I have come out of crying mode and am cross again. "A big mistake."

"What can I say?" Christian rakes his hair. "When you went to Jemma's, I was still feeling really rough from the night before." He looks decidedly sheepish. "I decided to roll myself a joint to see if it would take the edge off. Tanya is very streetwise," Christian looks up at me, and there is a hint of irony in his eyes. "She knew straight away what it was. Against my better judgment, she persuaded me to let them have a drag." He looks away again. "Or two."

"Even Elliott?"

"Especially Elliott. He said they'd tell on me if I didn't share it. So I did and they all sort of flaked out. I didn't know it would make them do that. It must have been good stuff."

"Or a really bad idea."

"Don't you think I know that!" Christian looked bleak. "I wanted to be one of the gang. I wanted them to like me, Ali. It was silly. I didn't think it through, but I thought that would be the end of it."

"So?"

"So, when I got home, I realized I hadn't got my stash. It must have fallen down the back of the sofa or something. Maybe Elliott lifted it when I was asleep."

"Don't try to blame my children for your stupidity!"

"I'm not," he says. "But I could hardly ring Ed up and ask if he'd have a rummage round the cushions to see if I'd left it behind."

"You might as well have done."

"There was only enough left for one more joint. Maybe two. It didn't even occur to me that they might try to smoke it."

"There's a lot that doesn't seem to occur to you, Christian."

"That's not fair," he argues, his expression pained.

"It was stupid and totally irresponsible."

"Yes," he agrees. "But it isn't the end of the world."

"It might be! Ed is threatening us—*us,* not just *you*—with the police, Social Services, withdrawal of access rights." Eternal damnation.

"Don't you think he's overreacting?"

"Overreacting!"

"Ali, Ali." Christian is trying to be measured. "They smoked some dope, got wasted, and if they had any sense, they wouldn't have tried it again. And I've apologized. If you think it won't make matters worse, I'll apologize to Ed."

"I don't think you realize the seriousness of this," I say harshly. "You have no idea what it's like to be a parent!"

"No, I don't, Alicia. You're right. I have absolutely no idea of what it's like to be a parent. And that's because I'm twenty-three years old and have never been in this situation before. But, in my defense, I feel that I have tried really, really hard to understand what it feels like and, up until now, I thought I was doing pretty well." Christian stands up. "And now I'm going to bed."

And with that he walks out of the room, leaving me with my mouth open and my cup of tea well and truly forgotten.

CHAPTER 62

Neil would have been very jealous. Up to a point. Ed sat back in his chair and folded his arms. He was on location in the garden of a sprawling manor house in the heart of the Home Counties, directing a promotional video for Sit-Down Showers—a device which no one who is fat, over fifty and terminally unfit should be without.

The idea was that if it was all too much of an effort to stand up for the three minutes required to shower, why not sit in a cozy, plastic armchair while you lather up your bits instead? If you were actually infirm rather than just lazy, this would be of great benefit, but the powers-that-be at Sit-Down Showers wanted to stress the glamour and labor-saving elements of their products rather than the fact that they'd come in a bit damn useful if your legs were buggered.

To illustrate this, they'd chosen a lithesome twenty-year-old brunette called Bonnie, with barrage balloon breasts and a 1970s curly perm, to "model" a Sit-Down Shower, involving her, of course, in getting her extremely scanty bikini and her curly perm very wet. Bonnie's legs were definitely not buggered, but it was becoming abundantly clear that her brain probably was. They were on take 472 or something—Ed had lost count and the will to live—and she had yet to manage saying anything other than "Shit-Down Sowers" before dissolving into fits of giggles.

The first few times, the crew had roared, which was a big mistake, because she'd then played it for laughs for half an hour. Then, when they'd lost interest, she'd gone for the sympathy vote, and now didn't appear to be able, even if she was willing, to nudge her needle out of the groove it was stuck in. Ed felt tempted to go and slap her across the face to snap her out of it, like they do with hysterical women in films.

Neil would have found this all very amusing. And this is where they differed. As brothers, they had never shared the same taste in women. Neil liked airheads. He liked woman whose breasts were more evident than their brains. The subtle charms of wit, conversation and intelligence didn't score highly on his brother's eligibility chart. Neil would have enjoyed just looking at Bonnie, despite the fact she was having trouble stringing one sentence together. Perhaps that was why Neil could never hold down a relationship, because he always ended up with women who were the complete opposite of his ideal. All his serious relationships had been with hard, controlling women who had tried to change Neil and ultimately dumped him when his inability to morph into someone else became apparent.

It had taken them hours to rig up a working shower cubicle in the middle of a garden just so that viewers would immediately make the connection that it was much more natural and wholesome to take a shower rather than a filthy old bath. The main problem had been to protect the shower from the intermittent bouts of rain that had also brought proceedings to a halt.

Trevor sidled up to him. "Shall we break for lunch?" he suggested. "See if she can get her gob working after that?"

"Good idea." Sandwiches, soup and tea had been set up in a tent at one side of the garden for the crew, and Trevor ambled off to tell the lads that they could take a break for half an hour, during which time they would, undoubtedly, all take turns chatting up Bonnie.

Orla had been watching from the sidelines, networking with the various luminaries of Sit-Down Showers who had turned up ostensibly to see how their advertising budget was being spent, rather than admitting that they were taking the opportunity to ogle Bonnie, who had on relatively few occasions graced page three. She, too, made her way toward him. "Lunch?" Orla said.

"Not yet." Ed waved his mobile. "I've a few important calls to make."

"Want me to bring you a sandwich?" This was possibly the nicest Orla had ever been to him, and he wondered if she sensed the coolness in their relationship since the "bedroom" conversation.

"I'll follow you in a minute," he said, forcing a smile. "Won't be long."

Ed fingered the envelope in his pocket and, when Orla was safely out of harm's way, pulled it out. Even the sight of it gave him a shiver of something. Trepidation? Pleasure? He wasn't sure. But he *was* sure he recognized the writing on the envelope, he just wasn't certain it was Ali's. Maybe she'd tried to disguise her handwriting. Maybe she'd even got Jemma to write it. He opened it and slipped the gold-edged invitation from inside, his fingers not entirely steady, shaking like a schoolboy's. There were only three things written on the card, in the same flowing hand:

The Ivy
Saturday 8.30
Please Be There

Ed stared at it, deep in concentration, eyebrows knitted together in a frown. It could only be Ali. This was exactly the sort of thing she would do. Or the sort of thing she used to do. She was always secretly arranging surprises for his birthday or special occasions—over the years he'd been treated to flying lessons, white-water rafting, rally driving, hot-air ballooning, weekends in Paris, Rome, Milan. You name it, he'd done it. He only had to mention, in passing, an interest in some new experience, and Ali had dutifully organized it. So much so that he would have been more surprised if there hadn't been a surprise. Birthdays had always been fun times with Ali, and had made him feel very loved, very special. A lump came to his throat. Perhaps he hadn't said so at the time.

It would have cost her a lot to have made a gesture like this. Not just financially—which wasn't a mean consideration with the prices at somewhere like The Ivy—but the emotional cost would have been huge. They had always promised themselves to go there, but had never quite made it. Could it be that she was making the first tentative step toward reconciliation? There was a part of him that really hoped so. He'd felt terrible after their meeting yesterday, and this must already have been in the post. Ed ran his finger round the wavy gold edge. He'd been a bastard, and Ali had looked fantastic and as if she wasn't missing him at all, which had made him want to be even more of a bastard. She'd phoned this morning to give Christian's version of events of the dope-smoking discovery, and he'd done nothing more about it other than ground the children for the rest of their natural-born lives. Yet.

Besides, she was hardly likely to be all mysterious and stump up for The Ivy if all she wanted to do was discuss divorce, was she?

Orla returned bearing a plate of curled-up cheese sandwiches on tired white bread and a cup of tea. "Your tea's going cold," she said.

"Thanks," Ed said.

"I wanted to show you how much I love you." She kissed him on the cheek, and Ed scanned the garden to check that no one was watching, resisting the urge to brush away the damp circle she had left behind.

Orla sat down beside him. Ed turned sideways and attempted to tuck the invitation into his pocket without her noticing. Her eyes flickered across the card, and he wondered if she had managed to read it.

"What's that?" Orla asked.

Ed shook his head. "Nothing."

"Then why are you looking so guilty?" She laughed lightly and handed him his lunch.

"It's from Ali," he admitted.

Orla frowned. "Bad news?"

"I don't think so," Ed said with a smile, and lifted up a corner of his sandwich to see just how little cheese lurked beneath. He bit into the flaccid bread absently. It had to be Ali. Who else could it be?

CHAPTER 63

It was a cold day in Covent Garden market. The sun had given up trying to come out and was hiding behind some big, black blowsy clouds. Business was slow despite the calendar creeping steadily toward the start of the tourist season proper. Weather was the main thing that kept them away, Christian decided. That and the ridiculous prices that now made London one of the most expensive capital cities in the world.

When you could easily pay more than a fiver for a glass of cheap plonk in an overrated wine bar, having a stunning, original portrait in charcoal by a talented but as yet undiscovered starving artist for not much more was a bloody bargain. Christian shifted on his triangular canvas seat and carried on sketching aimlessly. None of the street entertainers were busy today. Even the best of the magicians had only attracted meager audiences. Today, you would have to be prepared to sweat blood to make enough to cover the price of your pitch.

And he was pissed off to start with, anyway. Ali had slept with her back to him all night again. So he, in turn, had slept with his back to her. It was like going out with Rebecca again. And he'd sort of expected older women to behave differently. He didn't know in what way, but he didn't think they'd sulk.

It was fair to say that they'd been very cool with each other since last week, when she'd found out about the dope business. And he could see Ali's point, it was just that he could see his own point rather more. Rebecca and Robbie thought it was hilarious, and he had to admit it made him smile to think about it. Ali had made out that it was all seedy and sordid, but it wasn't. He and the kids had enjoyed a bit of naughty, forbidden fun, nothing more. Where was the harm in that? He could see that it looked bad, of course—particularly when the little buggers had tried it out again for themselves. Kids these days!

He didn't know what to do to win her round. She'd been very gloomy—going to bed early, not saying much, sitting in the corner with one of her self-help books rather than join in the conversation. If he was the sort of bloke who bought flowers, he probably should have gone and bought her some flowers. This is what he hated about relationships, and was more than likely why he was crap at them. It was all very well when it was swimming along all lovely and floaty, but it was when the hard work of keeping it all together started that he found it all a bit much. Should it be an effort to love someone? Christian sighed inwardly. He looked over to the Covent Garden Café, the place where it had all started. Perhaps Robbie was right. Should he have let it drop then? Before they were too entangled. Before he had realized the solid blocks of responsibility that built her life. It wasn't the age difference between them that mattered as such, it was the commitments one seemed to acquire with the passing years, the developed sense of duty, the family ties which seem to tighten with age rather than slacken off, the upsetting of the apple cart of a well-defined place and status in society. If Ali had been thirty-eight, single and unencumbered, where would the problem be?

Ali seemed so special, so beautiful, he thought that all they needed to do was hold hands and they could fly to the moon together. And now all they were doing was getting bogged down by the daily grind of simply existing together. Did all relationships end up like this?

Christian clapped his hands together. His fingers were cold. Perhaps he should go and have a coffee at the Covent Garden Café for old times' sake.

"Hello." A voice broke into his thoughts, and he looked up, hopeful at long last of a customer. "It's me," the girl said.

"Oh, hi." It took him a minute, but it was the one with the black

Lycra from the nightclub. The one he'd taken home the night that Ali had turned up out of the blue.

"It's Sharon," she said shyly, as if she was sure he would have forgotten. Which he had.

"I was just passing. Shopping," she said by way of explanation. "New shoes." Sharon studied her feet. "I'd forgotten you worked here."

And he wondered absently if she had.

Grinning, she pulled her coat round her. "How are you?"

"Fine," Christian said. She looked different from how he remembered her. There was little makeup in evidence and her face was naturally pretty now that it wasn't overpainted, with a small upturned nose. Her hair was mousy, parted in the middle, and she swept it back with her hand. Christian wondered if she had changed the color. The flared denims and sheepskin jacket she wore were more hippie chick than vamp and it suited her better. She seemed less certain of herself, more vulnerable. Not like a Sharon at all. She looked younger too. Nineteen at the most? Maybe eighteen?

"Are you still with that older woman?" she asked too brightly.

Christian paused for a moment, tidying his charcoal. "Yes."

"Oh." A shadow of disappointment crossed her face. "That's nice."

"Yes." Christian returned his gaze to his sketch. "That could have been a bit…awkward for me," he said. "Thanks for being so…understanding."

She shrugged. "That's okay."

"I appreciate it," Christian said.

"Anytime." They both laughed at the absurdity of her offer.

"Maybe not," Christian acknowledged ruefully.

"Well, it's been nice talking." Sharon chewed her lip. "I usually go to The Gallery on Friday nights or The Ministry of Sound. If you're ever around."

"I'll remember that," he said, and she looked at him as if to say fat chance.

"See you then," she said, and turned to walk away.

Christian let her take three or four steps. "Sharon," he called after her. "I was just going for a quick cappuccino. Want to join me?"

She looked back, grinning. "Yes. I'd love to."

Christian picked up his pad and, with his charcoals, tucked them in his rucksack. He balanced his Back In Five Minutes sign on his easel. "Come on, then," he said, and he took her arm and steered her briskly toward the Covent Garden Café. "If you've got time," he said, "I'd like to sketch you later. On the house."

"I'm not busy." She was trotting to keep up with him.

"It's good for business if people see me at work." Christian's mouth spread into a slow, lazy smile. "You have a very beautiful profile," he said.

CHAPTER 64

There is an awful lot to worry about in this relationship. There's fifteen years' difference between us and, although that doesn't seem too huge in the scheme of things, it does alter some things intractably.

When I was twenty-three and already well into motherhood, Christian was an eight-year-old boy, which is not something I want to dwell on. When I'm sixty, Christian will only be forty-five, and that's a huge difference too. Most women of sixty look like they've had a lifetime of clearing up after kids, husbands and washing-machine floods—which they invariably have. Whereas forty-five-year-old men are in their first flush of maturity, a delicate graying of the hair, perhaps a little thinning on top, a softening of the waistband, but generally they look in pretty good nick because they've been cosseted by one of the aforesaid women who because of it will, later in life, look totally knackered.

Take Ed. He is looking fabulous. If we weren't teetering on the very verge of divorce, I'd probably still fancy the pants off him. And he was well cosseted in the years I devoted myself to him. I wonder, when I'm old and gray—will Christian be around to look after me? When I'm seventy, he'll be a mere fifty-five, and by that time I might be so riddled with Alzheimer's that I won't even remember who he is. My God, I might mistake him for one of my own children. So you see, although the spacing of the years doesn't change, the age gap grows ever wider.

Should I care? It didn't prevent Anna Nicole Smith, aged twenty-five, from marrying billionaire oil tycoon J. Howard Marshall, a very unsprightly ninety, who looked to be in an advanced state of decay long before he was dead. But then, young woman and old man isn't uncommon—it does, however, very rarely happen the other way round. You don't often see wrinkly old women with smooth-cheeked young studs. And it very rarely happens to people who haven't got a few million tucked away in the back of their cupboards.

Perhaps it's because I'm sitting in a doctor's waiting room that I'm worrying about bits falling off me. It was a terrible shock when I found out I needed glasses—apart from the obvious horror of discovering that you do look exactly like your mother when you put them on. I know there are exceptions to aging without all your body parts sagging or falling off. Take Joan Collins, I hear you cry. She could be the role model for *How To Be a Sex Kitten at Any Age.* At sixty-seven she's still a size eight and prancing around in stockings and suspenders. And her boyfriend is absolutely decades younger than she is. I don't suppose it worries her one jot.

Goldie Hawn isn't looking too shabby, and she must be knocking on a bit. But then I was never as glamorous or as gorgeous as those two, not even in my prime, which is supposed to be sort of now. And Jane Fonda put us all to shame, didn't she? Leaping around like a mad thing, going for the burn when she was well past being a spring chicken. Aerobics has never been my thing, either. Oh God. I don't want to grow old, it's too depressing.

"Alicia Kingston!" Dr. James comes out of his cubbyhole and shouts my name. I fold my twenty-five-year-old copy of *Country Life,* showing ten-bedroomed houses in Surrey for one and sixpence—not that I was reading it anyway, I was just looking at the pictures—and follow him.

Shutting his consulting-room door behind me, Dr. James glides across the terra-cotta carpet, installs himself behind his big black Ikea desk and smiles his professional concerned smile. "How are you?"

"Fine, thanks." What a stupid thing to say in a doctor's consulting room, but we all do it, don't we?

"Elliott?"

I nod. "Still in one piece."

"Good. Good." I am on chatting terms with my doctor mainly because I've spent so much time in here with Elliott and his various injuries. I'm amazed we escaped the "At Risk" register. "So," Dr. James says, "what can I do for you?" He leans forward on his desk, expectantly.

"I'm not sure, really," I say weakly. "I just don't feel great. I'm not sleeping very well. I've lost my appetite. My periods are shot to pieces. And I've got a permanent headache."

"There's nothing specific wrong?"

Isn't that little list enough? "Well..." How can I explain that I have about as much energy as an off-duty sloth, despite just having returned from two wonderful weeks on holiday where I did fuck-all but bake myself on a sunbed.

Dr. James stands up and, looking purposeful, snaps on his stethoscope. "Let's give you an MOT, shall we?"

He checks my heart, and I'm glad to find out that I've still got one. "On the scales," he orders.

I hate this bit. "Lost weight?" Dr. James asks.

"Have I?" I have. Loads. Yippee. Even after two weeks of gorging myself on holiday. So there are some benefits to feeling like shit.

He takes my blood pressure. "It's a bit on the high side," he mutters, "but nothing too much to worry about. We'll keep an eye on it. When did you last have a smear test?"

I hazard a guess. "Two years ago?"

Dr. James taps expertly at his computer keyboard. "Seven, to be exact," he says with a frown. "We'll do one now, then."

Oh, good. I'm on my back, knees bent up and apart before you can say "lack of dignity." The fact that I can't stand anyone rooting around that particular part of my body with a tube of KY Jelly and a cold metal prod is probably one of the reasons I've put off having a smear test done lately. Plus today it seems even more painful than ever. I don't mention it because Dr. James will probably just tell me I'm tense. Who wouldn't be?

"Don't leave it so long next time," Dr. James says as I'm getting dressed. He is scribbling out a prescription.

"It could be stress, Alicia."

"Really?" Tell me something I don't know!

He stops and looks up at me over the top of his glasses. "I heard about you and Ed," he says sympathetically.

"Well, yes," I mumble. I wonder if he has heard that Ed is threatening to prevent me seeing the children at all because I'm an unfit mother, that my young lover is one step down from a crack-cocaine dealer and that I've lost my cushy job because I was too unreliable to turn up for work when required.

"On a stress scale of one to a hundred," he continues kindly, "divorce is right up there at the top."

Divorce!

"It's only a few points behind bereavement and marriage," he says without irony.

Divorce! I want to tell him that I'm not getting divorced, but I have a horrible feeling that I might be. I want to tell him that I no longer have the strength to deal with all this turmoil and that I want to go back to my safe little life and my safe little house and my safe little job typing invoices for safe little Kath Brown. I want my children back and my husband back and I have no idea how to do it, and if I'm not to sink slowly below the shifting sand beneath me, I really, really need some advice.

Dr. James looks at his watch. It's time for his next patient. He hands me the prescription. "Here, these might help," he says.

"Thanks."

"Nice to see you, Alicia." He is keying the name of his next patient into his computer.

"Yes." I smile automatically, stand up and walk to the door. And I know that it will take an awful lot more than a soppy tablet with a great long name and a million side effects to sort this mess out.

CHAPTER 65

Neil was spring cleaning. Which was okay as it was that time of year which could still just about be classed as spring—not that the seasons bore much in the way of distinction from one another these days. They were all wet and gray and neither too hot nor too cold.

He had considered getting Molly Maid in, but recent experience had told him that if there was something potentially unsightly to be uncovered, it was better that you discovered it yourself and not have your shame exposed to someone young and nubile. The incident with Jemma, the pizza and the porn video was still weighing heavily on his mind.

The bath had been cleaned until it shone like something very shiny indeed, and he'd even polished his taps, which now sparkled so much that he could see his face in them. Albeit a rather distorted face. He felt like something out of a Mister Sheen advert, whipping around with his duster, spraying potpourri-scented loveliness into the air. Neil could see why women were so attracted to housework. It was terribly cathartic. He'd got down on his hands and knees and had scrubbed the kitchen floor. He'd even pulled out the cooker and was startled to see the amount of rotting and dried detritus lurking there, particularly when he hardly ever used the thing—but he could now understand where the man who invented Pot Noodles had drawn his inspiration from. And let's face it, it had to be a man.

The glass thing that goes round in the microwave had been removed and treated to a brisk rubdown with a Brillo pad, and there had been enough food stuck fast under there to feed a family of five for at least a week.

The bedroom was a bit of an eye-opener too, and he could categorically state that discarded rubber did not start to rot, even after two years. There were underpants under his bed that looked like they'd been there since the late Jurassic period, when dinosaurs still roamed the earth. It was quite possible that the carpet needed something stronger than fumigation, and for the first time he wondered about moving out of the flat. He was doing all right, workwise. Okay, so he wasn't desperately inspired by his daily grind, but it paid his bills and then some. Perhaps the act of cleaning had made him more aware that he needed to sort out other areas of his life.

Hugging his Mister Sheen to him, Neil came to a momentous decision. He was going to reinvent himself completely. He was going to be dynamic, forceful, organized, possibly even neat. He was going to cancel his account at The Canton Garden and start eating rabbit food. He was going to stop wearing ten-year-old faded jeans and buy only Paul Smith suits. Paul Smith did make suits, didn't he? Anyway, posh suits. If he wanted to attract rich, powerful women, he was going to have to act as if he were rich and powerful himself. He was going to stop photographing snot-nosed schoolkids and do sexy fashion shoots. He wasn't sure how, but with his new dynamic attitude and his power suits, the big breaks would come his way as surely as night follows day. And, finally, he would force Ed into playing squash at their weekly meet rather than going to the pub to talk about it.

Just as he was about to consider stopping for a well-earned coffee break, the phone rang. It was Jemma.

"Hi," she said.

"Hi." He'd gone off Jemma. Not in a heart way, but in a head way. Her voice still did very strange things to his anatomy, but a relationship that had already involved him in wearing flared trousers, getting a cup of tea lobbed in his face and brazening out a pizza-and-porn experience was not a relationship that was heading in the right direction, was it? Even he could work that one out. And he was the man who'd stayed with Arabelle Hinton-Green for nearly a year after she'd told him he was a no-hoper and they were going nowhere.

"Is everything okay for tomorrow night?"

"Tomorrow night?" This phone table would be next for the Mister Sheen Domestic Exterminator treatment. Neil tucked the phone under his ear and started to leaf through the mounds of paper. He tutted to himself. There were petrol receipts here from 1982! And my, how cheap it had been! You could go there and back on a tankful for less than thirty quid and still have change for chips on the way home. Those were the days!

"Tomorrow night." Jemma sounded stressed. "Ed. Ali. The Ivy!"

"Oh, that," Neil said. There were envelopes franked with a 1997 postmark that he hadn't even opened. Neil slid his thumb under the flap of brown paper of one and started to tear it apart.

"Are you listening, Neil?"

"Of course I am." It was a bill for a missed dental appointment. Neil ran his tongue round his teeth. They all seemed okay. No worries there.

"Did you write the invitations out nicely?"

"Yes," he said. "I used my best felt pen."

"Did you put what I said?"

"Yes. I put what you said."

"Nothing else?"

"Like what?"

"I don't know." Jemma's voice was turning into a screech. That woman should relax more.

"No. No. I didn't put anything else," he assured her.

"Good. Good." He could hear Jemma mentally biting her nails.

"Don't worry," Neil said laconically. "It'll be fine." God, there were all sorts here. Car insurance reminders. Pension info—he'd been meaning to start one for ages. Since 1992, it appeared. The *Sunday Times* Wine Club joining offer from 1995—probably out of date by now.

"And you put first-class stamps on them?"

Neil gasped and halted in the process of sifting through his letters. A small white envelope had stopped him in his tracks.

"What's wrong?" Jemma was immediately suspicious.

"Nothing." Neil glared in terror at the envelope.

"I thought I heard a funny noise."

"I farted," Neil said, thinking that he had nothing else to lose.

"Oh." He heard her sniff. "You *have* checked the restaurant booking?"

"Yes," he said.

Jemma sighed worriedly. "I hope it goes well," she said. "You do think we've done the right thing, don't you?"

"Yes."

"You're sure?"

"Yes. Yes." He was trying to control his breathing. In, out. In, out. In, out. "Look, Jemma," he gasped. "I have to go now. There's something I have to do."

"Oh. Okay." Jemma sounded put out, but he couldn't worry about that now. "I can't wait to find out how they get on. I really hope this brings them back together, Neil."

"So do I," he said.

"All our scheming will have been worth it."

"Yes," he said. "Bye." And he hung up, tugged off his apron, grabbed his keys and raced down the stairs. In his hand he clutched the small white envelope. The one that contained Alicia's invitation to The Ivy. The one that he'd written on just as Jemma had instructed. The one that had a first-class stamp on it. The one he had forgotten to post. He had to get round there now and deliver it before it was too, too late.

CHAPTER 66

Ed was in the kitchen, with a large glass of Dutch courage in his hand. He wanted Ali back, and to do that he had to have his mind free from clutter to concentrate on it. And, he hated to admit it, by clutter he meant Orla and the lovely Nicola Jones.

Telling Orla would be tough. She wouldn't take this kindly. His vision of sharing a beer with Harrison Ford, convivially slapping him on the back and maybe, just maybe, barbecuing a few steaks together was blurring at the edges, becoming indistinct and hazy. It was never going to happen now, his dream of setting Hollywood alight with his sheer brilliance. Once he ditched her, Orla would make sure that it would never happen. It was going the way of all his other dreams—playing for Manchester United, captaining the England cricket team, having a number-one smash hit, keeping all his hair until he was sixty, getting through Christmas without going overdrawn. He just hoped the dream of getting back with Ali was worth it.

He phoned Orla's flat, knowing full well that she would be out. Age was turning him into an emotional coward, he knew he should have done this face-to-face, it was the right thing. He just couldn't bring himself to do it. Orla's soft American brogue sounded tinny on the answerphone.

"Orla," he began. "This is a terrible way to do this. I know I shouldn't. But I'm English. I can't help it. Orla… I need… I need you… I need you to understand that I have to end this. This… This… I have to end it. There's a chance that Ali and I might get back together. A remote chance, but I have to take it. I know now it's what I want. I have to do it for the kids. For Ali. For me. For a thousand other reasons that I'm not sure you'll understand. And I'm really sorry. Really, really sorry. I thought it might work out between us, but… Well. I'm sorry. Really, I am. I hope you'll find someone who'll make you happy."

Ed hung up. The last time he remembered dumping anyone was when he was about fifteen, and it didn't seem to have got any easier. He took a slug of his drink and his fingers were trembling. Oh, well. Going for the double. Nicola would be more simple. There wasn't the guilt involved there, none of the complications that came with working alongside Orla and having to continue a business relationship, at least for the time being. Nicola was delightful, but she was as wispy and as insubstantial as her dresses and her pretty blond curls. He needed a woman with substance, not someone who could be blown away on a stiff breeze. He should have known better than to get involved with her, particularly when his heart had never really been in it, and it was cruel merely to use someone as a benchmark.

With a bracing swig of wine, Ed dialed Nicola's number. This time, the well-rehearsed speech flowed better. "Nicola," he began, "this is a terrible way to do this. I know I shouldn't, but it can't be helped. Nicola, I can't see you again. Not in the romantic sense. There's a chance that Ali and I might get back together, and I know now it's what I want. I have to do it for the kids, for Ali and for me. And I'm really sorry. Really, very sorry. I hope you'll find someone who'll make you very, very happy."

Ed replaced the receiver and sat back, rubbing his hands over his eyes. The kitchen door creaked open, and Elliott came in. He sat down on the stool next to Ed, one finger inserted in the hole where Barney's eye used to be.

"Does this mean that Mummy's coming back to live with us?"

"You shouldn't earwig on other people's conversations, Elliott. What have I told you?"

"I wasn't earwigging!" his son said indignantly. "I was tiptoeing past like a quiet little mouse, and my ear fell against the door. And you were talking very loudly."

"Well, don't do it again," Ed said.

"So, is Mummy coming back?"

Ed sighed. "I don't know, Elliott. But I hope so."

"I do miss her, Daddy."

Ed put his arm round his son. "So do I."

"What will Christian do when Mummy comes back? He won't have anyone."

"What a shame," Ed said.

"I know," Elliott said brightly, "perhaps Christian could have Miss Jones or Orville, now that you're finished with them."

"Elliott, you and I must talk about the fundamentals of dating sometime."

"Now?"

"It can wait." Ed finished his drink. "Now I must go and get myself spruced up. I'm going out."

"With Mummy?"

"Yes," Ed said, only hoping he was right. "One of Tanya's friends is coming to baby-sit."

"But we haven't got a baby?"

"You will be good, won't you, Elliott?"

"I'm always good," he said with a tut.

Ed stood up. "That, Elliott, is a matter of perspective." He checked his watch. Time for a long, relaxing soak in the bath and a quick shave.

"Daddy?"

"Yes, Elliott?"

"Will we still see Christian if Mummy comes back to live here?"

"I don't think so."

"Why not?"

"Mummies and daddies don't work like that," he said.

"Oh." The smile disappeared from his son's face. "I do like Christian, you know."

Cut out my heart and watch me bleed, Elliott!

"He's a lot of fun."

"I'm fun too," Ed said.

"But you can't skateboard."

"I'll pay for you to have lessons."

Elliott's mouth turned down some more. "That isn't the same."

"Then I will learn, Elliott," he said. "Watch this space." I will bloody well learn!

There was a tinkling of glass behind him and Ed spun round. A brick had come through the kitchen window and landed in the washing up bowl in the sink with a dull splash. Elliott had gone white. Ed rushed to the hole where the window used to be in time to see a familiar figure disappearing out of the drive at a run. The flowery roller blind flapped in the breeze, its pom-pommed edge tapping rhythmically against the window.

"Are you okay?" Ed asked.

Elliott nodded, for once at a loss for words.

Ed fished the brick out of the onetime soapy water. There was a note attached to it with string. Ed picked the knot open and unfolded the dripping note. YOU BASTARD was all it said.

"Bollocks," he said with a sigh.

"Daddy, it isn't nice to swear in front of children," Elliott gasped, clearly having recovered his powers of speech.

"This is one of those rare exceptions."

"Who did it, Daddy?"

"Miss Jones," Ed said flatly. Seemingly, the wispy, insubstantial Miss Jones had not taken her dismissal very well.

Elliott folded his arms and puffed heavily. "I'm going to have to change schools, aren't I?"

Ed squished the note in his fist and tossed the house brick back into the water. "Quite possibly," he said.

CHAPTER 67

Neil was completely and utterly out of breath by the time he reached Alicia's house. Which was ridiculous, because he'd driven all the way there in the car.

He'd parked a little way down the street, partly because he wasn't exactly sure which was the right house and partly because he didn't want Alicia to peep out of the window just as he approached and catch him in the act of hand-delivering her should-have-been-posted invitation to dine at The Ivy. He plucked the envelope from the passenger seat and fingered it gingerly. God, Jemma would gnaw his balls off and eat them for breakfast if she ever found out that he'd forgotten to post the bloody thing.

Where was his brain? He knew how important this was, and yet he'd still nearly managed to cock it up. All it had done was strengthen his resolve to turn himself into a new all-singing, all-dancing powerhouse, not some twit who couldn't even be trusted with something as dangerous as an envelope. And to that end, as soon as he'd delivered this little time bomb, he was off to buy himself the nattiest suit in Christendom and bugger the expense.

With a quick and overly melodramatic check that the coast was clear, Neil got out of his car and crossed the road. Ed had told him ages ago where the house was, and he only hoped he'd remembered correctly and that some batty ninety-year-old next-door neighbor didn't turn up at one of London's swishest restaurants instead, expecting her Prince Charming to be sitting there. How on earth had he let Jemma persuade him into all this in the first place! Because he was hoping that it would result in him relieving her of several articles of essential clothing at some later date, he seemed to remember. Bloody testosterone had a lot to answer for!

Neil crouched down slightly, acknowledging that it probably made him look even shadier than if he'd walked upright and confidently to the front door and just shoved it in. The theme tune to *Mission Impossible* started playing in his head, every potential curtain twitch alerting him to the danger of discovery. He should have known that no curtains would be likely to twitch, as no one in London was the slightest bit interested in what anyone else was doing anyway. But this was too important to mess up now that he had come this far—and so close to messing it up.

As he reached the right front door, he spun round, checking he wasn't being followed. He crouched lower and inched his way toward the letterbox, easing the flap open gently, gently, like a bomb disposal expert disarming a fuse. The flap lifted with an I-want-oiling creak, Neil took the invitation and squeezed it through the draft excluder inch by careful inch. When the letterbox had accepted its prey, Neil lowered it down, carefully, carefully, coaxing its creaking hinges to a state of calm and quietness. The envelope was inside. The letterbox was in the closed position. And Neil sighed with relief at the same time as his mobile phone went off, sending him three feet into the air.

"What?" he yelled.

"It's Jemma."

His heart was pounding against his rib cage, and his knees had gone as weak as if he'd seen Britney Spears naked. Adrenaline as well as testosterone is bastard stuff. "Oh," he said breathlessly.

"Neil. You did remember to post those invitations, didn't you?"

"Yes," Neil panted. He could quite safely say, without fear of contradiction, that he had.

Robbie was having a beer and watching *The Weakest Link.* "Did you hear a phone, Becs?"

Rebecca looked up from her nails. She blew delicately on them. "No."

"I did." Robbie pushed himself out of the chair. He went over to the curtain and pulled it back. "There's a bloke on a mobile phone crouched down on our path."

Rebecca looked worried. "Do you think it's someone we owe money to?"

Robbie curled his lip. "Could be."

"What's he doing now?"

"Leaving," Robbie said. "I'll go out and see what he was up to."

He went out into the hall, and Rebecca heard the front door open and close. Robbie came back in carrying a small white envelope. "He's gone," Rob said. "Seems as if he delivered this. It's addressed to Alicia."

Rebecca held out her hand and he gave it over to her.

Robbie sat down again and stared at the television. "Where is Ali?"

"Upstairs," Rebecca said. "She's not very well."

"She's looked a bit off-color all week," Robbie said.

"Christian's up there mopping her fevered brow. He's just taken her some soup."

"That boy has got it *bad*." Robbie wagged his beer bottle and then jumped up. "Slash," he said. "Can't stand the excitement of the normally meek and mild Anne Robinson being a dominatrix."

When he'd left the kitchen, Rebecca examined the envelope. If she had time, she probably would have steamed it open. Looked like it was something interesting. Maybe an invitation. She held it up to the light and tried to peer through it. Call of nature presumably completed, Robbie's footsteps thumped back down the stairs.

Quickly, Rebecca ripped the envelope into little pieces. "Goodbye, Alicia," she said. "*You* are the weakest link!" And she stuffed the tiny shreds of Ali's invitation to The Ivy down the side of the sofa.

CHAPTER 68

The famous Ivy was housed in a very unprepossessing building. It was down a rather seedy, litter-strewn side street opposite St. Martin's Theatre where Agatha Christie's *The Mousetrap* had been playing since time began. But, despite running for nearly half a century and the fact that it must, by now, be more jaded than a lapdancer's knicker elastic, there were still smiling crowds milling around waiting to see it.

The restaurant was swathed in scaffolding which did little to enhance its appearance, which was dreary on the best of days. The windows were dark, leaded, diamond-shaped panels in jewel tones, like the coat of a harlequin or the stained-glass windows of a particularly modern Catholic church. You could see nothing of the inside through them. Not a hint. Ed knew, because he had spent an awfully long time trying to peer through to see whether or not Ali had arrived yet. He nibbled his fingernails uncertainly. Ed was nervous. That much was clear. Otherwise he wouldn't have been hanging around outside, eulogizing about the bloody windows.

Decked out in his best suit, bathed, shaved, doused in smellies, Ed was wearing a red rose in his lapel, which he thought added a humorous touch to what was potentially a very tense meeting. The rest of the bunch was hidden furtively behind his back. He wasn't a natural flower-buyer—but then, which man was? He always felt a bit of a twat walking through the street with flowers. It was too poofy for words, even though they usually had the desired effect, which was well worth the effort. He didn't know if red roses were the right thing to buy given the occasion, but what the hell? They were Ali's favorites—as far as he could remember. Ed scratched his chin. Or had she said she hated red roses? Bugger!

Ed clicked the tension from his neck. It was best to get all his clicking over with before he went in, as it always drove Ali barmy and he didn't want her irritated before the evening got under way. This was ridiculous! It was more nerve-racking than his first date with her! Mind you, he'd had a cold then—which she'd kindly given to him—and the whole thing had been conducted through a fug of Benylin Expectorant. Tonight, he needed a clear head, as he didn't want to put a foot wrong. And, before he could think better of it, Ed wrenched the door open.

CHAPTER 69

Orla hummed quietly to herself as she clanked her way up to her apartment in the elevator. She was laden down with carrier bags filled with things she didn't need, but then that was the joy of retail therapy, and she had certainly needed some. Ed had been avoiding her all week, she could tell. Whenever he saw her coming, he'd dived into one of the editing suites or pretend to be deep in conversation with a bemused-looking Trevor. It was driving her to distraction, and she could put her finger exactly on the minute she knew it had all started to go wrong.

It was after that conversation about the children. She had handled it badly, but then it isn't every day that you have three children foisted upon you, Ed should appreciate that. She could deal with this. They could work it through. Ed was too good a director. Too good in the sack. Too good a catch all-round for her to mess up now. She'd never been in what you would call a "long-term" relationship—three months had been the extent of her dating stamina. But then the only men she dated had turned out to be self-centered, mamas' boys with suspect homophobic opinions.

She was going back to the States, but there was no way she was going back without him. Maybe they could all go to family therapy, it was one strand of counseling she hadn't yet tried. Whichever way, the years were passing far too quickly for her to continue being choosy, and this was just one little blip in an otherwise very sunny horizon—or three little blips, to be precise.

Ed hadn't asked to see her tonight, but then she'd preempted it by saying that she would be unavailable, so that she wouldn't feel too abandoned and perhaps that might give him something to think about. After all, he had given her plenty to think about. She'd seen the envelope he'd had at the Sit-Down Showers shoot which had made him blush like a guilty schoolboy. It looked like an invitation, and she'd tried to scan it quickly before he'd had a chance to push it back into his pocket. It was impossible. The writing was too neat, too small. Had it been from Alicia, as he'd said? Or was it something entirely different? Did she know Ed well enough to trust him? Probably not. Whatever it was, she knew instinctively in that small hollow at the pit of her stomach that it was something Ed was trying to hide from her.

Orla turned her key in the lock, barged her parcels through the door and kicked it shut behind her. She dropped them all on the floor in the hall. Drink first. Deal with unnecessary purchases later. The red light on her answerphone was blinking furiously at her and, stripping off her coat, Orla clicked the play button. She went through to the kitchen and opened the door to the fridge, pulling out a bottle of ice-cold Vodka Absolut. It was her mother's voice.

"Hi, honey. Mommy here." Orla reached for a shot glass from the cupboard. "I'm glad to hear you're coming home, honey. I'm missing you." She went on to say an awful lot about nothing, ending with: "I'll catch you later, honey. I hope you're out having fun. Kiss. Kiss."

Orla downed the vodka, enjoying the sensation as the freezing liquid heated up the back of her throat. Her mother never missed her. It was the first time she'd phoned in months, which usually meant that she was between boyfriends and had time on her hands. She'd made her fortune as a theatrical agent and now spent her time bedding twenty-five-year-old actors, offering them the earth and dumping them again before she had to stump up so much as a grain of sand. And who could blame her? Nice work if you could get it.

The second voice stopped the second shot of vodka on its way to her lips.

"Orla..." It was Ed. And he sounded terrible. Truly terrible. Distraught. The tape hissed and crackled, so that she couldn't catch the first bit clearly. Orla turned up the sound. Ed's voice was still faint. "I can't help it. Orla... I need... I need you..." The tape cut off, beeping enthusiastically, and whirred itself back to the beginning. Her mother, yammering on about Brett or Bradley or whoever it was this time, must have used up all the goddamn tape.

Her mother's voice piped up again. "Hi, honey—"

"Damn," Orla said, and punched the buttons until Ed's message kick-started again.

"Orla... I need... I need you..."

Orla replayed it again. "Why do you need me?" she shouted at the answerphone, straining to listen through the crackling.

"Orla... I need... I need you... I need you to understand..."

Again the tape, uncaring of its impeccable timing, rewound itself. Damn. Damn. *Damn!* Whatever it was he needed her to understand, he sounded pretty damn desperate about it. Orla downed the belated shot of vodka and punched out Ed's mobile phone number. It went straight to his messaging service, so she hung up and started pacing the hall. She had read *The Rules,* and you were never, ever supposed to return men's calls, particularly when they sounded desperate, as it would make you seem just as desperate. But then, *The Rules* had never worked, otherwise she wouldn't still be single and desperate. Orla clenched her fists. That wasn't a good idea. If she contacted him by phone, he could just fob her off with any old excuse, make light of his message.

"Orla... I need... I need you... I need you to understand..." the message played of its own volition. She snatched up the receiver again and bashed the handset with it. "Why? Why? *Why?*" she shouted. "Why do you need me now?"

Orla nibbled her fingers, a habit she'd long since forced herself to abandon except in times of extreme stress. She wasn't used to being at a man's beck and call. This would put a whole new slant on the relationship. Maybe it was time to abandon any defenses and enter into this relationship wholeheartedly. Time to throw the rule book in the trash can where it belonged. One final nibble and she'd decided. She had to find him, wherever he was. Orla abandoned the vodka and shrugged into her coat once more. He needed her and it was urgent. Of that, there was no doubt. And if he needed her, she would damn well go to him.

CHAPTER 70

Neil was admiring his reflection in the mirror. "I feel good," he sang to himself in the style of James Brown, straightening the lapels of his brand spanking new Paul Smith suit. "I knew that I would..." He tried a few exploratory dance steps. "I feel fine, like a glass of good wine...." He gave a twirl. "Da, da, da, da!"

Neil adjusted his tie. "If you looked any sharper, mate, you'd cut yourself to ribbons," he said and winked cheekily at himself. He could have nearly bought himself a new Hasselblad camera for what this little bit of schmatter had cost, but it was worth it. He felt like he'd just walked off the set of a Will Smith film.

When he'd finished admiring himself, Neil tried Ed's mobile phone again. It was still switched off and Neil had left half a dozen messages on Ed's answering service and his brother hadn't replied to any of them. But then, Neil didn't feel confident that he'd left the most coherent messages imaginable as he hadn't wanted to give the game away.

It was fast approaching the witching hour, which was eight-thirty in this particular case. He hoped Ali had finally received her invitation, although he couldn't have done a lot more than actually press it into her hot little palm. And that too would have given the game away. Neil caught a glimpse of himself again.

God, he was looking good! Supposing Ali had got her invitation, but she wasn't able to go for some reason—although what reason would keep Ali from The Ivy, or food in general—he couldn't quite imagine. Why had he ever got involved in all of this? Neil chewed his fingernails and sighed out loud. What if, despite their brilliant planning, this all went belly-up? It would be hell for Ed if he was sitting there alone. He would never forgive Neil for his involvement. Although Neil, of course, would try to shift all the blame onto Jemma.

Neil stared at himself again. He couldn't stand here all night admiring his new image, he had to do something. Something constructive. But what? A light went on in his brain, and Neil clapped his hands together with glee. He would go and lurk outside The Ivy, just to make sure they'd both turned up. Though how he would explain what he was doing there if either of them saw him would take some creative thinking. Neil slipped his car keys into his snazzy new pocket. He would give it some brainpower on the drive there.

Regretting the fact that he hadn't had time to polish his one and only good pair of shoes, Neil bounded downstairs to his car. For once, the Citroën didn't show its usual charming reluctance to start and roared into life at the first turn of the key. Well, perhaps not roared…

As Neil set off down Camden High Street, he had an extremely good feeling in his bones. He'd had the same feeling the day that Manchester United beat Bayern–Munich, 2–1, in the 1999 European Cup Final—both goals scored in extra time—and you didn't get that kind of feeling very often. He fizzed with positive vibes. As he passed an Esso station, he decided to pull in and buy some flowers in case his clueless brother hadn't thought about it. But then his clueless brother didn't know who he was meeting and could, quite possibly, be excused a certain amount of cluelessness. Neil ran into the petrol station Late-Nite shop and there, right beneath the stack of cornflakes, the stale-looking bread and the few remaining battered and tattered *Daily Mail*s was the most beautiful bunch of red roses wrapped in rich purple tissue paper. Neil snatched them up and winced only slightly as he paid for them. As he sprinted back to the car, thoroughly delighted with his second extortionate purchase of the day, he noticed that the pretty blond cashier was smiling coyly at him through her security window. Neil blew her a kiss. This was definitely going to be his lucky, lucky suit.

CHAPTER 71

Inside, The Ivy had the tasteful air of a rather old-fashioned gentleman's club, all dark mahogany paneling and crisp white linen. There was a subdued hum of good-natured conversation, the occasional restrained ha-ha-ha of genteel laughter. The waiters moved silently, as graceful and as haughty as swans. Everyone was in couples, lovey-dovey holding-hands couples. Ed smiled quietly to himself. This was evidently not a hen-party type of place. This was a place where you came to impress a new love, get engaged or even try to patch up a shaky marriage. Looking round made him acutely aware that he was alone, and he felt conspicuous because of it. Ed glanced at his watch, nearly eight-thirty. He hoped his "mystery" date wasn't going to be late, acknowledging ruefully that Ali's punctuality had never been one of her strong points.

"Drink, sir?"

"Yes," Ed said. "Please." And he snapped his attention back to the menu. It ought to be champagne, as he hoped to God they'd have something to celebrate by the end of tonight. An end to all this madness, this mayhem and misery, this minor indiscretion. The start again of life as he used to know it. Ali could have been shagging the entire lineup of *NSYNC, and thoroughly enjoying it, and he wouldn't care as long as she agreed to come back and he didn't have to carry on living without her.

Ed ordered a bottle of the finest fizz, blanking the pain that this would cause his credit card. If the interior decor failed to make your pulse race, then the prices on the menu certainly would. The food was rather eclectic fare, influenced too much by *Ready, Steady Cook* for his liking. Not that he was hungry. His stomach was twisting and turning like wet washing in a tumble dryer. And he would be glad when the champagne arrived—as it did on cue—since his mouth tasted like one of yesterday's socks. The waiter poured him a glass and looked meaningfully at the conspicuously empty place opposite him and at the red roses by his side.

"Would sir like me to leave another glass?"

Ed checked his watch again. Perhaps it was fast. It was a quarter to nine and there was still no sign of Ali. "Yes. Yes, please," he said. Why would she go to the trouble of setting this up if she didn't intend to show?

The waiter put the rest of the champagne in the ice bucket and left. Ed wet his lips. It tasted good—even at a zillion quid a sip. If he'd known Ali was going to be late, he'd have stopped at All Bar One across the road and had a few beers. The first glass of champagne went down without touching the sides, and Ed helped himself to a second glass from the ice bucket. He sat and twiddled his fingers and tried not to stare at the other diners.

At nine o'clock the waiter reappeared. "Would sir like to order?"

The champagne was half-gone and the bubbles were blowing his stomach up like the gas in a hot-air balloon. Ed looked round at the lovey-dovey couples again. This was too heartbreaking to bear. "No," Ed said. "I won't be staying for supper." He smiled bravely at the waiter. "I think I've been stood up."

The waiter's sympathetic look said, "Tell me about it!"

"I'll just take the bill for the champagne."

He wanted to get out of here as quickly as he could—all this ambience was making his eyes water. How could Ali have done this to him? He signed the bill with a hasty signature and went to leave. His legs felt like they were weighted with lead, and they were trembling slightly as they did when he'd overdone it a bit on the squash court. Perhaps this hadn't been Ali? Perhaps someone else, someone with a cruel, cruel sense of humor, had set him up to deliberately embarrass and humiliate him. But who? The whole thing bore the hallmarks of an Alicia-style surprise. Would he have been taken in by it otherwise? Whoever had done it, he wanted to punch their lights out. When he found out who it was. And he would. Make no mistake.

Ed took the half-empty bottle of champagne from the ice bucket—there was no way he was leaving that here—and his rapidly wilting bunch of roses. Forcing himself to walk slowly out of the restaurant, Ed stared grimly ahead. There was no way he wanted to make eye contact with the other *It's A Wonderful Life* diners, and they, thankfully, seemed to be avoiding noticing his plight. He wanted to go home and lick his wounds, not have salt rubbed in them as someone had unkindly done.

The restaurant manager nodded as he pushed through the harlequin doors. "Good evening, sir."

"Is it?" Ed said and walked out into the street, taking great gulping breaths of what passed for fresh air in London as he did.

Outside on the street, an old woman huddled in a filthy, once-tartan blanket, a mangy old dog curled round her feet.

"Spare a pound for a cup of tea," she implored, thrusting out a hand that hadn't troubled soap for some considerable time.

"Here," Ed said. He gave her the bunch of red roses and, with a final swig, the half-bottle of champagne. Peeling a twenty-pound note from the bills in his pocket, he parted with that too.

The old woman let her toothless mouth drop open. "You're a gent," she cried ecstatically, clutching at her ragged coat. "A kindhearted gent."

"I'm not," Ed said bitterly. "I'm a mug. A first-class mug." And he strode off down West Street trying not to break down. To top it all, he couldn't remember where the hell he had parked his car.

CHAPTER 72

Orla was standing outside Ed's house, hot and bothered, apprehensive and having raced across London to get here. Loud music pounded out into the driveway. After much knocking of the knocker, ringing of the bell and foot-tapping outside on the gravel, Elliott eventually opened the door.

"Hello," he said warily.

Orla crouched down. It was always good to get on a level with kids.

"Have you dropped something?" Elliott said, looking at the gravel.

"No. I haven't." Orla smiled brightly. "Remember me, Elliott?"

"I'm not an idiot."

"Of course not." Orla stood up again. This one would be the first to get straightened out with therapy. "I'm looking for Daddy," she said.

"Your daddy or my daddy?" Elliott queried.

"Your daddy." Orla kept her smile in place. "Is he home?"

"No." Elliott studied his feet.

"Do you know where he's gone?"

"Yes."

"Would you mind telling me?"

"I'm not supposed to talk to strangers."

Orla laughed. "I'm not a stranger."

"Tanya said you're very strange."

"Did she?" Orla narrowed her eyes. Next in line for therapy, she vowed. "Please tell me where your daddy is, Elliott. It would be very helpful of you."

Elliott puffed. "It'll cost you a fiver."

"What?"

"Five pounds," Elliott reiterated, folding his arms.

Orla felt plumes of smoke coming out of her nose. "Elliott..." she started. "Never mind." She rummaged in her purse and reluctantly handed over a five-pound note.

Elliott put it in his pocket with an angelic smile. "He's gone to The Shrubbery."

"The Shrubbery?"

"Haven't you heard of it?"

"No, I don't think I have."

"It's a posh restaurant," he informed her. "Very posh."

"Oh, I see," Orla said. "Do you think you might mean The Ivy?"

"I might do," he replied. "I'm only four!"

"Right." Orla sighed. "I'll try The Ivy." She started to turn back toward her car.

"You should say thank you," Elliott said.

"Thank you." The smile was too much of an effort. "It's been nice meeting you again, Elliott," she said. "And a pleasure doing business with you. I'll enjoy telling Daddy. *Your* daddy."

Elliott leaned insolently on the door frame. "You wouldn't dare."

"Just watch me," Orla warned as she headed back toward her car.

"He's gone to The Shrubbery with Mummy," Elliott shouted after her. "*My* mummy." And he closed the front door firmly behind him.

CHAPTER 73

Why is it you can never find a parking meter when you want one? There must have been thousands of the beggars stretched in a line all across London, but never just where you needed one. And tonight had been no exception. Neil had parked a million miles away from the restaurant and was now dashing through the streets, battering hapless passersby with his roses, racing to The Ivy.

The sidestreet was deserted, the restaurant shrouded by a framework of rusty iron. There was no point hanging around outside, as they should have ordered and be halfway through their starters by now—shock over, loosened up, laughing, joking, talking over old times. God, he hoped so.

Neil swung the door open and was greeted by a smart black-suited man whom he assumed was the restaurant manager. He was glad he was wearing his Paul Smith suit and not his usual garb of jeans, not necessarily clean, and polo shirt.

The man armed himself with his professional greeter's smile. "Can I help you, sir?"

"Do you have a table booked in the name of Kingston?"

The manager ran his finger down a page of bookings on his desk.

"It was for eight-thirty," Neil offered helpfully.

The man frowned. "I'm afraid you're rather late…."

"It's not for me," he said. "It's for my brother." Neil tried to peer over his shoulder. "And his wife. I wondered if they'd arrived?"

The manager studied his bookings some more. "One moment," he said tight-lipped, and disappeared into the restaurant. Neil tried to catch a glimpse of the interior, but it was impossible. True to his word, a moment later the man reappeared, a waiter at his side.

"Mr. Kingston left in rather a rush," the waiter said when prompted. "About five minutes ago. I'm afraid his guest didn't turn up."

Neil's heart sank to his unpolished shoes. "Was he okay?"

The waiter looked for confirmation that it was all right to breach client discretion. The other man gave a barely discernible nod. "He seemed rather…disappointed," the waiter said.

"Disappointed, about-to-slit-his-wrists disappointed?" Neil asked.

The waiter looked for the go-ahead again. "Disappointed, about-to-slit-someone-else's-wrists disappointed," he said.

Neil sucked in his breath. "Thanks," he replied earnestly.

"You're welcome." The waiter disappeared gratefully back to his post.

"I'm sorry," the manager said.

Neil pursed his lips. "Me too." And he stuffed his bunch of bloodred roses into a conveniently placed leather wastepaper bin.

Misery washed over him. Ed would batter him to a pulp with his cricket bat if he ever found out that it was Neil and Jemma who'd dreamed up this fiasco. And why the hell hadn't Ali showed? Perhaps she was hopelessly in love with this young toy boy of hers after all. Perhaps it wasn't just a flash in the pan. Perhaps they should never have interfered in other people's lives. How, by all that was holy, he was going to break this news to Jemma he had no idea. And this was supposed to be his lucky, lucky suit!

He turned to go out of the door, and as he did so, a stunningly attractive woman rushed past him, causing the heavy, well-oiled door to ricochet on its hinges. She turned and stared at him. Her hair was almost black, frothy, like a feather boa piled on top of her head, and her strong, wide mouth, emphasized with a slash of red lipstick, was unhappy. Fine lines creased her soft white forehead into a frown. Her black eyes were shuttered, inscrutable, and they flicked over Neil blink-clicking like the lens of a camera. She was tall, beautiful and utterly, utterly out of his league. The strains of Rossano Brazzi singing "Some Enchanted Evening" from the film *South Pacific* reverberated very loudly in Neil's head. He checked the speakers in the foyer—they were playing some twinkly classical stuff. Neil banged his ear.

"Sorry," she said in a resonantly New York accent. "I'm in a rush."

"Me too," Neil said, wishing that Rossano would shut the flip up. He stood and held the door open gormlessly.

"Thanks," the woman said, flicking her tongue across her full lips.

Neil decided that he had died and gone to heaven and that the inevitable bollocking that would come his way from Jemma would be well worth it for this moment alone.

The restaurant manager engaged his professional smile again, although Neil noted that it seemed less of an effort for this particular customer.

"I'm looking for a Mr. Ed Kingston," she said, brushing a stray curl from her eyes.

The manager cast a nervous glance at Neil. The woman turned round and followed his gaze.

Neil felt himself flush. "So was I," he said.

The woman's frown deepened. "And you are?"

"His brother."

The woman raised her eyebrows. "Really?" she said. The frown stayed in place. "I'm Orla." She held out her hand. "Pleased to meet you."

Neil looked at her hand and back at her face. Rossano Brazzi's exquisite rendition of "Some Enchanted Evening" screeched abruptly to a halt.

CHAPTER 74

I am curled up on the bed, clutching my stomach. A thousand knives are slashing away at my insides. I've been here for hours now, alternating between throwing the duvet off as I boil over and pulling it back on as I turn into a shivering wreck. My forehead and hands are like blocks of ice. In case you are in any doubt, I am not a well person.

Christian is standing over me pale-faced, plucking at his T-shirt and perspiring nervously. "What can I do?" he says.

"I think I need you to call the emergency doctor." I barely recognize my own voice, it croaks out in a whisper like a frog with a sore throat.

Christian's eyes are bleak, and he might or might not be in focus. "What emergency doctor?"

"At the practice you're registered with. Don't they have an emergency number?"

"I'm not registered with a doctor," he says. "I'm never ill," he adds apologetically.

It only serves to make me more aware of our age difference. Christian is in that blissful gap between the conquering of childhood illnesses and the onset of age-induced meltdown. He is at the age where he believes he can abuse his body unmercifully and it will never let him down. But it will. They all do in the end.

Like mine. I roll in pain. I know exactly what's wrong with it. Or I think I do. Dr. James phoned me yesterday when he'd received thc results of my smear test and told me his fears, unleashing mine. He told me not to worry, which I didn't until he told me not to. It's like telling someone not to blink, isn't it? The minute you think about it, you can do nothing but blink. And I am blinking worrying, that's for sure. I have an appointment with a specialist next Wednesday, but I'm not sure that I'm going to be able to wait until then.

"Can you drive me to the hospital?"

"Are you sure you need to go?"

The words I need to say to Christian won't come to my mouth. They are stuck in my throat, lodged, unspeakable.

"It could be something dodgy you've eaten," he offers brightly.

"I don't think so." The room is starting to go swimmy and soft. The commando screaming out of the ceiling becomes a hazy khaki blob. "Can you drive my car?"

"Er…no," Christian says weakly. "I'm banned."

I groan.

"Drunk driving," he says. "I've got another year to go."

"I can't wait that long."

"I didn't mean…" he tails off.

"What about Robbie? Or Rebecca?" See how desperate I am?

"Neither of them drive," Christian says feebly.

Why should they? They live in London and don't have children to ferry around.

Another wave of pain crashes against me. "Ring for a taxi," I say, clenching my teeth.

Christian chews his lip. "I haven't got any money."

"I'll pay," I say. "Just do it. Do it now."

Christian rakes his hair, breathes heavily through his nostrils and walks out of the room.

I try to sit upright and fail. I fall back onto the bed and try not to hold on to the thoughts that come unwanted. I'll pay. No truer words have ever been spoken. Believe me, there's no such thing as a free lunch. And there's no such thing as a free drawing either. Everything in life has its price, and now I'm being asked to pay up.

CHAPTER 75

Neil eventually took Orla's hand. "Hi," he said.

The smile came back and so did Rossano Brazzi. The woman of his dreams stood before him, and Ed, the lucky bastard, had snaffled her up first. Some blokes had all the luck. And his brother seemed to have more than most. This bloody lucky suit was proving a disaster!

"Do you know where he is?" Orla asked, extracting her hand from his. Her fingers were long, slender pianist's hands.

The restaurant manager tried to make himself look busy.

"No," Neil said. "He'd gone by the time I got here."

"Why did you come?"

Tricky one that. "Er..." Neil said while he floundered around his brain looking for inspiration.

"He was meeting Alicia, wasn't he?"

"Yes," Neil said, nodding. Wool would not be pulled easily over this one's eyes. "I wanted to check everything was okay."

Orla shrugged. "That's thoughtful of you."

They stood and looked at each other. Orla's face softened. The black eyes charged with flecks of electricity. "What now?" she said, gesturing with her arms.

"I don't know," Neil answered.

She gave a half-laugh and twisted one of her curls. "I guess I'll go home to a frozen pizza."

"Me too," Neil said.

Orla clapped her hands together. A tight, uncomfortable movement. "Oh, well."

The restaurant manager cleared his throat. Neil glanced up at him, and the manager flicked his eyes toward the restaurant door. A light clicked on in Neil's brain.

"Unless..." he said.

Orla tilted her chin. "Unless?"

Neil laughed. "No. No. No. I don't know what I'm thinking of!"

She laughed back. "What?"

"Well." Neil fluttered his eyelashes. "We could have dinner together."

Orla glanced at the restaurant manager.

"I'm sure we could find you a table," he said encouragingly.

Orla laughed again. "Shall we?"

"Why not?" Neil was magnanimous.

"If you'd like to go through, madam," the manager said to Orla, indicating the door.

As Neil passed him, he whispered, "Cheers, mate."

The manager picked the beautiful bouquet of red roses wrapped in purple tissue from the wastepaper bin, dusted them off and gave them back to Neil with a wink. "Good luck, sir."

"I think I'll need it," Neil said, tugging at his tie. But then, he was wearing his lucky suit.

CHAPTER 76

It isn't possible to die of happiness, I've learned. It is, however, entirely possible to die of cancer.

I pull my hospital gown round my knees, which bares my bottom to anyone who cares to look. Not that there is anyone else here, apart from the consultant gynecologist who's probably seen it all before and a little bit more. He is sitting looking at me after his calm, cool bombshell announcement, waiting, presumably, for some response from me.

There's a big empty space where the comforting thud, thud, thudding of my heart should be, and I swear it takes ten whole minutes for the next beat to kick in. What if I have a heart attack and die of shock before the cancer has a chance to kill me? I laugh out loud at the irony, and the consultant lowers his head and studies his notes.

This is a truly horrible room. The tiles are supposed to be white and clinical, but they're grubby, gray and cracked all over the place. I'm on an examination table which has a rip in it where I can see the stuffing coming out, and that can't in any way be classed as hygienic, can it? And this tissue paper I'm sitting on is revolting. It's more crumpled than I could have made it, and there are already faint yellow stains on it as if someone has used it before, someone with a more leaky disease than me. Goose bumps creep all over my skin and I really want to get off, but my legs won't move.

The consultant comes round his desk and perches uneasily on it. He crosses his legs and then his arms. I think he is trying to adopt a relaxed pose. So am I, and we are both failing.

"You have a very good chance of making a full recovery," he says softly. "An excellent chance." I want to remind him that's not what he said a minute ago. A minute ago he said I had ovarian cancer. A minute ago he said it was at a very advanced stage.

He smiles grimly at me and continues, "You're young. You're fit. You're healthy." Is he talking to the same person? I resist the urge to look round in case there is someone else behind me who *is* young and fit and healthy. I'm not young and fit. And I'm definitely not healthy. I'm as old as the hills and I have a disease, I want to say. I have a disease that's silently eating me away inside.

"We must move quickly," the consultant says. He is young and fit. He looks like he's just come back from Barbados or Antigua. Some exclusive holiday resort. Sandals, maybe. He is bronzed and athletic-looking. He looks like he swims or works out. His sheer healthiness is out of place in this hospital full of sick people, in this small, airless room with a sick person. "I want your permission to operate straight away." He is wearing the most awful tie. Whoever told him it matched that shirt was color-blind. I wonder if he has a wife who helps him to get dressed. Perhaps she's the one that's color-blind. "Ali?"

I look up. He's folding and unfolding his arms and legs as he talks as if he's doing some big, invisible origami. "Ali. I want to prepare you for surgery tomorrow."

I know I should say something, but I can't. I nod instead. I want it out of me, this thing. This thing that Dr. James put down to nothing more than stress.

I spent the entire evening being ignored in Casualty, waiting for a bed to come empty so that I could be "observed." I had this horrible thought that they were either going to parcel up someone and send them home before they were ready because they weren't quite as sick as me or that they were waiting for someone to die so that I could nip between their sheets. I have been reading far too much about our Third World National Health service in the *Daily Mail* to feel comfortable here. Anyway, at around three in the morning, when someone did finally "observe" me, they decided I should have been "observed" a lot earlier. About five years earlier, I think.

The consultant glances at his notes. "You've got three children?"

I nod. I am hanging on to them by a thread, I want to say, because my husband thinks I'm an unfit mother. It was all I ever wanted to be—a wife, a mother, to have a lovely husband, three children and maybe some roses round the door.

"Had you planned to have any more?"

I don't know whether I nod or shake, but I feel my head move. I can't even plan what I want for dinner tomorrow night these days. I try to conjure up images of children that may or may not be born, but fail dismally. I just can't think that hard.

"Is there someone you want me to contact for you?" he says. "Do you need to discuss this?"

What would be the point? Who would I discuss it with? Not Ed. Why should he care anymore? Besides, even the sight of a blood-stained plaster makes him go pale. Not Christian. How could he understand anything of this? He is another young, fit and healthy specimen. He has no idea what it is like to have your traitorous insides do the dirty on you. How could he possibly advise me on the best course of action? And, as I see it, I don't have a choice. It's do or die. Literally.

"Do you have children?" I ask.

The young, healthy consultant looks embarrassed. "Not yet."

"When you do," I say wearily, "make sure that you treasure them."

My eyes fill up with tears and I feel one roll out, over my cheek, in a cold, self-pitying trail, and I watch it splash in slow motion on the hard vinyl tiles. It is followed by another and another and another, until there is a great, long stream of them. I feel as if my heart is about to snap in two. I stare at the tears pooling at my feet. This floor looks like no one has taken a mop to it in a long, long time.

CHAPTER 77

It was persistently raining. Drips of rain from Ed's porch were running down and hitting Neil squarely in the middle of his head, and he didn't feel like moving out of the way. He felt as if it was what he deserved. Water torture from Ed's porch. Water torture and kneecapping with a baseball bat. And he was probably going to get both.

He'd wanted to ride over on his motorbike, but it wasn't a bike-riding sort of day. Rain seeped inside all your exposed bits, face, neck, wrists. It ran down inside your boots making a water feature of your toes. Soggy leathers took days to dry out. If, however, he had been able to ride round on his motorbike, it might have given him time to sort out in his head exactly what it was he wanted to say.

Ed opened the door.

"Bro!" Neil stood and dripped cheerfully at him, relieved to see that he wasn't yet carrying anything that could be classed as an offensive weapon.

"Bro," Ed replied flatly. He stood aside while Neil went in. Ed followed him into the kitchen. There was a bottle of whisky standing on the counter, and in the light Ed's eyes were looking red-rimmed and bleary with alcohol. "Drink?" Ed asked, pouring himself another one.

"No thanks, mate," Neil said, shaking his head. "Designated driver."

"You don't mind if I do?"

"Well…don't you think you've had enough?"

Ed looked up. "No."

Neil wished he had something to fidget with, so he started to wring out a wet bit of his fringe. "It's not the answer, is it?"

Ed sat down on a kitchen stool, whisky poised. "To what?"

Neil shrugged. "Anything…"

"In particular?"

The oblivion of whisky was very tempting. "What happened last night?" Neil ventured.

"I sat in and watched telly," Ed said. He fixed his brother with a stare.

"I've got some bad news, some very bad news, some very, very bad news and some really, truly awful news," Neil blurted.

"Have you been taking drama-queen lessons from Elliott?" Ed said over the top of his glass.

"I'm serious, bro."

"Go on, then," Ed said, topping up his whisky. "Do you want to tell me in reverse order in the time-honored tradition of Miss World contests?"

Neil looked uncertain. "I don't think so."

Ed slid farther down toward the counter. "Shoot."

Neil took a deep breath and opened his mouth.

"This wouldn't have anything to do with The Ivy?"

Neil looked shocked. "How do you know?"

Ed shrugged. "As the bloke who rang the bells at Notre Dame said, 'It's just a hunch.'"

"Jemma and I set it up. Mainly Jemma," Neil added quickly. That would pay her back for the cup of tea in the face.

Ed turned his eyes from his bottle. "That's the bad news?"

Neil nodded. "I came down to see you, but you'd gone."

"You'll realize then that Ali didn't turn up?"

Neil nodded again. "There's a reason, mate."

"Why doesn't that surprise me?"

"A good reason."

Ed's glass faltered slightly on the way to his lips.

"She's in hospital, bro."

A spark of concern flashed in Ed's eyes, and he was instantly sober. "Is she hurt?"

Neil chewed his lip. "Not hurt," he said. "Not as such. This is heavy-duty, man."

"How heavy-duty?"

"She's got the big C, Ed. Cancer. They're operating tomorrow."

Ed stood up. "Take me to her. She'll need me."

"That was the very bad news," Neil said. "The very, very bad news is that she doesn't want to see you."

Ed sat down again. Heavily. He looked like someone had punched him in the stomach. His breathing was labored. "Why?"

"I haven't a clue." Neil put his hand on his arm. "Women, eh?"

"Women," Ed agreed.

"Who needs them?" Neil tried a jocular laugh and failed miserably. The bleak look in Ed's eyes said that he did. At least, one particular woman.

"So," Ed said with a heavy sigh, "if that was the very, very bad news, what's the really, truly awful news?"

"I'm shagging your girlfriend," Neil said earnestly.

"Orla?" Ed said, his mouth turned up at the corners.

"Yes," Neil answered grimly.

Ed started to laugh, a tight little giggle that turned into a hearty guffaw. Neil stood and watched helplessly as his brother laughed and laughed, laughed so hard that he cried and the tears rolled unabated down his sad, tired face.

CHAPTER 78

I had a tumor the size of a grapefruit, apparently. Why are all tumors the size of grapefruits? Why not any other citrus fruits? Lemons? Limes? Kumquats? Is a kumquat a citrus fruit? Or tennis balls? You never hear anyone say they had a tumor the size of a tennis ball, do you? Anyway, it's gone now. All of it. Along with quite a bit of my insides. But apart from the fact that I feel like I've been kicked up the bottom by a horse and my emotions are whirling on the breeze with all the control of a stunt kite, I'm absolutely fine. That's the wonder of modern anesthetic for you.

Christian, on the other hand, is not fine. He, like most of the male population, does not cope well with illness. Hospitals make him break out in a cold sweat. He says the smell of stale urine makes him want to gag. Not mine, I hasten to add.

He is sitting by my bedside looking bored, and he's already eaten most of the grapes he brought in. Visiting hour is torture. Christian looks up at me wanly.

"Cheer up," I say. "I'll be out in a couple of days." I can't wait.

The hospital food is great, providing you like beans and chips for every meal. And it's one of those mixed wards, where they let geriatric old men wander round at night with their pajamas all undone. There are several shades of hair tangled round the bathroom plug hole, and the loos are crying out for the want of some Toilet Duck. If you didn't come in here with an illness, you would, without a shadow of a doubt, go out with one.

A few months ago I could have been ill in a cream-and-terracotta room that looked like a window design from Habitat, with my very own spotlessly clean shower, and had prawn sandwiches with the crusts cut off for afternoon tea and Baileys on demand. I had private health care under Ed's scheme with Wavelength, but I don't know if Ed has cut me out of it now that we are "estranged," and because I came in as an emergency, I didn't really have the time or the inclination to ask.

Ed hasn't been near, and I think that's mainly because I told everyone I didn't want him here. And that was partly true. I am just about holding all this together, and I really don't think I could have coped with him feeling sorry for me because I'm feeling sorry enough for myself. And I didn't want him to want me back for all the wrong reasons, which he might have done if he'd seen me like this. There's nothing quite like having an armful of intravenous drips to bring on a bit of misplaced sympathy. Do you know what I mean? There's a part of me in all this that just wants to pretend none of it has happened and to wind the clock back, about three years probably, to a time when all we had to row and worry about was whether we needed a conservatory built or not.

I didn't want the kids to come in either. It's not that I don't miss them desperately, I do—they're the only children I'll ever have now, and I want to hug them to me and love them. But I didn't want them to see me sick and worry. And I didn't want them to catch anything deadly either. As I said, the whole thing has just screwed my emotions up completely. Facing your own mortality is nearly as scary as the length of the checkout queues at Ikea.

Jemma is clip-clopping her way down the ward, and Christian looks relieved. It means he can slope away early. Jemma is flushed and has on her careworn look, but despite that, she is dressed from head to toe in antique silk and looks like she's going to a gallery opening rather than hospital visiting. She's missed the tea trolley, which she'll be miffed about. It's only seventy pence a cup, and they use at least one tea bag per hundred patients. So no cutbacks there!

Christian stands up. He and Jemma nod curtly at each other. "I'll be off," Christian says, and he pecks my cheek and rushes away without another word.

Jemma sits down in his vacated utilitarian lime-green plastic seat and starts to cry. I reach out and stroke her hair. She'll start me off too if she's not careful. "Hush, hush," I murmur softly, and reach for the box of Tempo Aloe Plus tissues on my metal bedside cabinet. "Don't worry about me." I tilt her chin and smile my bravest, if slightly tearful, smile. "I'll be fine."

Jemma sniffs unhappily. "I'm not worrying about you," she says, taking one of my tissues. "You're always fine. I'm worrying about me."

I stop stroking her hair and lie back on my pillow.

"Supposing I can't find anyone to have babies with?" she continues. "Cancer sometimes runs in families. We used to eat the same breakfast cereal. Suppose that does it?"

"Don't be stupid."

"You're all right—you've already got three children. What if I haven't had any by the time my insides decide to pack up? I can't find anyone who will commit to me."

"So stop going out with married men." In this mood, Jemma would make Good Samaritans want to take a long run off a short cliff.

"It's easy for you to say that, you're married to one. Well, you were."

Thank you, Jemma.

"Do you know how many prams I saw today, Alicia?"

"No." But I'm sure you're going to tell me.

"Nine," Jemma says emphatically. "Nine prams."

"Nice."

"Nine prams and seven cute, chubby little toddlers."

"Any surly teenagers?" I inquire.

"No," Jemma snaps. "None." My sister eyes my grapes covetously, and I move them away from her. "Now that you're staring death in the face, Ali, it's made me realize that I'm not getting any younger either."

"God forbid," I say.

Jemma starts a renewed bout of crying. This is a two tissue flow. "He's left me," she wails loud enough for even the deaf geriatrics to hear. They pull their attention away from *General Hospital,* which is blaring out of the lone ward telly, cunningly positioned ten feet up the wall so that no one can quite see it.

"Sssh," I say. "Who?"

"My Swiss banker." Her sniveling has never been done in dulcet tones. "I've always wanted a Swiss banker."

"Why?"

"Because they're rich and sophisticated and have apartments overlooking Lake Geneva and ski lodges in Zermatt."

I tut. "Why has he left you?"

"Oh." Jemma's lower lip quivers. "Eric said he couldn't go on living a lie."

I can't hide my smile. "Eric?"

"So." Jemma scowls. "No one's perfect!"

"So, presumably, Eric not only had a crap name but a wife too."

Jemma tosses her hair. "The marriage had been dead for a long time."

"Let me have a guess." I can do waspish along with the best—anesthetic or not. "The minute alimony was mentioned, they thought they'd give it another try."

Jemma has the grace to look slightly abashed. "Well…"

"How often are you going to go through this, Jemma?"

"You're a fine one to talk."

"At least I've only cocked things up once."

"And at least you're admitting it now," she snapped. "You and Ed make me want to bang my head against the wall in frustration." Don't I know the feeling! "You're both too damn stubborn to back down. That's why Neil and I arranged the meal on Saturday…."

"What meal?" I'll have you note my senses are all still on full alert despite my pain.

"Oh." Jemma looks round for help.

"What meal?" I have her cornered. There are fifteen minutes left of visiting time before she can escape.

"We want you to get back together, Ali. For your sake and for the kids. You have three lovely children who you're destroying because you're both too damn cussed to say you're sorry. The world is full of people with children, and you all just take them for granted."

I am so choked that I can't speak.

"We arranged for you and Ed to meet at The Ivy."

"No one told me," I say when I find my voice again.

"Neil sent you an invitation."

"I didn't get it." There are cogs whirring slowly in my brain, and maybe I'm not as sharp as I think.

"Well, it doesn't matter." Jemma shrugs. "You couldn't go because you were in here." Her gaze takes in the worn blue nylon curtains which don't quite meet and the eiderdown which has a design in ten-year-old black currant juice on it.

"Did Ed go?" My mouth is dry.

"Yes," she says.

"And he sat there all alone?"

"Yes."

"And he knows that I'm in here?"

"Yes," Jemma says. "Yes, yes, yes to all of the above." Patience is a virtue Jemma doesn't possess. "He wants to see you, Ali."

"No," I say. "I couldn't handle it. I'll see him when I'm better."

"And who's going to look after you?"

"Christian."

"He might be as gorgeous as George Clooney, but I'm not sure he'll have his bedside manner. What if you've got to have chemotherapy?"

"We'll manage."

"Come to me," she pleads.

"I can't think of anything worse."

"Go to Mum's then. She'd love to fuss round you."

"The cancer wouldn't have to bother, she'd kill me with kindness," I protest. "I just want to be alone."

Jemma takes my hand. "Please sort this out with Ed," she says. "Or one day you will be alone."

"Get your own glass house sorted out, Jemma," I snap tiredly. "Then you can throw stones." Sometimes the truth hurts, doesn't it?

She stands up. "I shouldn't have messed Neil around," she says.

"I won't say I told you so."

"He's a really nice guy."

"He could have given you what you want, Jemma."

"Maybe it's not too late," she says tentatively.

"He's very forgiving."

"I threw a cup of tea in his face," she says.

"Maybe he's not that forgiving," I say, and we both start to laugh.

"Ali." Jemma is serious again. "If you'd got the invitation and this hadn't happened, would you have gone to meet Ed?"

I scratch the intravenous drip which is going into the back of my hand, turning it a nice shade of blue, so that I can avoid looking at my sister. "I don't know," I say, but in my heart I know exactly what I would have done.

CHAPTER 79

Neil was giving his studio the new, improved Neil Kingston patented power treatment. Well, he was threatening it severely with a large bottle of Fantastik and a rag. He looked round the studio. It was drab, dingy, definitely lacking a woman's touch and shrieking, over the dirt, that a less-than-successful photographer hung out here. That said, it had served him well. In some ways he'd be sorry to see it go. There was a spider in the corner by the kettle, called Harriet, who had lived here untrammeled for years. He would miss her. Except when she occasionally took to crawling out of the milk carton.

The whole place needed a coat of paint and some new backdrops, and he wondered if he would find the time to do it. Unlikely. This whole thing with Ali's illness had made him stop and think. He'd always been a never-do-today-what-you-can-quite-easily-put-off-until-tomorrow merchant. His plans, if you could even grace the loose meanderings of an alcohol-fueled brain with such a formal title, had all been five-year, ten-year, sometime-maybe-never plans. But this had suddenly made him realize that one day, when you weren't expecting it, your dance card would be marked. And it would be marked, in indelible ink, with *The Last Waltz*.

It was a sobering thought. Along with his newly acquired Paul

Smith suit, he was now going to be a live-every-day-as-if-it's-your-last man. Because one day he would be right.

The doorbell chimed, making Neil turn round. Jemma stood in the doorway. She looked gorgeous. The sun was strong today. It was the sort of sun that holds a promise that we might, just might, for once be in for a long, hot summer. It was bleaching her hair to a honey-golden sheen, the color of the inside of a Crunchie. She swept it from her face. "Hi," she said.

"Hi."

"I was just passing." She glanced at the traffic gridlocked outside the studio. "Thought I might be in time for pizza."

If it was supposed to be a joke, it wasn't funny. Neil put down his Fantastik. "Not today."

"Oh." Jemma came into the studio and looked round, trailing her hand over a group of dusty albums of particularly awful wedding photographs from years ago that he'd thought were state-of-the-art when he'd taken them—you know, couple trying to push Rolls Royce, bride with garter on full show, ushers throwing top hats in the air, terrible, terrible, cringe-making stuff. They were destined for the bin. All of them.

"How's Ali?" he said.

"You know Ali," she sighed, fiddling with her car keys like worry beads. "Toughing it out. She's got her invincible shell on, but cracks are starting to appear. That woman will have me in an early grave. I could kill her."

"Bad choice of words, Jemma."

"I know." Jemma pushed her hands into her pockets and kicked aimlessly at the scuffed vinyl floor. "I'm so worried about her, Neil. We really messed up with her and Ed, didn't we?"

"We tried. We could do no more than that. You never know, it could have worked."

"Yeah." She sat down on the one bare corner of his desk. "Sometimes you never know what might happen unless you're prepared to take a risk."

"Yeah," Neil said flatly. "I'm known as Neil 'Too Risky' Kingston."

"I wanted to apologize again for the cup-of-tea thing," Jemma said.

She was an attractive woman, Neil thought—even if she did have a fuse shorter than your average firework.

"Bad day." She laughed cheerlessly. "Bad life."

"Well..."

"It won't happen again," she said. "Promise. Perhaps we could go out for dinner one night next week...."

"I'm very busy," Neil said.

"It wasn't a personal thing," Jemma said too hurriedly. "I wanted to do a portfolio of my clothes for an advertising feature. Glossy magazine. I thought you might like to take the photographs. That was all. Nothing in it."

He savored the words "glossy magazine," silently rolling them round his mouth like a fine wine, and let them go. "Like I said, Jemma, I really am very busy."

The doorbell clanged again and Ed walked in. He looked older, grayer and more awful than Neil had ever seen him.

"Bro!" Neil went over and hugged him.

"Good afternoon, conniving brother," Ed said, clapping him on his back. He turned to Jemma. "And you must be his lovely meddlesome assistant?"

Ed clearly hadn't bought the bit about it all being Jemma's fault.

"We were only trying to help," Jemma said miserably.

Ed glared fiercely at them both. "I'm not sure I've forgiven you two yet."

"Life's too short, Ed," Jemma said, getting up to kiss him. "It was all done with the best intentions."

"Yeah, yeah," Ed said, hugging her. "How's Ali?"

"You should go to see her."

"She didn't want me to, remember?"

"Alicia doesn't know what she wants," Jemma tutted. "She's not great, Ed. She's pretending she is, but I know her better than that."

"The kids are missing her."

"Go to see her," Jemma instructed. "She's going home tomorrow."

Ed's face darkened. "Where does she class as home now?"

"Christian's place. She wouldn't come to me. She wouldn't go to Mum's. Anyone can see she's not thinking straight."

Ed hunched his shoulders into his jacket.

"Go round there, Ed. Tell her you love her. Get her to come home. To your home. *Her* home. She needs you."

"Do you never stop interfering in other people's lives?" Ed said.

"Only when they stop making a complete mess of it themselves."

"She's right, Ed," Neil offered.

"Who asked your opinion?" Ed said, kicking listlessly at one of the packing cases Neil had lined up against the wall. "What's this? Doing a moonlight flit?"

Neil took a deep breath. "The studio's up for sale." Both Ed and Jemma turned to look at him. Neil spread his hands. "I'm moving on."

"Pastures new?" Ed said.

"You could say that." Neil swallowed hard.

"Why didn't you say something?"

"Well, it's all happened very quickly." Neil had gone very hot. "I might as well tell you both while you're here."

Jemma was smiling inquisitively. Ed's frown was about to get a few millimeters worse.

Neil tried a laugh, but it came out as an uncomfortable snort. "I'm going to California," he said. "To Los Angeles."

He was right about Ed's frown. And now Jemma had one to match. Neil looked at Ed and their eyes locked.

"With Orla?" Ed asked.

Neil nodded. "With Orla."

Jemma put her hands on her hips. "Who the hell's Orla?" she said.

CHAPTER 80

Christian is helping me out of the taxi. After a fashion. He has already dropped my handbag and its contents into the gutter, and I think I might just be about to follow it. "Get my purse and pay the driver," I say. I'm really trying to hang on to my temper, which is being stoked by pain and pity.

It's all very well sitting there like Lady Muck in hospital surrounded by grapes and tissues and bottles of Robinson's Barley Water, but it's a bit of a shock when you've suddenly got to start maneuvering up and down stairs and in and out of taxis in the manner of a sprightly young thing. They wanted me to stay in hospital for an extra couple of days, but I think I was about to turn into a chip, so made my excuses and my escape.

Christian seems less certain about me being home. He is doing a lot of huffing and puffing, which is never a good sign, is it? He huffs and puffs a bit more as he pays the taxi driver and then huffs and puffs me into the house. Everything is as black as pitch. Including my mood.

"Do you want to go straight to bed?" Christian says, propping me up under one arm.

"Yes." I am totally exhausted and almost wished I'd chosen the rigors of another plate of hospital chips instead.

We start off up the stairs. "Put the light on," I say, realizing for the first time that the sun rarely shines in this house. "I can't see a damn thing."

Christian stops, halting the minuscule progress we've made. "I can't," he says.

"Can't what?"

"I can't put the light on."

I lean against the banister. "Why?"

"We haven't got any electricity."

"Has there been a power cut?"

"Only in this house," Christian says.

"What?"

"We've been cut off, Ali."

I face him, and he looks like he wishes he wasn't here. I know exactly how he feels. "Haven't you paid the bill?"

"No."

"Why not?"

"We haven't got any money."

"How can I recuperate in a house that hasn't got any power?" I can feel this horrible hysteria rising inside me.

"You'll be fine," Christian says quietly.

"I won't be fine," I shout. "How can I wash properly if we've no hot water? How can I even have a cup of tea?"

"We're boiling pans of water on the cooker," he says. "We've still got gas."

"For how long?" I slump down onto the nearest stair.

Christian looks at the floor.

"I'll pay the bill," I say, forgetting for one blissful moment that I have no job and am not going to be able to work for the foreseeable future. "How much is it for?"

"I don't know," he mutters.

"How long does it take to get these things put back on? I've never been cut off before." I look accusingly at him.

"It isn't that simple," Christian says.

"Why not?"

"It isn't exactly our house." He scratches his head.

"Then phone the landlord."

"We haven't exactly got a landlord either."

"What?" With hindsight I blame the anesthetic for all this.

"We're not exactly supposed to be living here."

I stop myself from saying "what" again.

"We're squatters, Ali," he says, as if it's the most natural thing in the world.

"I'm living in a squat?" I can barely hear myself. "But I thought squats were derelict council houses with rats and urine-soaked mattresses on the floor?" Surely they can't be rather grand Victorian terraces in swishy little backstreets lined with Porsches?

Christian blows a snort of air out of his nose. "Get in the real world, Ali."

I am in the real world. I know because everything hurts far, far too much for me to be imagining it. My voice is still wobbly. "Isn't that illegal?"

Christian rakes his fringe nervously. "Some people view it like that."

"Mainly those involved with the law," I remark icily.

"Well…"

Let me tell you, I am the person who thinks all asylum seekers are no-good scroungers. I am the person who has never been flashed, not even once, by a speed camera. I am the person who has never had a parking ticket, and I can tell you in London that is an extremely rare beast. I am the person who wouldn't even dream of dropping an empty crisp packet on the pavement. I, Mrs. Law-Abiding Citizen of the Century, am a squatter.

Christian tries a disbelieving laugh. "How did you think we managed to live in such a smart place?"

I stare up at Christian, and he looks exactly like someone I've never, ever seen before. My voice has almost deserted me. "I thought you had rich parents."

"I do," he says. "But they loathe me."

And, at this moment, I can't say that I blame them.

CHAPTER 81

Ed was sitting watching Ice Cool Chew-Chew Mints dive into a vast blue plastic swimming pool filled with iced water—to illustrate, of course, how refreshing they were. They had already done seven takes, and the Ice Cool Chew-Chew Mints were all very pissed off.

It was, however, making Ed smile. Which was nice, because not a lot had made him smile lately. The last take had been pretty much perfect, but as Ed watched the Ice Cool Chew-Chew Mints being fished out of the swimming pool, he thought he might make them do it all over again just for a bit of fun.

"Once more from the top," Ed shouted, nodding to Trevor with a barely concealed smirk.

Orla slid into the seat next to him. "There was nothing wrong with that, Ed Kingston. You're doing this for spite."

"Half of them were late this morning," he said. "They're paying for it now."

"In spades," Orla said as she watched the Mints form a shivering queue to jump in all over again needlessly. Ed settled back in his chair, folding his arms across his chest.

"Are things okay between us?" she asked.

"Yes," Ed said, eyes still on the Mints.

"You don't mind that I'm in love with your little brother?"

Ed shook his head. "No. Not at all."

"Or that I'm taking him halfway across the world?"

"No."

"Is that because you were never really in love with me?"

Ed looked at her. "Would you mind if that were true?"

"Yes," she said sadly. "A little."

Trevor was loading more ice into the water and making sure that the bobbing polystyrene penguins were all the right way up. The Mints were jumping up and down in a vain effort to get warm.

Orla studied his profile. "Neil's a lot like you."

"He's not," Ed said. "Neil's nice. You're better off with Neil."

"He'll do well in Hollywood." Orla stretched out, lifting her hair. "I'll make sure he has lots of work."

"Good," Ed said. "Good."

"There's a job still open for you," she said. "If you want it."

Ed shook his head again, more emphatically. "No. I need to be here." Harrison Ford will have to wait. Possibly forever.

Orla touched his arm. "How is Alicia?"

"I don't know," Ed said, realizing that he was fed up with hearing secondhand reports. "But I'm going to find out."

"She's a very lucky woman, Ed. In a lot of ways."

"Yeah," he said. She must be slapping her thighs and thanking the Lord for chemotherapy. But he knew what Orla meant. She was lucky that she was going to survive. Lucky that she'd been blessed with three beautiful children. And he was a lucky man. Lucky to have loved Alicia. Lucky to still have the chance to tell her. It had just taken him a long time to work out quite how lucky he was. Perhaps too long.

Reluctantly, the Mints were inching their way along the diving board, jostling fractiously as they went. Despite himself, Ed started to grin again.

The Mints were launching themselves into the ice-cold water, splashing and scattering the polystyrene penguins and polar bears strewn on the surface.

"I did love you, Ed," Orla said softly.

But he was laughing too hard to hear her. Or if he did, he chose to ignore it.

CHAPTER 82

My insides feel as if they've been scrubbed out with one of the white nylon bottle brushes that you can only buy from Kleenezee catalogs. Going to the toilet every ten minutes aided and abetted only by candlelight does not make for a peaceful night's sleep, I can tell you from bitter experience.

Christian is sitting at the side of me on the bed, proffering a cup of pan-boiled tea and a bowl of Sugar Puffs. He strokes the hair gently from my face and whispers, "How are you feeling?"

"Like shit," I say crisply.

"You didn't sleep very well?"

"No." I resist the urge to point out that he, *au contraire,* slept like the proverbial baby. Why is it that men never, ever have disturbed sleep no matter what the crisis? And, God knows, I tried to disturb his sleep. I kicked him, pinched him, punched him, ground my big toe into his ankle. Fruitless. All of it.

I take the Sugar Puffs, not with a good grace, and I don't even like Sugar Puffs—they're so sweet they make your face suck in and your fillings itch—but I am starving, which I take as a good sign. How can I possibly still have cancer *and* a good appetite?

"Try to get some more sleep," he says, and kisses my forehead. "I'll see you later."

"Later?"

"I'm going to work."

"Work!" I abandon the Sugar Puffs and any attempt at frailty. "Work? You're supposed to be looking after me, Christian. I've just come out of hospital. I've just had a major operation. I could do with a forty-foot crane to help me get out of bed."

"I have to go to work, Ali. I'm going to lose my pitch otherwise. Even starving artists have to play by the rules of hard commercialism these days."

Now I'm starting to panic. He is so totally unaware of my needs. I want to scream at him: *I haven't just broken a fingernail, you know! I've got more stitches than a bloody patchwork quilt!* "How will I manage?" I sound so pathetic.

"Becs is here all day. She's doing some work from home. She'll look after you."

"That's like leaving me to the tender loving care of Dr. Crippen!"

"You'll be fine."

"Stop saying that! I won't be fine. I need you, Christian. If you love me, you won't walk away from me now."

"I do love you, Ali." I can feel a huge "but" coming on and it chills my blood.

"But?"

"But..." Christian twists the camouflage duvet in his fingers. "I'm finding this very difficult to cope with."

"You are?"

"I know. I know. You must think I'm very selfish."

"You can't have relationships that don't have ups and downs, Christian. It's times like these that test how strong your commitment to each other is."

"I've never done commitment very well," he says, and his eyes wander round the room. The room in the house that belongs to someone else. Someone else who doesn't even realize that there are strangers in his home having this conversation. "And I never realized how many commitments you had when we got involved."

"You did."

"I *knew* about them for sure, but I had no idea what it would be like living with them on a day-to-day basis. I like things to go along smoothly, Ali. Without hassle."

"But that isn't real life."

"Then maybe I'm not ready for real life." I can see he's been giving this a lot of thought, which scares me because Christian rarely seems to think about anything beyond the next meal. "Maybe I want to run wild with Robbie and Rebecca for a few more years. Maybe then I'll be ready to settle down." He looks at me and hesitates before he says the next words. "Maybe then I'll want kids of my own."

Christian's knife cuts deeper than the surgeon's. "Is that what this is all about?"

"Partly," he admits.

I try to ignore my instincts, which are telling me to shout "I don't believe it!" very loudly. "But you can't stand children," I point out calmly. "They were one of the obstacles."

"And you've done a great job of convincing me otherwise."

"So much so that now you think you'll make a great dad?" I am failing to keep the bitterness out of my voice.

"I don't know if I'll make a great dad, but I would like to try."

"Fabulous."

"You've shown me what family life can be like, Ali. I never had that as a child. I was shunted from one boarding school to another, seeing my parents when I could be fitted in around lunch engagements and weekends at the Hunt. I never wanted to do that to another person."

"But you can walk away from my kids?"

"I never said I wanted to walk away."

"What else is there to do, Christian? There's nowhere for us to go from here."

"I think we were all into this too deeply, before we had a chance to really think it through," he says, and I have never heard him speak truer words. Christian rubs his hands over his eyes. He looks pale and tired, as if he hasn't been sleeping too well while I've been away. I push down the question that comes to my throat. "This is the wrong time to be talking about this, Ali. I have to go. Let's talk about it later."

"By candlelight?"

"I guess so."

"How romantic!"

"I'll try to come home early," he promises, but the words have an empty, empty ring.

He leans over and kisses me. "I do love you, Alicia, Ali Kingston."

And I realize that what Christian thinks is love and what I consider to be love come in entirely different packages. He stands up, slings his Nike backpack over his shoulder, blows me a kiss goodbye and walks out.

My Sugar Puffs have gone soggy. They are floating about on top of the milk like dead flies. My pan-boiled tea has developed pond scum. I think I've probably been looking at the wall for a long time, but I'm not sure. I hear Rebecca clonk up the stairs and she pushes the door open.

"Finished?" she says, looking at the untouched breakfast.

"I'm not hungry," I say and try a smile.

"Are you okay?"

I laugh a little. "I've been better."

There is a spark of barely concealed glee in her eye. "You didn't expect Christian to hang around and look after you, did you?"

I sink back into my pillow. "I had hoped he would."

"Christian can't cope with anything that disrupts his life."

Yes, I'm beginning to realize that, and I think he isn't the only one. I regard Rebecca coolly.

"Rebecca. Did a letter come for me a few weeks ago? Something that might have looked vaguely important?"

She puts on a defiant teenager face, and I remember that she is only a little older than Tanya. Her chin juts aggressively, challenging me. "Yes."

"What happened to it?"

"You'll find it in pieces down the side of the sofa," she says.

"Why?" I ask.

"I want you out of here." Her eyes fill with tears. "You're spoiling everything." She sniffs petulantly, not realizing that she has probably just shot herself in the foot. Had she delivered my invitation to The Ivy, it might have solved her problem. Or would it? There's really no way of knowing now. "Everything was fine until you came along."

"I thought it was over between you?"

Rebecca's mouth forms a tight line. "We would have got back together. It was only a matter of time. It always is. And then you came along. You think he's wonderful, but you have no idea what he's really like," she continues, fists clenched into tight little balls. "He's still sleeping with that other little tart," she spits, getting into her stride. "And with anyone else who'll have him."

Weariness cngulfs me. "And with you," I add.

Rebecca flushes, the bloodred hue of those who stand guilty as accused. "If you know," she says, "then why do you still love him?"

I have asked myself that question a thousand times. "For the same reasons that you do," I tell her quietly.

"Then we are both very stupid women," she says, picking up the Sugar Puffs and the stone-cold tea. "And that's probably all we'll ever have in common."

I feel an amazing sense of detachment, despite hearing more revelations than there are in the Bible in the last half hour. I am floating outside myself, allowing my thoughts to swim freely. Perhaps this is what it's like to experience drowning. Having the water fold over you, weightlessly relieving you of all pain. It is not an unpleasant feeling and, at this moment, I envy those who walk knowingly into the waiting sea, never to return.

We all start off with the best intentions in life. How easy it will be to fall in love, marry, raise children, live happily ever after. We are all convinced that we won't make the same mistakes our parents did. We are all determined to raise our children steeped in the kind of nurturing that we may or may not have had ourselves. So sure that we will do better than the generations that have struggled to do the right thing before us. But where does it all go wrong? Why do we end up pursuing our own needs at the cost of theirs, citing their resilience, their acceptance, and leave them instead flailing around on a flimsy raft of uncertain emotions?

I can see that Christian has been damaged and I too have been damaged by my own childhood, where I was loved and molly-coddled and spoiled to the nth degree. One of us is wounded by emotional neglect, the other by emotional suffocation. How finely the balance is set. My upbringing has left me with a feeling that I ought to be able to do exactly what I want. But life is never that simple, is it? And I wonder what harm I am doing, have already done, to my own three darlings in my own well-intentioned and below-par way.

I have softened toward Rebecca, despite her having just dealt a killer blow to the shreds of my fragile, fantasy romance. We have both been drawn like moths to Christian's flame and we have both had our wings badly singed. And, whereas I am old enough to know better, she is young and still learning the hard way.

So. Let me recap for you. My toy-boy lover who everyone warned me was utterly, utterly wrong for me has proved them all right. My husband is running round trying to make Hugh Grant look like a monk. The lovely Rebecca has, herself, scuppered the best chance she had of getting me out of here. Here being the squat I am, presumably, squatting in. My sister has lost both Neil and her Swiss banker and is broody. Christian, the child-free zone, has discovered the joy of children and the fact that his biological clock might just be ticking too. I, in finding out that I'm no longer able to have children, am discovering just how important it is to me to be a mother. Have I left anything out? Probably. I bet Madonna doesn't have days like these.

I must try to relax and not think about what the future may hold, but in my book relaxation is one step away from paralyzing boredom. I pick up yesterday's *Metro* newspaper from the bedside table and flick halfheartedly through it. On page three I learn that Alan Titchmarsh has just been voted the sexiest man on British television, knocking second place rival George Clooney into a cocked hat. Now I know that the world truly has gone mad.

CHAPTER 83

Ed leaned against the city-blackened railings across the street from Christian's house. He wished he were wearing a trilby and maybe a trench mac and had a cigarette that he could light moodily with a Zippo lighter. But he didn't. So instead of lurking mysteriously and glamorously, he just hung around in the hard-edged shadow of his Mitsubishi Shogun, looking slightly furtive.

Also, the sun was shining, whereas his mood was more suited to swirling fog, lamplight and sinister shifting dusk. A cooling breeze ruffled his hair, and the scent of traffic fumes was building up nicely from the crush of cars in Notting Hill Gate. He'd left the shoot early, having subjected the disreputable Ice Cool Chew-Chew Mints to the iniquities of cold water torture more times than was absolutely reasonable. He'd probably get complaints from Equity, but it had been worth it to raise his spirits, which would otherwise have stayed languishing around the doldrums somewhere.

He was struggling to come to terms with the Orla-and-Neil thing. His brother wasn't prone to flights of fancy, and Ed suspected that this might be one. Selling up your entire life on a whim and a whirlwind relationship was a pretty big step. And he worried about Orla's motives. She was too driven and too dynamic to last the distance with someone as lackadaisical as Neil. What would happen when she tired of him, as she eventually would?

But then, who was he to pour the cold water of reality on someone else's dreams? How could he tell Neil that he thought it wouldn't last? Maybe it would. He had thought the same about Ali and the starving artist, but here they were, months down the road, still at the impasse between marriage and divorce called separation, with neither of them seeming to want to make the first move toward disentangling the life they had shared together.

There didn't seem to be much in the way of activity inside Christian's house, and he wondered if Ali was alone or whether she had company. Whichever way, he'd come this far and would tough it out. For the sake of civility, he would try to avoid pushing Christian's teeth down his throat. Unless he was really provoked.

He'd been standing here for half an hour already—trying to pluck up courage to see his own wife, for heaven's sake! If he hung around any longer, he was likely to get arrested for loitering with intent, so he crossed the road, rapped firmly on the knocker and tried to convince his legs that they really would like to stop shaking.

A young woman, who looked like she'd been crying, opened the door. "Is Alicia Kingston at home?" he asked.

The girl nodded and stood to one side.

It was a nice house. Not terribly homey, but smarter than he'd expected.

"Top of the stairs," the girl said.

"Is she alone?"

She smiled briefly. "Yes."

Ed climbed the stairs. He should have brought flowers. Or chocolates. Or grapes. Or something. But he hadn't, and it was too late now. There were four doors at the top of the stairs and only one was ajar, so he pushed it open slightly and, knocking tentatively, stepped inside.

Ali was asleep on the bed. The duvet was pushed down by her feet and she was wearing a white cotton nightdress which was stained with drops of blood. She was lying on her side with a pillow jammed between her knees, just as she'd done when she was pregnant with all three of the children. Her face was as pale as her nightgown, and her jumble of gold curls was spread out over the pillow. Dark lashes emphasized the hollow shadows under her eyes.

The *Apocalypse Now* theme of the decoration made her seem all the more small and fragile, as if she were being held hostage here against her will. Ed's throat tightened and his eyes started to burn, hot and prickly. How had they ever come to this? What on earth was she doing lying alone and sick in some stranger's bedroom, done out with all the taste of a ten-year-old? He wanted to lie down beside her and take her in his arms and never let her go again.

There were jeans hanging up at the side of the wardrobe. Trendy, slim-hipped men's jeans. Jeans that he never would have fit into twenty years ago, let alone now that he was fast approaching middle-aged spread. A packet of Durex Extra Condoms Ribbed for Sensitivity and Sensation mocked him from the bedside table. Ed pressed his lips together grimly. He shouldn't be here. Ali hadn't wanted him to come. She'd made it abundantly clear that it was over between them. He should leave now and make his excuses later.

He looked back at his sleeping wife. Ali opened her eyes. "Hi," she said, as if she'd been expecting him to be standing there.

Ed's voice wouldn't come. It had lodged somewhere deep down in his chest and was refusing to budge. He cleared his throat. "Hi."

Ali patted the bed and he sat down facing her. She'd lost weight. Her arms were like sticks and her collarbone jutted out beneath her skin. She tried to push herself up on her elbows, but gave up and sank back on her pillow. "Here, let me help," he said, and eased her upright, plumping the pillow behind her.

"How are you?" he said.

Ali bit her lip, tears filling her eyes.

"Oh God," Ed said and wrapped his arms round her. She collapsed against him, sobbing into his chest, painful, racking sobs, and he could feel the tears soaking through his shirt. "I love you, Ali," he murmured into her hair. Alicia cried louder.

He held her away from him and looked into her sad, tear-stained face. "Come back to me," he said.

Ali nodded. "Yes."

"I love you, Ali Kingston." Ed smoothed her hair. "I always have."

"I love you too," she whispered and clung to his neck.

Ed held her tight, letting the relief flood through him. "Let's go home."

Alicia wiped the tears from her eyes with the back of her hand and smiled weakly. "I'll get my things," she said.

CHAPTER 84

Christian walked briskly from the Tube station. It had taken him ages to get home. Covent Garden Underground station was probably the busiest in the world at this time of year. He'd queued for ages amid the throngs of Japanese, American and French tourists to get in one of the lifts, and then had endured his nose being pressed up against a million sweaty armpits as he chunked his way up to Holborn to change to the Central line.

He'd tried to get away earlier, but for once there had been a queue of people waiting to sample his talents. Typical. The one day he'd wanted to leave was the one day in months he'd had a constant stream of business. The tourist rush had finally and mercifully arrived, but Ali would be furious, and what was worse she'd think he didn't care. Christian checked the money in his pocket. Perhaps this would go some way to appeasing her. And some serious appeasing was called for, he'd been such an uncaring bastard that morning. This was all a bit much for him to handle, but he'd been thinking about it all day, and he wanted to let Ali know that it would work out all right in the end. They would find a way to cope.

And he was going to get his act together. Now. Right now. She'd given up too much to be with him. There was no way he could let her down now when she needed him, and he'd let too many good things slip through his hands to risk Ali going the same way. He needed to get back on track and start trying to be a responsible citizen of planet Earth.

As a start, he'd phoned Sharon and told her it was over, which was a shame because she was sweet. She'd cried a lot, and he'd felt like a complete heel. There were always going to be plenty more fish in the sea, he just had to remind himself that from now on he was going to have to let them swim by unhooked.

And the children thing wasn't the end of the world either. It would probably be years before he wanted them himself, and in the meantime he'd be more than happy to make do with Elliott and Thomas and Tanya, who would certainly keep his hands full. And when the time came, there'd be some way round it, surely. God knows what advances there would be in technology by then. They'd probably be able to nip down the road to Sainsbury's and buy a couple.

Christian walked briskly along Notting Hill Gate, the sun warm on his back after the chill of the Underground. There was a newsagent's at the corner of the road, and Christian darted inside. He was going to buy Ali some magazines and chocs, stuff to keep her mind occupied while she was recuperating. It was a nightmare having to leave her with Becs, but they needed the money and he'd talk to her more fully about it tonight, convince her of his point of view.

He scanned the shelves. She was probably a bit old for *Cosmo,* which Becs always had her nose in, a bit young for *Women's Weekly.* God only knows what he should get. What experience did he have of women's magazines? He tried to avoid anything that had the words "pregnancy" or "menopause" on the front, which was a bit of a tricky one. Best to steer a wide berth round bunions and breast-feeding too. Were women really interested in these things? After hopping up and down the row in agitated indecision, Christian alighted on *Good Housekeeping,* which according to the cover blurb featured nothing more politically sensitive than "Packing the Perfect Summer Picnic," "Pickled Pink—Ten Ways To Preserve Your Onions with Red Wine" and "Could Your Carpet Be Harboring a Deadly Disease?" Other than being certain that their carpet would be harboring a deadly disease, there was surely nothing contentious there? Hurriedly, he snatched a copy from the shelves.

Chocs were just as much of a minefield. Milk Tray and Dairy Box were pensioners chocolates, Black Magic a dodgy choice if you didn't know whether the intended recipient liked dark chocolate or not. A Terry's chocolate orange was cheapskate and smacked of Christmas. Anything called Celebrations or Good News was definitely bad news if you'd had a row. Why couldn't they categorize chocolates as minor tiff or major bust-up, then everyone would know where they stood. After much hum-ing and ah-ing, Christian settled on the relative safety and conservatism of a box of Quality Street—mainly because he liked those best himself, and if Ali didn't feel up to eating them he would.

He was itching to get home now, but Mr. Akash wasn't itching to serve him. Christian joined the growing queue of customers, all eager, it seemed, to chew the fat about their day's business, and regretted at this moment that they had the only chatty newsagent in London at the end of their street.

Eventually it was his turn at the counter. "You're looking very pukka, mate," Mr. Akash said.

"I'm feeing pretty pukka," Christian said with a smile and he bundled the Quality Street and *Good Housekeeping* magazine into his backpack and with a spring in his step set off to nurture and nurse the life out of Ali.

CHAPTER 85

I can quite honestly say that the next few minutes pass in a blur. One minute I'm lying in bed wishing the duvet would fold over me and eat me in the manner of a 1950s B movie, and the next Ed's standing there like some latter-day knight in shining armor. And it may be a trick of the light, but he's all bathed in this shaft of sunlight like whatshisname in *Highlander.* And now you think I'm going mad because of all the tablets I've taken. Perhaps I am. But I know that I've never made a more sane decision than agreeing to put an end to all this unnecessary madness and go home with Ed.

Within a flash he's lobbing my clothes into a holdall like a thing possessed. Then he helps me to struggle out of bed, and it *is* a struggle. Even the ridiculous sense of excitement that's growing inside me can't give my wobbly feet wings. Instead, my flight consists of me hobbling round the bedroom, wincing feebly. Ed hands me my dressing gown. "Put this round you," he instructs. "I just want to get out of here."

He looks all manly and masterful and he's striding about grabbing anything that looks remotely lacy that might belong to me.

I give up trying to find something else to get dressed in and submit to the dressing gown.

"Ready?" Ed says.

I nod and, despite being burdened with a bulging holdall of no mean weight, he scoops me up into his arms and carries me toward the door. I put my arms round his neck and have not the slightest fear that he will drop me or that he'll let me fall. He's strong and certain and I've never felt safer. As we reach the door, I look back at the room with its beautiful antique furniture and its bleeding commandos on the walls, and there is absolutely no trace of me. None whatsoever. It looks like I have never been here at all.

Ed carries me down the stairs and past an openmouthed Rebecca holding a grubby tea towel. "Goodbye," I say over Ed's shoulder.

Rebecca moves toward us. I can't read the look on her face—it's a mixture of fear, elation, relief and regret. "Ali…" she starts, but I don't want to listen to what she has to say and my husband is clearly not intending to stop. We burst out of the house and into sunshine so strong that it hurts my eyes.

"Top pocket," Ed pants.

And I fish about until I find the car keys and flick the lock open. Ed dumps the holdall on the pavement and, one-handed, opens the car door and lowers me into the passenger seat. Tugging at the seat belt, he feeds it across me gently, tenderly, and then sprints round to get in on the other side. As he starts the car, I notice his hands are shaking, and I don't think it's from the effort of carrying me. His cheeks are wet with tears, and I reach up and brush them away with my fingertips. He grips my hand and kisses it fiercely. "Okay?" he says gruffly.

I nod, unable to speak. I feel as if we're fleeing from a prison. Just the two of us. We've dug the tunnel together and we're out. Out on the other side of the big, big wall. We've made it. We're free. We're going home.

CHAPTER 86

Quickening his pace and resisting the urge to sing in public without the bolstering effects of beer, Christian swung round the railings, onto their path and in through the front door, which was already open. He dumped his backpack in the hall and it in turn spewed the chocolates and magazine onto the floor.

"Hi, honey, I'm home," he shouted and, snatching up his peace offerings, started to run up the stairs.

"Christian." Rebecca came out of the kitchen. She was red-eyed and pale-faced and she twisted the power bracelets on her wrist nervously.

He stopped midstride. "What?"

"She's gone."

He looked blankly at her.

"Ali's gone," she repeated.

"She can't have," he said. "She's not well."

"Her husband came." Rebecca hugged herself and avoided his eyes. "He took her home."

Christian raced up the stairs, burst into the bedroom and it was empty. Just as Rebecca said, Ali was gone. All Ali's toiletries had gone from the top of the chest of drawers. The stuff she had always thrown over the Lloyd Loom chair—gone. He flung open the wardrobe. Gone. Gone. Gone.

The bed was made. No crumpling of sheets, no imprint on the duvet to show where she might have been. Christian lay down and stared at the ceiling. The ceiling with the commando's foot crashing carelessly through. She was gone. His mind was so numb it refused to process anything else. Ali was gone. Gone. The copy of *Good Housekeeping* slipped out of his fingers and fell to the floor with a clatter. She would never know how to pack the perfect picnic or pickle her onions using only the power of red wine. Clutching the Quality Street to his chest, Christian Winter squeezed his eyes shut and cried for the loss of the one good thing in his life.

CHAPTER 87

What can I tell you? I'm lying on a sun lounger in the garden enjoying the longest, hottest summer since 1976. I am covered from head to foot in Factor Overcoat suntan lotion, because cancer is now a very real thing to me, and having got rid of it from one place, I don't want it springing up somewhere else through my own stupidity. And stupidity, like cancer, is something I know a lot more about than I previously did.

The chemotherapy stripped my gorgeous, gorgeous hair from my head, but it's growing back and I've given up on wigs and Amish headscarves. I think it's going to be curlier than ever and a deeper shade of ginger biscuit, if that's humanly possible. By the time I've got a full head again, I'm going to look like one of those rusty wire-wool pan scrubbers. But guess what? I love it. And it just goes to show that the old chestnut "you don't know what you've got until it's gone" is right every time. I think I'd better buy shares in John Frieda Frizz-Ease, though.

And it's not just my hair that I've developed a new appreciation for: The grass is greener, the sky is bluer, the birds are tweetier—and if you think that's corny, then I really don't care; it's true and I hope you'll just take my word for it and that you never have to find out in the way I did.

I look at my family and feel such a surge of love for them that

I could cry with joy. Elliott is in the sandpit, trying to convince Harry, next door's dog, that sand is a really great diet, and I'm pretending not to notice. Tanya is lying on the grass plugged into her CD player, kicking her bare feet complete with orange-painted toenails in the air. She is growing up fast and has turned into the model teenager. She knows where the kettle is, what a duster is for and has even tidied her room on a weekly basis. I am overjoyed by this turn of events and wonder how long it will be before I'm shouting at her and she's telling me that I'm the worst mother in the world because all of her friends are allowed to do everything that she isn't. Not too long, I suspect. And I'll welcome it, because then I'll know we are finally back to normal once more. Thomas, unscathed it appears by his dalliance as a drug addict, is reading the latest Harry Potter. *Harry Potter and The Ten Million Quid in the Bank*—or something like that. Perhaps I ought to write a book. Or perhaps not.

I had a note from Kath Brown offering me my old job back, and I think I may well take her up on it when I'm fully recovered and have enough hair not to scare away her customers, seeing as she's had the sense to grovel. I knew all along I was indispensable.

A card came from Christian too. It had a cartoon cat vomiting on the front and inside it said SORRY in big, theatrical letters. And I guess that just about sums it up, really. Inside there was a ticket for a pawnbroker in the East End. A pawnbroker who had custody of my engagement, wedding and eternity rings. And I now know how Christian paid for our wonderful romantic trip to the Maldives, by pawning my rings. I showed the tickets to Ed, who, without a word, got in the car, drove to the address on the ticket, retrieved my rings at vast expense and put them back on my finger, where I hope by all that is good, that they will always remain.

I retrieved my drawing from the back of the wardrobe and tore it up in case there was a time when I was ever tempted to think that I really did look like that and remember it with fondness. I wonder one day will I go back past the house in Notting Hill to see if they are all still there peering at each other through the gloom or if Christian has moved on to invade someone else's life. But I don't blame him for any of this, not at all. I lay it all squarely at my own feet. It takes two to tango, but I should have been more aware of the trouble that slow dancing with a stranger could bring. Especially a stranger who was a beautiful, heartbreakingly irresponsible boy.

I see a bright future for us all—Ed, Elliott, Thomas and Tanya. They are my life, and I can't believe how much I took them for granted. You can be sure I won't ever do it again.

Ed comes out of the house, through the conservatory, bearing a tray of cold drinks. He has taken a month's leave of absence from work to look after me, and it's brought us closer than we've ever been. The other thing I'll never take for granted again is the luxury of time, and we're going to make sure that we have plenty for ourselves.

Wavelength have decided to set up a subsidiary film production unit to find scripts from new, young British writers, and Ed's going to head it up. Although I think he'll really miss the commercial and promotional video side, this will give him a new challenge to look forward to.

Ed sets down the tray and hands me a glass of lemonade. He gets more handsome with age or, like the birds and the grass, perhaps I just see him differently now. I kiss his hair, which is warm from the sun. He smiles up at me. "I thought we'd have a second honeymoon," he says. "When you're feeling better."

I stroke his cheek, enjoying the feel of his skin. "I'd like that."

"Can I come?" Elliott says as he runs down the garden as if this is the only glass of lemonade he's ever seen.

"The idea of a second honeymoon," I say, "is for mummies and daddies to spend some time alone without pesky children."

Elliott pulls a disgusted face. "Just remember," he warns sternly, "if you're going to do that gushy stuff, we don't want to end up with a baby brother just like me."

"I don't think there's any chance of that, Elliott," I say. Ed and I look at each other, and we both start to laugh.

CHAPTER 88

Orla came out of her inner sanctum, leading Harrison Ford into the main office. She shook his hand. "I'm really pleased you're on board," she said earnestly.

Neil was surprised how much the actor looked like Indiana Jones in real life. Though not quite as dirty. Or as sweaty. And he was wearing a white linen jacket, not scruffy leather.

"I'm delighted," he drawled.

"We'll set up the filming in Prague. I guess we'll be in Europe for about a month," Orla said.

"Great." Harrison is clearly unfazed. But then, a man who has wrestled snakes and Germans with his bare hands is unlikely to be stressed by a mere trip abroad.

Orla strode across the room, happy to be calling the shots. Neil smiled benevolently. "This is my partner," she said, placing a reaffirming hand on his shoulder. "Neil Kingston."

"Hi." Neil held out his hand. "Pleased to meet you."

"Likewise," Harrison answered, and nearly crushed his knuckles with his firm grip.

"My brother worked with you years ago," Neil said. "On *Raiders*. He was in Special Effects."

Harrison looked decidedly blank.

Neil shrugged it off. "You probably won't remember him."

"Not Ed?" Harrison said, his million-dollar, mega-star smile widening.

Neil laughed. "Yes."

"Ed Kingston?" Harrison's eyes widened. "You're Ed Kingston's brother?"

Neil laughed more nervously. "Yes."

"He's a great guy! I loved working with him. We were like brothers."

"Really." Neil thought his voice sounded sickly.

"How is he?"

Neil shrugged. Never, ever again would he take the piss out of Ed for telling Harrison Ford stories, and he would apologize, just as soon as he could, for ever doing so. "He's fine."

"Call him," Harrison insisted. "Let's call him."

"Now?"

"Why not?" Harrison said. "What time is it in England?"

Neil looked at his watch. "It's about tea time."

"Tea time?" Harrison guffawed. "You guys crack me up. Tea time! So call him. Let's interrupt his tea."

Neil looked at Orla for approval.

"Call him," she said.

Harrison clapped his hands together in excitement. "Boy, would I like to shoot the breeze with Ed again."

This, Neil couldn't wait to hear.

Harrison turned to Orla. "Do you know Ed?"

"Well…" Orla said.

"Ed's a great guy. Can't we get him on this shoot?"

Orla looked at Neil. "Well…"

Neil picked up the phone.

Ed heard the phone ringing from the garden. He put down his glass and kissed Ali on the cheek. "Back in a mo."

He went into the cool of the kitchen and picked up the phone. "Ed Kingston."

"Hey, bro," Neil said. "It's me."

"Neil." Ed settled himself on the nearest stool. "How's it going?"

"Fine, fine."

"And Orla?"

"Fine, fine," Neil said impatiently. "Ed, listen. You'll never guess who I've got here who wants to talk to you!"

"Who?" Ed said, scanning the calendar. Maybe they could go out and visit Neil later in the year, if Ali felt up to a long flight. It was worth thinking about.

"Here," Neil said. "I'll pass him over."

"Hi, Ed," a deep voice drawled. "It's Harrison Ford here. How're you doing?"

Ed smiled to himself. All his dreams of Harrison Ford and taking Hollywood by storm had long since evaporated and, surprisingly, he had never felt more content. It would be him and Ali from now on, and nothing else mattered. "Yes. Very funny, Neil. Ha, bloody ha." And with a chuckle, Ed hung up.

He went back out into the garden grinning to himself and sat down beside Ali. She was looking better all the time, stronger, happier. He hoped that all of their bad times would be behind them and that everything in the garden would be rosy once again.

She put her book down and glanced up at him over the top of her sunglasses. "Who was that?" she asked.

He squeezed her hand tightly. "No one," he said. "No one at all."

CAROLE MATTHEWS

Carole Matthews believes everyone should reinvent themselves every ten years in order to keep young. Carole has taken this to extremes: secretary, aroma therapist, TV presenter and now a bestselling writer.

She describes herself as a typical Gemini—daydreamer and realist—whose passions include cooking, Tai Chi, dance, fast cars, cycling, gardening and travel. Carole is a self-confessed evening class-aholic and dedicated film fan who follows Feng Shui and horoscopes when all else fails.

In between all this, she also finds time to write hugely entertaining novels and scripts for television and film. Not surprisingly, she is a stranger to housework.

Carole lives near London, England, with her laid-back boyfriend and irascible cat.

RDIBIOCM-TR